The Girls
from the Local

Rosie Archer was born in Gosport, Hampshire, where she still lives. She has had a variety of jobs including waitress, fruit picker, barmaid, shop assistant and market trader selling second-hand books. Rosie is the author of several Second World War sagas set on the south coast, as well as a series of gangster sagas under the name June Hampson.

Also by Rosie Archer

The Munitions Girls
The Canary Girls
The Factory Girls
The Gunpowder and Glory Girls
The Ferry Girls
The Girls from the Local
The Narrowboat Girls

ROSIE ARCHER

The Girls from the Local

Quercus

First published in Great Britain in 2017 by Quercus
This paperback edition published in 2018 by

Quercus Editions Ltd
Carmelite House
50 Victoria Embankment
London EC4Y 0DZ

An Hachette UK company

A CIP catalogue record for this book is available
from the British Library

PB ISBN 978 1 78648 355 3

10 9 8 7 6 5 4 3 2 1

Typeset by CC Book Production

Printed and bound in Great Britain by Clays Ltd, St Ives plc

For my dad, who told me
'Travel broadens the mind' and
'You're never alone with a book'.
How right he was.

Chapter One

January 1944

'C'mon, Merv, open up this door!'

Ruby Garett watched her friend Marge pound on the heavy glass door of Gosport's High Street's public house while shouting for the landlord to wake up.

She felt as if she was in a dream, her head whirling, her thoughts muddied. How could her mother be gone? How was it possible her home and all her belongings had been blown to kingdom come? It was all the fault of that madman Adolf Hitler!

'Merv! Come down!'

Ruby held back her tears as Marge thumped and yelled.

She heard the sound of the bolts scraping back, and the

door opened to reveal Merv's ugly face. His sleep-filled eyes showed Ruby they'd roused him from his bed.

'Wasser matter?' He blinked. 'It's two in the morning, whatjer want?' The smell of male sweat mixed with Lifebuoy soap wafted over them. 'I sent you two home ages ago.'

Marge pushed past him and swept inside, dragging Ruby with her and leaving Mervyn Tanner on the doorstep scratching himself.

'Shut the door, quick. It stinks of cordite out there.' Marge, small, feisty, shook her dark curls and took charge of the situation.

Merv stood there, a big man who was running to fat, his huge belly barely held in by blue and white striped pyjamas. Marge stared at his broken nose that leaned to one side; a relic of the boxing ring.

'Ruby's been bombed out and her mum's gone as well. You gotta let her stay here, in one of your rooms—'

She got no further, for the big man stepped forward and enveloped Ruby in his arms, pressing her to him. 'Poor little bugger,' he said, and without a moment's hesitation, 'Of course you can stop here.'

Ruby, who up until then had tried to keep her emotions under control, burst into tears at his kindness.

'Oh, thank you,' she wailed, sagging against him. 'We went

dancing at the Connaught Hall. Marge was walking me home, but there was a raid and we had to go into the shelter near the Criterion picture house.' She used a hand to wipe the drip from her nose, sniffed, then stepped away from him. 'We left after the all-clear and when we got to Alma Street there was all these ambulances, ARP men and the WI making tea and handing out blankets.' She paused. 'Mrs Symonds from number five rushed up to me and said, "Your mum's copped it, Rube, an' your house is a pile of rubble . . ."' Remembering was too much and once more she crumpled, the tears falling fast.

Marge took over. 'We couldn't believe our eyes. Where Ruby's house used to be there was an empty space. The ground was still smoking.' She wiped her hand across her eyes. Ruby knew she was upset for her. 'Funny thing was, the washing was still on the line!'

Ruby whispered, 'Mrs Symonds said they took what was left of my mum to the mortuary . . .' Marge pulled her close.

'She 'as to go there tomorrow, Merv, the ARP man said.' Marge was hugging Ruby tightly.

Mervyn ushered them into the main bar and parked himself behind the counter. He slopped brandy into three glasses, not bothering with the silver measure.

'A nice drop of this is what you need.' He downed one and pushed the other two across the bar. Over the top of the bar was a wooden sign that said, 'Enter as a Stranger, Leave as a Friend.' Mervyn believed in that sign.

'Ruby, I'm sure your mum didn't feel a thing,' he said. 'Drink that up.'

Eighteen-year-old Ruby felt like she'd never be able to smile again. Why did this awful thing have to happen to her mother, who'd never hurt a fly in the whole of her life? She'd brought up Ruby alone, keeping her clothed and fed by doing any job that came her way. Ruby's dad had disappeared when she was a baby. Her mother had been her rock, the woman she looked up to.

Ruby swallowed the drink straight back. The alcohol scorched her throat as it went down. She wasn't used to spirits.

Merv stroked his chin.

'What about you, Marge? Are you going to bunk in with Ruby?'

Ruby was aware that when her friend worked late she often spent the night at the pub sooner than walk home in the dark and wake her nan and her two kiddies, five-year-old Tony and the baby, Chrissie.

'If that's all right with you, Merv?' She gave him a big smile. 'I'd have taken Ruby home with me, but we haven't got the room.'

Marge lived in a tiny flat in Albert Street. She had a husband, Alf, in the army, but he wrote as seldom as he sent money home. Her nan looked after the children while Marge worked to keep them all.

'I don't know how to thank you, Mervyn, you're very kind.'

Merv coloured up at Ruby's words, pulled back the empty glasses and slopped in refills.

'It's the least I can offer one of my best barmaids,' he said. 'Drink this, then get to bed. I ain't going to say it'll be better tomorrow, because something like this takes time to sink in. But you're welcome here, the pair of you.'

Ruby knew Mervyn had a soft spot for Marge. Her glossy curls, rich red lips and her enthusiasm for life had captivated the middle-aged man shortly after he'd taken her on. She was hard-working and popular with the customers, especially the men, who often included her in their rude jokes. Men felt easy in her company. She had something that made them gather around her like moths to a flame. Ruby always felt better when she and Marge worked together.

The alcohol and her tears had made Ruby very tired.

'Take her upstairs, Marge,' said Merv kindly. Ruby looked at the now empty glasses on the bar and already everything that had happened to her tonight seemed more like a scene from a film than reality. Still wearing their coats, Marge gripped Ruby's arm and led her away from the bar, out into the wide hall and up the thickly carpeted stairs. Ruby's legs felt like they were made of rubber. She caught a glimpse of her reflection in the big wall mirror. Her own face looked back at her, but there was something different about it. In the space of a few hours her life had been shattered. She would never be the same again.

Marge's arm was tightly clasped about her waist. Ruby knew she was lucky to have such a good friend.

Mervyn Tanner allowed himself to sink blissfully down into the deep feather mattress. He sighed and looked at the alarm clock; three more hours before the draymen arrived with the wooden barrels of beer from Brickwood's Brewery. He'd already unlatched the bolt and opened the wooden hatch to the outside chute, which led to the cellar, so that they could roll the barrels down – if there were any. In this bloody war with all its shortages, promises of beer meant nothing. He needed to be down there to sign for the delivery, but that was three blessed hours away. Another sigh of pleasure escaped.

Until his thoughts turned to Ruby.

Marge was right to bring her here. After all, she worked here so she might as well live in. Sylvie had a room along the corridor. They'd get on all right, eventually. Grace, the cleaner, a big hefty woman not at all like her name, had the room between. Trouble was, Sylvie thought herself a bit hoity-toity because she had a voice that enabled her to sing in some of the other pubs and clubs in Gosport. But she was a quick and nimble barmaid, which was just what he wanted on busy nights in the Point of No Return.

It was a rare night when they weren't packed, thanks to the dockyard, the naval yard, the pongos from St George's barracks, the air force at Lee-on-the-Solent and the Allies off the ships that docked in Portsmouth, just over the water.

Sometimes there were so many foreign tongues in the bar, including the Americans from their stores base at Southampton, that he had to pinch himself to remember he was in Gosport!

Mervyn tossed and turned.

He couldn't get the look of sadness that had settled on Ruby's face out of his mind. Perhaps he shouldn't have given her so much brandy? A cup of tea might have been better. Still, the girls knew where the kitchen was; if they wanted tea they could make it themselves. After all, he had plenty.

Bags of loose Brooke Bond Divi had fallen off the back of a lorry right into Lennie Stark's possession and naturally some of it had come Mervyn's way, for a fee, of course. Fancy the government only allowing two ounces of tea a week per person! Nobody could exist without a decent cuppa, could they? Cups of tea were what the English needed to win this war, everyone knew that.

He thought about the surprise American and British landings at Anzio that he'd heard about on the wireless. They were trying to stop supplies getting through to the 100,000 German troops at the Garigliano front and meeting little resistance.

He'd also listened to the announcer telling of the RAF bombers dropping 2,300 tons of bombs on the Nazi capital of Berlin. We'll get them blighters yet, he thought. We'll stop that dirty swine Hitler from invading.

Memories of the Great War ran through his brain. Twenty, he was, when they sent him to France. All that mud and all that bloodshed, all them bodies!

He was one of the lucky ones, he knew that. The damn gas had got hold of him and after the war he could barely fight his way out of a paper bag, let alone win a bout in a ring! He'd had the world in his hands and it had all been snatched away from him. Still, he'd had a bit put by to buy this place, hadn't he? That gas had frightened him, though. Even now, all these years later and in a different war, he insisted that all his girls keep their gas masks beneath the counter in the bar while they were working, in case of a gas attack.

He'd met and married his Joanne and she'd been a good wife, until that bloody bomb landed on the picture house in Stoke Road and she'd died along with all the other poor buggers. He still missed her. Told her that when he took flowers up to the cemetery.

Shame they'd never had kiddies. He'd have liked a couple running about the place. Marge sometimes turned up with her two little 'uns. He liked to spoil the boy with crisps, little bugger that he was!

There'd been a few women sniffing about him. He knew it wasn't him they wanted; it was the pub they were interested in. Well, look at him, ugly old bugger. That's what boxing does to a man, Mervyn thought, takes away his good looks; takes away his brain as well, sometimes.

He slept.

Chapter Two

Mervyn crawled out of bed. Already the draymen were rolling barrels and he could hear the clip-clop of the horses' hooves shuffling on the cobbles and their snorting as the animals breathed in the cold January air.

Downstairs in two seconds, he was pulling his braces over his shoulders, watching the two burly blokes at work.

'Mornin',' he called.

'Did we wake you?' Jonas Bennet paused, his hand on a cask and laughed, his red face even more scarlet than usual with the effort of the heavy work and the brisk wind blowing up off the Solent.

'Cheeky bugger,' Mervyn replied, but he knew he'd been caught napping. A bit more banter followed and then Mervyn went back inside to make tea after signing the delivery chit.

The kettle hadn't boiled when Lennie Stark pushed open the kitchen door and poked his head inside.

'Got some spirits, if you want them?' His voice was like gravel. Merv thought anyone could see where his son Joe got his good looks. They both were as tall as lamp-posts, with deep brown eyes and dark curly hair, Lennie's with a bit of grey at the temples, but it only seemed to make him more manly. Lennie eased himself into the warmth of the kitchen. 'I got whisky, gin, bourbon. And if you don't want it, the Flying Fox'll have it!'

'From the American stores at Southampton?'

'Ask no questions an' I'll tell you no lies.' Lennie grinned. 'Want it or not?'

'Of course I'll bloody take it.' Mervyn went over to the big old Welsh dresser and took out his wallet from a drawer. He also kept a stash in a National Dried Milk tin at the back of the cupboard, but he didn't advertise that fact. He extracted some notes, looked up at Lennie, who frowned, added another note, watched Lennie grin, then passed the money to his mate. Without a word the money was transferred to Lennie's wallet and he left the kitchen, reappearing moments later with a cardboard box containing the spirits which he offloaded on to the table.

'Good stuff, that is. The American lads gets it for next to

nothing from their stores, but they comes down to Gosport, in here, an' buys it at inflated prices,' said Lennie.

Merv, filling the teapot said, 'We all got to make a livin'.'

Lennie grinned again. 'Don't forget there's a war on.'

'I hadn't forgotten,' Merv said. 'When's that lad of yours coming home?'

'You know they don't let us know nothin' about what them glider-boys gets up to. An' even if I knew, I couldn't tell you, "walls have ears" an' all that. You pouring out that tea, or are we going to sit and look at it?'

'I thought Joe went in the army?' Merv shuffled towards the dresser and took down cups from the hooks.

'Like I said, it's hush-hush.' Lennie parked himself down on a stool at the table.

'Well, I've got his girl upstairs.' Mervyn lifted his head to denote his bedrooms. 'Poor little bugger lost her mum last night an' all her belongings.'

At first Lennie looked cross, then worry etched itself over his face. 'Why didn't you send her round to me?'

'That would be like sending Red Ridin' Hood straight to the bleedin' wolf. Anyway, she's all right. Marge is with her.'

Lennie relaxed his features. 'Thank goodness she's safe. Our Joe thinks the world of her. She's a nice girl, is Ruby.'

'Yes, and too nice for you to sink your teeth into while

Joe's away.' Everyone knew Lennie Stark chased anything in a skirt. Merv knew that Joe was different, a one-girl man. He and Ruby had got together a few months ago. Since Joe had left Gosport they'd been exchanging letters.

Merv thought he'd catch old Percy the Post and let him know any letters due for Alma Street could be left on his hall table. He'd make sure Ruby got her post, that was the least he could do.

'Good cuppa, this.' Lennie licked his lips.

'I'd be surprised to hear you say anything else, considering I got the tea off you.'

Lennie slapped his knee and laughed. 'I got to go. Tell that girl she knows where I am if she wants anything, anything at all.' He winked at Mervyn. Underneath that checked suit Lennie Stark had a heart of gold, hidden somewhere.

'Will do,' said Merv. He watched Lennie get up and move towards the door, then he took down another two cups and began filling them with tea. He grunted as Lennie called goodbye and once out in the hallway Mervyn began climbing the wide stairs to the bedrooms above the bar. He liked that he could smell polish through the stale cigarette smoke from last night. Grace was a bugger for polishing.

He knocked on the door, after setting the teas on the carpet. Marge called, 'Come in.'

When he stepped inside he saw Marge was dressed, but Ruby was a lump in the double bed.

'She didn't sleep well last night,' Marge said. 'Only to be expected.' She eyed the tea. 'That's kind of you. Ruby'll be glad of that; always makes a person feel better, don't it?'

As if on cue, Ruby opened her eyes. Mervyn saw they were puffy and heavy-lidded. She'd obviously cried herself to sleep. 'Hello,' she said drowsily.

'Stay up here as long as you like. You ought to have a couple of days off, you've had a big shock,' Mervyn said, putting one of the cups on the small table by the side of the bed. The other cup had already been claimed by Marge.

'No! I must work. I'll be all right once I'm behind the bar.' Mervyn was surprised at the sharpness in Ruby's voice.

'Well, sometimes work helps, but only if you're sure.' He looked at Marge. She passed him back her empty cup and he saw she'd changed her clothes from the ones she'd worn last night. He was used to her spending nights in this room. When they had a lock-in in the bar and she worked late, Marge usually stopped over. Her nan preferred that to her getting home, making a noise and waking them all up. The flat was small and baby Chrissie woke at the slightest sound. Marge kept a few clothes in the wardrobe and toilet things in a drawer.

He turned to go. Marge caught his eye and whispered, 'Thanks.'

As soon as the door had closed on him, Ruby got out of bed and drank her tea. She'd worn her petticoat as a nightdress.

In the corner of the room was a sink and she spotted a brand new toothbrush on its surround.

'Mervyn usually keeps a few toiletries for his overnight guests. There's soap, Gibb's Dentifrice and I've sorted out a few clothes of mine you can wear,' Marge explained, then stared at her, concerned. 'You sure you want to work?'

Ruby nodded as she turned the tap, listening to the water gurgling in the pipes.

She bent over the sink and lathered her hands with soap and began washing. 'I keep thinking that if we hadn't gone dancing last night and we'd stayed at my house, then maybe my mum would still be here . . .' She thought of all the servicemen she'd danced with while her mum had . . . had . . .

'Stop that, Ruby,' snapped Marge. 'If we'd stopped round your house my kids could be without a mother now!'

Ruby pressed the towel she was using across her eyes. 'Oh, Marge, I'm sorry, I never thought—'

'Well, just thank your lucky stars we're alive. Get dressed —' she pointed to a pile of clothes on a nearby chair — 'and I'll come with you to the mortuary when we've finished here this afternoon.'

Ruby, chastened, finished washing, then she put on Marge's clothes. She stared at herself in the mirror, glad she and her friend were of a similar height and shape. 'I think I'll ask Merv if he can give me a sub so I can buy some clothing and a few things I need.'

She went over to Marge, put her hand on her arm and looked into her eyes. 'Thanks,' she said. 'For being such a good friend. I dunno what I'd do without you.'

'Shut up, you silly moo.' Marge was embarrassed. 'You've got to write and tell Joe what's—'

'No can do,' said Ruby. 'He's moved on from the training camp and as yet I don't have his new address. I'll have to wait until he writes to me.'

Ruby pulled Marge's hairbrush through her hair and winced at a tangle.

She was glad she was going to serve behind the bar. It might stave off that dreadful feeling she had, like a thick band of steel was squeezing her heart every time she thought about the loss of her mum.

'I suppose this room'll be ours now,' Marge said. 'We can't have separate rooms, otherwise Merv won't have hardly any left for bed and breakfasters.'

'You don't stay here often, though, do you?'

Marge shook her head. 'Only when absolutely necessary. I'd much rather be home with my family. But I'm the only wage earner, so I can't afford to say no to overtime, can I? Anyway, it'll be nice us bunking in together sometimes, won't it?'

Ruby didn't relish staying on her own. There would be too much time to think. As if reading her mind, Marge said, 'After we've been to the mortuary, you can come home with me before my nan starts worrying.'

Ruby nodded. Marge was now kneeling on the bed with her compact against the iron bedpost, as she spat on her little mascara brush and coated her eyelashes. She paused, upended her handbag on the bed and said, 'Whatever you haven't got you can borrow from me.' She liberally sprinkled herself with perfume and offered the little bottle to Ruby.

Ruby smiled at her and sat down on the stool in front of the dressing table. The room smelled faintly of polish and strongly of Marge's scent. The double bed dominated, with a wardrobe along one wall and an easy chair in the corner. The slightly open sash-corded window looked down over the street where the market was almost in full swing. Laughter, noise and the sound of metal bars clanging as the stallholders set up for the day made her feel less isolated.

'My mum loved the market . . .'

'Fine,' broke in Marge, 'but you mustn't dwell on what's happened. You need to grieve, but don't let sadness swamp you.'

Ruby knew she was right. She outlined her lips with bright red lipstick, sighing because she'd nearly used it all. Make-up was difficult to get hold of, especially red lipsticks. She'd heard that Hitler hated it, so almost every woman in England painted their lips as brightly as possible. The war was now in its fifth year; would it never end? she wondered. She stood up and surveyed herself, wearing the pink fluffy jumper with the puff sleeves and the grey wide-legged trousers that Marge had lent her. Once again, she thought how lucky she was to have such a loyal friend.

Chapter Three

'Check your gas masks.'

Marge winked at Ruby. Mervyn said this every morning. The bad experience with gas that had left him with lung damage after the Great War had made him doubly careful, so he wanted to be sure that if Adolf Hitler sent planes over that dropped gas along the south coast his staff would be ready. The girls looked beneath the counter, then nodded at him.

'Humour the daft bugger. After all, he's only looking out for us.' Ruby smiled at Marge's words. They both knew Mervyn was a good boss.

Ruby had put her cup of tea at the back of the bar. Both she and Marge had eaten toast for breakfast. Ruby surprised herself with her hunger and had carried through another cuppa from the kitchen to the bar; she couldn't drink tea when it was hot and had to leave it until it grew cool. She started polishing some glasses with a tea towel while Marge excused herself, saying, 'Won't be a minute.'

Out the window Ruby could see the regulars lined up in the cold, waiting for Mervyn to open up. Marge had waylaid him as he went to unlock the main door. The wireless was on. Bing Crosby was crooning away and Ruby checked the bar top to see that the drip mats and ashtrays were all clean and in their usual places.

Through the window she could see Ol' Tom rubbing his gloveless hands, so she got his tankard down from the overhead shelf and put it ready to pour his mild as he stepped into the warm bar. Alec and his brother Alan were stamping up and down, all muffled up against the cold. She dived beneath the counter and put the cribbage board ready. Both of them would stay until lunchtime, playing at the table in the corner. Then they'd go along to the Dive café for a bite to eat. They didn't drink much. Both men were in their seventies, unmarried and regular as clockwork with their custom.

Margaret Bell was also hovering. Her fur coat looked ready for the knacker's yard, thought Ruby. It reminded her of that song, 'Stick It on the Wall, Mrs Riley,' about a woman who had a similarly ancient beaver coat and, like Margaret Bell, was never seen without it.

Standing across the road was a tall straight man wearing a trilby rakishly pulled over one eye and a puce mackintosh topping a blue suit. His long face and dark eyes gave him a mysterious look. Beneath his arm was a folded newspaper.

Ruby knew the newspaper was the early edition of the *Evening News* and Richard Williams was a reporter for this esteemed local newspaper. He also wrote Westerns that were published under the pseudonym Hank Wilson. They were very popular. He'd wanted to call himself Hank Williams after an American singer he'd heard once, so he'd told Ruby, but his editor had dissuaded him, reminding him that if and when Hank Williams became famous, he might not appreciate the fact an English writer had stolen his name. A small shiver ran through her body. There was something about Richard Williams that unnerved her. Was it because he never mixed with the rest of the clientele? His accent was not of the slangy Portsmouth twang; he'd obviously attended the kind of schools that Gosport people never had the chance to aspire to and it showed in the way he often left behind newspapers with the difficult crosswords completed. He'd also confided that he hadn't been able to join the forces because he had a heart defect.

Now, he caught her looking at him through the window

and he smiled, sending a flutter through her body. She nodded back, then reached up and took his tankard from the top shelf, ready to serve him when the pub's doors were finally opened.

'Here you are.' Marge breezed up in a cloud of lily of the valley, waving a white note beneath Ruby's nose. The sharp scent momentarily masked the bar's smell of beer, polish and stale cigarettes.

'Where did you get that fiver?'

'Off Merv, where else? He said pay him back whenever. After we've been to my place to see my kiddies, we can go back into town and see what we can find in the shops and market.' Marge looked expectantly at Ruby, who was quite overcome with emotion. 'You did have your ration book and identification in your bag last night, didn't you? You didn't leave your papers in the house?'

Ruby shook her head. She'd need clothing coupons if they could find anything decent to buy.

'Thank you,' she sighed. She knew Marge could twist Mervyn round her little finger. Anything Marge ever desired was never out of bounds with Merv. Then she suddenly grinned. 'I turned me knickers inside out this morning, so it'd be nice to have some clean ones!'

'Dirty cow,' laughed Marge. 'Sorry I didn't have a spare

pair. Ever heard of washing 'em?' She dived beneath the counter, found Ruby's handbag and stuffed the note inside.

'You serving or not?' Ol' Tom was grinning at Marge when she looked up. Their shift had begun.

'Guinness, please,' Richard Williams said. He held Ruby's gaze. She'd already placed his tankard beneath the pump. The Guinness took a long time to pour but she knew he hated the bottled stuff. 'I heard about your misfortune,' he said quietly. 'I'm sorry. If there's anything I can do . . . ?'

'That's kind of you,' said Ruby, suddenly realizing that the bomb that had taken away her mother and home would naturally be a talking point amongst the customers, until, like most gossip, it too died a death. She'd just have to put up with the talk, the stares. People didn't mean anything by it; mostly they'd be concerned for her welfare.

Mervyn was behind the bar as well. At twelve Sylvie would arrive. Because she sang most evenings, she didn't work full time, unlike Ruby and Marge. For two hours most lunchtimes she helped out, as it was the pub's busiest time. When she sang in the pub in the evenings, people turned up to listen and Mervyn was happy with the extra custom.

'Take a drink for yourself,' Richard said.

'Thank you, can I have it later?' Ruby nodded towards her tea at the back of the bar. Richard nodded. Like other customers, he was aware she might not take the drink in alcohol but would probably take his money and then put a bottle cap at the back of the bar. At the end of her shift, Mervyn wouldn't mind her and Marge exchanging the bottle tops for cash from the till. It was one of the perks of the job and as long as his barmaids didn't take liberties, Mervyn trusted them.

'Are you all right? Got a place to stay?' At last she was able to put his drink in front of him.

'Merv's letting me stay here,' she said, taking the money he proffered. Richard's eyes hadn't left her face.

'That's all right then,' he said. 'But if you want anything . . .' His voice tailed off.

While he'd been waiting he'd put on his spectacles. The dark frames made him look even more intelligent as he walked over to his usual table. A gust of laughter suddenly filled the bar, along with a squeal from Marge. Ruby could hear American voices now. The till pinged and a voice in her ear whispered, 'He likes you.'

'Shut up,' said Ruby and Marge laughed. Ruby knew her face had coloured up.

'Well, he does, I can tell. You could do a lot worse, a writer with a house in Alverstoke. Though you might bite off more than you can chew with him.'

'He's years older than me,' spluttered Ruby. She wondered what Marge had meant by that last remark.

'That doesn't matter,' Marge insisted. 'He's really good-looking in an Ashley Wilkes kind of way. But I ain't never seen him in here with a woman.'

Marge was referring to the Lesley Howard character from the film *Gone With the Wind*.

'S'pose so,' admitted Ruby. 'Merv said he used to look after his sick mum. I think he's a bit deep.'

'That's cos he writes novels,' said Marge, as though it explained everything, then she moved off to serve a customer at the end of the bar.

'Pint of mild?' repeated Ruby.

She'd got caught up in serving customers. She wondered who'd told Richard about her mother. That was the trouble with Gosport. News got about like jungle drums were informing everyone. Still, she thought, while they were talking about her, they were leaving someone else alone. She'd been right to work today; she knew it would do her good.

In a quiet moment she wiped down the bar and then put the rum bottle back on the shelf; it had been almost in constant use this morning. She looked across the sea of customers and saw Marge collecting glasses. They worked well together, she thought. Mervyn was leaning across the bar talking to a regular, but as if feeling Ruby's eyes on him he looked up and mouthed, 'All right?' She nodded. He was a good bloke, was Mervyn.

Suddenly she felt a hand on her arm, moving her to one side, and a figure was taking a box-like object from beneath the bar and waving it at Mervyn.

'He's got eyes in the back of his head, just showing him my gas mask's with yours,' said Sylvie. The smell of Californian poppy was strong. Her perfume, like everything else about her, was well over the top.

'Hello, Sylvie,' Ruby muttered. She had no intention of telling the girl about her mother. She couldn't warm to Sylvie. But then she'd never liked her at school either, mostly because every chance Sylvie got she bullied people, and it was Ruby who'd taken the brunt of that bullying.

One particular time Ruby was on her knees in the playground, with a circle of Sylvie's cronies around her jeering and yelling. Ruby had always been a slight child. Sylvie had put her thumb and forefinger around Ruby's wrist, encircling it. Because her fingers met, she was calling her Skinny Lizzie and implying her mother didn't feed her. Ruby's mum worked hard providing a stable home. Ruby's dad didn't exist in her life, whereas Sylvie's dad was convinced his daughter was going to become a world-class singer to rival Vera Lynn. He paid for her to have singing lessons.

Just when Ruby thought her shame would never end, a boy from the class above pushed aside the chanting girls and was about to raise his hand to Sylvie, then thought better of it and said, 'Get away, Sylvie Meadows, you're a disgrace.'

Sylvie's eyes had filled with tears but she'd slunk away, her friends following. That boy was Joe Stark and everyone knew that Sylvie had her heart set on him as a boyfriend. He was every bit as good-looking as his dad with his dark curls and long-lashed blue eyes. But Joe was more intelligent – he was never without a book stuffed in his back pocket.

Joe had helped Ruby to her feet and walked her home after using his grubby handkerchief to wipe the blood from her grazed knees. Sylvie never bothered her again after that. She totally ignored Ruby at school. It was as if Ruby didn't exist.

When Ruby began working at the Point of No Return and discovered she would be doing shifts with Sylvie, at first she was terrified. A leopard never changes its spots, her mother had told her many times.

That first night in the bar, Sylvie had greeted Ruby as if they were long-lost friends! Ruby, politely, never referred to the past.

Sylvie's singing lessons had paid off. She now entertained at several venues in the area and was paid well for it. Sylvie had turned into a beautiful young woman, choosy with her friendships. Now, receiving a nod from Mervyn, she sauntered to the end of the bar to serve a couple of estate agents.

'I forgot she was working twelve till two.' Marge's mouth turned down at the corners and she made a face at Ruby.

After serving the men, Ruby watched as Sylvie stared at her reflection in the mirrored glass behind the coloured bottles at the back of the bar. One of her long red fingernails picked at a bit of imaginary something on her immaculately made-up face. 'Oblivious to anyone except herself,' said Marge. 'Watch her with her bottle tops.'

Then a flurry of customers sent the four of them scuttling as they hurriedly served people. It was the lunchtime rush.

'Just for once I'd like to serve something really glamorous like we see being asked for in the bars at the pictures,' said Marge.

The air was thick with the stench of beer and cigarette smoke, so thick it could almost be cut with a knife.

Ruby had just emptied all the drip trays into the special slops pail. Mervyn would later filter this into the cask of mild. Every publican did it; some customers suspected, but never really knew where the slops went. A pint of Mervyn's mild was the best in Gosport.

'All we ever sell is beers and spirits,' said Ruby, commiserating with Marge as she now washed glasses in the sink beneath the counter. Marge picked up a tea towel and began drying.

The wireless broke off from playing dance music and the news came on.

'Did you hear that?' Now the rush had slowed again Mervyn was back sitting on the customers' side, drinking a well-earned half pint of bitter. 'The Nazis are planning an Aryan race of blond-haired blue-eyed perfect people. They're breeding children specially . . .'

'Me an' Ruby'll be all right then,' chipped in Marge. 'We got the looks. Dunno about you an' Sylvie though.' She began to laugh.

Sylvie, who was collecting dirty ashtrays, stopped what she was doing and glared at Marge. 'Hitler wants blonds,' she said.

'Don't say much for ol' Hitler himself then, with his rat's tails hair and mousy moustache, does it?' joined in Ruby. She turned to Marge. 'An' anyway, you can't make anything else besides a gin and orange, Marge, so what you want to serve cocktails for?' Ruby was teasing her friend.

'Shut up,' Marge laughed. 'I got a book at home on cocktails.'

'Best place for it, at home,' said Mervyn. 'Can't see Ol' Tom asking for a cocktail, can you?'

They all started giggling and once again Ruby thanked her lucky stars she'd decided to return to work straight away.

Chapter Four

Ruby stared down at her mother's face. It was serene. She looked like she was asleep, but Ruby knew different.

'Not a mark on her body,' said the mortuary attendant. 'Happens that way sometimes.' Then he added, 'I'll leave you alone for a while. I'll be outside with your friend if you want anything.' He closed the door after him and left Ruby sitting on a chair next to her dead mother. Did she want anything? She wanted this pale, frail, blonde woman to be alive again. To laugh, to dance around the kitchen with a young Ruby clutched to her bosom. But Ruby couldn't have that, could she? That part of her life was gone. Now she had to make her own way in her life. The thought was daunting.

Damn Hitler to hell, she thought, stroking the cold hand, willing the heat from her body to warm her mother's skin. She'd admired her mother so much that words couldn't describe her feelings. Her mother had been her anchor. Now, without Jane Garett, Ruby was adrift.

Just for a moment she thought she could hear her mother's voice. 'Be strong,' it was telling her. She looked at the wax-like fingers. Her mother's wedding ring glistened in the dull light shining down from the high window.

On an impulse Ruby slipped the circle of gold from the cold finger, surprised the ring could be removed so easily. Then she put it on the third finger of her right hand. Apart from memories, the wedding ring was all she had left of her mother. The tears rose but she knew crying was self-indulgent. Hadn't her mother told her to be strong?

Ruby rose, bent down and kissed the cold lips. Then she turned and opened the door, inhaling a cloud of cigarette smoke from the attendant's Woodbine.

Marge jumped up from the bench. 'You all right?'

Ruby nodded at her, then asked the attendant when she could bury her mother, giving her address as the Point of No Return.

Later, as they picked their way over a bomb site adorned with a broken bedstead and a stuffing-less armchair, Marge asked, 'How you gonna pay for a funeral?'

Ruby shrugged. 'I don't know, but I will.'

They walked arm in arm from Clarence Road to Albert

Street. It was a cold, clear day and because it was January it would be dark in an hour or so. There was no need for words between them. Ruby liked that she could be with Marge, silent, yet Marge still seemed to know her thoughts.

Near the coal yard in Albert Street, not far from the railway line, they turned into an alley that was the only entrance to Marge's two-roomed home.

Marge unlatched the back door that led into a room containing a sink, a big old-fashioned cooker, a sofa that doubled as her bed and a large Welsh dresser hung about with crockery. Beneath the sash window that looked down towards an outside lavatory at the bottom of a long thin overgrown garden was a small table and a couple of kitchen chairs. A fire burned brightly in the grate and a little woman in a grey dress sat in an armchair. Her grey hair was plaited and looped over the top of her head and in her arms slept a pink-cheeked child with dark curls and chubby limbs. The woman put her finger to her lips and went, 'Shh!'

Marge and Ruby froze.

'She's been a bugger,' whispered the woman. Propped against the chair was a walking stick. With her free hand she pushed her spectacles higher on her nose. 'Awake all night and I've only just got her off.'

'She won't sleep tonight,' warned Marge. 'Tony?'

'On his way home from school, I hope,' said Marge's nan. 'An' don't look like that, Emmie Higgins is picking him up, along with her Tommy.'

Ruby felt Marge relax. Marge went over to the kettle, shook it and then set it down on the stove. She lit the gas with a Swan Vesta and the flames popped.

Ruby looked through the window at the monstrosity of a mangle sitting in the long grass. A bowed line held a row of surprisingly white terry towelling nappies blowing gently in the wintry breeze.

'Shall I bring in the washing?' she asked.

'Would you, Rube, there's a good girl.' Ruby didn't think Marge's nan could stir from the chair and the fire. Marge gave her a grateful look then began setting out mugs on the table.

Outside, Ruby let down the line, ready to gather the nappies. She thought how strange it was not to be going home to the house in Alma Street and her mother. There'd be no more changing her clothes in her comfortable bedroom or kneeling on the floor in front of the mirror propped on a chair so she could put on her make-up. She supposed she must now treat the room above the pub as her home. She realized how lucky she was to have somewhere to go, a comfortable bed to sleep in.

With an armful of dry nappies she turned to go back to Marge's kitchen. Her fingers brushed against the wedding ring.

Her father must have loved her mother at one time, the ring proved that. But why did he leave? Where did he go? She barely remembered the man who'd held her in his arms, that fragrant pipe-tobacco smell that came to her sometimes to remind her of him. Some men simply left their houses and their families and disappeared, but why had her father been such a man?

When she was small she'd asked her mother where her daddy was. The curt reply had been, 'He left. He's not coming back, so don't ask again.' But she'd seen the pain in her mother's eyes. Ruby never asked again, and now she'd never know.

Once back in the warm crowded room, Ruby draped the nappies over the fireguard to air. She saw Marge had taken off her coat and changed places with her nan. Ruby watched as Marge planted a soft kiss on her daughter's forehead.

The rattle of mugs at the table and the sound of pouring tea caused Marge to say, 'When we've had a cuppa, we'd best get down the town and see what we can find to clothe you. Shall we get some chips in the Devonia? I'm starving.' The clipped way she spoke made Ruby realize that while she'd been gathering the washing Marge had told her nan about the bomb and her mother.

'Starving? That's your own fault,' Nan barked. 'I didn't

know what time you'd be home, Marge, an' I promised Tony tonight we'd have faggots and mash, but that's for later.'

Ruby realized by the unusual atmosphere that Nan didn't know what to say to her about her mother, so for now had decided to say nothing.

A mug of tea was slapped into Ruby's hands.

Marge made a face at her nan, but Ruby witnessed the love and understanding flow between them. They both knew she wouldn't want to talk about her mother's death.

Back at the pub, Mervyn had impressed on Ruby that she was to cook and eat whatever she found in the kitchen. The slice of toast she'd eaten for breakfast was grumbling away in her stomach, reminding her that she was still hungry.

'Mum!' A whirlwind of a small blond boy swept into the room, closely followed by a red-headed friend with freckled skin and arms and legs that were too long for his clothes.

Immediately, the baby, Chrissie, opened her eyes and started wailing. Marge lumbered to her feet, pushed the crying child into Ruby's arms and pulled the blond-haired boy into a tight embrace.

'Hello, my love, how was school?' The boy was pushed away again so that Marge could look him over. Then, happy nothing was amiss except for a torn jumper and baggy socks, she hauled him back into her arms.

'You're squashing me!' Tony said and struggled away, shrugging himself out of his unbuttoned coat and leaving it in a heap on the floor. 'I won a race at school. Mr Fellowes said I might get in the team. What's a team, Mum?'

Tony had Marge's pointed chin and blue eyes. He stared at her, waiting for her to enlighten him.

'It means your teacher can see you're a very fast runner and he might want you to run for the school in a race with other boys, when you're older.'

'Pooh! I can run to school now,' answered the boy. 'I don't have to wait until I'm six and with the others.'

Nan was laughing. She stepped back from the cream and green cupboard with the pull-down table where she'd been cutting bread. 'He's a card, ain't he, Rube?' She didn't wait for an answer but held out two halves of a slice of doorstep-thick bread, dripping with condensed milk. Each lad took a piece, murmuring in unison, 'Cor, fanks.'

The old woman leaned across and picked up her stick, then said to Marge, 'I ain't pushing you out, love, but if you wants to get some bits in the town before the market closes you'd better go.' Marge struggled into her coat and Ruby handed the plump baby back to Nan, who said, 'She's filled her pants, I can smell it from here.' Then in a more serious tone she said very quietly, 'Sorry about your mum, Rube.'

Ruby smiled at her. 'Thanks,' she said.

'You're welcome here any time,' Nan added. 'If we'd had more room, you could have come here.'

Ruby knew the second room of the flat was a bedroom filled chock-full of a double bed, cots and bedding. The two-room so-called flat was really the bottom half of a terraced house, for which the landlord charged Marge an exorbitant rent of fourteen shillings a week.

'She's all right at the Point,' said Marge, leaning forward to kiss her nan's forehead. 'I'll see you later.'

She turned and gave a wink to Tony who was busy licking his fingers while holding his *Dandy* comic. Marge grinned at the other lad, then pushed Ruby through the open door and out into the back yard.

As soon as they reached the pavement Marge said, 'I've changed me mind about chips. I'm not hungry no more.'

Ruby said, 'I'm not daft, I saw the pile of money you left on the table. That was your tips, wasn't it? You was leaving money for Nan.'

Marge coloured up. 'We're a bit short at present, I haven't had any money from Alf for ages.'

'Yet you asked Mervyn for money for me?' It never ceased to amaze Ruby how deep the older girl's friendship went for her.

'We both get paid at the end of the week and things will be better then,' said Marge, tucking her arm through Ruby's. 'C'mon, let's get down the town. We have to be back by six for work.'

They walked past gaps in the houses where Hitler's bombs had fallen, past St George's Barracks, past Weevil Lane where the armament factory stood near the water's edge and the Canary Girls worked, so called because of the gunpowder that affected their skins, making them look yellow. They went on walking past the mortuary, where Marge didn't say anything about Ruby's mother, but she squeezed her arm to give Ruby confidence.

And then they were in the midst of the market with stallholders calling out their wares and the smells of fruit, vegetables and fish vying with the scents of bath salts and cheap cleaning products.

Ruby hadn't said anything, but when she'd managed to find a few second-hand bits of clothing at Paddy's stall and discovered enough toiletries to tide her over, she was going to treat Marge to Dutch eel and chips in the Devonia fish shop. With some bread and scrape and a cuppa the meal would set them both up nicely for the evening shift.

Ruby admired Marge. Thrown out by her mum at fourteen

for falling pregnant after experimenting with a boy at school, her nan had taken her in, looked after her and the baby, Tony, when he arrived, screaming and yelling, into the world. Marge had had to leave school and earn a living, so Nan became her childminder. When all her friends were discovering dancing and make-up, Marge was working extra shifts at Green's Bakery.

The lad who'd impregnated her had moved away, not interested in her or the baby. She now had no idea where her boy's father was and didn't care. At eighteen she'd met a soldier at a dance at the Connaught Hall and after a whirlwind courtship married him. She'd forgotten servicemen spent a lot of time away from home. Lonely for Gosport, she'd left the army accommodation at Aldershot to live once more with her nan, her mother meanwhile having disappeared with a spiv called Harry who used to have a fly pitch at the market.

On one of Alf's rare visits home Marge once again fell pregnant and the four of them crammed into her nan's tiny flat posed problems. Severe rheumatism meant her nan couldn't work, but Marge, now over eighteen, was able to earn for them all. Just as well, she'd told Ruby, for after Chrissie was born, Alf didn't come home so much and sent money irregularly.

Her nan was a godsend; she loved and looked after Chrissie and Tony, though she spoiled the little boy shamelessly.

All this Marge had confessed to Ruby one rainy evening at the pub when the miserable weather had kept the punters away.

'I'm not telling you because I want sympathy,' Marge had snapped. 'I'm explaining because I like you, but letting you know I can only offer friendship, I don't have the funds to go gallivanting over to Portsmouth or to Southampton to dances, but I'd like us to be mates and sometimes go to the Connaught or Lee Tower ballroom. An' even that won't be regular, because when I got time off I need to be with my nan and my kiddies. But you're welcome to join us.'

So they'd settled into an easy friendship that meant a lot to Ruby.

Picnics in the local recreation ground, walks along Stokes Bay and paddling in the cockle pond with Tony, Marge and Chrissie, became activities that Ruby loved. The two girls became more like sisters.

Far from the glamorous life Sylvie purported to be leading.

Going to dance halls in Portsmouth and Southampton to sing, wearing clothes that were glittery, escorted by men old enough to be her father was quite alien to Ruby and Marge. Yet Sylvie bragged all the time about the expensive and flash cars she'd ridden in and the meals she'd eaten in posh restaurants.

Ruby's mother, Jane, had been a quiet person, still working

at part-time cleaning jobs up to the day the bomb fell. She preferred Ruby to go and enjoy herself while she was happy to sit at home knitting or reading with the wireless on, though she adored it when Marge brought the children round or they all went out for walks together.

Working at the Point of No Return meant there was always something going on, people to talk to and to laugh with. Ruby enjoyed working for Mervyn, even if it was hard on her feet.

Sometimes she and Marge practically collapsed with exhaustion. Then they pursued easier hobbies at each other's homes, played Snakes and Ladders with Tony and Nan, or helped Jane Garett in her beloved garden. The war dictated their everyday lives, as it did for all people.

'I'm not paying three coupons for a pair of silk stockings.' Ruby was horrified. 'No, I don't care if they will soon all get snapped up. I'll put gravy browning on me legs and use me eyebrow pencil to make a line up the back, like I usually do.'

'Look at this dress.' Marge held out the green wool dress that was the exact shade of Ruby's eyes. 'I've still got forty coupons left from me allowance,' said Ruby, fingering its softness. 'It is lovely.'

They were in Fleure's in the High Street. 'Can you afford it?' Marge was curious. Ruby had had quite a spend-up, including buying liquorice sticks for Tony and a fluffy toy cat for Chrissie. Toys were hard to come by, so Ruby had said she just had to buy it for the little girl. 'Try it on. I know it will look lovely on you.' She unhooked the frock from its hanger.

'But it's too nice to get beer spilled all over it.' Ruby thrust the dress back at her.

'I was thinking you'd knock Joe's eyes out when he comes home and sees you in that.'

A sudden thrill coursed through Ruby's body. It was a lovely dress. And though there'd been few letters from Joe, eventually they'd let him come home on leave, wouldn't they?

'There's a mirror over here.' The elderly assistant with the victory-roll hairstyle showed her to a quiet corner where Ruby could try on the dress without the other shoppers gawping at her.

Trying to ignore her greying underwear, Ruby pulled the dress over her head. It felt soft, like duck down against her skin. She opened her eyes and looked at herself in the long mirror. She was transformed!

'You look a treat,' gushed Marge. 'You got to buy it. I got coupons to spare if you need them.'

Ruby ran a hand over her slim hips. The skirt clung in all the right places. She looked at the assistant, who amazingly hadn't said a word but simply stood smiling at her until, 'That dress was made for you,' came from her lips.

Ruby shuddered as she paid for her goods and once outside they both realized the day had disappeared.

'I think you've done well,' Marge said. 'If you give me those two pairs of trousers and those three blouses you got off Paddy, I'll get Nan to take them in to fit.' Ruby nodded. Nan was good at sewing. Marge was carrying the two pairs of second-hand shoes she'd got off the Greek's stall. In a brown carrier bag was the cheap underwear Ruby'd purchased from Woolies.

Ten minutes later they were sitting in front of two large plates of Dutch eel and chips. Ruby took a deep breath in, smelling the fragrant meal.

'Good thing fish ain't rationed.' Marge took a slurp of tea and wiped her mouth. 'Still, the shops can't always get hold of it, can they?'

Ruby waved her cup of tea in the air. 'To you,' she said. 'Best friends for ever.'

'You're bloody daft, you are,' said Marge.

But too late – Ruby had seen the tears in her friend's eyes.

Chapter Five

'He ain't gonna jump no more,' came their raucous voices as Joe prepared to jump. Fortified with a single pint of beer each, the airborne troops were still considered the relatively new weapons, and the one device that came into its own was the parachute. Joe would be floating down through the sky, egged on by Prime Minister Winston Churchill who'd decided to take the enemy by surprise – but first the men needed training.

The Parachute Regiment, a small elite group, was going to be thrust into the heart of the German enemy lines ahead of the main force. Only the cream of the crop from the men who applied were chosen. Some, like Joe, hadn't applied but were selected. Only the bravest, the best, were recruited. Backgrounds didn't come into it. Working-class men stood alongside the public schoolboys. The paras were the airborne infantrymen of the British Army. Their back-up, the First Airlanding Brigade's gliders, provided additional support as back-door entry into enemy territory.

Towed over enemy countryside and then cut loose to float down, the gliders would carry heavy equipment, including jeeps and small tanks, thus providing greater mobility, along with the infantrymen, to fight further and faster.

These, then, were the airborne cavalry.

Joe was scared. He knew it wouldn't be normal if he wasn't frightened of falling through the air, dependent only on a parachute to get him safely to the earth. But practice makes perfect and he'd told himself to trust the girls who'd packed the chutes. His life was in their hands.

If he met the stringent criteria of this training, then his beloved country's well-being would be in his hands. This was his fifth jump. Anyone failing a jump from an aircraft was sent back into the army – that's if he lived!

The door was open.

And then the air currents were rushing past his face, stretching his skin; too late now to be scared. He had to rely on his apparatus. Gone were the sounds of the men's voices, replaced by his own, 'If you're going to die, you can't do a bloody thing about it,' and the wind took his words away.

And then the ground was coming up to meet him.

Remember your training, do what that bastard Sergeant Cecil Howard had drummed into him at Colchester. Roll with it, be as one with the wind, the air, the earth.

No use wishing he had a second parachute to rely on. They cost sixty pounds each and the government had decided an extra chute was a waste of money.

And then he was down! Rolling, safe, unhurt. His silk parachute floating, drifting, seconds later around him on the ground, ready for him to gather and dispose of. His feet were on English soil, Brize Norton, to be precise.

Joe let out a huge sigh of relief.

At the Airborne Corps in the green grass of Herefordshire, operations were being planned by Major General Roy Urquhart, Commander of the First Airborne Division. Training, intensive and detailed, was carried out here but nothing happened without Montgomery's say-so.

That was all Joe knew. Rumours were rife. Joe was fed up with not knowing his next step. He dreaded his next run-in with Sergeant Howard. Why? Because he had to take all that the bastard dished out. Howard was his senior officer. Joe had to do what he was told, even if he thought Howard was an arsehole most of the time. The bloke had it in for him. Said he was a Gosport lout and not worthy of the maroon beret and badge with its wings and a parachute.

But Joe would bide his time, he'd show the bastard he was worth all this training. He thought of the argument yesterday because he was late for drill. He'd been to the office to double check on his post. Joe couldn't understand why Ruby hadn't written to him. It wasn't like her to break a promise.

Of course his dad had written and told Joe about the bomb devastating Ruby's home and killing her mother. The poor girl must be almost out of her mind with grief. He'd written to her straight away. Told her about the forty-eight-hour pass he was getting so he could be with her and see his family. Thank God she had her mate Marge, she was a good 'un, was Marge. His dad had told him Ruby was living at the pub. Mervyn would see she was all right. Of course he was worried about the girl, she'd crept into his heart and made her home there. He couldn't get her out of his mind.

The army postal office had told him categorically that if there'd been letters for him, he would have received them.

When he got back the others were lined up on the training ground and he'd made a show of himself joining them. Apologies didn't count. That bastard Howard wanted to show him who was boss. So Joe had been made to spend the afternoon cleaning the bogs with a bloody toothbrush! God, how he hated the sergeant's booming voice, his red moustache, and his sarcasm.

Joe saw his mate land on the soil in a flurry of creamy parachute silk. Vinnie gave him a thumbs-up sign. Joe nodded back. Now he could do with a second bloody pint!

Dick Haymes was fighting a losing battle singing 'You'll Never Know' against the noise in the bar. As Ruby looked at the clock she saw it wouldn't be long before Sylvie swanned on to the parquet flooring where the microphone was and began singing. There was no denying the girl had a voice. It reminded Ruby of Billie Holiday, all soulful and smoky. Sylvie had caught Ruby on the stairs when she'd got back from the town with her purchases from the market.

'I've been buying some stuff to wear,' admitted Ruby.

'I'm wearing a new dress tonight,' broke in Sylvie, looking down at Ruby's assorted jumble of bags. 'None of that Utility stuff for me. I had the dress handmade to fit. You're so lucky being a standard size. My bust being bigger than yours makes it difficult for me to wear cheap clothing.'

Ruby sighed. Why was it everything that came out of Sylvie's mouth was a put-down? She was too tired to think up a retort, so she merely smiled and said, 'I'll look forward to seeing you in it tonight.' She carried on up to her room and began putting her new things away in the wardrobe and in the drawers.

A pair of wide-legged dark trousers on Paddy's stall had caught Ruby's eye. She was going to team them with a frilly white blouse that looked as if it had come from the same source as the trousers.

'All good quality an' all tidy,' Paddy had said, his long white beard ginger in places from the cider he drank. For once, both Ruby and Marge had believed him.

Marge rarely wore the same clothes behind the bar in the evening that she'd worn in the mornings. Fastidious about the few clothes she had, she kept herself neat and clean at all times. Even though Marge's priority was feeding and clothing her children, she still liked to look nice.

Ruby began washing at the sink. She'd already checked the hall table where Percy the Post left letters, usually brought in by Sylvie during the busy lunchtime period. There was nothing from Joe.

Well, no matter, she thought, when tonight's shift was over she'd sit in bed and write him a letter telling him she loved him and how she felt about the bomb. If there was still no news tomorrow, she'd give the letter to his dad to post in with his, when Lennie next wrote back to Joe.

It couldn't be easy for the servicemen, she thought, not knowing where they were to be billeted, or to which part of the world they would go to fight. She understood the need for secrecy.

What with everything that had happened, Ruby hadn't had time to think much about Joe. But she was sure she loved him. Secretly, she'd always loved him. Oh, she'd had other boyfriends, not that many, but enough to know that none of them ever matched up to Joe Stark.

She'd thought she didn't stand a chance with the good-looking lad. And her mum had told her off many times for mooning after him, saying he'd break her heart. Break her heart? He never knew she existed!

After that time at school when he'd warned off Sylvie, he'd always been in the background, keeping an eye on her. Like she was some silly little kid that needed looking after! But he'd never approached her. Of course, Sylvie, being pretty, had caught his eye and Ruby had seen them kissing in the back row of the Forum picture house. But then Sylvie had always been hanging around him.

Sylvie hadn't been his only girlfriend.

When she'd told her mum, Jane had said, 'He's playing the field, sowing his wild oats.' Ruby, then, hadn't really known what her mother meant. But it did seem to confirm he didn't want a regular girlfriend.

One day, when she hadn't been working at the Point for

long, he'd come into the bar with a noisy crowd of lads. He'd stood looking at her as though he'd never set eyes on her before.

He waited outside until she'd finished work, then he'd asked solemnly if he could walk her home. She had agreed, why not?

He hadn't kissed her goodnight, but a week later when he did, Ruby knew it had been worth the wait.

'Don't you fall for him,' her mother warned. 'He's like his dad, anything in a skirt . . .' And so Ruby held a small part of herself back from him.

'Don't worry, Mum, I can handle him.'

It didn't take Ruby long to find out those words were the most ridiculous she'd ever spoken. Joe had crept into her heart even though she was aware of his reputation as a heart-breaker.

Joe enrolled in the army. The war separated them. At first there were no letters because, as his father explained, for the first few weeks his son would be practically a prisoner at Colchester. The army regulated the men's lives and to minimize homesickness, little contact with the outside world was the norm. The day finally arrived when a letter came from Joe. He said he thought of her all the time. Ruby hugged that letter to her heart.

But then his letters stopped.

Joe had been moved from the barracks, but he'd begged his father to let Ruby know that as soon as he was settled with a proper address, he would contact her. He had been chosen for the parachute regiment. He then apologized to his father because that short letter would be the last he would be able to send for some time.

Since then, silence for her.

'Percy the Post knows where you are, love,' Mervyn said. 'Any correspondence won't go astray.'

'What did you expect?' Sylvie was quick to point out. 'He's like his dad, he'll never settle down.'

'Take no notice,' warned Marge. 'She couldn't hold on to him, so she's jealous. We know he's joined some crack regiment that's all hush-hush. Eventually you'll hear from him. He's not like that bag of shite I married.'

So Ruby decided she'd heed Marge's words.

Alfred Sugden had taken on Marge with her little boy, married her, gave the lad his name so he wouldn't grow up a bastard, but as soon as Chrissie was born everything changed. Despite this, Ruby knew deep down Marge still had feelings for Alf.

Ruby now brushed her hair until it shone, using the hair-brush she'd bought in the market. She stared at herself in the big floor-length mirror.

'Cor! You look nice,' said Marge, coming in from the bathroom.

Marge had spent a long time making up her face. The red puff-sleeved jumper and maroon skirt emphasized her slimness.

'So do you,' returned Ruby. But her own new clothes only served to remind her that she'd lost her mum.

All the time Marge had been away from her, Ruby had kept thinking about her mother. If Marge hadn't come in when she had, she'd have found Ruby crying.

Marge threw her towel over the back of a chair. She put an arm around Ruby's shoulders.

'It's all right, it's early days yet,' she said softly. 'Let's have another look at you.' She pushed Ruby to arm's length and then said, 'It's your lipstick. It's not vibrant enough.' She rummaged in her bag and came up with her own bright red one. 'Put this on, it'll go lovely with the black and white.' She handed the gold tube to Ruby and watched while she first outlined her lips then filled them in. 'That's better,' she said.

Looking at the bedside clock she added, 'We'd better get down to the bar. Mervyn'll have a fit if we're not there when he opens up.'

*

Ruby had served half a dozen people when she turned to find Richard Williams standing there with a brown paper parcel. She smiled at him, reached up for his special tankard and started filling it with Guinness. He pushed a parcel across the bar and said, 'One of the women at the *News* was selling lengths of this. I hope you don't think I'm being presumptuous, but knowing you'd lost all your belongings I bought some for you.'

Ruby'd never accepted presents from previous boyfriends. She'd even found it hard to let them pay for tickets for the pictures or bus fares when they'd asked her out. Joe had told her off for her independence.

Her mouth opened to say 'I can't accept that' when she saw the disappointed look begin to work its way over his face. It was a bit like a dog who was expecting to be kicked. She suddenly realized he meant nothing but kindness because he knew all her clothes had gone up in smoke. So, instead, Ruby smiled and asked, 'What is it?'

'Take a look,' he said, immediately looking happier. She unwrapped the brown paper to find a long length of parachute silk inside. Her fingertips felt its softness.

'Oh, it's lovely,' she said. Ruby didn't ask how the girl at his place of work had come by the material. That was something one never asked. It ran through her mind that there was enough silk to make camiknickers for both her and Marge, a couple of blouses, maybe even pyjamas. She thought of the rough cotton knickers she'd purchased in Woolies earlier, then imagined this lovely material close to her skin. 'I don't know what to say,' she added. His Guinness was ready, so Ruby set it in front of him, careful of the lovely cloth.

'Thank you will be enough,' he said, delving into his pocket for coins to pay for his drink.

'It's really kind of you,' she managed. Then she transferred his money to the till. 'Thank you,' she added.

'It's only a bit of material!' He laughed and moved to his usual table. With a warm feeling, Ruby wrapped up the parcel and put it beneath the counter near the boxed gas masks.

Chapter Six

'Vinnie, are you getting your post all right?'

Joe was lounging on his bed, Vinnie, his mate, was playing Patience, the cards spread across his army-issue blanket. Joe let his novel slide from his fingers. He quite liked the character Philip Marlowe and was reading the third book by Raymond Chandler, *The High Window*.

Vinnie scratched his ear. 'I write, but it's hit and miss whether I get answers. I've been putting this address down, but we both know we're likely to be moved on any day now, and maybe they delete addresses anyway, like they delete stuff we're not supposed to talk about.'

Joe sighed. 'We're kept in the dark like mushrooms.'

Both men were relaxing after a route march that morning. It was raining outside, the wind throwing the raindrops against the barrack-room window like hailstones. Most of the men had gone into town where the pubs, girls and a possible punch-up beckoned.

Joe had confined to barracks for answering back to his nemesis Sergeant Howard. Well, he didn't so much answer him back as make a slight noise like a laugh when the sergeant had mispronounced a word.

Howard had ripped into him: 'Think you're bloody clever, eh? Well we ain't all had the benefit of your Gosport schoolin', so you can stay behind this afternoon an' think about what subordination means.'

Joe had stood to attention. 'Yes, Sergeant.'

Those two words had been a sort of apology but inside he was seething. Howard was watching his every movement so he could take him down a peg. But why? One of the other blokes said Howard had lost his only son in France and ever since he'd tried to take his bitterness out on someone, anyone. Joe just happened to be the target of his unhappiness.

Vinnie had declined the offer of boozing and women. He was going to try to telephone the nursing home where his girl worked. His calls didn't always get through, but he said he just wanted to hear Jocelyn's voice.

Now he said, 'I understand what we're about to undertake is highly confidential, so much so we ain't even been told yet, but letters mean so much, don't they?'

Joe picked up his book. 'My girl's mother copped it in a raid. I only want to make sure she's all right.' He began to read.

Ruby held the fragile French knickers against herself. 'It's been a long time since I had anything so lovely to wear. You're a marvel, Nan.' She planted a kiss on the older woman's cheek.

'I got camiknickers for the both of you, a blouse each, not the same style, you've got ruffles, Marge got a pussy-cat bow. Pyjamas for you an' I hope you don't mind but I saved the scraps – well, silk is too precious to waste, ain't it?'

'What did you make, Nan?' Marge was changing Chrissie's nappy and taking a long time over it because she was blowing raspberries on Chrissie's fat tummy and the child was convulsing with laughter.

Nan coloured up. She let the beautifully made pyjama top slide through her fingers.

'Come on, show us!' Marge was teasing her.

Ruby guessed that after making up all these beautiful articles of clothing there'd be precious little silk left for anything of value. Her eyes moved to the treadle sewing machine in the corner of the crowded room. Nan had had it for years, it was her best friend, she said.

'Come on!' Marge was insistent. Nan looked at her, then went over to the machine and from a box beneath pulled out a garment with embroidery stitched prettily near the elasticated legs. She held up the knee-length bloomers.

Ruby could see she'd cleverly cobbled together small pieces of material hardly useful for anything.

'I hope you don't mind, Ruby. I ain't never had no silk underwear.'

Ruby stared at the wrinkled, worried face. She stepped across the room and put her arms around the woman's skinny body. 'Nan, they're lovely, you wear them with my blessing.'

Marge looked up from Chrissie's quivering belly. 'You saucy woman. Just don't let no German soldier see them, he might use them as a barrage balloon!'

Sylvie ran her hands over her hips. Her nails, dark red and long, were the exact same shade as the dress her dressmaker, Mrs Gardener, had made to Sylvie's specifications.

Ellen Gardener lived in Mayfield Road. To look at the outside of her shabby terraced house you wouldn't think the woman living there could run up such lovely clothes. But then, dressmaking wasn't the only talent Ellen Gardener possessed.

Sylvie had been thirteen when her father had taken her to see the woman. Money had changed hands. Sylvie, still in her gymslip, had climbed up on to the table in the stuffy kitchen.

'Lay back, love, after you've downed this.' Sylvie was handed her first ever drink of gin and orange. The taste of the baby's special sweet juice that drowned out the enormous dollop of cheap gin in the cracked cup had become her drink of choice ever after.

Already, her head was fuzzy as she stared at the kitchen ceiling, making mind patterns of the cobwebbed whitewash that was flaked and grubby. She could see her navy blue long-legged bloomers on the chair on top of her satchel that held her geography homework. At the back of her throat, the sweet-sour of the orange juice lingered.

She thought of her father, in his suit, sitting on a chair in the front room. His elbows were on his knees, his head in his hands, his fair hair flopping through his fingers. He had looked such a miserable figure that she'd wanted to reach over and put her hands on his shoulders and say, 'Don't worry.'

She didn't move. She'd been told to lie still.

It didn't seem right to be lying on a place where people ate their meals. Her with no knickers on and her legs outstretched. Just like the woman with piled-up yellow hair had advised.

The woman had thick mascara that made her eyelashes clump together. Her father didn't allow her to wear make-up. 'That's only for tarts,' he said.

Ruby Garett must be a tart, then. Her mother allowed her to wear the faintest smidgeon of mascara along with that pale peachy lipstick that didn't even look like lipstick.

Ruby Garett with the long dark plaits that Joe Stark had playfully tugged in the playground. Ruby Garett had whirled round, her hands on her skinny hips, and given him a mouthful! He'd stood there, taken it and then laughed at her before sloping off with his mates. Sylvie wished Joe would tug her long dark hair. She wouldn't scream at him.

'You might feel a twinge,' said the woman, leaning over her. Sylvie could smell Evening in Paris. She knew that scent. Her mother used it. Sylvie was sickened by the smell and thinking of her mother made her think of her grandfather. It was her mother's father who had the money that paid for their house, for her daddy's expensive car and his visits to the golf club.

The woman had a long silver needle-like instrument and she was pushing one hand down on Sylvie's stomach while probing up inside her private parts with the metal thing.

Sharp pain dug its fingers in both sides of Sylvie's lower abdomen. She gasped. That was more than a twinge. It was a dragging sensation a bit like period pain, but a hundred times worse. She screwed up her eyes.

'Is she all right?'

That was her dad's voice from outside the kitchen door.

'Nearly over, I'm just going to flush her out.'

Now a rubber tube was going up inside her. The same rubber tube she'd seen attached to a pump thing lying on the draining board alongside some egg-smeared dinner plates. She'd wondered what that thing was for. Flushing out, the woman said.

The gin made Sylvie feel like what was happening to her was really happening to someone else. A bit like she was at the pictures, watching a film. Only she was the star and could feel the pain!

Now she could smell soapflakes, sweet and clean. Lux perhaps?

'I'm lifting your legs a little higher, love.'

Sylvie could hear the sound of the pump, swish, swish. Then warm water was running out of her. She was embarrassed. It was like she was weeing without wanting to go.

'All over, love.' This was directed at Sylvie. 'Did you bring the sanitary pads?'

Sanitary pads? It wasn't her period. But then it had been a while since she'd had to use her sanitary belt with the pins and a pad.

Sylvie stared at the woman.

Her father was standing by the table now, fumbling in his jacket pockets. His face looked funny, like he'd been crying. Sylvie's head was swimming, round and round like a goldfish in a bowl. The woman was pulling the rubber tube out. It felt like her insides were flowing out with it. She tried to keep her mouth shut but the vomit squeezed through her teeth as she heaved herself up and was sick all down the table's corner. It dripped onto the specked lino.

Sylvie didn't know what happened after that. Only that she was in her own bedroom in their nice house in Alverstoke, St Mary's Road.

Light came from the table lamp that had been left on especially for her.

Sylvie stumbled out of bed, her nightdress wet and dark with blood. The pains from her insides were like hot coals. Was she going to die? Sylvie cried out. She wanted a towel to wipe herself and a fresh pad.

She must stop the blood, maybe then the pain would end. She staggered to her dressing table and pulled open a drawer to find her sanitary pads. Inside, with her other coloured ribbons, was the very first ribbon her daddy had bought her. As she sank to the floor, she remembered. 'Let me tie it in your hair,' he'd said. 'Sit on my lap.'

He'd taken a long time to put the new ribbon in her long dark hair.

'You look so pretty, Sylvie,' he'd said. His voice was all funny.

His fingers found the gap between the skin at the top of her legs and her white panties. She didn't like the thick warm thing he took from his trousers and made her touch. But it made him happy and she liked her daddy to be happy.

He wanted her to be a singer like her grandmother, his mother who had been on the stage and who was dead now.

Sylvie's mummy was a very busy lady. She worked for the church. She wasn't always at home, but her daddy was. His job allowed him to spend loads of time at home. He had an office somewhere that really belonged to Grandfather.

Her father arranged for Sylvie to have a voice coach. She sang scales and did them over and over again.

As she stood at the sink, Sylvie remembered again that she had felt grateful her father had finally allowed her to be alone in the bathroom. She washed between her legs, trying hard not to faint again because of what had come away from her.

Earlier when she'd cried out, her father had come in and had wrapped the awful stuff in paper and taken it out to the garden to burn. Then she had washed, showered, and shampooed her hair.

Her father was always buying new ribbons for her long hair.

Sylvie sang in front of judges, waiting with other girls in rooms with polished furniture. Sometimes it took ages to get to the venues in Daddy's car. Sometimes they had to stay in hotels. Always he bought her new ribbons. Her life became singing, travelling, school, and always Daddy.

Her mother was in Paris when Sylvie was taken to the abortionist in Mayfield Road.

When her father rang the doorbell and the woman came to let them in, Sylvie's father had stated that she was beginning to show and something needed to be done. 'Something needed to be done', those were his words. Sylvie saw the woman was wearing a black blouse that was incredibly beautiful and she asked her where she had bought it.

'By trade I'm a seamstress. I make all my own clothes and for anyone else who'll pay me.' Sylvie remembered the woman looking meaningfully at her father. 'This is only a sideline,' she'd said, showing them both into the kitchen. Sylvie never forgot the blouse.

After her father had changed her bedding because her sheets were covered in blood and Sylvie was back in bed with a towel beneath her, and another wrapped around her freshly washed hair, she'd said to him, 'If you ever touch me again, not only will I tell Mother, but Granddad as well.'

Sylvie had bundled all the hair ribbons she'd taken from the drawer into his hands. Then she shook off the towel from her head and with it came her sheared hair.

Her voice tuition continued. She won singing competitions.

Much later, when Sylvie was older, she visited Ellen Gardener with material and plans for new clothes. She'd never forgotten the beautiful blouse. Sylvie never saw evidence of Mrs Gardener's 'other work'. And that was how she liked it. Her own abortion was never referred to.

Now, in her room at the Point of No Return, nineteen-year-old Sylvie admired her figure in the long mirror. Tonight, after singing in the Star, she was being taken out for a late dinner by a very rich gentleman who had sent her flowers. He looked a bit like her father. But then Sylvie liked older men, apart from Joe Stark, whom she adored.

Chapter Seven

Richard Williams turned the electric light off in the hall before he settled in his workroom. Electricity cost money. He saw no sense in leaving a light on when there was no one in the room.

Using an Underwood portable typewriter, he sat for a couple of hours until finally writing 'The End' at the bottom of the manuscript for another Hank Wilson potboiler. Classical music issued from the wireless. In the corner of the room was a baby grand piano. It had cost him an arm and a leg, but then he liked spending money on Leon. He poured single malt whisky into a glass and sat back contentedly.

He knew he wasn't writing great literature, but fifty thousand words, a hero, a pretty girl, Indians, a hanging post and a small-town prison break-out plus countless denominations of life and its problems in the Wild West enabled him to put money in the bank while living off the wages the *Evening News* begrudged paying him for his services.

The Underwood was his friend. He'd managed to shave the price of it down from a friend at the paper who was selling because he'd got the push from working on the newspaper and badly needed the money.

This was Richard's seventh Western. Apparently men of a certain age gobbled them up. But novel writing wasn't as glamorous as people thought. It was putting your backside down on a chair and getting your imagination to flow. It was lonely, which was why he'd settled on the idea of a partner, the possibility of a wife.

He was good-looking enough to elicit nudges and winks from the copy girls at the Portsmouth newspaper, but those were silly girls, giggly girls. Which was why he'd set his sights on Ruby Garett.

He noticed one of his three sharply pointed pencils was out of line with the other two. He straightened it and sipped at his drink.

Ruby was young, fresh and naive, but not stupid. She was also unhappy and alone.

It was a stroke of luck that simpering Elaine, who took in the advertisements, had come into the office with the bundles of parachute silk from her American boyfriend. He didn't ask how her boyfriend came by the material, he didn't care. But he bought the silk at a rock-bottom price. It would be a nice little sweetener for Ruby. Bit of luck that bomb devastating her mother's house. She was in no position to refuse handouts, under the guise of friendship, of course.

He'd heard that Joe Stark was interested in her.

That didn't bother him too much. Joe Stark was like his father. In like Flynn, then on to new pastures.

How Emily Stark put up with her husband's philandering was nobody's business, but she did. Emily Stark, the mouse who stayed at home while her handsome lion of a husband roared away in town.

That wasn't going to happen to Ruby, once he'd got her. He would keep her in his pretty house, in the way in which she'd soon become accustomed. A week in Cornwall, new clothes occasionally for her to wear to the works' dances, not expensive stuff; just pretty fripperies that women liked.

And of course a few pretties for the love of his life, Leon, who would once again be able to live with him.

There was plenty of room for the three of them in this large house. Some of the furniture was antique. Good stuff, not Utility rubbish. The big rooms allowed for privacy, the garden too. But could he pull off such a scheme? Love and desire made him want to take the chance.

He pulled the quarto paper and its copy from the typewriter and shuffled them into two neat piles, one for his publisher, one for him. He didn't often make mistakes and ruin sheets of paper: mistakes cost money, paper cost money. He preferred to spend his money on Leon.

Leaving the room, he turned off the light before going into the kitchen. Waste not, want not. He might have another whisky and think about Leon and the future.

Mervyn sighed at his good fortune. The boxes holding the bottles of assorted spirits had come from Lennie Stark at exactly the right time. How Lennie got hold of so much stuff he didn't want to know. 'They fell off the back of a lorry' was good enough for Mervyn. Through this war Lennie Stark had been a good mate to him. It didn't faze Lennie, he seemed to be able to lay his hands on the strangest objects. Spectacles, petrol, toys, babies' items, food, and if it wasn't already stored at his home he could deliver in a day or so, for a price, of course.

Mervyn sighed again, contentedly. He'd finally persuaded Ruby to accept a loan to pay for her mother's funeral. Of course he hadn't done that for Ruby but for Marge. He wanted to let the young woman see that he could be relied on in times of need.

Of course, he could afford to pay for the funeral without Ruby paying him back but she'd never have accepted the payment as a gift, neither would Marge, so a loan it had to be.

The spirits had come in handy, not only to sell in the bar, but also to serve to guests when he arranged a small gathering after the funeral, to wish Jane Garett well on her heavenly journey. If a job was worth doing, it was worth doing well.

He'd already given some money to Grace so she'd set up a buffet table with sandwiches and dainties. In his larder there were tins of salmon and ham, courtesy of Lennie, crying out to be gobbled up. And he was sure that lad of Marge's, young Tony, would appreciate the bars of American chocolate that had come from the USA stores at Southampton.

He thought of the little boy, inquisitive and spoiled and not frightened to answer back. Just like his mother, though you couldn't call her 'spoiled'. It was a pity Mervyn didn't see as much of him as he'd like. A kid like that should be taught how to defend himself properly. Especially at school when the bigger boys began to bully him, as they no doubt would. He was a pretty boy, with Marge's pointed features. Yes, he'd get a ribbing or two, sooner or later. Maybe he'd put it to Marge that he should teach the boy a few boxing moves. He still had the gloves he'd worn as a kid. Bit old-fashioned now, but they'd do to spar with.

A gust of loud laughter vied with Frank Sinatra's voice and Mervyn remembered he was supposed to be helping out in the busy bar. He went through the hall and into the smoke-filled room.

He spotted Emily Stark sitting with her mate Flora in the corner. She was giggling. Flora was showing her some knitting and Emily was shaking her head. She was still a pretty woman, was Emily, soft spoken, slight of build and with a remarkably clear complexion. She was always nicely dressed.

'What's this then, knitting for the soldiers?' Emily burst into another giggle that was overshadowed by the laughter from the crowd of sailors at the bar.

'Don't think any soldier would need a baby's bootee.' Flora showed him the dropped stitches. 'Got so many holes in it my daughter'll never know how to put it on the child.'

'Cor,' he said. 'I didn't know that was a bootee, I thought it was a dishcloth!'

Emily slapped his hand. 'You're awful, you are,' she said.

He was about to tell her that her husband had not long left the Point of No Return by his kitchen door, then decided against it. She and Lennie didn't seem to have a lot in common these days, only their love for Joe. He'd often wondered why Emily put up with Lennie's carryings on. Once, a while ago when Lennie was knocking off a bus conductress and it was common knowledge to all, including Emily, he'd asked her why she didn't leave him.

'I got a lovely home, he's kind to me, lets me do what I want, when I wants, and if it wasn't for him I wouldn't have my Joe. Lennie's like a big kid, got to go on proving something to himself. Besides, he always comes back to me.'

He'd thought at the time that Emily had her husband taped.

Now he looked over at the bar, caught Marge's eye and made signs that she was to bring over a couple of drinks to the two women, on the house. He grinned at Emily. Of course she still had Lennie taped.

There were a tidy few in tonight, Merv thought. He lifted the wooden hatch and got behind the bar and was straight into serving some sailors brown ales.

After putting the money in the till he looked at the two piles of bottle caps at the back of the bar. Marge's was near the fruit chopping board, in its usual place. Fruit chopping board? That was a laugh! Gone were the days when he offered pieces of lemon with the gin – getting hold of fruit was about as likely as Father Christmas turning up! He didn't mean plums and apples and pears but proper fruit: oranges, bananas; he couldn't remember the last time he ate a banana. Maybe he could ask Lennie? Wonder what young Tony would make of a banana?

Marge had a neat little pile of drinks money to come back to her tonight. Good for her, he thought. Ruby kept her pile of bottle tops near the bottle of lovage. He smiled, about the same number of caps each. They were good girls. He marvelled once more that when Sylvie worked behind the bar her pile of tops grew quickly. He wasn't stupid, she often stuck a top there even if she hadn't been bought a drink. But then, he didn't begrudge her too much, she drew in the crowds when she sang.

'Come to do some work, have yer?'

Marge was being cheeky. He could see the perspiration on her forehead.

'You don't know what hard work is, missy,' he retorted, filling up Amos's tankard as it was shoved across the counter.

'Barrel's gone,' sang out Ruby. She was standing at the pump of the Brickwood's Best, a straight pint glass only half filled beneath the tap.

'Just going to the cellar,' he called back and saw she was apologizing to the old couple. It wouldn't take him long to change the barrel.

The sudden noise of the siren made him swear. They'd hardly got over the last raid and here was another one. Still, as soon as he'd finished in the cellar he'd be back in the bar.

The cellar was cold but scrupulously clean.

Within minutes, job accomplished, he was climbing the wooden steps back upstairs. Some customers had left for the public shelter, most preferred to wait it out in the pub. The blackout curtains were pulled tight against the taped windows and as he passed he flicked the thick curtains across the door.

The huge thwump, too close, sent slivers of ceiling white falling like snow onto the floor. Someone screamed. There was a scramble to get beneath tables and into corners, as if an extra layer of wood would save a life. The roar of planes above cut out the wireless music. Another bomb crashed, and splintering sounds followed by glass shattering heralded more screams. Then the lights went out, leaving the roaring fire in the big fireplace the only way to see what was happening.

Merv lifted the hatch and another huge bang caused him to drop it, the hatch clattering back to the bar top.

'You all right?' he shouted to Marge and Ruby.

Through the gloom he could see the two girls had their arms around each other at the far end of the bar. They were crouched beneath the sink. Big frightened eyes stared back at him. Marge nodded frantically. Mervyn was hoping against hope those bloody bombs hadn't landed anywhere near where Marge's kids were.

'C'mon, you two,' he said. 'Set some tots on a tray and take a whisky round to everyone to settle their stomachs.'

He could hear the planes retreating now and unless he was mistaken, it was to be a short, sharp attack.

'Those bloody Jerries,' he said to no one in particular, 'they come along the coast and bam, bam, bam, hoping to get the dockyard, a warship moored up, maybe the bomb factory. Silly buggers, they won't defeat us.'

He went over to Marge and took the whisky bottle out of her hands. 'You're spillin' more than you're getting' in the glasses, love, I'll do it.' Marge gave a huge sigh of relief. The wireless suddenly came back on and Frank Sinatra began crooning away again.

Marge gave him a small smile. 'Are you all right?' she asked.

Little bugger was always looking after other people when she needed someone to look after her, Mervyn thought.

It was definitely quieter outside now and the front door was opening and closing as people left or returned. Mervyn could hear the bells from fire engines and ambulances. A customer had come up to the counter where Ruby, tongue between her teeth, was conscientiously still pouring whiskies. A shadow loomed over the bar.

'Is one of them for me?' Joe Stark asked.

Chapter Eight

'Why haven't you written?'

'I have, blame the post, not me,' Joe said to Ruby, running his fingers through his dark hair and grinning widely. 'Well, until a little while ago when we were told we were going somewhere hush-hush, so I thought I'd better wait . . .' He leaned across the counter and kissed Ruby full on the lips.

'Oi! What you doin' to my bar staff?'

Merv leaned over and whisked the tray of small glasses away so he could deliver them around the bar and give Ruby a bit of time with her young man.

The all-clear sounded and Merv called back, 'See, Marge, it was something and nothing, that raid.'

Marge shrugged, turned to Ruby after acknowledging Joe with a big smile, and said, 'This shift's nearly over. Why don't you get off with Lover-Boy, I can clear up.'

Before giving Ruby a chance to say anything she yelled towards Mervyn's broad back, 'Ruby can go, can't she, Merv?'

His tray of drinks was less than half full now and Ruby could hear him saying, 'Take a nip to settle your fears about those blasted enemy planes.' He heard Marge's voice, turned and said, 'What leave you got, young Joe?'

'I had a forty-eight-hour pass, but that bastard of a sergeant mislaid my train ticket so I had to hitch.' Joe tutted. 'I reckon he mislaid it on purpose. I'd have been here sooner but—'

He got no further for Ruby leaned across and whispered in his ear and Joe looked towards the back of the bar where his mother was rising to come and greet him.

A few bounds from him and Joe had picked her up and spun her around like she was a little girl.

'Put me down, you great oaf,' Emily squealed, but everyone could tell she was pleased by his embrace.

Ruby heard Joe say, 'I'll be back later tonight, Mum, if that's all right with you? I want to walk with Ruby for a while. My kitbag's already at home and I've seen Dad. It was him told me where everyone is.' Joe gave his mother a big sloppy kiss on her cheek and called to Marge, 'Sort me mum out with another drink.'

Ruby saw Marge nod and Joe went over to her and slipped some change on the counter. Mervyn looked over and said, 'Are you two still 'ere?'

'Won't be a moment, see you outside, Joe.' Ruby squeezed Marge's arm as a thank you then pulled up the bar-flap and was running upstairs to get her coat and scarf. When she came back down, she went straight out of the main door to find Joe stamping up and down on the pavement to keep his feet warm. His big boots were making quite a racket. She flew into his arms. Ruby felt the warmth of his scratchy uniform as she snuggled into him.

'I'm sorry about your mum, Rube,' he whispered. 'But I'm glad you're staying here.' He nodded back towards the pub.

'Everyone's been ever so kind,' Ruby said. 'I don't suppose the army'll let you come back for the funeral?'

He shook his head. 'Doubt it. All I know is we're going overseas. A few of us who signed up got taken out for parachuting and now my training's almost over we're off on some mission.'

'Your mum and dad must be very proud of you, Joe. Well, I am an' all.'

He twisted her round so they were face to face and he asked, 'Really? Are you really proud of me, Rube?'

Ruby looked into his earnest eyes. He might look like a

man, be as tall as a man, but inside he was like a boy and wanted her approval.

'Joe,' she said, 'I've done a lot of thinking since Mum, since Mum . . .' She gathered her thoughts. 'I think I've always known deep down that I cared for you, even when we was kids at school . . .'

His breath was warm on her cheek as he bent towards her. It was like a million fireflies warming her whole body. At this moment, with Joe, in his arms, she felt she was where she belonged.

'I know, Rubes,' he breathed, 'but I had to be called up and leave Gosport to find out what I think I've known all along—'

'And what's that?' she interrupted.

'That I love you, Ruby Garett.'

Ruby took a deep breath and stepped away from him. Now her head was reeling. It was as if nothing around them existed, just her and Joe. She stared at him, then cuddled back into his scratchy blouson and put her hands up to his neck. The forces had done a hatchet job on his lovely soft hair. It was so short it was stubbly. For a moment there was silence while his eyes searched her face.

'Ain't you got nothing to say, Ruby Garett?'

'Only that I love you an' all.'

For a moment he looked as though he disbelieved her words, but then he gave a kind of strangled whoop! He lifted her up and whirled her around like she had seen him do to his mother. When he set her down he began leading her as though they were on a polished dance floor and not the pavement near the cinema. He made her dance in the street with him, off the kerb, into the road, whirling her around, neatly avoiding a cyclist who irritably rang his bell at them.

And then they were still. Laughing, kissing, any place they could find to put their lips on each other, until Ruby pulled away.

'The pictures are turning out, don't you make a spectacle of me, Joe Stark.'

A man and woman passed them on the pavement and Ruby and Joe stepped out of their way. Cigarette smoke followed the couple. Then Ruby was back in Joe's arms.

The cinema was emptying out quickly now, noise and laughter insinuating itself into the cold night air. A fresh gust of cigarette smoke wafted along the pavement.

'C'mon,' said Joe, 'let's walk.'

Stepping arm in arm along the High Street towards Walpole Park and the boating lake, every so often Joe stopped and showered her with small kisses. Ruby felt so full of love for him that she was sure her heart would burst.

'We keep hearing that we're leaving barracks tomorrow, tomorrow, then the next day comes an' we're still practising dropping out of planes . . .'

Ruby gasped. 'Ain't you scared?'

'Of course I'm scared, we're all scared. We're fed up with everything being put on hold, whatever everything is, and we're frightened of fighting and dying—'

'Don't you talk about dying!' Ruby's voice was fierce.

'Oh, I'm sorry, Rube. But sometimes it's worse not knowing where we're ending up . . .' He stopped once more and beneath the moonlit sky that still smelled of cordite and burning from the earlier raid, he pulled her into his arms, bent his head and kissed her lingeringly.

When the couple came up for air Joe said, 'There's all kinds of rumours about what's going on over the channel in France. Then I come home and find Gosport's like a building site with barbed wire along the seafront, foreign Allies everywhere, trucks and military stuff parked in the streets and all that reinforcing they've done to the shoreline down the ferry. What's goin' on?'

'I asked Mr Williams, he's a reporter for the *Evening News*, about all the activity at Hardway, Stoke's Bay, and

Lee-on-the-Solent,' answered Ruby. 'He said he couldn't tell me, even if he knew, but he thought it had something to do with our boys being pushed nearer the coast over in France, by them Germans.'

Joe nodded. 'We got to get them poor buggers out of France, they're like sitting ducks.' He shrugged. 'We don't want them Germans invading.'

She agreed with him and then it struck her how little time they had together. Forty-eight hours, he'd said, and God knows how much time had already passed. She wished she could spend part of the next day with him but she had to work. She couldn't take time off, Mervyn had already been so kind to her, allowing her to stay at the pub and arranging the funeral of her mother. As though reading her mind, Joe said, 'Don't worry, I'll come into the Point before I leave tomorrow. Better let me mum cook me a slap-up breakfast, then I'll have a chat with the old man before I get back to barracks.' She smiled and nodded at him. Everything would be all right, wouldn't it?

They began walking along by the cockle pond. Swans were huddled together for warmth. One stood up and shook its huge wings, then settled down again. Ruby clung to Joe, suddenly scared.

'I wish we had somewhere warm to go,' Joe said. 'But I'm

not taking you home while my mum's still in the pub and my ol' man's there to ogle you.'

'It doesn't matter, Joe,' Ruby said. 'I could take you back to the pub, I've got a room upstairs . . .'

'No!' His voice was hard. 'It only needs to get about that you had a man in your room and people will talk. You know what they're like. Besides, why break Mervyn's trust in you?'

'It looks like you've thought of everything,' she said.

'I have,' he conceded, 'and it'll be different when I can put a ring on your finger.'

Ruby gasped. 'What? Get engaged?'

He twisted her around again. 'That's what you do when you love someone. You put a ring on the girl's finger to stop other blokes from wanting her.'

Ruby laughed. Love was one thing, she hadn't thought of engagements. Didn't that lead to a wedding?

'You really mean this, don't you? Or are you having me on?'

For a single second she was frightened of his answer, but she needn't have worried for he said, 'I'm not like my dad, Rube. I take after me mum and believe it or not she loves him and he, in his own way, loves her. You won't find me messing you about.' He gave a small cough. 'Say you'll wait for me, Ruby Garett?'

'You're serious, aren't you?'

'Course I am, I've played the field an' I'm ready to be with the girl I've loved all me life. You.' He was studying her face intently. 'I don't expect you to be like a nun an' never go out. In fact, I want you to go out and enjoy yourself, but I'd like to think of you waiting for me when I get back.'

'Oh, Joe,' she said. 'I promise I'll wait for you.' She suddenly thought of her mother's wedding ring that she was wearing. It hadn't kept her father from leaving, had it?

Joe smiled and it was like a light had suddenly shone in a dark room.

'An' I promise I'll come back for you,' he said.

The moat near the swimming pool was full of dark water. An iron gate set in the wall on Haslar Road that led to the bridge over the lake was partly open. Inside the gate, grass and bushes led the way to a mound that overlooked the sea. A long time ago, Ruby knew this area had been part of Gosport's defence system of the old town. Ramparts from the walls jutted from the earth and she could hear the swish-swish of the tide in the cockle pond. This was the haunt of lovers. Tragedy Bank, a secret place and hidden from the eyes of Gosport's town dwellers.

Despite the cold on a grassy knoll Joe pulled her down

and into his arms. Ruby felt nothing could ever harm her again. Joe pushed her gently aside and began feeling in his breast pockets.

He got out his wallet and opened it and took out a white note.

'You're my girl now and I'd have brought you something today if I hadn't been too busy trying to hitch me way home.' He felt for her handbag, lying on the grass, clicked the fastener and slipped the money inside. Then he said, 'I'd like it if you'd keep in touch with me mum. I'm gonna keep on writing to the both of you, but by the looks of things I won't have no proper address for a while. Will you do that? Pop in and see her sometimes?'

'Of course I will. I don't need paying to go and see your mum, Joe.'

'Dad and her already know I've got feelings for you,' he added.

'That's good, but I don't want money from you, Joe,' she repeated. She felt for her bag, intending to hand him back the note.

'It's not money, like money . . .' He stumbled over the words as he stilled her hand. 'When everything's back to normal, we'll get hold of a little house, maybe one of them new-fangled prefabs everyone's raving about, and tie the knot and if I've been sending you money, it'll be like our bottom drawer. What d'you think?'

Her heart was overflowing again. 'I think it's a lovely idea,' she said, then, 'C'mere, you.' Ruby's hands had begun to act of their own accord. Heedless of the cold she was unbuttoning his thick blouson jacket and then her fingernails began undoing the small buttons on his shirt, unfastening them from their buttonholes. She bent her head to kiss his warm skin, surprised at the hairs covering his chest. He was making small groaning sounds. Then Joe was above her, pushing back her coat and Ruby was shrugging her clothes from her body as if her main goal in life was to put as much of her bare skin against Joe's as was possible. Now his hands were on the buttons of her trousers and soon they too were discarded. He sat back to look at her.

'God you're beautiful,' he said. Then, 'And what have I found here? Silk? French knickers? You saucy little thing.'

Ruby began laughing. 'Marge's nan made them up out of some parachute silk one of the customers gave me.'

'Well, I hope he didn't think he was going to see them.' Joe found her mouth again and kissed her hungrily.

'What makes you think it was a bloke?' Ruby twisted away. She knew Joe was making a joke about the silk. All the same, she felt a little frisson of something like fear pass through her. But when she found Joe's tongue snaking back deliciously inside her mouth, everything flew from her mind except how lovely these feelings were that she'd never before explored.

Ruby could smell the male muskiness of him as Joe found a nipple after expertly removing her bra. His tongue began to work on it. Her hands were in his hair. Her eyes open to the darkness about them as Ruby breathed him in through every pore of her body.

Joe was whispering something to her. Ruby didn't know what it was, neither did she care because she was tasting, smelling, hearing, feeling him and replying, 'Yes, this way, like this.'

Joe's mouth was a thing apart, and just when she felt they could get no closer, he was inside her, filling her up, then moving, at first slowly as if he was frightened of hurting her. Then she was urging him on, his movements now more assured, a steady stroke, plunging into that bottomless well of herself. A strange emotion was growing inside her, begging for release.

'Yes,' Ruby cried, 'I never thought . . .'

Those words floated out in the night with other different sounds, words of love as Joe arched his body and thrust into the core of her. Ruby felt her mind, her soul, her body was spilling out.

A sob was wrenched from her at the same time as Joe gripped her, holding her close.

'That was your first time,' he said quietly, later. 'Wasn't it?'

Ruby had no strength to answer immediately, she was thinking, So that's what it's all about. She managed to nod.

Her head was whirling, she could no more have stopped what had just happened than fly to the moon. He was fastening something around the third finger of her left hand.

'This will have to suffice until I can buy you a proper one. You will still marry me, won't you?'

Ruby looked at the circlet of plaited grass.

Joe was staring into her eyes. 'We'd better get dressed before we catch our deaths,' he said. 'My little love, I'll take care of you, you're all right with me.'

Chapter Nine

Ruby was serving customers and watching Joe sitting at a table talking to his parents. Every so often he looked up and their eyes connected, saying words they had no need to speak. She looked at the clock. In another ten minutes, Joe had to leave to catch the ferry that would take him to Portsmouth Harbour station where he would board a train to return to his barracks.

She had no idea when she would see him again, or even if he would return. But she had his promises.

The talk in the bar had been of the banning of travel from Ireland to the south of England. The Irish leader said such action would damage his country's neutrality. Nobody wanted the Germans on English soil and the enemy was pushing nearer the coast of France all the time.

After putting money in the till, Ruby looked across the

bar. Her heart sank. Joe was on his feet, his kitbag over his shoulder, and now, after a hug with his mother and a handshake with his father, he was coming towards her.

'Walk him to the door, girl.' Mervyn held up the wooden flap so she could pass through.

Out in the hallway, she was surprised to see Joe's eyes were damp with tears.

'I don't want to leave you, Rube. Not now when I've only just found you.'

And then his lips were on hers. She could smell coal tar soap mixed in with his familiar musky male smell. And suddenly she realized she wouldn't be smelling his skin any more, maybe not for a long while. Inside her, tears rose. But she knew she couldn't send her Joe away with tears down her cheeks and a miserable face so she took a deep breath and said, 'Get out there in the cold and begin walking to the ferry.'

'All right,' he said cheerfully, 'I know when I'm not wanted.'

Ruby swung him round. 'Don't say that, I want you more than I've ever wanted anyone in my life before.' She put her hand up and showed him her finger adorned with the twisted grasses. 'See my ring? It means you and I are joined for ever.'

Joe caught her hand and kissed the strands of dried greenery.

'Course, I can't wear it all the time,' she said. 'It'll fall to pieces, but I'll keep it safe till you come back to me.'

She was kissed with such force she feared for her teeth, and then he was gone! The cold fresh air coming through the open door was the last reminder he had been home that weekend.

'Check your gas masks.'

Marge groaned. Nevertheless, she foraged beneath the counter until her fingers reached the square case. She bent down and peered at her name.

'Mine, Ruby's and Madam's,' she said, meaning Sylvie. 'All present and correct!' Facing Mervyn, she did a mock salute.

'By rights I should make you carry them everywhere, just in case we get a gas attack . . .' Mervyn frowned.

Now it was Ruby who groaned. She, like many other people, hated carrying the thing and had abandoned her mask under the bar. The only time she ever thought about it was when Mervyn mentioned it.

'I've noticed some women have decorated the cases and use them like shoulder bags.'

Marge caught Ruby's eye and winked. 'Very nice they look too,' she said in answer to Mervyn's remark. Then she knocked Ruby on the arm and dissolved into giggles.

'You won't be laughing when you're middle-aged and gasping for breath . . .'

'Depends what I'm doin' what's making me short of breath.' Marge could just about get the words out for laughing.

Ruby knew Mervyn was only making sure his barmaids would be safe.

He walked away from the bar in despair. 'I give up, I really do,' he grumbled, leaving the bar to unlock the front door and let the punters in.

Marge stuck her hands in the pockets of her grey trousers and said, 'Do you fancy going to the Connaught tonight?'

'Is there a dance on? We're working . . .' Ruby thought about the music, the lights, she could have a drink of shandy. She wasn't a drinker, but after all the enthusiastic jitterbugging the American lads were so good at, lemonade mixed with beer was the best drink to cool a person down.

'I reckon if we clear up quick, Merv'll let us go early. It starts at seven but no one gets there until later and if we roll up about ten, ten thirty, we'll still have plenty of time to dance before they chuck us out at twelve.'

Ruby could see the excitement in Marge's eyes. 'You got that beautiful new dress an' you ain't put it on yet.'

Ruby didn't need reminding but she asked, 'What about your nan? Will she be all right with Tony and Chrissie?'

'Actually it was her idea. I been a bit down just lately. There never seems to be enough money to go around. She told me to get out an' put a smile on my face! She also said it would do you good.'

'Well, we won't have to pay to get in, will we?' Ruby said.

Every so often the hall held dances where girls didn't have to pay an entrance fee. The servicemen paid to go in and the management hoped the enticement of free admission for girls meant bigger ticket sales.

'You ask Mervyn, then, you know he's got a soft spot for you.' Ruby winked at her friend and Marge retaliated by sticking out her tongue.

They were still talking about what to wear to the dance when Ruby was interrupted by Richard Williams. He gave her a broad smile because she'd spotted him coming in and had already placed his tankard beneath the Guinness tap. She put his drink in front of him and he delved in his pocket for money.

'So, you're thinking about going to the Connaught tonight?'

Ruby realized he must have overheard. 'Should be a laugh,' she said, adding, 'There's an American cruiser in the dockyard,' as though that explained everything.

She thought he looked very dashing today, a bit like Richard Widmark, only with spectacles on. 'Take a drink for yourself,' he said. She saw he had put the exact money for his drink and a small amount extra for hers on the counter.

'Thank you,' she said, putting the money in the till and then scrabbling around beneath the dusters, bottle openers and boxes, looking for a bottle top. She found a stray one and put it at the back of the counter to start off her pile of tips. She mouthed at Richard, 'I'll have it later.' He laughed, and carrying his drink he walked over to his regular table and sat down, taking the newspaper out of his pocket.

'Miners are striking,' he called over. 'That'll mean there'll be no coal. Munitions factories and trains'll be paralysed, just when we need as much industry as possible to help us win this bloody war.' He rattled the broadsheet.

'Not right, is it?' called back Ruby. She'd heard the news on the wireless so felt able to make a comment. 'But the Welsh reckon their mines have harder seams so it's more difficult to remove the coal and they're worried about their rights for cheap fuel.' She broke off the conversation to serve another customer. When she next glanced at Richard Williams, he was smiling at her.

'How d'you know that?'

Marge pushed past her to pick up a straight glass.

'Heard it on the wireless,' shouted Ruby.

'Well, I get my coal for free, as well you know,' whispered Marge, looking about in case anyone was listening.

'Yes, and one day you'll get caught sneaking through the hole in the wire fence of the coal yard and helping yourself to a bucketful!'

'Got to catch me first,' laughed Marge, whirling away.

Ruby knew Marge wasn't the only culprit who stole buckets of coal from the huge piles at the railway yard. It seemed every time the owner mended the high fence, miraculously another hole appeared in it! Of course, it didn't make it right that Marge stole, but Ruby knew the price of coal was atrocious and Marge would never let Nan and the kids get cold. So often, when Marge got home late from the Point of No Return, she'd go off in the dark with her bucket.

Ruby smiled to herself. She was looking forward to the dance tonight, especially since her mother's funeral last week had been so awful.

It had rained all day when they'd buried Jane Garett at Ann's Hill Cemetery. There'd been about twenty mourners. Friends of her mother, come to pay their respects. Nan had ventured along, pushing the big old pram. She reckoned pushing the pram helped her to walk. Tony was at school so there was no fear of him running all over the graves.

The schools had closed when some of the children had been evacuated, but they'd opened up once more when many of the little ones came home again.

'There's no way Tony's going anywhere without me,' Marge had said, so Tony had spent the entire war with her.

Mervyn had closed the bar for the morning. A big notice proclaimed, 'Closed Due to Funeral', and was inserted in the front window of the Point, but when the mourners were invited back to the pub for the wake, Ruby had dissolved in tears in his arms.

'It's a big day for you, Ruby,' Mervyn said, when he opened up again. 'I quite understand if you'd rather stay away from the bar.'

'No, I'm better when I'm around people,' she said. But the funeral had done one good thing for Ruby. It had brought closure on her mother's death. She knew her mother would tell her to get on with her life. Ruby could almost hear her saying, 'Laugh and the world laughs with you. Cry and you cry alone.'

She began to smile again.

'You heard from Lover-Boy?' Marge grabbed at a tea towel and began drying the half-pint glasses that Ruby was washing during a lull.

'He put in a page for me when he wrote to his mum. Only because I told her to ask why I hadn't heard from him. She said he told her he writes regularly. I haven't been getting his letters, I suppose it's this blessed war. Anyway Joe said whatever they were supposed to be doing had been cancelled again.'

'So he's not actually fighting?'

'Only with the American Air Force lads when they go to the village pub.'

Marge began laughing.

'You can laugh, but he can't say anything personal when it's in a letter to his mum, can he?'

'S'pose not,' said Marge. 'Are you going to serve her, or shall I?'

Margaret Bell sashayed across the floor towards them. Ruby gave her a big smile.

'Just come from the butcher's,' she said. She had a wicker basket and something wrapped in newspaper inside it.

Ruby nodded in reply, thinking that if she took off that damned fur coat and put it in the doorway it would walk over to the bar by itself. 'Stick it on the fire, Mrs Riley,' hummed Marge as she flicked a tea towel at Ruby.

Ruby poured Margaret Bell a drink and was rewarded with a pile of change left on the counter.

'What you got for dinner, then, Mrs Ril— Mrs Bell,' Marge called out.

'Half a pigs 'ead, dear. I told him to leave the eye in. It'll see me though the week.'

Ruby heard Richard Williams laugh.

Marge had left her 'dollin' up' clothes, as she called them, in Ruby's room, and at ten o'clock Mervyn told the girls to go and get ready. It was raining, a quiet night, and Ruby knew it was unlikely that there'd be a rush of customers now.

At half past ten, arm in arm, the girls sauntered into the big building on the corner near the town hall. Cigarette smoke rushed to greet them and Ruby wondered why on earth she'd bothered to get up early to wash her hair. The small band on the podium was playing swing music and Ruby began to tap her feet on the floor.

'We was lucky to find this little table,' said Marge. Ruby thought how pretty she looked. She'd worn the new silk blouse with the pussy-cat bow and matched it to a flared skirt that had long been a favourite of hers. Her best black court shoes were shiny with polishing and she'd pinned a yellow flower in her hair that Nan had made from scraps of material. In *Picturegoer*, Marge had seen a photograph of Dorothy Lamour wearing one just like it.

Ruby wore her new dress and it felt soft against her skin. There hadn't been time to wear it for Joe, he'd come home one day and was gone the next, but she'd keep it for best so he could see her in it the next time he had some leave.

The large hall was packed with lads from all the forces, and some Gosport lads were standing drinking near the makeshift bar: two tables pushed together with jugs of orange, water and home-made lemonade on top. Tonight they were also selling cups of tea from a big silver urn. Alcohol wasn't allowed, but every so often the men disappeared outside to fill up from bottles of beer and other alcohol they'd bought with them and stashed away, hidden in the bushes and gardens.

'Go and get two lemonades,' Marge said.

Ruby fought her way through the crowd dancing a waltz and bought two small lemonades in big glasses from the grey-haired woman serving drinks and managed to get back to the table without spilling any.

Marge said, 'I remembered you said you fancied a shandy.' From her big handbag she took a bottle of Brickwood's pale ale with the top already flipped off and pressed on again to stop it spilling. Beneath the table, out of sight of other people, Marge mixed two drinks.

'C'mon, take one,' she said, passing Ruby a glass. 'An' I'm

putting the bottle beneath the table so we can have another drink later.'

Marge had barely taken a mouthful before a Canadian hauled her to her feet to dance.

Ruby sat back on her chair and relaxed. The room was hot, sweaty and smelled of stale perfume and cigarette smoke. But she thought it was nice not to be at everyone's beck and call like she was behind the bar. The drink was cool and tasty and she took another mouthful.

'I s'pose you won't want to dance with a civilian when there's all this foreign talent about?'

Ruby looked into the eyes of Terry Barnet, a lad who'd been in the same class as her at school. He pulled out the chair vacated by Marge and sat down, hoisting his trousers at the knees so they wouldn't bag.

'Hello,' Ruby said. To the best of her knowledge Terry didn't drink; well, she'd never seen him in the Point of No Return. 'Where have you been hiding yourself?'

He looked very smart in a dark suit. His eyes were deep brown pools and she suddenly remembered the crush she'd had on him. He'd once taken her to the pictures but she'd been so shy she'd hardly said a word, even though he'd bought her toffees. That had been their one and only date.

'I've been working in a garage.' He thrust out his hands

and she saw the ingrained marks of oil around his nails. 'I'm always scrubbing at these but the dirt never comes out.'

'You shouldn't worry about that,' she said. 'It's honest, clean dirt.'

He grinned at her. 'Want to dance?' There was a lull in the music as the band changed tunes.

Ruby put down her drink and stood up. She'd forgotten how tall he was.

As soon as he had her in his arms he began quickstepping around the floor. She was just about to ask him if he was going into one of the services when he said, 'Next Tuesday I'm in the navy.'

'How does your mum feel about that?'

'Not happy. We lost my brother Ted an' she's convinced I'll be lost at sea, like him.'

'You'll have to prove her wrong then,' she said. He was light on his feet and whirled her around competently. 'You're an expert, where'd you learn to dance like this?'

'My sister Pat made me dance in the kitchen with her. She's funny, is Pat, got to be the best at everything, but it's done me some good as the girls like a turn on the floor with me.'

'You'll do well when you get leave in the navy, then.'

He laughed again. 'I saw you with Joe Stark the other weekend. I thought you had more sense, Ruby.'

Ruby's heart fell. Did everyone know she was now Joe Stark's girl? Not that she minded, she loved Joe, didn't she? But some Gosport people were so nosy and liked to tell you what they thought, even when it didn't concern them.

'What d'you mean by that?' She lost her rhythm and stumbled against him. The silver glitter ball in the centre of the ballroom circled and twinkled.

'Oops,' he said, side-stepping cleverly to put her back on track.

'Sorry,' she said. 'But I need to know why you've said that.'

He took a deep breath. 'You're not stupid, Ruby. We all know what he's like. The girls reckon he's hot stuff, he gets into their knickers, then they don't see him again. Well, you only got to look at his dad, ain't you, to see the apple don't fall far from the tree?'

'Shut up! You know nothing about Joe Stark!' Her voice was loud and it cut through the band's music as she stopped dancing, put her hands on her hips and glared at him. The look on his face was of pure horror – she was showing him up! In the Connaught of all places! Ruby stomped away, leaving him standing there, unsure of what to do or where to go. When she got back to her seat after elbowing through the crowd Marge was sitting down.

'Whatever's the matter with you?'

'That damn Terry Barnet reckons Joe's leading me on.'

'Calm down. What's it got to with him?'

Marge pushed Ruby's glass towards her and Ruby grabbed it and glugged it all back. 'Oi! Hang on, we've got to make this one pale ale last all night,' Marge cried.

Ruby wiped her mouth, slammed down the glass and said, 'He said Joe gets into girls' knickers and then he don't want them any more . . .'

Marge broke in, 'You know that's not true.' She stopped talking then and stared at Ruby. 'That weekend, you didn't . . . you and him?'

Ruby was sitting quietly, her hands clasped together, her face immobile.

Marge seemed to crumple before her. 'Oh, Ruby, you daft 'a'porth. You never . . . never . . .?'

And now Ruby was nodding. Then she looked down at the table and put her finger on a drop of beer and traced it on the wooden top.

'I couldn't have helped meself even if I'd wanted to. He was so . . . so . . . comforting.'

'You don't give it away because it's "comforting"!' She could tell Marge was angry.

Tears were now spilling from Ruby's eyes and coursing

down her face. A wet spot reached and darkened her new green dress.

Marge said, 'Stop that! What's done is done! You going to spoil that dress as well as spoiling yourself?' She stopped speaking. It was as though she had suddenly realized what she'd said. 'Oh, Ruby, I didn't mean . . .' Her hand shot across the table. It was almost, thought Ruby, as if she and Marge were cocooned in their own small world as Marge grabbed at her hand and held on tightly.

'Do you really love Joe?' Marge's voice was firm.

Ruby nodded.

'Do you believe he loves you?'

Without hesitation, the grass ring swam before Ruby's eyes, his promises, his kisses.

'Yes, I do.'

Marge seemed to shrivel as she let out a big sigh. 'Then you got nothing to worry about. But if you let the reputation of Joe's father and common gossip get to you, your love for each other is going to disintegrate, it'll wither and die!'

Her voice was raised at the word 'die'. But it did the trick. Ruby knew her friend was right. She also knew what she and Joe had was special.

Loud clapping broke into her thoughts and she realized the dance music had stopped, people were relatively quiet in the large hall and Mr Prout, the leader of the band, was talking into the microphone and waving his white-gloved hands about as he announced, 'And now we have, for tonight only, Gosport's songstress, Sylvie Meadows!'

Chapter Ten

'It's like living on the edge of a precipice. One day it's all go, "Get ready, boys, we're off tomorrow". Then it's, "Sorry, lads, it's not today, you can have a few hours' pass to make up for the disappointment",' moaned Vinnie.

'You get passes, all I ever get is work to do around here. When I do get a pass it's for such a short time I can barely get to the village pub and back.'

Joe gave an extra polish to his rifle butt. He missed Ruby and he was fed up with having to stay in the camp. There had to be some reason why his letters weren't getting through to her. It could be something to do with the special ops their sergeant had been talking about. Everything was all very hush-hush. That's why he'd taken to enclosing a page or two to Ruby in with his mother's letters. He'd talked to Vinnie about his lack of mail, but Vinnie had told him he was lucky to get any letters at all.

He thought of his telephone call to the Point of No Return. He'd been lucky to have the receiver picked up by Sylvie, who was just going off to sing at some place. She told him Ruby had gone dancing. And she was good enough to advise him of the best times to ring to catch Ruby when she was in the bar. So far he'd not had much luck, though. Nearly every time it was Sylvie who answered and bless her she always had some excuse as to why Ruby wasn't at the Point. Still, he was glad Ruby wasn't sitting indoors moping around.

His friend Vinnie was examining himself in a small hand mirror, looking at his immaculate white teeth, of which he was inordinately proud. Vinnie stretched his mouth and turned to Joe.

'Well, you do provoke the sergeant.' He sighed. 'It's like some tug-of-war between the two of you, him giving you orders and you trying to find ways not to obey. Why can't you get it into your thick skull he's superior to you and you must do as he tells you?'

'It's superior to make me run around the exercise yard with a bloody great pack on me back until I collapse, is it? It's superior for him to say, "I'll make you wish your mother was here so you'll cry, 'I want me mother,' and then I can tell you, Sonny Joe, 'You want your mother? Well, while you're here at the barracks, I AM YOUR BLOODY MOTHER!'"'

Vinnie sighed again. 'If you got a death wish, go on as you are.'

'I never signed up to be a para. I thought I was in the army. Then I'm told they don't need me but the paras do. I wouldn't mind, but I'd like leave to go back to Gosport to see my Ruby.'

'An' I want to win the football pools.'

Joe knew Vinnie's girl Jocelyn had sent him a Dear John letter, so he didn't have much patience with Joe whining about Ruby. Vinnie foraged around in his drawer and threw a paperback at Joe that landed on his bunk.

'What the hell is that?' Joe picked up the odd-shaped book. It was wider than it was tall, and made of cheap wartime materials, but the cover of *A Tree Grows in Brooklyn* by Betty Smith was exactly the same as he'd spotted in bookshops.

'That, my friend, is an ASE, designed to fit inside a serviceman's pocket, breast or hip. Cheaply produced for wartime reading and made to be read until it falls apart.'

'ASE?' Joe was flicking open the pages; the book was small but perfectly readable.

'Armed Services Edition, made for the Americans to take into battle. There's loads of titles. What d'you do when you've got to hang around waiting for this or that? Most of us read, except carrying an ordinary book around is much too bulky, so these little beauties fill the gap. Have you read it?'

Joe was studying the format, the writing. 'No, is it a girl's book?'

His friend laughed. 'No it's not. It's about the American Dream, but I guarantee you'll be laughing as well as crying. It's like a good letter from home, that book. Put it in your pocket and hang on to it. When I get more I'll pass them on.'

Joe grinned at him. 'Trust the bloody Yanks to get in first.'

Vinnie gave him a mock salute. 'I'm off now. See you later, try not to antagonize Cecil!' He laughed, a cloud of cologne wafting towards Joe, then he said, 'You ever wondered why the sergeant's so hard on you? Apart from you bein' a dickhead?'

Joe shook his head.

'I reckon he knows you're a bit special and worth movin' up in this group. An' if he can rile you into showing your true worth, he'll be vindicated.'

Joe looked at him. 'You don't half talk some bleedin' twaddle,' he said.

The whisky bottle was almost empty. If he wanted more he had to go to the stores and book it out. That would necessitate getting from this office, to the main gate and along to 3rd Battalion out in the rain. Not a problem when he wasn't legless but he was and if he ventured outside this room everyone he met would know he was pissed.

Cecil Antony Howard resisted the urge.

He ran his fingers around the edge of the silver frame. The blond boy with his arm thrown casually along the back of the model toy car he was sitting in stared back at him from the photograph. Eddie would pedal away, moving the vehicle swiftly down the concrete path at the married quarters, a look of determination carved on his baby face.

'He'll get knocked down on the road.' Joy wouldn't let it be.

'Everyone knows there's kids galore here out on the streets. Nobody drives fast.' As usual he had the last word. Of course the roads were safe. Joy was being a natural protective mother.

Eddie would grin his lopsided smile and his little feet would pedal up and down, up and down . . . Jesus, he could pedal fast.

Cecil didn't bother with using his glass, just upended the whisky bottle and drank from it. Funny how when he'd had his very first taste of whisky it had burned all the way down his gullet; now it tasted as ineffective as tap water.

He swallowed, cleared his throat and drained the last dregs. He looked at the empty bottle, its familiar paper logo proclaiming its strength, its suitability to rival and surpass all other brands. Bloody tosh, he thought. It got the job done, didn't it? Blotted out the past and made him stop thinking about his son. For a little while, at least, he could crawl inside the bottle and forget. But it didn't last. What was it they said? One drink is too many and ten not enough?

His boy had been enough for him. His Eddie had been everything for him. No fear, that lad. From the toy car he'd graduated to roller skates, a bike, a motor bike. Speed held no fear, why should it? From a lad Eddie would take things to pieces, find out how they worked. When Eddie knew how it worked the object held no mystery. And Joy worried.

But he was proud of his boy, his inquisitive mind, his probing fingers, his lack of fear.

Cecil was prouder still when Eddie joined the Royal Engineers.

The bomb squad handled hazardous explosive devices that needed to be made safe. The Luftwaffe and their ZUS-4Os had fuses designed to maim and kill.

It was a summer's day in 1940 and *boom!*

Suddenly, his boy, his fearless, beautiful Eddie, was no more.

It wasn't Joy who couldn't hold it all together. It was him. Cecil Howard, now a wreck of a man who distanced himself from the one person who still loved him.

No more Eddie, then, no more Joy. But the whisky was there. Cecil was proud of the fact he could keep his drinking a secret. It was under control. Until, like tonight, it wasn't.

But what made today different?

Joe Stark.

Joe Stark, and yet again news from the powers that be that they weren't sending any of his lads on the drop. But wasn't that a blessing?

His lads had missed the chaos that came after the Allied German reserve regiments went running around the countryside looking for landed troops.

More than nine hundred C-47 transport planes had appeared above the Cotentin Peninsula to drop the US 101st and the 82nd Airborne Divisions. With most of the drop zones unmarked, the pilots had become lost in cloud. The heavy flak from the enemy broke their formations. But the paratroopers were ordered to drop.

Some dropped in the bloody sea and two planeloads were dropped in the centre of Ste-Mère-Eglise and were shot dead, while their chutes remained tangled in bloody telephone wires.

Yet again, orders for his lot to remain at barracks.

It wasn't common knowledge yet how bloody lucky they were to be alive.

And Joe Stark, ignorant Joe Stark trying to act the big man. Moaning because he was fed up doing nothing, and acting like a clown, only concerned with getting home to his bit of Gosport stuff.

He didn't realize what a gift he had. Didn't realize he could be a better man than Cecil Howard could ever aspire to be. Bloody silly young bugger! If Joe Stark thought he could best Cecil Howard by railing against him he had another think coming. Whether Joe Stark knew it or not, he was like his Eddie.

Eddie. Cecil turned the heavy frame on its face. Eddie was gone. Joe Stark was here. And whether he wanted it or not Cecil Howard was going to make a man of the silly young bugger.

The empty whisky bottle rolled across the desk and fell unbroken to the floor.

Sergeant Cecil Howard, his head on his arms, slept.

Ruby snuggled further down, but the lower she wriggled the warmer it was. It was uncomfortable having so many blankets on the bed in June. Mervyn liked to make sure his guests were well looked after. That included her and Sylvie.

Grace gave all the rooms a clean-up and stripped the beds after each guest had eaten breakfast and left the Point. It was nice, Ruby thought, not having to worry about cleaning and polishing, and washing sheets, but she might ask Grace to leave off some of the bed coverings.

The talk in the Point for days now had been the D-Day landings. Now it all made sense why Gosport had borne the brunt of so much work on its beaches. Paratroopers and gliders carrying equipment began landing on the Normandy shores.

Apparently over a hundred Germans were killed, many captured and the paras lost seventy men, some dead, some wounded.

Bomber Command began the last of its pre-dawn attacks on the port north of Caen and Ouistreham. Then the cruiser HMS *Orion* began shelling the gun emplacements of Gold Beach.

The beach assault was met with fierce resistance from the enemy. But our boys were marching to free France from the hated Germans. Heavy fighting was continuing around every beachhead as the enemy retaliated. As far as Ruby knew, Joe had not been involved in any of this. The news bulletins came from the wireless and the bar was full of gossip from the newspapers.

The last letter she'd had from Joe had been enclosed in a letter to his mother. This seemed to be his method of corresponding with her. It was all right, she supposed, but there was hardly any reference to how he really felt about her. Ruby could understand why. No bloke would reveal his innermost thoughts to the girl he loved, knowing his mother would read his words first, would he? But a page enclosed to her, inside his mother's letter, was better than not hearing from him at all.

'Joe says he writes regularly to you,' his mother insisted. 'He gets your letters.'

Ruby felt his letters to her were jinxed.

Since living at the Point, several communications had been forwarded to her. An electricity bill for a house no longer standing, and letters of condolence had reached her via the hall table after being addressed to Alma Street, so Ruby knew that Percy the Post had his re-deliveries all in hand.

She wrote straight back to Joe, using the same address that his mother used. Everyone, including guests at the Point of No Return, left stamped letters on the table in the hall and they were collected daily by Percy.

She tried so hard to believe Joe really did love her. The words Terry Barnet had flung at her still rankled.

But the practically loveless words handed to her from his parents made it difficult for her to believe his love was all-consuming.

'You got to remember all the secrecy of this D-Day attack,' Joe's father advised. 'Careless talk costs lives.'

Terry Barnet's words about Joe simply wanting to get into girls' knickers floated around uneasily in her brain. Was that why he didn't answer with proper letters of his own? Were the few lines enclosed to her merely a salve because she'd given in to him? Only she hadn't 'given in', had she? No, she'd embraced the act of love with every fibre of her being. Then she hated herself for even thinking Joe had lied to her.

She thought back to the last time she'd seen and heard Sylvie Meadows sing, at that dance at the Connaught.

The girl had appeared in a skin-tight silver dress that perfectly matched the silver ceiling globe flashing across the room. Sylvie had stood quite still, waiting for the applause to disappear. There was something quite magical about her slight body, her dark hair in a victory roll with a white gardenia pinned above one ear.

'Bet they ain't real flowers,' Marge had hissed.

Ruby didn't care if Sylvie had bought them in Woolies,

the effect was fairylike, the young woman was a vision for the men on leave to remember.

Then she began to sing. Her deep voice, throaty, the emotion pouring out of that slim body like it needed to let the world know she wanted her lover to come back to her. She told the audience that song wasn't out yet on 78 rpm but would soon be for sale countrywide, not sung by her, but by Billie Holiday. Sylvie was singing it as a tribute to her idol.

To tumultuous applause she sang 'All of Me' and when she started on 'Georgia' there wasn't a dry eye in the place. The servicemen whistled, stamped their feet and shouted.

And as Sylvie moved, sinuous as a snake, Ruby wondered why a man like Joe wanted a girl like herself when he could have Sylvie?

'They went around together,' she said to Marge, expecting her to know exactly what she was talking about.

And Marge did. She answered, 'Sylvie's name was often linked with Joe's. I heard she gets fags and booze off his dad now.'

Ruby was well aware of Lennie's nefarious interests. Didn't Mervyn buy black-market goods from him?

Now Ruby got out of bed and went to the dressing table. Tucked inside a hanky down the side of the drawer was the grass ring. In an envelope were banknotes, money that had been enclosed with the notelets from Joe to his mother. It was mounting up nicely now, her 'bottom drawer'. See, he did love her, he did, she thought.

Her fingers moved over the dried grasses, brittle and prickly. She thought of the earnest look in his eyes as he had placed the makeshift ring on her finger.

Tomorrow she would try and get through to him on the telephone. His mother had given her a number to use in emergencies. The only time she had used it, the emergency had been that she longed to hear Joe's voice.

A clear, educated male voice had told her he was unavailable.

Ruby closed the drawer.

The grass ring in its cotton protector she slipped beneath her pillow. She climbed back into bed.

Tomorrow was another day.

Chapter Eleven

Address not known. 'The bugger,' swore Marge. 'An' he never even bothered to disguise his writing.' She threw the returned letter to her husband Alf on the fire without opening it. After all, she knew what it contained: two pages begging for money from him. She'd seen the back of the envelope had been steamed open, read and resealed.

Marge bent again towards the fire and holding a cloth around the handle of the iron, took it from the fire's embers and rubbed it across the piece of old towelling to get rid of the smuts. Standing at the small table doing the ironing wasn't her favourite way to spend a Sunday evening off, but chores had to be done and kids' clothes ironed.

She heard a cough from the bedroom. Nan had a terrible cold and it had made her crotchety. Marge had packed her off to bed early after she'd bathed Tony and put him down for the night. She listened carefully but heard no more coughs. Good. They were both asleep. She looked at Chrissie, spread-eagled on her back in her long white cotton nightie. She practically filled the pram now. She was going to need a proper bed, the pram would be too small for her shortly.

There was a tickle at the back of Marge's throat. She ran the hot iron over Tony's grey flannel shirt. He needed some summer clothes. Where was she going to find the money? The tickle expanded and made her cough. Please don't let me be coming down with Nan's cough, she thought. A cold was the last thing she needed.

The rent man was coming tomorrow. She owed four weeks' rent and only had three. She couldn't ask Mervyn for a loan. When Tony had kicked through the toes of his shoes she'd asked Mervyn for money and he'd given it to her straight away. But she hadn't paid him back yet. No, she couldn't ask him again, it was out of the question.

She heard Nan cough again. Marge had left water at the side of the bed. What Nan needed was linctus. Perhaps she could borrow five bob off the rent to go to the chemist before she went to work tomorrow?

If she didn't have all the rent anyway what did the extra five bob matter?

She thought of the sleazy little runt, Flint, who would call tomorrow morning. He collected the rents for the bloke who owned several houses in the street.

Mrs Ogden at number three had said how accommodating Mr Flint was. She'd owed two weeks and Mr Flint had concocted some story to the owner. Mrs Ogden still lived at number three, so that particular story must have been true.

Usually Nan paid the rent when Marge had left for the Point. If Marge sent Nan shopping for cough mixture, maybe she could have a chat with Mr Flint? She could explain to Mervyn why she was going to be a bit late. He wouldn't mind.

Chrissie stirred. She threw out an arm and it knocked against the side of the pram. She quivered but stayed asleep.

Marge set the hot iron back in the grate, grabbed her purse with a few coins in and ran out of the flat to the telephone box. It would only take her five minutes to phone Mervyn.

'Why have I got to go to the chemist? I feel awful!'

'You know very well whatever linctus I bring back won't be the right one. So you'd better go and get it yourself.'

Marge pressed half a crown into Nan's hand. Nan sneezed.

'I wish you'd sneeze into a hanky.'

'*I wish you'd sneeze into a hanky*,' parroted Nan. 'Very la-de-da, I'm sure!' She glared at Marge. 'Ain't you supposed to be at work?'

'I'm going in later today.'

Nan looked at the coin in her hand. 'Send the old ones out to die first,' she moaned. Then her rheumy eyes brightened. 'Want me to take the baby?'

Marge's eyes moved to Chrissie. She was still asleep. She marvelled that the little girl wasn't crying.

'No, I haven't washed or dressed her yet.'

Nan shuffled off, click-clacking with her stick. Marge knew by the time she reached the chemist she'd have stopped to talk to so many people it would be ages before she returned. Marge heard Nan stop at the back door and cough as soon as the cold air hit her. She turned towards Chrissie and bent down and kissed her cool forehead. Then she looked in at Tony, who was still asleep. He could sleep for England, he could, she thought.

'Rent!'

Marge hurried through from the untidy bedroom to find the man already standing in her kitchen. That was one of the things she hated about him. Just because he collected the rents, he thought it gave him the right to walk in unannounced. He must have passed Nan on the street.

'C'mon, I ain't got all day.' His ratty eyes went to the mantelpiece where the rent book with the money inside it sat.

Marge was there before him. 'The thing is Mr Flint, I . . .' She took a deep breath. 'I ain't got all the rent. Most of it, yes. But . . . But . . .'

His black eyes were looking her up and down and his thin mouth was sucked in like a cat's behind.

'What am I supposed to do about it?'

A strand of his heavily Brylcreemed hair came adrift from the rest and fell over his face, and he pushed it back with a big-knuckled hand.

'I . . . I . . .'

'C'mon, spit it out.'

She knew he was enjoying her discomfort. 'I was wondering if there was some way you can allow me to let me rent roll over . . .'

'Roll over? It's only women what rolls over, when I've finished with them!'

He was laughing at her. With his mouth wide open she could smell his eggy breath.

He stopped laughing and looked her up, then down, very slowly, just like she was for sale in a shop window. He pulled on his chin like he was stroking an imaginary beard while thinking. Then he began unbuckling his leather money pouch. Marge's heart was beating so fast she was sure he could hear it.

'Well, Margie love, I like a little tickle on a Monday morning, what d'you say?'

Marge wasn't stupid. She knew exactly what he meant. Her stomach roiled at the thought of being anywhere near him, let alone having him inside her! But what could she do? Where was she to get the rest of the rent money?

'If I do, how do I know you'll mark my rent book as paid?' Oh, God, how she hated herself for even thinking she could do such a thing!

His eyes were glittering. He'd put his grubby leather bag on the table and was coming towards her. He licked his lips.

'Because I'll mark the rent book as "Paid in Full". You keep what's on the mantelpiece.'

Chrissie stirred.

Marge stared at the pink and white child. 'I'm not going in the bedroom,' she said. 'I got a little 'un asleep in there.' Besides, how could she think of her clean bedding being sullied by this man?

'I likes a kneesie wobbler against a wall, I can get it right up inside . . .' There was a smirk on his face.

'. . . I could probably find the rest of the money by the end of the week.' Marge was playing for time.

'I ain't calling back on a wild goose chase. I've heard that tale too often.'

'All right . . .' said Marge, hoping to shut him up. The quicker he got it over with, the sooner her life could get back to normal. She could wake Tony and get him dressed then.

She walked towards the back door where that part of the wall didn't have anything standing against it. He followed. With her back to the flowered wallpaper she began hitching up her skirt and taking down her French knickers. She prayed that Tony would stay asleep.

'Ooh! They're tasty. Silk panties. I'm hard already.' He leaned in towards her. His nearness made her want to vomit, but she waited while he quickly fiddled with his buttons and she felt the small member find its way into her creases.

He began moving.

With one hand flat against the wall he was pushing into her.

'Ohh! That's nice, that is, you smell lovely . . .'

And now he'd begun to thrust harder. His other hand was also helping him balance against the wall. He wasn't a big man, more or less the same height as her. Marge felt his hand drop and grip the cheek of her behind as he was slapping himself in and out.

She was holding her breath, willing him to hurry up and

finish when, 'Marge!' She heard the voice before the foot-steps sounded.

'Agh!!!!'

He'd come. He leaned back and the thing fell wetly away from her just as, 'Marge!'

Nan's croaky voice was louder and her footsteps nearer.

Marge's skirt fell down around her knees as he leapt away from her. She could feel his slime on the inside of her thigh.

'Get out,' she hissed. He'd turned away and was fiddling with his flies. Then in a bound he moved towards the fire-place and flicked the money from the rent book. Fingers quick as a monkey's paw he grabbed his heavy money belt and was just buckling it when Nan's stick tapped its way over the tiles and she pushed open the door.

'Why aren't you answering me?' Nan began and stopped when she saw Mr Flint running a hand through his greasy hair.

'Well, I'll be off then,' Flint said. Marge had to remind herself to breathe.

He didn't have a hat, but he tipped his forelock politely towards Nan and moved around her to leave the room.

'Didn't know you was 'ere . . .' Nan said scathingly.

'Well, I'm a busy man, I am.' He left the room. Marge felt

all the air leave her body, like she was a rubber tyre blown up and then had a pin pushed into it.

'He reminds me of a ferret,' Nan said. Her eyes narrowed. 'I've never liked that greasy bugger.' She'd hooked her stick against a chair and was looking fondly down at Chrissie, still sleeping in her pram. Nan's fingers clutched at a bottle of linctus.

'Neither have I,' said Marge.

She realized then the bastard hadn't written a bloody thing in her rent book and he'd taken her money.

Ruby didn't feel well. She'd said, 'Excuse me' to Marge and rushed upstairs to the bathroom, where she'd been violently sick down the lavatory pan. She didn't like using the outside lavatory that all the customers used; there was always a stink of urine emanating from it no matter how many times Merv whitewashed the place or scrubbed it.

She wiped her mouth and looked at herself in the mirror.

How funny. She felt as right as rain now. She looked all right. There was a pink flush to her cheeks. A bit tired, but that was to be expected, Merv had had a couple of lock-ins so she'd had a few late nights.

She wondered where Marge had been earlier this morning. It wasn't like her to be late coming in and when she had appeared, she was in a right mood, banging about and rubbing the counter with a polishing rag as though she wanted to make a hole in the wood. Merv didn't seem surprised that Marge was late, so Ruby guessed there must have been some kind of family emergency.

Ruby popped into her bedroom, cleaned her teeth at the little sink, powdered her nose and retouched her lipstick. Then she went down again to the bar. It was slow today.

She looked at her solitary bottle top. Ol' Tom had bought her a drink. Her eyes went towards Marge's space where she piled her tops. Five? How could she have been bought five drinks when Ruby had only been out of the bar for five minutes? She glanced about the bar. Four customers. Two women, two men and of those one was Ol' Tom. Something wasn't right.

Marge had taken down some dusty, fancy, little-used glasses and was washing them in the sink. They tended to get on with cleaning jobs in the bar when it was quiet.

'What you up to?' Ruby poked her in the back.

Marge almost dropped a glass. 'What?'

Ruby wasn't going to beat around the bush. She was Marge's mate and it wasn't like her to steal – especially not from Mervyn. There must be a reason why Marge needed the extra money.

'You ain't been bought them drinks.' Ruby spoke softly and looked towards the bottle tops. Then she looked at Merv, who was sitting at a table reading the *Mirror*. She uttered the words so quietly that no one else could possibly hear.

'What d'yer mean?' Marge frowned, but her face betrayed her. She went cherry red.

'If you was Sylvie I'd have expected it. But you're straighter than a beanpole.'

Marge put her hand to her forehead, her fingers wet with soapy water. Bubbles dripped down her cheek. She sighed. Ruby handed her a clean tea towel. Marge wiped her face, then said very quietly, 'I've got into a bit of money difficulties. With no cash coming from Alf and Tony starting school I've been taking from Peter to pay Paul and now it's all gone upside down.' She gave a big sigh. 'I haven't paid back what I owe Merv so I didn't like to ask him for more . . .'

'Why didn't you ask me?'

'You?' Marge was looking at her like she had two heads. 'You ain't paid for the funeral yet . . .'

'No, but he's taking a bit from me wages each week for that. I've got some money that Joe's been sending me.' She swallowed. 'My bottom drawer, he called it. I haven't had any communication from him for a while, you know what the blasted post is like, but what about I give you five pounds? Will that help?'

Ruby was horrified to see her friend burst into tears.

'Oh, you don't know how much that will help me.' Marge blew air out of her cheeks. She flapped the tea towel across her wet face, then she grabbed hold of Ruby's hand. 'You're an angel in disguise, thank you.'

'Look,' said Ruby, staring at her, 'I got more money if you need it and I don't care when you pay it back.' She tried to look stern. 'You got to promise me something, though?'

'Whatever's that?' Marge was frowning.

'You got to put them bottle tops back an' only take them out again for genuine bought drinks.'

Marge leaned across Ruby and scooped up the bottle tops and threw them all in the waste box.

'Better?' she asked.

Ruby squeezed her around the waist. 'Much better,' she said.

The door opened with a clatter and in came Richard Williams. His eyes sought Ruby's and she smiled at him. She was just about to say 'Hello' to him when Marge whispered to her, 'I'll make sure any money I have off you I give back before your baby really starts to show.'

Chapter Twelve

Richard Williams sat down and opened the late edition of the *Evening News*, folding the broadsheet so he could handle it easily while lifting his Guinness.

Both barmaids were preoccupied this lunchtime. Almost as if their minds weren't on their jobs. He could understand it with the older one, the one with curly hair, Marge. After all, she had a couple of kiddies and an old woman to look after. But Ruby had been looking peaky lately too. He wondered if she was finding it difficult to come to terms with her mother's death.

He thought back to the night of the dance at the Connaught Hall. After eavesdropping on their conversation he'd decided to go along himself.

He'd spotted the pair of them supping home-made drinks like a couple of naughty kids. He'd watched them being asked to dance, surprised that Ruby was so nifty on her feet.

He'd been on the point of surprising Ruby with his appearance when that young whippersnapper had pulled her up to dance.

For a while she'd looked as though she hadn't had a care in the world. But then something had sparked her up the wrong way and she'd stomped off the dance floor.

They'd left as soon as the other barmaid that worked here, that singing one, had finished crooning into the microphone like it was a lollipop she was going to swallow whole. Still, he had to admit that, when dressed up, that Sylvie was classy.

The other week when he was on a job for the paper he'd spotted her in Winchester, eating lunch and cosying up to Councillor Eddington. Richard was there to cover the forth-coming election, but Eddington looked like he wanted to cover Sylvie.

Sylvie Meadows. Voice like an angel, morals of an alley cat, so Mikey at the *News* said.

Ruby had looked great at that dance, she was wearing a dress he'd never seen her in before.

Now he turned to page three and the big story about the landings. People couldn't get enough of what was happening in France. The byline was his. A smile touched his lips. Why was it, no matter how many times he'd seen his name in print, it always gave him a thrill when he spotted it again?

He looked at the clock on the wall. Ten past twelve and he was finished for the day. He idly moved his trilby hat over the table and lifted his drink. He'd have a second pint before he went home to that big, empty house.

His book, *Hanging at Cripple Creek*, was almost ready to send off. He'd run through it again tonight for mistakes, then put the pages in the empty typing paper box, which he could send to the publishers tomorrow. He'd had an idea about a stranger turning up in town and getting involved with a rancher who was losing cattle. He was eager to start working on it.

He wondered what was on the wireless tonight.

He wondered what Leon was up to. In a way he was glad the lad's deafness in one ear and a heart that beat irregularly, due to the rheumatic fever he'd had as a child, had kept him out of the services. It didn't affect the way he could play the piano, though, he thought proudly. He missed the young man. He hated that he couldn't be with him all the time. Odd days and nights weren't the answer. If only the law was kinder to homosexuals they could live openly together, couldn't they? He told himself to stop thinking about things that could never happen, it would only provoke his jealousy and it was hard to keep that particular green-eyed monster at bay.

The sun was shining through the big bar window and he could feel the heat on his hand.

Halfway through the year already? Perhaps at the weekend he'd cut the lawn and paint the back fence. There was always something to do in a house. He looked towards the bar where Ruby was standing near the till. She looked so sad and, funnily enough, so alone.

The phone was ringing. Sylvie staggered out of bed, grabbed her silk dressing gown and threw open her bedroom door. Mervyn didn't like his staff to answer the phone, but he consented to Sylvie picking up the receiver as she needed to attend to her bookings. The telephone was at the bottom of the wide staircase.

'Hello?'

'Is that you, Ruby?' The man's voice was one of abject misery.

'No, Joe. Ruby's not here again.' She could almost feel his unhappiness. 'It's Sylvie. If you want to leave a message I can give it to her when she gets back, but I'm not sure when that will be.' She hesitated. 'As far as I know she's gone on some trip with a lad home on leave called . . .' Sylvie was searching around in her brain, 'Terry,' she said. 'Terry . . .'

'Him as joined the navy?' The question came quickly from him.

'Yes, home on leave, he is, home on leave.' Sylvie heard the impatient tone as Joe said, 'Sure, me mum told me he'd joined up.'

Sylvie gave a sort of sigh as the lie found a bed to sleep in.

'Can you tell her I'll phone again as soon as I can? Things are hotting up here.'

'Of course I will, Joe. And how are you?' Without waiting for his reply she said, 'I hope you're going to a few local dances. I never knew your Ruby was so nifty on her feet, she was dancing at a place I was singing at. Looked lovely, too, Joe, new dress and everything.'

Sylvie suddenly realized she was talking into a telephone where the caller had hung up. She smiled as she replaced the receiver.

Just then the front door opened, letting in a gust of cold night air. Mervyn breezed through. 'Got another date to sing?' He flung the words at Sylvie as she galloped up the stairs.

'You could say that,' called Sylvie.

Upstairs again, Sylvie sat on the end of her bed and ran the silver-backed hair brush through her straight hair. She stopped and looked at her dressing table where the brush's fancy silver mirror and comb resided on a glass dish. The set had been a present from Colin Buckleby. Sylvie had hated his flabby paunch as he'd wriggled around on top of her in that hotel in Hastings. She shuddered. He was a means to an end, she thought. He'd taken her to a few very posh places.

How wonderful would it be to lie in a proper bed with Joe Stark and his magnificent body? When she was younger she hadn't really known what she'd wanted. Joe Stark was a diversion then, a pretty boy to sleep with while she was looking for a man with money. But then she found out that the men with money were ugly, fat, or 'had families who must come first'.

But now, if her plans went the right way, this time she could show him how a real woman made love. The money part was easy: she made her own, received presents, or stole it.

Humming, Sylvie began brushing her silky hair once more.

Richard Williams let himself into his detached Alverstoke home. Vectis Road was a nice, quiet place to live, near Western Way, where some of the crème de la crème of Alverstoke lived. His garden gave the house a secluded feel.

Of course, seclusion was fine for his mother before

she'd died. He'd been able to push her wheelchair out in the sun, knowing she wouldn't be overlooked by nosy neighbours. Dementia is a terrible illness, it robs that person of their whole personality. In return, it gives back a different persona that is so far removed from the original that it's frightening.

It was the rages Richard hated most. When his mother had absolutely no idea who he was, and thought he was trying to kill her!

He remembered the doctor's words:

'I can find her a place in a home where she will be adequately looked after and it will enable you to continue to work. You can visit whenever you want. Alverstoke has an abundance of homes such as these.'

'I can't bear the thought of putting her away.' That was only partly true. All the time his mother was in the house she was his alibi. He was free to have Leon stay without fingers being pointed.

Richard had eyed his doctor with disdain as he'd continued, 'It's not "putting her away", it's making sure that the rest of the time she has left she can live without you being in fear of her hurting herself. A fit man such as yourself shouldn't be changing another adult's nappies and soiled bedlinen . . .'

Richard had waved the good doctor's views away. His mother had cared for him, he said, he would care for her.

Nevertheless, he had visited such an establishment, mainly to see what alterations he might need to do to the house to make sure his mother could either roam at will without fear, or be constrained should he need to be absent for any length of time. He was lucky in that a lot of the time he could work from home on his trusty typewriter, then either send or telephone his pieces in to the *Evening News*. He had at his disposal a wonderful library, started by his father upon his marriage to Gwendolynne, his mother. And of course the library in Gosport was quite familiar with his requests for obscure information. Writing his Westerns was a solitary occupation that was also undertaken from home.

'I can manage,' he'd assured his mother's doctor, knowing he could rely on the medical profession for help should he so require it.

A local builder was hired to make alterations to rooms his mother would have access to. Unfortunately, a knee injury prevented her from walking too far without the aid of either a stick or her wheelchair. She loved the sun, so was able to spend hours in the garden, pottering about or simply sitting with her face raised towards its heat. Richard made sure the house and garden were entirely safe and secure. His passion for cleanliness and order was paramount.

Put his mother in a home? He wouldn't hear of it.

Naturally, all the time she was living in the house, Leon was free to come and go without arousing suspicion. He thought of the happy evenings he had spent in his workroom, researching or writing while Leon played on the piano he'd had installed especially for him.

Richard went through to the kitchen. The Aga was a godsend in the winter and provided not only a means to cook, but heat that powered radiators both upstairs and down. Now it stared back at him, shiny and sullen.

He opened up the glazed kitchen door that looked over the expanse of tree-laden garden. The trees gave shade from the fierce sun; a hammock was strung between an oak and an ancient apple that still gave passable fruit. Sometimes he swung in that rope hammock and thought about plots for his novels. He remembered too the memories of Leon lazing companionably there. Why couldn't he have those happy times back again?

Fresh air flooded into the house, which had been closed up since he had left earlier that morning. He'd driven down to the Gosport ferry, crossed the water by boat, then caught a bus that landed him outside the *News* office. Sometimes he drove his car around through Fareham to his place of work, but there didn't seem to be a great deal of point in driving when he usually had a staff car at his disposal, complete with cameraman if he was needed, to travel to newsworthy venues. Besides, why waste his own petrol allowance when he could use the newspaper's petrol account? Nevertheless, this afternoon he would give his car a quick polish. The Ford 7W, a two-door, had been bought brand new by his mother in the late 1930s and she'd driven it until her left- and right-hand signals had become confused. What Richard liked about the car was that it started first go almost every time.

While waiting for the kettle to boil he went upstairs to open the bedroom windows. He must remember to get his shopping in from the car as well. It was worthwhile wandering through the market when the traders had almost finished selling for the day. They often sold remaining food cheaper. The tomatoes would be fine with some bacon he had in the larder. Waste not, want not.

His own room was at the front of the house; it looked out over the quiet road. It was carpeted and had fitted wardrobes and a half tester bed, and he always felt this room was the nicest in the house. His mother's room had looked over her beloved garden. There were two other bedrooms, little used nowadays.

There was no doubt about it, he surmised, this house was beautiful. His mother had loved it too. But she was gone now. The cellar steps had put an end to her suffering.

Richard could hear the steady whistle of the kettle downstairs.

He was alone in a beautiful family home, where normally a woman would preside and children would play in the grassy garden. He thought about Ruby Garett. He'd spent a great deal of time watching her. If he wasn't mistaken, she was in the family way. Common gossip had her dating that Joe Stark. One only had to look at his father to recognize the son. She'd certainly seen the last of that fly-by-night, that's if he made it back from the war in one piece.

He could do a lot worse than ask her to marry him.

Ruby was still shaking. She was sitting on the end of her bed and had just locked the drawer that contained her Post Office savings book and the cash she kept in her bedroom, along with the grass ring. She handed Marge the white note.

'You sure that's enough to tide you over?'

Marge nodded. 'It's fine, I'll give it back as soon as I can.'

Ruby said clearly, 'What d'you mean, "before my baby shows"?'

Marge tucked the money inside her purse. 'I'm not stupid.

I've had two nippers meself. It hurts that you haven't confided in me, especially as you're quite far along—'

Ruby broke in, 'You can't tell nothing, I'm fine—'

'Oh, yes? You've been sick. The smell of fags makes you heave. One minute you don't want anything to eat, the next you're wolfing down chips like they're going out of fashion. I was like that with my first. An' you're tired all the time!'

There was a sudden silence in the bedroom, then Ruby burst into tears and twisted herself into Marge's arms.

'I thought my periods had stopped because I've been so miserable about Mum dying . . .'

Marge pushed her to arm's length and stared at her. 'Really? Did you really?'

'Yes, it was only the once, you see . . .'

'It only takes the once, you silly mare. I got to keep away from men because as soon as I look at a pair of trousers I falls for a kiddie!'

Ruby knew Marge was trying to make her feel better. A funny look had come over Marge's face. She'd coloured up, then added briskly, 'If you're being honest with me and it was that one time, then it's too late to get you seen to.'

'Whatever do you mean, "seen to"?'

'There's a woman lives in Mayfield Road who does abortions—'

'I'm not having an abortion!' Ruby was horrified.

'No, I know you're not. That's only safe up until three months, an' you're further gone than that.' Marge looked as if she was thinking. 'Gin and a hot bath. Nan said that worked for her. Quinine and pennyroyal tablets from the chemist . . .'

'I don't want to get rid of Joe's baby!'

'I think it's too late for that anyway. But where's Joe when you need him?'

Ruby turned away. The shock of accepting the news had sent tears to her eyes. 'That's a horrible thing to say . . .'

'Face facts, little girl! Where is he?' Before Ruby could open her mouth, Marge carried on, 'Has he been home to see you? No! Has he properly answered your letters? No! Well, if that don't prove he's a fly-by-night like his father, what does?'

Ruby stared at her. Every word Marge said was true. Wait a minute, he did write! He put notes in with his parent's letters, didn't he? He sent her money.

She glanced towards the locked drawer. Well, he had been sending her money, but it had mysteriously dried up of late. His mum said Joe really would prefer a proper letter from Ruby as well as the notes she enclosed with her own letters to her son. Ruby couldn't understand why he wasn't getting her letters when she left them ready-stamped for Percy to pick up from the hall table. Why oh, why did this blessed war make the delivering of letters so difficult?

'I can't understand it,' she'd told Sarah. His mother had sniffed, like Ruby was at fault.

Ruby now stared hard at Marge, who had suddenly become silent beneath her gaze.

'I have no intention of getting rid of the baby,' she repeated.

'Earlier you were insisting you weren't pregnant!'

'Now I know I am. And I want to keep it.'

Marge put her hand to her head. 'Do you realize what's at stake here? A baby when you're not married means the end of the world as you know it. Where are you going to live? Here? I don't think so. Mervyn might feel sorry for you and let you work as long as possible, but he won't want a baby cluttering up the place and you know it. This place is his livelihood. You'll need money. Where's that coming from? Think you'll get a place to live? Well, think again. "No unmarried mothers" means just that! You'll be shunned. Think you'll get another job? Think on, the moment you say you've got a baby the job vacancy will have mysteriously become filled.'

Ruby saw the tears in Marge's eyes as she continued. 'I know first-hand what it's like with kids an' no father around.'

'My baby has a father . . .'

Marge bent down and looked under the bed, then she went to the window and peered behind the curtains.

'I don't see no father.'

Ruby couldn't hold back her tears. Marge put her arms around her.

'I'm sorry, my love. I just want you to realize you might have to bring this little one up on your own,' she murmured softly into Ruby's hair. 'It will be no picnic.' She pushed Ruby away and looked her up and down. 'I'm here for you. Whatever happens, I'm here for you. We'll manage somehow.'

Their arms around each other, the girls cried.

After a while Ruby pulled away. 'Don't tell anyone,' she begged.

'My lips are sealed,' said Marge, 'but pretty soon you'll begin to show even more.'

'I need to tell Joe . . .'

Marge nodded. 'I think you'd better,' she said.

Chapter Thirteen

Lennie was counting out packets of twenty cigarettes into stacks of two hundreds, but the soft packets didn't stand together too well and kept falling over.

'Bloody American rubbish,' he muttered, looking at the picture of a cowboy wearing a big hat and hurling a lasso on the front of the packets. 'Can't beat a proper fag, a Woodbine,' he muttered.

There was no one to hear him so he carried on counting. He'd make a nice profit on these, he thought.

Maybe he'd offer some to Merv. Most of these would go to the Green Dragon, though. He didn't like the taste of them himself. He wondered if he should save some for his boy, Joe, then discarded the idea. Joe was always banging on about one day Merv would get caught, then he'd go down the line, end up in Winchester nick. Lennie smiled to himself. They had to catch him first!

The knock at the front door made him lose count. He swore and waited for his wife to answer the knocking. Then he remembered she'd gone to the next street to see her friend May, who had a cold. Lots of colds about, he thought; summer colds.

Lennie moved, scraping his chair along the lino, and took his time going down the passage to the front door because his braces had slipped down over his shoulders.

'Hang on,' he said, 'don't knock the bloody door down.' He confronted the beautiful vision on his doorstep as the door swung back. 'Hello, what can I do for you?' He was suddenly aware he was wearing a collarless shirt, and needed a bath.

'Can I come in?'

He stepped back, ashamed he hadn't thought immediately to ask her inside.

'Of course, love. To what do I owe this delightful pleasure?' He could smell expensive perfume drifting from her and into the passageway, which was still reeking with the remnants of the sausage and mash that they'd eaten for tea.

He stood aside and she click-clacked in her high heels up

the passage and into the kitchen. She turned to face him and he saw the look of sadness on her pretty face.

'Whatever's the matter?'

Lennie pulled out a chair so she could sit down. Then he realized he'd invited this young woman in with packets of American cigarettes stacked all over the kitchen table, still, it wasn't as though she'd not had stuff off him before.

'Bit of business,' he murmured, remembering he didn't have to explain himself to her, not in his own house.

'How long have we known each other, Lennie?'

She'd never called him by his Christian name before. It was always 'Mr Stark'.

'Since you was knee-high to a grasshopper,' he said. 'Want a fag?'

The girl nodded. 'I shouldn't, I know, but it calms my nerves.'

He pushed three packets of twenties across the table towards her, then pulled out another kitchen chair and said, 'Put the fags in your handbag and sit down. If you've come to see the wife, she's not here.' He ran his fingers through his silky hair that was still luxuriant. 'Gone visiting the sick,' he explained.

He watched as she sat carefully across from him and crossed her legs at her knees. He thought he saw a glimpse of stocking top! Then she surprised him by putting her hand on the table top and starting to rise.

'I'm sorry. I shouldn't have come. It's really not any of my business . . .'

His hand shot across the table and covered hers. The warmth of her skin made his blood tingle.

'Sit down! And for God's sake put them fags in your bag.' She sat down again and made herself comfortable after unclipping her bag and putting in the cigarettes.

'You're very kind,' she said, making him feel as if he was suddenly ten foot tall.

'Neighbourly is the word,' he said.

She looked him straight in the eyes and smiled. Her teeth were white and very straight. Like little pearls, he thought. And that heavenly perfume she was wearing was making him feel quite unnecessary. It was real perfume, none of that Woolies stuff that choked a bloke.

'Well, what can I do for you?'

She took a handkerchief from her open bag and dabbed at her cheek. 'I'm not one for telling tales, but I can't sit by and see a friend being taken advantage of . . .'

Lennie's ears were on high alert.

'No,' she said, shaking her head so that her shiny hair

swished and fell immaculately back into its glossy style. 'You'll think badly of me for coming round here.'

'I could never think badly of you. Why, when you and our lad used to hang about together I often thought something would come of it bu—' He faltered.

'So did I, but all that's in the past. Though we do talk on the phone now and then . . .'

His ears pricked up. So the little bugger was stringing her along as well as young Ruby, was he? He smiled. Like father, like son.

'You can tell me anything,' he said, leaning across and patting her arm. She moved forward and her full breasts jiggled together in the sweetheart neckline dress.

'It's easy to see how much Joe loves the girl. I often answer the phone, you see, even when she's there. Ruby puts her finger to her lips, pretending she's out.' She mimed the act for Lennie. 'I'm a very straight girl and I don't like her deceiving Joe when she's often out with that young sailor . . .'

'Is she?' Lennie realized his grip on her skin had hardened. 'I'm so sorry,' he said, suddenly flustered. He moved his hand from her arm.

He could see she hadn't wanted to tell him, hadn't really wanted to come to the house. She was dabbing at her eyes as she rose from the table.

'I'm really sorry. Whatever must you think of me?' Again she was staring into his eyes, her long mascaraed lashes wet with tears. She turned away. 'I must go,' she said with a sniff. 'It's just that I've always cared for Joe and I don't want to see him hurt . . .'

'Of course you don't, my love.' She was leaning in to him now and he could feel himself growing hard. He pushed her away, ashamed. Taking her hand, he led her towards the passage and the front door.

'You did right to come round, my love. Don't you worry about a thing. I'm going to sort this.'

He gave her a peck on the cheek, then opened the door. When he closed it, he was cursing his body for showing him up. He hoped she hadn't noticed anything. She was a nice girl, Sylvie Meadows. She'd done right to tell him his boy was being two-timed.

He'd hardly got back into the kitchen when he heard the key turn in the lock.

'Who was that I saw coming out of here?' His wife was striding up the passageway, her normally placid face white with anger. 'It was that Sylvie Meadows, wasn't it?'

She threw the light shawl that had been covering her shoulders against the cool night air over the back of a chair. 'Are you up to your tricks again?'

'Calm down, love,' Lennie said, sitting back at the table and patting the chair next to him for her to sit. He was glad the evidence of his bulging delight in seeing Sylvie had quickly disappeared. 'The girl came round here hoping to see you.' Not quite the truth, but it will appease the wife, he thought.

'Oh, and why's that?'

She plonked herself down beside him and was staring hard at him through narrowed eyes.

'Have you seen Ruby lately?' he asked.

'Only in the pub. Things seem to have cooled between them. Joe's stopped sending her money, said he couldn't be really be sure she was receiving it as he don't get letters from her, only the scraps she gives me to include with mine. I told him I always gave her the money and the notes. She hasn't been round here for ages . . .'

'Just as I thought . . .'

'What d'you mean?' Her eyes were still boring into him.

'Ruby's doing the dirty on him.'

'Well,' the word was followed by a long drawn-out sigh, 'I thought something was wrong. Ruby gave the excuse she wasn't coming round here because she was tired, too many lock-ins, she said.'

'Well, she ain't too tired to be going off with that Terry Barnet.'

'No!'

'Yes!'

His wife's mouth clamped itself into a thin line before she spoke again. 'An' that Sylvie's been tryin' to smooth things over? Is that why she came round here to see me?'

He nodded, watched as his wife slipped her nail beneath the top of a packet of cigarettes and shook out a fag. She lit up and puffed away.

'I always said him and Sylvie would have made a good pair,' she said.

'You've got to tell him about the baby.'

Ruby looked at her friend.

'How can I when I don't get no letters, nothing, now?' She polished the already shining counter.

'Tell his mum then and let the jungle telegraph do the rest.' Ruby knew Marge was like a dog with a bone some-times. Worse since she'd worked through a sniffly cold that she swore Nan had passed on to her.

'How can I do that? She's gone all funny on me. Don't speak unless I talk first and when I asked her if she had a letter from Joe for me she said, 'You needn't worry your head about Joe.' I'd have tackled her about that, but there was a queue at the counter waiting to be served and I could feel Merv's eyes boring into my back.'

'Perhaps your beloved Joe has got himself another girl?'

Ruby felt the tears prick at the back of her eyes.

'He wouldn't do that.'

Marge turned away and began to serve a customer. When she was finished she said, 'An' you've got to tell Merv. He mustn't be the last one to know, not after all he's done for you.'

Ruby knew she was right.

When she was in bed at night she was certain she could feel her baby move inside her. Wouldn't it have been awful if she'd sat in a bath, drunk on gin? Or taken them dangerous tablets? What would have happened if she'd gone to that woman down Mayfield Road and she'd done the operation to take her baby away? Despite everything, Ruby had feelings for her child and she knew she already loved the tiny being.

Ruby was alone now. Marge cared deeply for her, but Ruby knew she had problems she wasn't sharing with her. Often she'd catch Marge staring into space, then when Ruby spoke Marge didn't appear to hear her. She'd asked what was troubling her but all she'd got in return was, 'Nothing.' Merv was the same as ever, bluff, hale and hearty. The pub was doing well, especially on the nights that 'Gosport's Songbird'

Sylvie Meadows sang in the bar. Even Ruby had to admit the girl had a wonderful voice.

It hadn't been so wonderful the other morning when Ruby had been in the bathroom and Sylvie had barged in. She'd called her a fat sow!

Sylvie had come downstairs later moaning that Merv should put a lock on the bathroom door.

'I barged in on that fat sow washing her hair. Imagine if that was some bloke happening on me in the bathroom? I'd be mortified,' Sylvie had said.

There was no love lost between her and Sylvie.

Ruby knew she had to heed Marge's advice. Soon she must tell Merv. Ruby put her hands over her stomach.

'It will be all right, my little one,' she said. 'We'll manage, somehow.'

Since the giddy highs of D-Day, everyone thought the end of Hitler was in sight. Churchill privately admitted that neither the German people nor the German army were about to roll over. He wrote in a memo that Hitler would be fighting into the next year. The belligerent Montgomery wanted to thrust forward, sweeping northwards through the Netherlands to try to outflank the Germans and their defences. His plan was to descend into the Ruhr Valley and for the Allied forces to drive hard towards the Rhine, grabbing a bridgehead on the other side before the Germans managed to reorganize themselves to react.

Eisenhower, however, thought it a 'bold plan'. To the American Airborne Division he gave the job of taking Eindhoven and the bridges at Grave and Nijmegen, and to the British the more difficult task of capturing the bridge at Arnhem.

This was a task the British 1st Airborne were up for. Disappointed at missing out on the D-Day landings at Normandy, they were more than ready to do their bit.

The men embarked on their mission with fervour. The fact that they had been told to stand down so many times had only added to their keenness to get the job done. To a man they had unshakeable belief in themselves, none more so than Joe Stark.

Although not scheduled to take off until ten a.m., Joe was woken up at an unearthly hour. Parachutes had been drawn the previous evening and inside their tents each man slept alongside his chute.

'It's a bloody quagmire out here,' Vinnie said. The mud was clinging to everything. It had been raining all night.

Told by the sergeant to get their breakfasts, they queued in the rain with their mess tins. Then it was trudging back to their tents with their bacon and baked beans, thick slices of toast, salted porridge and strong tea.

By torchlight their equipment was checked and with dawn breaking Vinnie and Joe clambered on board the trucks that were dispatching them to the airfield.

Vinnie said, 'We've practised this so many times and then been let down, I reckon we could all do this blindfolded.'

'We've got further than this before and been made to turn back,' Joe agreed, watching the truck behind the lorries carrying the men that held their chutes, all chalk-marked and ready.

Eventually Fairford, a place in Gloucestershire, came into view and there on the airfield were twelve black bombers.

'Bloody hell, our carriages await,' said Vinnie.

Their gear was checked off. Two hand grenades, a bomb, two ammo pouches, combined pick and shovel, water bottle, mess tin, camouflage net scarf, rifle: the list seemed endless and heavy. Joe, like the rest of them, had a Mae West in case the target was overshot and he ended up in the drink. He had fags and chocolate and a bloody folding bike.

'I reckon we got twenty stone of gear tied to us,' Vinnie mumbled above the roar of the plane's engine when they were strapped inside, lined up, airborne and almost ready to bail.

'It bloody feels like it,' Joe said. He was seated on the floor facing Vinnie and had pulled number eight. Sergeant Howard was going to jump after him.

'Bloody uncomfortable, this,' muttered Vinnie.

'I think they designed planes to be uncomfortable when we're sat here with all this gear so we're always glad to get out when the order comes,' said Joe.

Sergeant Howard's face was inscrutable.

Joe was worried about what would happen at the jump, they all were. Signs of nervousness filled the cabin. It was claustrophobic and sweat was running down his neck.

'We got far to go, Sarge?'

'About twenty minutes,' Howard said. Time was going by so slowly. Joe felt he'd been in the air for ever.

He knew they were all glad to finally be doing something besides practising jumping. Getting ready to leave the barracks and then being told it was all off was soul-destroying.

If that had happened once or twice it wouldn't have been so bad, but it was time and time again. So now nerves were stretched to breaking points. Every time the back-down had come, the men had been rewarded with twelve-hour breaks and passes to go home. Fine, thought Joe, if twelve hours was enough time to get home and see loved ones. Even then there was the terrible wrench of being pulled away again when it was time to leave. Joe couldn't do it. He couldn't travel home with anticipation at seeing Ruby high on his list, only to have to leave almost immediately after greeting her. So he stayed in barracks, walked about the town or read. He'd had quite a few long chats with Sylvie on the phone.

The older she got the more she seemed to understand him.

He hadn't liked her nature when he'd been younger and out for all he could get from girls. He'd got what he'd wanted from Sylvie all right. Age seemed to have mellowed her. She understood how he felt when he couldn't get hold of Ruby. Sylvie's empathy showed. And just what was Ruby playing at?

She'd been a virgin that night at Tragedy Bank. She'd led him to believe he was the only man for her. What was she doing taking so many nights off from the Point to go out dancing?

Sylvie had assured him there was probably nothing in Ruby's meetings with Terry Barnet. But he had the feeling that Sylvie was hiding something, covering up for Ruby. When he tried to get her to talk more about Ruby she clammed up, said it wasn't her place to talk about her mates. He admired her for that. Sure, it frustrated him not to be able to get at the truth of what was happening in Gosport, but she was lucky to have a good friend like Sylvie who didn't tittle-tattle.

Time was dragging now. The minutes seemed like hours. The juddering of the plane, the rank atmosphere inside and the feeling of gloom, yes, that was it, gloom, pervaded everything.

Then the silence was broken as the pilot's voice came over the intercom.

'The hatches will be opened to blow in some fresh air. It's a beautiful day down there over the Dutch coast. Should be a piece of cake, your drops, so good luck!'

Hooking up began. A dispatcher began moving between the two lines of men, checking the parachutes were properly hooked to the line that ran the length of the plane's fuselage. As each man exited the aircraft the canopy was triggered automatically.

Then the flaps of the jump hatch opened.

Sunlight and air, fresh and cold from the bright morning outside, streamed briskly into the plane.

Joe stood and eased his way closer to the hatch. He was dripping with sweat, a combination of fear, apprehension and excitement. He waited for his place in the queue of jumpers. Vinnie ahead of him, Howard behind.

Through the hatch the earth seemed to be rising to meet

him. Joe knew each man was in his own private hell as thoughts flashed through their heads. Yet each had been trained to ignore them and concentrate on the job in hand.

The plane was beginning to lose some of its height in readiness for the drop.

The small red light above the hatch was blinking on then off, on then off. The red light magically changed from red to green and silently the men began moving along the line, then disappearing. As if in a dream sequence, Vinnie turned, gave Joe a huge wink, then the rushing air seemed to suck his friend away before his eyes.

Below, Joe could see men scrambling, on the ground, tidying their chutes. The first of them had already reached their destination.

Then Joe was in the hole. Air rushing about him. The hole was gone. Joe struggled in the cold, stinging air. Dangling, legs, arms, all awry, he twisted and jerked to free his parachute lines. At the periphery of his vision the next man to drop was also out of the hatch. But something was wrong.

Sergeant Howard's fall speed was much too fast!

Chapter Fourteen

'This is to notify you that your tenancy agreement is being rescinded with effect from September the first—'

'What the hell does that mean?' Nan interrupted Marge.

'Wait until I've finished reading and then I'll tell you.' Marge's hands were shaking as she looked at the letter that had arrived a week ago and that she'd been unwilling to think of or even to tell Nan about.

'That, Nan, is Mr Barclay's posh way of saying he wants us out of here.' The absolute relief of the secret she'd kept and now was able to spill out was tremendous.

Nan frowned. 'But we got nowhere else to go! Does he say why? Our rent's always been paid without fail . . .' She paused. Then she bit at her bottom lip before saying, 'Tell him we'll pay up what's owing, I got a little bit under the mattress . . .'

'It's no good, Nan. I didn't want to worry you, but this isn't the first letter an' when I offered to pay extra, even though I had no idea how I was going to get hold of it, he told me he wants both these flats vacant so he can remodel them to charge more rent. The fact I'd got a bit behind paying was the lever he wanted.'

'But how did you get behind with the rent? You've always said, rent, bills, food, in that order. That's how we manage on the little we gets . . .'

Marge let the letter fall to the table. She tuned out from Nan's voice. Nan was going to go on and on and one thing she couldn't stand now was an inquest on her inability to get that rat-faced Flint to mark her rent book up to date. The bastard had pocketed her rent money, and there wasn't a thing she could do about it. Why would Mr Barclay believe her when he wanted the two flats vacant?

She sighed.

If it was only herself who needed a place to live she'd ask Mervyn if she could share with Ruby. But two kiddies and Nan in the pub as well? No, that wouldn't do at all.

She didn't want to tell Nan she'd already gazed at notice-boards in shop windows. No joy there. No unmarried women, no kids, no coloureds, no pets, no Irish. The list was practically endless. Where were people supposed to live?

'I went down the council offices.'

Nan stopped talking.

'I told 'em I was on their list and asked about them new prefabs they're building at Bridgemary and at Clayhall.'

Nan's eyes were bright, expectant. Marge carried on. 'They said they could help if I'd got bombed out, but not while I still wasn't homeless . . .'

'Didn't you tell them we was going to be homeless?' Nan's voice was at screech level.

'Course I did!'

Nan slammed into the bedroom and the thin wail from Chrissie told Marge the noise had woken the child.

'For God's sake,' she said, too quietly for anyone to hear. There was little point in ranting and raving. What's done was done and she had to find them somewhere else to live. She wasn't going to tell Nan that one of the first things she'd done was to write a letter to Alf and tell him of the predicament they were in. The letter came back, 'Not at this address', and as usual it had been steamed open and read and stuck down again. Alf must think she was daft!

Nan stayed in the bedroom. Marge knew the old lady had to come to terms with what was happening in her own way.

Luckily Marge already had her evening change of clothes hanging over the fireguard, a green skirt and a lighter green jumper that was thin so she wouldn't get too hot working in the stuffy bar.

She knew Nan would wait for her to leave before she came out. Marge smiled to herself; her nan didn't mean anything by shutting the door on her, it was just her way of coping with things. She heard Chrissie giggling. Nan was playing with her. Everything would be all right. She'd come out from the bedroom later and call in Tony who was playing with his little friend on the bomb site.

The warm evenings seemed to be coming to a close now, but it was still plenty light enough for kids to play in the streets.

Marge walked along the High Street and then pushed open the main door to the bar.

'Hello, Ruby,' she said, treating her mate to a big smile that she didn't feel like giving.

Marge's worries were paramount, but serving behind the bar meant being polite and cheerful. So for a while she could almost forget that she and her family were about to be evicted from their home.

She wasn't sure whether it was wise or not, but she was going to try to keep her problems to herself. Ruby had enough on her plate without worrying about her. And Marge knew if she so much as breathed a word to Merv he'd go on about her being extremely stupid not to have paid her rent in the first place.

The trouble was, when your kids needed clothes and food, that's exactly what you spent your money on. Everything else had to be put on a slow burner. People who never had kids didn't understand the true cost of them and how their clothes were forever being outgrown.

Ruby was talking to Richard Williams. There was something about the man Marge didn't like.

Tim Bracknell, the estate agent, was in for a swift pint before he went home to his missus. He worked for Landings, the biggest letting agent in the south and was in charge of letting the caravans. He was deep in conversation with the man who was converting the café at Stokes Bay.

The place had taken a hit in the last raid, been put up for sale and sold quickly, along with three caravans on the highly esteemed site near the café.

Marge had even been along to the site one afternoon to see if she could rent a caravan.

The woman in charge of the site had looked down her nose at Marge pushing Chrissie in the big pram.

'These are holiday lets, young lady. For hire only. There's no provision for people' – when she'd said 'people', her eyes had narrowed like she was looking down on Marge – 'no provision for people to live in the mobile homes all the year round. If we had any lettings vacant, which we don't, the maximum length of stay is ten months in any one year.'

Marge felt she had been put in her place and despondently pushed the pram along the beachfront where the wire was broken down. She thought how much nicer it would be when all the barbed wire was gone from the beaches. The wire was supposed to be a deterrent against German landings.

Tim Bracknell now approached the bar. 'Two pints of Best, Marge.'

She gave him a smile and took two clean pint glasses and began filling them.

She thought about the snotty woman at the caravan site and wondered if she might ask Tim outright whether his friend intended letting the caravans. That woman only managed the site, she didn't know everything, surely?

Marge put both pints in front of him. 'Good head on those,' he said, his hand going to his pocket for payment. Marge took a deep breath. 'Look, I know anything I hear this side of the counter is private. But I couldn't help overhearing that you've sold three of the mobile homes on the Stokes Bay site. I have to get out of the place I'm lodging and wondered if it was possible I could rent one off you?'

He paused as he put coins on the counter and stared at

her. He puffed out his pink lips and let the air go out of them. He had auburn hair and freckles and his face was red from being out in the sun.

'Fallen on hard times, Marge?' He gave a silly laugh.

Why, oh, why had she expected him to help her? He was just like most of the fellers who came in the pub, always with an eye to what he could get out of any situation.

Marge thought, In for a penny, in for a pound.

'Actually, yes.'

He was in the process of turning away from the bar, when he looked back at her and set both pints down on a beer cloth and leaned across to speak softly.

'The site vans are dealt with in an entirely different way to renting houses. Gosport's got a housing shortage due to the bombing. You'll get no joy from the council because although they're building these new prefabricated houses, they're not ready yet. Can't get hold of materials to do up the places that are bombed . . .'

Marge knew all this already and tuned out. Why did he have to waffle on? Why didn't he just say no, and let her get on with it? But wait a minute, what was he saying?

'. . . It's not sited which means the water has to come from a nearby tap. It is waterproof but there's a long walk from the main road. If you like seclusion, you've got it.'

Marge said, 'You mean you've got something?' Her heart started banging against her chest so loudly she thought the noise of it would drown out Vera Lynn's singing.

'Let me take these over . . .' She watched his stocky figure move away, saw him speak to his friend, then leave the pints on the table and return to lean across the bar.

'Like I said, it's waterproof, four-berth, and you can cook by bottled gas. There's a heater, because right next to the sea like that it gets bloody cold at nights.'

'You mean you'll let me rent it off you?'

'Just said, haven't I?' He frowned. 'For a small consideration, of course.' He winked at her. Marge's heart dropped.

Here it was again: Let me in your knickers an' I'll be nice to you.

'How much a week?'

'We'll worry about that later,' he said. He raised his sparse eyebrows. 'Could be rent-free, we don't really use it any more, not since I bought that cottage down in Devon.' His voice tailed off. He was looking at her in a funny way. Almost as if she was a sweet in a candy shop and he wanted that sweet very much.

Marge thought of Flint and what she'd endured against the living-room wall and she shivered.

'You all right, Marge?' Tim Bracknell was staring at her.

Quickly she gathered her thoughts together. Supposing she was lucky enough to find a house to let, she'd need money up front for a deposit, then possibly as much as a month's rent in advance. She had no savings, no money and although Nan had let slip that she had some money in her mattress, it was hardly likely to be more than a fiver, more likely a ten-bob note. After all, where did Nan get money from?

She couldn't ask Merv because she still owed him money and she'd already borrowed two more pounds from Ruby to help outfit Tony for school. The rags he'd been wearing out to play during the summer weren't going to keep him warm in the winter. Suddenly, she didn't care what she had to do to put a roof over their heads.

'Yes,' she said, coming back to life again. 'Will you take me to see it?'

'Bloody hell, you're eager.' He seemed shocked. Then he said, 'How about tonight, after you've finished here?' He looked at his watch. 'I've got to leave after I've talked some more business with Matey,' he inclined his head back to his friend who was looking bored and had already drunk his pint, 'but I can meet you outside, about eleven?'

Marge nodded. It seemed a funny time to go and look at a caravan, especially in the dark. 'Are there lights?' she asked.

'They run off batteries, a sort of transformer,' he said. 'It's a caravan, Marge, not a bleedin' hotel.'

She could see he was getting cross. She didn't want to antagonize him.

'All right,' she said. 'Eleven.'

He put a hand on the counter and squeezed her arm. 'I'll bring a blanket,' he said softly, his face inches away from hers. She could smell the fish he'd eaten for his tea.

'Why am I this side of the bar, doin' your job?' Merv pressed change into a man's hand. 'Clean the counter.' He walked away from the mess of Guinness he'd created. Marge shrugged at Ruby, who was, Marge could see, adding up a huge order in her head. A crowd of factory girls had come in and they were all drinking something different. They were giggly and loud and looking around the bar at the men.

Merv's voice cut through their laughter. 'I hope you've checked your gas mask,' he directed at Marge.

She nodded violently. His question had nothing to do with gas masks, the old devil. She knew he didn't like either her or Ruby chatting up the men while working, but she couldn't be rude to customers, could she?

'Marge.'

She turned at her name; it was Richard Williams.

He beckoned her along the bar. 'Want a refill?' she asked.

'Not yet,' he began. He was wearing something that smelled spicy, some kind of aftershave, it was nice. 'I want to ask you if Ruby's all right?'

'Yes, she's fine,' Marge replied automatically and went to move away.

'I don't think she is.' His voice was quite firm. 'She's put on weight . . .'

'That's not a crime. Ruby likes chips.'

'That bloke she was knocking about with has ditched her, hasn't he?'

'You, Mr Williams, are very direct.' Marge tried to sound superior. 'But why are you asking me questions when you've just been talkin' to her yourself?'

'Because I think she's been let down by him.'

'Oh, you do, do you? And what does she say about it?'

'After she cried, or before?'

Marge glared at him, then stalked along the floor at the back of the counter to where Ruby was taking change from the till. She peered into Ruby's face. Sure enough, there were dark rings beneath her eyes, eyes that were bright with dampness.

'You been crying?'

Ruby pinged the drawer shut and handed over change to

a beefy blonde woman who tipped back a shilling at Ruby: 'Buy yourself a drink, love.'

'Thank you,' Ruby muttered and put the money in the till and then searched for a bottle top to join the pile she already had. 'They're a generous lot tonight,' she added. She hadn't answered Marge's question.

'What did you say to that writer bloke?'

Ruby said, 'Nosy, ain't you? He asked me when Joe was coming home and I told him I didn't know, because I hadn't heard from him. Then it upset me, what I'd said.'

'Look, you daft mare, if you ain't careful it'll all be out in the open about him not writing and the baby, everything, and what'll happen then?'

'Pint of cider, Marge?' called a thin young man, another regular who was tapping a coin on the wooden counter.

'Pint of cider, Marge, *please*?' Marge took a dimpled glass and began pulling on the pump. When the glass was topped up she put it on the counter. 'Politeness costs nothing,' she said, her mouth settling angrily.

The young man, eyes wide, handed her the correct money. 'Thank you,' he said with exaggerated diction.

'Turn around!' Ruby did as she was told and Marge stared at her. She was wearing navy-blue wide-legged trousers and a light blue knitted loose top with short sleeves. 'You look tired. Very healthy but overweight. Luckily it's all spread about and not stuck out in front. You got to be about seven months now . . .'

'What's this, a bloody fashion show? I pay you two to serve drinks, not talk about bleedin' clothes . . .'

'It's Ruby, she wants to talk to you.'

Ruby closed her open mouth.

'She wants to talk to you in private, now!'

Merv sighed. 'Whatever now?' he muttered, and pulled up the flap in the bar. 'We'll be in the kitchen if it's urgent.' He stared at Marge. 'Remember why you're here and try to serve a few punters instead of chatting them up.' After he'd said his piece he stood aside so Ruby had no choice but to go through the hatch, out into the bar and then through to the kitchen, with her boss following.

Chapter Fifteen

'Sit down, love. I'm not going to say I haven't guessed something's up. I got eyes in me head and ears that might be cauliflower-like, but they don't miss much.'

Merv pushed Ruby towards a chair and she sat down at the kitchen table. She was about to answer him when he spoke again.

'I've noticed too that you're not so pally with my mate Lennie, nor his missus?'

Ruby sighed. 'First, I want to thank you for taking me in after my mum died, you've been really good to me—'

'An' you're a good worker, Ruby,' he broke in. 'But I don't like dissent between my workers and my customers.'

'It's . . . it's . . . it's . . .' She took a deep breath. 'Joe seems to have left me high and dry. I've not had any proper word from him for ages.'

'The lad's in the paras. Even I know he can't do what he wants to do. I've heard talk of somethin' going on that they've been practising for ages . . .'

'Surely he could write and tell me?' Ruby knew her voice was high, accusing.

'Sometimes there's reasons beyond our control why we don't hear from our loved ones. You do still love Joe?'

She nodded, took a deep breath, then said, 'I need to tell him that I'm pregnant.'

For a while there was nothing but the ticking of the big old clock disturbing the silence. Then Merv let the air go from his body. It sounded like a balloon being punctured.

'How far along are you?'

'I don't rightly know, about six months, maybe . . .'

He looked her up and down. 'Now I know why you look so bonny. I thought I bin feeding you too much.' He tried a half smile to lighten the atmosphere, but it didn't work.

Merv pulled out a high-backed kitchen chair and sat down alongside her.

'You know you can't stay here?' His words were soft but Ruby heard them clearly. 'I got a business to run. I'm not a nursery.'

Ruby felt the tears rise for the second time that night. 'You've already been so good to me . . .'

'All I've done is give a good barmaid a home and lent her money. But you understand I can't have a squalling kiddie around the place. It's bad for business and not good for a little one to be brought up in an environment like this. Kids need fresh air, a garden . . .' His words tailed off.

'I understand,' she said.

He nodded. His tired, battered face looked haunted. 'You can stay until you've got somewhere else to go, then it's goodbye, Ruby. Have you got anywhere in mind?'

Ruby shook her head. He thought for a moment, then said, 'Have you been messing the lad about?'

Ruby, who'd been playing idly with a teaspoon, realized what his words implied. 'No! No, I bloody haven't,' she said. The spoon flew across the table and dropped to the floor.

'Steady on, I had to ask. It's not like Lennie to take against a pretty face. As you got nobody except Marge, who's strapped for space in her tiny flat, would you be agreeable to going to stay with Joe's people?'

Ruby leaned forward. 'I thought me an' his mum were pals. Of course I'd go there, like a shot. I've no idea why she's taken against me—'

Merv cut her off in full flow.

'I can't see them turning out their own grandchild. I take it they know nothing about the baby?'

Ruby shook her head. 'No one besides Marge and you know. If it hadn't been for Marge . . .'

Ruby knew she was running off at the mouth again, but it felt so good to have her secret out in the open.

Again he stopped her words by saying, 'Get back in the bar and do some work.' He suddenly grinned at her. Ruby saw that although his teeth had gaps in them, where presumably some had been knocked out while he was in the boxing ring, his remaining ones were very white and clean. 'Leave things with me. I'll do what I can, all right?'

Ruby slid off the chair, her face wet with tears. Merv gave her an awkward hug, then said, 'You can't go back in the bar like that; for God's sake go and put a bit of slap on and make yourself look presentable.'

She gave him a wet smile and went upstairs to her room. For a few moments she sat in front of the dressing-table mirror with her head in her hands. Then she took a deep breath, got up and went to the small sink, washed her face and cleaned her teeth. She sat down again in front of the mirror, pulling the hairbrush through her hair.

Nothing was settled yet. But it felt as if a load had been

taken from her shoulders. Thanks, Marge, she thought, you're a good pal.

After spitting on her mascara brush and darkening her lashes, Ruby began outlining her lips with New Dawn.

'What's the matter with you, Marge? You're like a fart in a colander.'

'Sorry, Merv, I just want to get out of this place.' She banged the tin full of cigarette ends into the rubbish bin and then wiped the tin around with the damp cloth. Marge looked around the bar; it looked clean enough. She'd swept up. She'd replaced the chairs beneath the tables. On her way out she'd carry the bin full of rubbish and empty it into the big dustbins near the chute used by the draymen. She knew she had to leave the place clean and tidy, but Grace would be in in the morning to polish.

Ruby still had her hands in the sink, working on the last batch of glasses.

Marge wasn't eager to meet with Tim Bracknell, but she was hoping to get it all over and done with.

It was five past eleven. She looked at the clock again, and it was still five past eleven.

'You coming to the kitchen for a cuppa, Marge?'

Sometimes the three of them would sit and put the world to rights over tea.

'If you don't mind, Ruby, I'd like to get off home.' Ruby had already thanked her for stepping in and making sure she shared the secret about the baby with Mervyn.

'Go on, bugger off then,' Merv boomed. 'Leave everything to us.'

It was meant as a joke. After all, Marge had already cashed up the night's takings and put in the float for the morning.

'See you tomorrow,' she sang out.

Once outside, Marge took deep breaths of the night air as her eyes scanned the pavement for the man she was going to meet. She shivered. The rain had stopped, but the night was chilly and she wore no coat. The street was silent and deserted.

Twin lights fluttered so palely she thought she might be mistaken that they were there at all, then she realized Tim had flashed the car's lights at her. She walked down the road towards him. Marge had no idea of the vehicle's make, only that it was ticking over quietly and was small and box-like. He leaned across, opened the passenger door and Marge got in.

She immediately smelled baby sick. So Tim was married, and had a child?

'Thought you was going to let me down,' he said.

'A promise is a promise, to me,' she replied. 'Where does your missus think you are?'

'Quite the Sherlock Holmes,' he said. She looked at him and a smile had lifted a corner of his mouth. 'I told her I had to go back to the office, I forgot some paperwork.'

Marge nodded and looked out the window. They were driving past the Forum picture house now.

'How are we going to see the caravan in the dark?'

'Look on the back seat, there's a flashlight.' She turned and saw he was right. It was next to a tartan blanket. She sighed. What the hell, she thought. He had something she wanted. She had something he wanted. It was a fair swap, but she had the feeling she would go on paying for longer than he would.

Then the car turned down Western Way in Alverstoke, past Vectis Road and out on to the main road towards Lee-on-the-Solent. He drove the car on to a small road that led to the barbed-wire-covered beach. They passed a disused bomb shelter, where the doorway was all boarded up, and then he parked on the gravel. Marge could hear the sea. It was too dark to see it, but she heard the pull of pebbles on the beach as the waves washed the water to and from the shore.

'Are we allowed here?'

It looked dark and creepy outside the car.

'Actually, yes,' he replied. 'This is common ground. A bit like Walpole Park, which isn't allowed to be built on, because many years ago it was deeded to the people of Gosport as a fairground. Much like Ewer Common,' he added. 'C'mon,' he coaxed, 'you won't see the caravan sitting in here.'

Once out of the car and with the torch in his hand and his fingers over the beam so that it wouldn't shine too brightly, he began walking along a narrow pathway that appeared to have brambles either side. Every so often he slowed and asked her if she was all right. They came to a clearing backed by trees and she saw the caravan.

'Oh!' It was such a surprise coming upon the small mobile home that she gasped. He felt along the top of its doorway and pulled down a key, opening the door.

'Let me go in first and I can put some light on the subject,' he said.

She smelled the mustiness from the place having been shut up, and the damp. But, she told herself, that was only to be expected. It was close to the sea and hadn't been used for ages, so he'd already told her.

She gasped again when the lamp was lit and she could pick out a double bed made up at the far end, a small sink and a square of gas rings that had a pipe disappearing through the wall of the caravan to the outside. There was what looked like a wardrobe, the door hanging open, and a table set up with benches.

'That table folds down and becomes another double bed,' he explained.

Actually, Marge thought it looked quite nice. It was tidy, and in the light from the lamp it looked clean. Carpet covered the floor and on top of the carpet was brown paper that still crackled beneath their feet, so the van couldn't be that damp inside, she reasoned. He checked the curtains were closed so no light would escape. Someone, his wife probably, Marge thought, had gone to great lengths to keep the small place clean and nice.

'You can't see them in the dark, but outside there's a wooden picnic table and half a dozen wooden chairs. We used to love coming out here but after the baby was born, Diane wanted something more permanent,' he added.

Marge nodded. 'So let me get this straight, I can cook by bottled gas. There's a heater to light when it gets cold and the lights are . . .'

'Take your pick,' he said, 'There's a generator or oil. Be careful of the heater – it takes a while to light properly, else it stinks of paraffin.'

'Sounds fair to me,' she said. 'How far is the nearest shop?'

Marge couldn't bear to think she'd have to trudge all the way back into Gosport.

'There a path runs along the top of the beach and in ten minutes you can walk into Lee-on-the-Solent.'

'Oh,' she said, thinking Nan would like that. She could manage that walk, using her stick.

'Well,' he said, 'what do you think?' He was looking at his watch, trying to make out the time in the dull light.

'I think it's lovely,' Marge said. 'When can I move in?'

He pressed the key into her hand. 'Any time.' Then he stared at her. 'Look, I have to get home. Why don't you come here tomorrow on your own in the daylight? If I'm out too long my wife will start asking questions. If you decide to move in, I'll pop round and see you sometimes.'

'For the rent?'

'If you want to call it payment for rent, that's fine by me.' He threw his head back and laughed. 'I'm not an ogre, you know.' He looked at her then said, 'I won't come unannounced, we'll agree a time, I'll catch you at the Point.'

'All right,' she said. After all, she needed somewhere to live, didn't she?

Marge knew there was a bus stop somewhere on the main road so she'd be able to get to work easily. He broke into her thoughts. 'There's stuff in some of the cupboards, welly boots, jumpers, books. Get rid of what you don't want.' He paused and looked serious. 'You're a nice girl, Marge, I won't bother you a lot. My missus has got a bit funny since the little 'un's been born.'

Marge nodded. She understood.

He waved his arm around the interior. 'If my wife finds out you're living here I'm going to tell her I had no idea you'd moved in, got it? I'll say you're a squatter.'

'All right,' she said after a while. The money she'd save on rent would help towards food and things for Tony and Chrissie. Her spirits began to rise.

He bent forward and awkwardly placed a kiss on her forehead. Then he said, 'I got to get back, let's go.'

She stood at the bottom of the wooden steps while he turned off the light inside. When he reached her he grabbed her hand to guide her through the bushes and back to his car. He went round the passenger side, opened the door and let her in.

'Our secret, eh?'

'Yes,' she said. 'Will you take me home, now?'

'No,' he laughed, 'I'll leave you in Lee outside the Tower Ballroom! Where else d'you think I'm going to drive you to?'

She laughed along with him, feeling more relieved than she'd felt in days.

Two boxes of assorted bottles of alcohol sat on Merv's kitchen table. His wallet was on the side and he'd just given Lennie payment.

'All I'm saying is I can't keep her here at the Point. It's not the right environment to bring up a baby.'

'And all I'm saying is I want nothing to do with the little tart. She can't go seeing that bloke in the navy and ignore my boy, then expect him to look on the kid as his own.'

'But the baby belongs to Joe.' Mervyn stood and faced Lennie. 'You're its grandfather!' Lennie looked very smart today in a suit. Merv wondered where he was off to.

Lennie poked him in the chest. 'You don't know that the baby belongs to my boy, you've only got her word for it.' He was shaking his head. 'She's made her bed, let her lie in it.'

'So you don't want to know?'

'That's right. My lad's been phoning her, she's never here!'

'Don't be bloody daft, where else is she but working behind my bar?'

'So Joe's a liar, is he? Doin' his bit for his country and lying about Ruby?'

'I never said that!'

'No! You implied it though.'

There was a fair bit of grimacing, puffing and snorting while the two friends faced each other. Then Lennie seemed to fall into a kitchen chair. He ran his fingers through his curly hair and said, 'She hurt him. To find out she's messing about with another bloke has near enough killed him. He's had problems in the paras and ain't been able to get home to sort things out. How d'you think it feels to know the girl you thought you was going to marry is carrying some other bloke's kid?'

'Not good, Lennie.'

Lennie shook his head. 'I don't want to see him mess up his life. Like I said, Ruby made her bed, let her lie in it.'

'I don't want to fall out with you, Lennie.'

'Well, let's leave it there then, shall we?' Lennie gave him a half smile. 'I got some Turkish fags out in the van – you want some, they're cheap?'

Chapter Sixteen

Joe didn't stop to think. He threw his arms out, around the man hurtling past him faster than he himself was travelling. And he hung on. The awful judder and sway as his chute opened in mid-air, then took the strain of double the weight, tightened the straps about his back, his groin. But he held fast to the man who'd jumped almost simultaneously along with him.

Joe's chute was now tangled and seemed to have become only partly filled with air. He was falling too quickly! By jerking and twisting, his body hurting with every movement, yet still with the sergeant in his arms, he managed to untangle the lines and felt the blessed relief of an upward draught and a gentle sway and bob as his parachute adjusted.

It was as though the two men were doing a dance, Joe thought. Locked together, like lovers, the length of their bodies pressed tightly together. Joe could feel the scratch of the sergeant's chin where already his beard was growing. He could also smell the alcohol on his breath.

Did the sergeant mean to jump to his death?

Why had he jumped without waiting for the safety light? Why hadn't his parachute deployed? Was he befuddled by drink?

Joe had to give it to the sergeant, he was bloody good at disguising the fact he'd been drinking. Up until now!

Joe's arms were numb. He dared not move them for fear they would unlock and his charge would slide through and crash to the earth below. It ran through his mind that he – they – might stand a better chance of survival if he could release some of the baggage he had strapped about him, but to do that he would have to use his hands. He couldn't take the chance.

The cold wind made his face sting and the rushing air took his breath away. Joe knew he must hold on to his unexpected cargo and let fate decree the ending.

A ploughed field was below. A ruined farmhouse to the left of him. He was on the edge of a small town. Please God let the farmhouse be empty and not full of snipers, waiting to pick them off one by one.

Parachutes lay like huge flat mushrooms to be gathered by eager pickers as his own chute hurtled earthwards.

'Brace,' Joe yelled. The sound of his own voice made him realize the man in his arms had not spoken a word. Now he must try to land so he would sustain as little injury as possible.

And then he was down on terra firma and the shock of the ground beneath him forced his arms apart and his charge fell on to the golden dirt. Joe opened his eyes and saw the sergeant lying in the earth.

Was he dead?

Joe struggled out of his chute, aware someone else was at his side, bundling up the slippery material. Oh, dear God! Had he tumbled straight into the arms of a German?

'You are British?'

Joe's heart leapt – the man was Dutch.

'We have been waiting for you.' The man was pushing his hand towards him, pumping at his arm. The sudden pain reminded Joe of his charge lying face down, inert.

Then the sergeant rolled over. 'My fuckin' leg,' he said. 'I'm sure it's broken.'

The Fox was packed. Lennie fought his way through the crowd to the bar.

Sam, the landlord, was on duty, with his girls trying to keep pace with the requests for drinks coming from all directions.

'Pint of Brickwood's when you're ready, Sam,' he called. 'Good crowd.'

'Always is when I get Sylvie in to sing,' Sam threw back at him.

Lennie wiped the sweat from his forehead with a clean pressed handkerchief that his missus always made sure he had on him.

The microphone was in the middle of the floor, as the Fox was only a small public house and unlike some of the larger places, there was barely room to swing a cat. But it was regularly filled with girls from the armament place at Priddy's Hard, and so near the ferry that Allied sailors always stopped off there for a drink on the way to and from their bases.

It was Lennie's second visit of the day. That morning he'd brought round some fags and drink. Tonight he was here to listen to Gosport's Songbird, Sylvie Meadows.

Lennie patted his inside pocket. There were six pairs of the finest nylon stockings in there. A present for Sylvie.

He smoothed his hand along his chin, surprised at its softness. Of course, he'd shaved twice today. And he was wearing a suit. He knew he looked good, because two women seated on the bench had already given him the eye. They weren't bad either, especially the redhead in the high heels. But he was after better and younger fish, not them two old trout.

He looked at his watch, then picked up his pint. Another few minutes, then the girl who could possibly become his daughter-in-law would be singing her heart out.

He couldn't get over his mate, Mervyn, asking him to take in Ruby!

He wondered if Sylvie knew the girl was pregnant. Thank God she had kept her eyes and ears open to what was going on at the Point. The last thing his boy needed was to be trapped into marriage by some young girl who wouldn't keep her legs shut. That young sailor had a lot to answer for. Lennie felt sorry for his boy, because he knew just how much he cared about Ruby. But by God the girl wasn't going to make a laughing stock out of Joe.

Lennie had heard the Allied troops were sweeping across Belgium. The only way to stop them German buggers was to make them retreat. The Allies so far had wrecked more than nine hundred German trucks and seven hundred horse-drawn vehicles. Lennie prayed with all his heart that his boy was safe. He'd had no word from Joe after Joe had said they might be flying to pastures new.

His thoughts disintegrated as the small band began playing and people began cheering.

The vision in a tight black dress was now at the micro-phone, and she was waving the people into silence. 'I Gotta

Right to Sing the Blues' started up and her voice, mellow, like melted honey, was holding them all spellbound. 'God Bless the Child' left the audience tearful. She looked a treat in that black dress. He'd got the glittery material for her from that posh shop in Southsea. She'd had it made up by a local woman living in Mayfield Road. That was Sylvie all over, she never forgot people who were kind to her. She'd told him the seamstress had been marvellous to her when she was a girl.

Lennie patted his inside pocket once more. He knew this vision, Sylvie, fancied his son, but what wouldn't he give for a crack at her himself?

Mervyn couldn't keep it to himself any longer. Ruby had a right to know she wasn't going to get any help from Lennie and his wife.

He knocked gently on her bedroom door.

'Come in.' Her voice was sleepy.

He wasn't going to mince his words. 'Don't get out of bed, I'll sit here on the side.' He sat down. She was like a dormouse, all cuddled up in the covers. He took a deep breath. 'Lennie and his missus don't want you round their house. They reckon you've been doing the dirty on their boy and the baby isn't his.'

He knew she was going to cry. He didn't see any point in

prolonging the agony, but he waited. He could see she was digesting his words.

'That's a lie. And how do they know anything?'

He shrugged. He had to strain his ears to hear her as she added tearfully, 'Have they spoken to Joe?'

'Bit of a problem, apparently. They haven't heard much from him. I read in the *Evening News* that the Parachute Regiment is chasing the Germans out of Holland. If that's where he is then who knows when anyone will hear?'

'You know as well as anyone, Mervyn, that apart from seeing Marge I rarely go out because I'm here working.'

'It's not me what's spreading rumours, is it, love? You tell me the child belongs to Joe, I believe you. You've always been honest with me. But it don't alter the fact I can't keep you here when you give birth.'

Ruby was sitting up. She wasn't crying now, but as soon as he walked out the bedroom he knew she'd burst into tears again.

'You want me to make you a cup of tea?'

She shook her head. 'Tea ain't the answer. I only wish it was. I can see now why Joe's mother has been giving me the cold shoulder. If I went to her on bended knees asking where he was, even if she knew, she wouldn't tell me.'

For a few moments there wasn't a sound inside the room, only the rain beating against the windows.

'I'm sorry, love, I really am.'

Mervyn stared at her. He felt awkward but he'd tried to find a home for her and now it was up to Ruby to sort herself out. He left the room, closing the door behind him. He heard her small voice say, 'Oh, Mum, I'm so sorry I've messed everything up.'

'Check your gas masks.' Mervyn's voice came over loud and clear.

Both Marge and Ruby poked beneath the counter and Marge said, 'Gas masks are here and so is Sylvie's, but she's not coming in today.'

Mervyn banged a dimpled-glass bottle on the shiny bar top. 'We're supposed to carry the means of saving our lives at all times!'

Marge raised her eyes heavenwards.

'Thanks for offering to help me pack stuff up,' she whispered to Ruby as he thumped around. 'I've got the loan of a barrow for tonight, but I have to get it back early in the morning. It's Paddy's barrow.' Ruby knew the bloke from the market would need his only means of transporting goods to Gosport market back as soon as possible.

'I can help you move in . . .'

'I don't think so. It's a fair old walk to the caravan and then you'd have to get back to the Point. I don't want to be the cause of your baby coming early. Have you been to the doctor's yet, made arrangements?'

Ruby looked confused.

'You must see the maternity nurse and get booked in to have the little one in hospital. You don't want to give birth behind the bar, do you?'

Ruby burst into tears.

'Seeing the nurse isn't that bad, she'll tell you what to expect—'

'I . . . I can't have it here, Merv says I've got to find another place.'

'OK, Joe's mum'll be on hand. She knows what it's like—'

'She don't want nothin' to do with me, says the baby don't belong to Joe!'

'What utter tosh!' Marge moved to the end of the counter to serve a customer, as Mervyn had now unbolted the front door and people were streaming in. When she returned she said, 'No wonder you been so down just lately. Don't worry. Something'll turn up.'

She walked away to serve Richard Williams and then came back again.

'Look, I ain't never seen this caravan what I told you about in the daylight, but if there's room there you can bunk in with us.'

Ruby fell on her neck. 'Oh, you won't be sorry, I'll be a babysitter so you and Nan can go out together, I'll—'

Marge grabbed hold of her hand. 'Look, I know it's got four beds but I don't know what condition stuff is in, so I can't make no promises, but I wouldn't see you on the bleedin' streets. Not like some!'

She'd aimed her last words at Mervyn, who was pouring himself a half of Brickwood's. Obviously unaware of what she was talking about, he looked up and smiled at her from along the bar.

'Merv's been good to me,' jumped in Ruby, 'but I can see where he's coming from. He's supposed to make money from this place, not turn it into a mother and baby home. He'll be a barmaid short, with no room for a new woman to stay and his customers'll be treated to a baby crying at all hours. He told me not to worry about paying him back any more money off me mum's funeral . . .'

'Good of him, I'm sure.'

Just then a man used a coin to tap sharply on the wooden counter to gain their attention. 'Two pints over here, ladies, when you've got the time.'

Marge glared at the man, but beneath her breath she said to Ruby, 'He can have the slops out of the tray for that, I can't abide blokes who tap on the bar top like that.'

Ruby smiled. The Brickwood's tray was already slopping over where Merv had made a hash of pouring his half pint. She wished she could be strong like Marge.

Marge had told her about the rent man and her having to leave her place. She'd also told her she was going to live in a caravan because it was all she could find. But no matter how much Ruby probed, Marge wouldn't tell her how she'd come by it. Never mind, her friend was going to try to squeeze her into the van as well. Ruby looked at Marge, tapping the fingers of her left hand on the top of the pump while waiting for the Brickwood's to top up in the straight glass. Ruby saw the drip tray was empty and laughed to herself. She knew how lucky she was to have such a good mate.

The wireless was playing a Bing Crosby song, and Ruby shifted her weight from one foot to the other. Her ankles were all puffy, and once upon a time she would have been jigging about to the music, but she so often felt tired now and all she wanted to do was sit down.

She felt fiercely protective towards the child inside her. What did it matter if no one except her wanted the poor little scrap? Whenever and wherever it was born she would love and care

for it. When was the operative word. Knowing little of concep-
tion and birth, it was difficult for her to comprehend exactly
when her baby was due. Early on she'd had a sort of spotty
period that she'd put down to grief. As best she could count
she had a few weeks to go yet, but it amazed her that she was
not huge like some pregnant women she'd seen. It really looked
as if she had a couple of blankets wrapped around her middle.
As if to reassure her everything was as it should be, the baby
gave a fierce kick. Ruby smiled to herself. Was it a boy? Or
maybe a little girl with dark curly hair like Joe's?

'If you have it in hospital, you can tell them you're not
married and ask for it to be adopted—'

She'd stopped Marge's words with a glare. 'If you can
manage with two children and an old lady to look after, then
I can look after one little baby.'

'Not makin' such a good job so far,' Marge threw back
at her.

Marge was right. She wasn't doing so well, but she would.
She rested her hand beneath her stomach and said softly,
'Don't worry, little one, it will be all right.'

This afternoon, when she got back from helping Marge
pack up her belongings in boxes and carrier bags and
stacking them on the cart, she would write one last letter to
the barracks. She realized now that Joe could be anywhere,

abroad, perhaps in Holland. But, who knows? Eventually that letter might get to him. He would believe her, she was sure of that. She would tell him the baby was his and that she could never love anyone the way that she loved him. If he didn't reply, it would be the very last communication she would send to him. She would put all her energy into looking after the baby and forget about blokes. It wasn't a good thing that her child would grow up without a father. Look how hard her mother had worked! Look how she, herself, had been ridiculed as a child. People had gossiped about her mother. A neighbour had called her mother unmarried scum during a row about Ruby playing two-ball on the neighbour's wall. Ruby's mother had been married! She looked down at her mother's wedding ring on her own finger. Ruby's father hadn't been around. Not that Ruby had really missed him. After all, how do you miss what you've never had?

'You going to stand there dreaming all day, Ruby?'

Ruby jolted back to the present and she stared at Richard Williams.

'Sorry,' she said. 'I was just—'

'Dreaming?' he finished for her. 'Well, I'd like another drink, please, and take one for yourself.'

Ruby smiled like the good barmaid she was and picked up his special tankard from the counter.

Chapter Seventeen

Renata Wilhelm was shaking the feather duvet out of the top window of her father's house in Oosterbeek, near Arnhem. She could feel the September sun on her face, still warm for the time of year. She let go of the duvet and allowed it to lie across the window box containing the last of the red geraniums. She would leave the bedding to air while she and her father went to church. She glanced at the heavens, deciding it wouldn't rain. She was glad, because her signal was necessary, but wet bedding was not.

A roaring sound filled the sky and it looked like a million flies had descended at once to flutter over the tall house and fields outside the village. Aircraft!

'Renata!' Her father was calling her. 'Come quickly! No time for church.'

Downstairs, he was holding on to the banister. 'We must

get to the air-raid shelter. The Germans in the village streets are running about like headless chickens, the Allies are here!'

'I think we'd be better off in the cellar,' she said. Her father found it difficult to walk and the nearest shelter was some distance away. 'We might get caught in the crossfire.'

Renata pulled a huge dresser that was poorly furnished with pots and crockery away from the wall. She unlocked the cellar door with a key from her pocket and one step at a time helped Piet, her father, to safely manoeuvre the steep incline to the bottom where cots were made up and boxes of food sat on a table.

'Stay here while I find out what's going on,' she said. Once back upstairs, Renata relocked the door, slid back the dresser, stopped for a moment to regain her breath, then ran to the bedroom and peered through the window; planes pulling gliders were filling the sky. She could hear her neighbours who had run from the village shouting for joy, 'Parachutists are falling! It's really happening! We're being saved!'

Her heart was thundering away in her chest. Was this really true? Was freedom coming from the skies? Then she saw people below, holding hands, dancing, crying with joy, singing.

Parachutes were drifting down with boxes attached to them. She knew different coloured chutes meant different supplies – medical, food, ammunition – so many parachutes, so many gliders, so many men.

Then the Germans were firing into the skies with their machine guns as if they could halt the shower of parachutes. They were shouting and then they began running towards the men in the fields. '*Die Englander*,' she heard.

Still keeping behind the curtains, Renata saw soldiers close by with badges with winged parachutes on their berets and jackets. It was the English! The English had come at last!

Joe was keeping the sergeant from toppling over, holding an arm tight about his waist. A Dutchman was carrying most of his pack and his chute had been quickly hidden with branches by yet another Dutchman.

'We have to leave this behind,' one was saying. Joe hustled away Cecil's heavy kit. He was only interested in helping his sergeant to safety. The noise of machine-gun fire filled his ears.

'Come with me to a safe place where someone will look at his leg.'

Joe knew that for better or worse he was landed with Sergeant Howard.

He had no idea where any of the others he had jumped with were. His descent had messed up the timing. Vinnie and the others could be anywhere now.

'Leave me and go with Matey,' Sergeant Howard said.

'Oh, yes, and have you on my mind for ever more? All you've ever done is try to bend me to your will, but now the boot's on the other foot and you have to do what I say.' Joe gripped the big bloke tighter and saw the Dutchman was running past the derelict house he'd spotted from the skies.

'Couldn't we rest a bit?' the sergeant begged. 'Leave me!'

'Not possible. Maybe that house is booby-trapped. Stay with me,' the Dutchman yelled back.

Still hobbling, Joe managed to half-carry his charge towards the outskirts of the village. The gunfire was louder. Was this a trap? Were these Dutchmen German sympathisers? Men were falling from the skies, fast and furious now. Joe had to dodge a huge square box that had almost dropped on him.

'I think that's classed as friendly fire,' said Howard, before his head fell forward in a faint. Joe thought he preferred Howard out of it. At least he was silent.

'Slow down,' he called.

'Not possible. I don't want any Germans to see where we're going. My people have been trained to be very careful. We won't be safe until peace has been declared.'

There was a church ahead. Dutch people were standing outside, hiding from the gunfire, but singing and shouting about the brave Tommies landing from the heavens.

The man ahead was scanning the tall houses. Despite the weight of his superior officer, Joe ventured a look skywards. He saw a quilt hanging over a window box. He thought he caught a glimpse of the curtain moving.

'Nearly there,' said the man. 'Stay here by this fence and I will come and get you, if it's safe.'

With relief Joe stopped and leant against the broken wood, his arm still around Howard. He took deep breaths. He couldn't see any Germans, only women, men and children laughing and singing through the gunfire.

The Dutchman had brought him this far and Joe was willing to take a chance the man would get them to safety so that the sergeant's leg could be looked at. In the distance he could see more parachutes falling. But he could also hear more rifle fire coming even closer.

Joe had no idea who the Dutchman was, or where he was taking him, but he felt he could trust him. Besides, what was his other option? Dump the unconscious Howard and run for safety? After all, what was the man to him? Simply a bloke who'd made his life a misery since the first day they'd met.

It wasn't in his nature to leave an injured man, but didn't some proverb or other say if you saved a man's life you were responsible for them for evermore? He hoped not!

And then the Dutchman was back at his side, minus Joe's gear that he'd obviously stowed away somewhere. He was alone, the other Dutchman had disappeared.

'Quick, there's no one but her and her father in the house.'

The man pulled the sergeant over his shoulder and with amazing strength for such a slight man, carried him across to the tall house where, as if on cue, the door opened, a woman stepped aside and they entered, the door closing behind them.

'Down in the cellar,' she commanded.

Though there was barely room for the three men, Joe and the Dutchman manoeuvred the sergeant down the steep steps towards an empty cot where he was unceremoniously tipped onto the bed. Joe expected the man to cry out with pain, but he was still unconscious.

'You stay with him. Father will tend to you while I make sure you weren't followed.'

The young woman was gone, her cloud of orange hair swirling about her shoulders.

Joe heard a key click in a lock and the scrape of furniture. He let out a big sigh. What had he done? Where was he? One thing he knew for certain was that he was locked in the cellar of a house in Oosterbeek when he should be on the way to Arnhem!

*

'You've been looking a bit peaky lately.'

'Have I, Mr Williams? Some customers have been saying I've never looked healthier.'

'I can sense when people are unhappy. You haven't been your usual chirpy self.'

Ruby grinned at him. She felt happier knowing that Marge would find a space for her in the caravan. It meant a lot to Ruby that she had somewhere to go. Now things looked on the up she confided to Richard, 'I have to leave the Point. But I'll be staying with Marge and the kids.'

She wasn't going to tell him all the ins and outs, but she knew the customers would wonder and gossip when she finally left so she might as well tell her side of the story the way she wanted it to be known.

He seemed eager to listen. 'But you can't leave!' he said.

His words were out before he could stop them, she could tell, so she explained more.

'I'm pregnant with Joe Stark's baby, but I haven't heard much from him since he joined the Paratroop Regiment. He could even be dead for all I know.' Ruby didn't know how she managed to let that last sentence out without shedding tears. But it was possible. He could be dead. That might be the reason he hadn't answered her letters. 'Anyway, I can't work for much longer and Mervyn needs a barmaid who can, so I'm going to bunk in with Marge.'

'But won't you be squashed together? What with the kiddies, her and her nan?'

Naturally, she hadn't breathed a word about Marge's eviction so Richard was imagining her sharing Marge's small flat.

He didn't know Marge was moving to a place even smaller than where she lived now, so she said, 'Oh, I expect it will all work out for the best.'

He took a long slow draught of his Guinness and stared at her thoughtfully.

'You don't have any other family?'

'My mum was all I had and . . .'

He put down his drink, carefully sat it on the drip mat, then said, 'I've got a big house that needs filling up . . .' He paused. 'I've been rattling around in it like a single pea in a pod since my old mum died.' He seemed to shake himself before he added, 'She was getting on and lost some of her marbles. I was almost at the end of my tether when she died. But I miss her, miss having someone to come home to. My house shouldn't be empty like that.'

His words tailed off.

Ruby couldn't help herself, she put out her hand and laid

it over his fingers. They were icy cold. And in that moment, she made a decision.

'Could I could come and stay with you? Only on the understanding I pay rent.'

As soon as she let out the words, she realized how hollow they were. Where was she going to get money from to pay rent if she wasn't working? She wouldn't be able to work when the baby arrived.

He said quickly, 'You could be my housekeeper?'

There was a period of silence while she thought about it. How soon he had mentioned the word 'housekeeper', almost as though it had been on his mind already.

He added, 'You could look after the house and me, but have your own big room and I'll pay you a small wage . . .'

He frowned again. 'It wouldn't be much . . .'

'I wouldn't care about that,' she said quickly.

'You'll need bits and bobs for the baby.'

'Of course,' she said.

But what about Marge? How could she tell her she no longer needed her kind offer of a home? Ruby knew she would take Mr Williams up on his offer because he lived in a big house in Alverstoke, he was a writer, she was promised a room of her own and a wage. She wouldn't get any money if she went to live in the caravan, would she? She'd be dependent on Marge, who could barely look after herself and her family as it was. Dear, kind Marge who would give away her last halfpenny if someone needed it. She thought that maybe Marge might be quite relieved that Ruby wouldn't be joining them.

'All right,' she said.

Ruby felt his hand move and he now clasped her fingers. She pulled her arm away.

'Strictly a business proposition,' she said.

'Oh, dear, yes,' he said.

Ruby felt relieved.

'You tell me when you want to move in and I'll arrange to come down here and pick you up in my car, once you've packed up your stuff.'

She nodded. 'That would be very kind of you.'

'Oi! There's a bloke down here gasping for a pint!' Mervyn's voice rang out, almost eclipsing the Andrews Sisters on the wireless singing 'Chattanooga Choo Choo'.

'All right, I'm coming,' yelled back Ruby. The fire inside her was burning brightly now that the question of her homelessness had been solved.

Chapter Eighteen

Ruby shoved the broken ornament beneath Marge's nose. It was a black native figure sitting by a drum, but the head had come apart from it.

'I've been meaning to mend that for ages. Won it down the fair, didn't I? No, I don't want it, there's no room for sentimentality. We can only pack the bare essentials,' Marge said.

'I bet you're actually glad you're not taking me, then?'

'Of course! I'm not saying I ain't been worrying about things, because I have. Don't forget I ain't seen the caravan in proper daylight.' Marge looked up from the four plates she'd put in the bottom of a cardboard box. 'Nan, put the kettle on,' she yelled.

Her nan poked her head out from the bedroom. 'What did your last servant die of?' No one took any notice of the old lady, so she hobbled over to the gas stove, shook the kettle, deciding there was enough water inside, and set about making tea. From the pram came a small whimper, Chrissie murmuring in her sleep.

'You didn't say anything to that writer chap about where I'm moving to, did you?'

'Give us a bit of credit, Marge. As if I'd do that! Your business is your business.'

Apart from wanting to keep her whereabouts secret because she didn't want to get Tim into trouble, it was a rule that the girls never told the punters where they were living. There were some very peculiar men in pubs, who followed girls home, so Mervyn made sure his girls were aware of the dangers and the need for personal secrecy. But even the best-kept secrets sometimes got out.

'I've told Merv I'm going to live with Richard Williams.'

'What did he say?'

'He seemed quite relieved.'

'Yeah! Well, he would do, wouldn't he? I got the same brush-off when I asked if I could move into the Point. He said, "If you was on your own, Marge, you could move in like a shot, but not with the old lady and your two kids." He said there wasn't the room and the punters wouldn't like the kids running about.'

'Well, at least I know he was telling the truth about not

keeping me on at the Point, because that man idolizes you, Marge, and if he wouldn't take . . .' Her voice tailed off.

Nan made tea and they drank it scalding hot, except for Ruby, who left hers to cool right down.

It had been decided that both Ruby and Nan were going to take the children on the Lee-on-the-Solent bus, getting out at the Tower and then walking back along the coastline to where the caravan was sited. Marge was accompanying her barrowload of stuff with the horse and Paddy.

Marge had wangled an hour off for her and Ruby, so it would be a late start for the pair of them on the evening shift. Nan would sort out the van and put the kids to bed. Ruby and Marge would return to the Point just in time to freshen up in Ruby's room.

Mervyn had unearthed an old sit-up-and-beg bicycle, mended a puncture in it and told Marge she was welcome to it for transport to and from work. Tony would go to school on the bus. Marge could put him on and he'd be collected at the other end at the school gate, as were some of the other children.

'There's not so much stuff as I thought there'd be,' Paddy said. His Irish eyes twinkled. He'd put the nosebag on Daisy, his shire horse, while they loaded up.

'We had to get rid of everything except the bare minimum because there's so little room,' sniffed Nan.

Ruby handed Paddy the box of pots and pans. Nan stood near the back door of the flat mumbling to herself and generally getting in the way.

A few battered suitcases full of children's clothes. A small trunk that Nan kept telling Paddy to be careful with. The pram had to be hauled aboard, but as Ruby was taking charge of Chrissie they'd filled the pram with all the stuff from the larder.

Ruby thought Marge looked worried stiff, though she was doing her best to be cheerful and was singing, 'It's a Long Way to Tipperary' at the top of her voice.

Tony was crying and moaning that he didn't want to leave his best friend.

At last they were ready for the off. A couple of neighbours had come out to wish them well and be nosy.

Nan then dropped her bombshell. 'I ain't going on the bus, I can't walk that far. Tony, you get up here with me.'

Paddy showed remarkable restraint and picked her up bodily, settling her on a couple of pillows. 'You can both ride then,' he said. At last he was able to shake the reins and Daisy began ambling down the street.

Ruby got a lift as far as the bus stop and then slid off

the back of the cart. With Chrissie – who'd recently began toddling – wearing her reins in case she tried to make a bolt for it, she sat on the wall to wait for the bus.

Ruby waved until the horse and cart was out of sight. She couldn't think of anything they'd forgotten. The flat had been swept until Nan had exclaimed, 'It's a darned sight cleaner now than it was when we moved in!' Chrissie was sucking her thumb. The little girl felt warm and heavy in Ruby's arms and made her think about her own baby. When she moved out of the Point she'd be taking her stuff in brown paper bags. She didn't have much.

She'd been buying a few bits and pieces for the baby for a while now but there was no pram, cot or toys like the stuff now trundling towards Lee-on-the- Solent on Paddy's cart.

Marge had been genuinely happy for her that she was taking a living-in job with Richard.

'Just you make sure you lock your door or put a chair beneath the handle. I reckon he's after you, an' I'm sure there's something funny about him.'

Ruby had laughed at her.

'I'm pregnant with another bloke's kid, don't be daft!'

Marge had rounded on her. 'But you won't always be, will you?'

Chrissie was now touching her face with wet fingers.

Ruby buried her face inside the child's neck, loving the sweet talcum-powdered smell of her. She thought about Richard Williams. He was all right. He'd been kind to her, hadn't he? She remembered the parachute silk he'd given her. She smiled. He was much older than she was. He was a different sort of man altogether to the boys she'd been out with in the past. He was certainly nothing like Joe. Ruby shivered. Perhaps it was just as well he was nothing like Joe.

She could see the bus coming. There was quite a queue now.

Ruby manoeuvred herself to a window seat so that Chrissie could look out. She paid the ticket collector, a big, hearty woman who stopped Chrissie from climbing over the back of the seat.

At the ferry she crossed the road to where the bus that went to Lee stopped, outside the Dive Café.

Chrissie seemed to be weighing more by the minute. But she was growing sleepy now and as soon as Ruby had settled herself on a seat, Chrissie stopped bouncing about and fell asleep.

The bus chugged through the town, back part of the way she'd already come, then along Stoke Road and out into the country. Ruby was able to see the true damage Hitler's bombs had done to Gosport. Bomb sites settled between rows of houses like teeth pulled from a gaping mouth. She thought of Joe, somewhere, fighting for his country. But thinking about him hurt her. They passed Browndown, and the rifle ranges that were all government land. Then the bus trundled along the road near the sea. She kept an eye out for Marge and Paddy, but thought they must have driven by some quicker route.

When the bus stopped at Lee Tower Chrissie woke up.

Ruby lifted her and, with the little girl's arms about her neck, stepped from the bus. She stood looking at the notices for dances to be held at the Tower Ballroom. The tall white building was beautiful inside and out. It looked across the sea and there was a semicircle of gardens in front of it.

Not only was it a ballroom, but there was a picture house inside, a café and an ice-cream parlour. The tower itself was an observatory where people could look out across the sea, almost to the Isle of Wight.

'Ice cream!' Chrissie had spotted the people eating cones.

'Hang on.' Ruby gripped the child's leather reins while she hunted in her handbag and purse for the money to buy the little girl a treat. She knew Chrissie would drip the blessed thing all down her, but she also guessed if she didn't buy an ice cream Chrissie would start screaming.

Eventually, with a vanilla cone each, they began walking

along the grass path that went back towards Browndown and the way she'd been advised led to the caravan.

It was cold now. Ruby knew the summer was over for another year, but with her friend moving and herself soon to take the plunge and live in Alverstoke, the future was to be looked forward to.

Pretty soon the boats out on the Solent were disguised by a misty dullness, but she was still going in the right direction.

Ruby stopped to mop up the ice cream that covered the little girl. On the narrow path that separated the road from the sea, and as brambles and bushes made themselves felt, she saw activity and lights ahead.

Tony saw her first. He came bounding up to her like a happy puppy.

'We've been here ages, slowcoach.' Ruby bent down, set her charge on her wobbly, tubby little legs and cuddled him. 'You've had ice cream,' he accused.

'You'd have had one an' all but you went on the back of the cart.' He scowled but couldn't contain himself for long.

'It's ever so nice,' he said. 'And Mum said I can have mates over later when we've settled in.'

Then Marge was walking towards her with a mug of tea in her hands. Ruby could see the steam drifting up from the cup. Her heart lifted and her face broke into a smile.

'We've made a good start,' Marge said, holding out the mug towards her. As soon as Ruby took the handle Marge sank down to her knees and pulled Chrissie into her arms. 'And my big girl went on a bus with Auntie Ruby?'

Chrissie started to cry. Marge laughed. 'That's her all over,' she said. 'Got to be the centre of attention.'

She said to Ruby, 'Fallen on me feet, I 'ave. It's lovely inside. Come and look.' She scooped up her daughter and walked back along the path with Tony at her heels.

The tea slopped perilously, so Ruby put the mug down on a small wooden table made out of tree trunks, next to which were similar home-made seating arrangements. Someone had gone to a lot of trouble to make the place attractive, she thought. The caravan was in the middle of a clearing that had obviously been well tended at some time.

Marge untangled Chrissie's sticky fingers from round her neck, saying, 'She can't come to any harm out here.'

'Hello, Paddy,' Ruby murmured. Paddy touched his forehead as a greeting and stood aside so Ruby could climb up the steps into the van.

She saw a carrier bag of Tony's toys on a table. A small light flickered from an oil lamp hanging in the centre of the ceiling. Ruby gasped. The surfaces were highly polished and despite Marge's bags, boxes and belongings strewn every-where, even she had to admit the van was lovely.

'Listen,' commanded Marge to everyone. Ruby held her breath. Then she could hear it; rolling up and down over the stony shore, the sea. 'Imagine going to sleep to the sound of that every night?'

'Brilliant,' said Ruby. She pushed a wicker basket filled with Chrissie's nappies out of the way and fell onto the cushioned seating.

'I don't know about bein' on me feet all tonight, but I'm fair whacked now,' she said. She suddenly realized someone was missing.

'Where's Nan?'

Marge started laughing after she told Tony to fetch in Ruby's tea. 'That's the only downside about this place. There's no lavatory. She's gone for a walk and a wee! There's a wardrobe in the van big enough to put one of them chemical toilets in, but there ain't one. I found a jerry inside there instead, for emergencies, like the middle of the night.' Marge wiped her hand across her face. 'Still, Tony thinks it's a brilliant place and he's all for doin' his business in the undergrowth.'

Ruby said, 'I'm glad I don't need to go.'

Marge said, 'That's you all over; when I was in the family way I needed a pee every five minutes.'

Just then Paddy yelled out, 'If you two want a ride to the Point, come now. I got to get ol' Daisy bedded down for our early morning market shift.'

From somewhere in the undergrowth Nan shouted, 'I'm here!' She was about to walk behind Daisy but thought better of it, so, holding her stick high, she carefully came round to the front of the large horse.

'I don't trust them big buggers,' she said.

Marge and Ruby were now outside again, and Marge asked Nan, 'You all right if I go? I'd really like to stay, but we can't afford for me not to go into work tonight.'

'For God's sake, I was mindin' kids when you was only a twinkle in your dad's eye. Me an' Tony can clear up and put stuff away. I'm not sayin' it'll be shipshape for when you get back, but we'll do our best. Just show me how to turn on the gas for the cooker, will you?'

Marge walked round to the back of the van where two Calor gas bottles were connected up to a hose and tap.

Paddy said to Nan, 'Best to keep things switched off when they ain't needed. Watch carefully.'

He fiddled about and Marge said, 'Well, that seems simple enough. What d'you think, Nan?'

'I could do that blindfolded,' the old woman said. 'Show

me again how these lamps work, just in case one runs out of oil and I have to use that generator thing.'

They all watched Paddy as he let down the flame on the lamp, then relit it. It gave a little pop as the flame caught again. 'I think one in this small space will be plenty. Want me to show you how the generator works?'

Nan shook her head. 'Reminds me of the days before we had electricity.'

'You should be all right then,' said Marge. 'Do you want me to show you how the heater works in case you get cold?'

'No thank you, dear, my poor ol' brain will explode with so much knowledge. Anyway, me an' Tony are going to sort stuff out, then have a wash and snuggle down.' She looked at the little boy for confirmation and he grinned, showing gappy teeth.

'You comin' or what?' demanded Paddy.

'Hold your horses . . .' began Marge, then she dissolved into laughter for Paddy was now indeed holding on to Daisy's reins.

'Get up on the cart, then you can haul Ruby up,' he said. 'Stop worrying, that ol' woman's been through the First World War an' seen more life than you, she'll be all right. An' you'll be back here again in next to no time. Got your handbag?'

Marge waved her clutch bag at him and made a space for Ruby to sit next to her.

'Wagons roll,' shouted Paddy.

Daisy clip-clopped an about-turn and Ruby had to pull her legs up quickly as a bramble pinged against the cart.

'Kisses everyone,' shouted Marge, and with everyone waving in the dim light, they were off.

'You're right, it's a lovely little caravan,' said Ruby, pulling her coat round herself. 'And you're lucky it's rent-free,' she said. She knew Marge would still have to scrimp and save, as it cost a lot to bring up a family on one wage.

'It ain't really rent-free,' Marge admitted. She was tying a headscarf around her curls.

'I thought you said—'

'I know what I said and I told you the truth. But I wasn't born yesterday. You don't get something for nothing in this world.' She put her hand over Ruby's ear and whispered, 'Tim's got me right where he wants me. I'm a sitting duck for him to snap his fingers and go running to have sex with him any time he wants.'

'No,' said Ruby, 'you've got it wrong.'

'I didn't come up the Solent yesterday in a bucket,' said Marge.

Chapter Nineteen

When Joe's eyes opened he thought he was still dreaming. He could smell bacon, and eggs. He took a deep breath, but when he let go and began to breathe normally the wondrous smell was still there. He turned his head and there on the other cot was Sergeant Howard, clean and washed, his bad leg splinted and raised by several pillows. The sergeant was snoring.

His eyes went to the door, which was wide open. From upstairs the wonderful smell wafted down tantalizingly.

He heard footsteps on bare wood and a flowery-scented woman with a cloud of bright hair sailed into the stark cellar bearing two plates, both piled high with food.

'Good, you are awake.' Her English was staccato but accurate. 'You are Tommy?' She held a plate beneath his nose and he struggled to a sitting position and looked longingly at the steaming food.

'No, I'm Joe,' he said, and winced as his fingers touched the hot dish that she'd had no trouble in holding.

'No, you are a Tommy?'

The woman took a salt cellar and pepper pot from her apron pocket, while still holding the other plate of food.

'Ah, yes, I see what you mean. You've thought of everything, including condiments.'

'And salt and pepper!'

He was about to say something but he saw her eyes twinkling and realized she was teasing him. She put the other plate on the top of a small table between the beds.

'This looks scrumptious,' he said. 'Better food than I've seen in days.'

'We have pigs that the Germans knew nothing about and hens we have kept up in the woods. And yesterday food fell from the heavens because of you Tommies.'

She smiled, showing strong white teeth.

'I have been stupid,' she said. The corners of her mouth went down. He couldn't imagine her being at all stupid.

'Why? What have you done?' He saw she was waiting for him to put some food into his mouth.

He chewed on the bacon and closed his eyes in ecstasy.

'I have brought down your sergeant's breakfast and he will

not be awake to eat it while it is hot. I'll put it in the oven for him,' she said. She moved to turn away.

'Don't go!' Joe said. 'Talk to me!'

She turned back. It seemed to please her that he was enjoying her breakfast. He waved his knife towards the sergeant.

'You have bandaged him up?'

She shook her fiery hair. 'Not me. My father is a doctor. He has, how do you say?' She seemed to search her mind. 'Splinted, put a splint on his leg, it is broken in two places, very bad. You have saved his life.'

And he nearly killed me, Joe thought, remembering how it had crucified him holding on to the man as they'd hurtled through the skies. He said nothing about that, but instead told her, 'He would have done the same for me.'

She smiled and made to walk away after picking up the hot plate.

'No, don't go,' he implored again. 'I need to know where I am and what's happening.'

'And I thought it was me you liked,' she quipped. 'I'm going to bring you some tea. Tommies like tea?' She smiled before she left.

He was so hungry that the food quickly disappeared.

The man in the other bed had neither moved nor wakened.

Joe supposed the woman's father had given him something to help him sleep. He marvelled that he himself had slept so deeply. Every muscle in his body burned like fire where he had held and carried Sergeant Howard.

He was just putting his empty plate on the floor when the young woman returned. In her hands was a mug of steaming tea and in her pocket he could see the top of a Woodbine packet. His mouth watered.

She put the tea alongside his plate and withdrew the cigarettes from her pocket, holding them out to him.

A few moments later he was breathing out smoke satisfactorily. Smoke rings floated towards the roof of the cellar. She had pulled up a small stool and now sat beside the bed.

'My name is Renata Wilhelm and you've been brought here because my father and I can get you home again, to England.' She smiled at the smoke rings.

'Wait a moment! I've only just got here and I've a job to do.' His free hand swept across his forehead.

'Quite so, but you can't leave your friend and he won't be able to travel alone.'

'He's no bloody friend of mine . . .'

'I think differently. You've got him this far and you'll want to make sure he lives.'

'I came to help you lot, not the other way around.' He

bent down to the floor, stubbed out his cigarette on his plate, picked up his mug of tea and drank noisily.

'So you're willing to go on to Arnhem alone and leave this man to the Germans who are still in this area? Not only will you be leaving a defenceless man, you will put me and my father in a difficult position. Already the enemy suspects us.' Joe suddenly remembered the duvet slung across the window box, a splash of colour. 'That was your sign, wasn't it? The duvet means this is a safe house?'

'Of course.' She smiled at him. 'And the longer you are here,' she looked towards the other bed, 'the more difficult it will be for us to help others, should they need it. We will not keep you longer than necessary.'

'But our objective is Arnhem—'

'*Was* Arnhem,' she interrupted. 'You cannot leave an injured man.'

He unhooked his finger from the mug's handle after he had put it back on the floor, and looked at her.

She wasn't pretty in the traditional sense, but her hair made one think she was beautiful. He could imagine that, when she was younger, she had been taunted about her freckles and pale skin at school.

'So the man who brought us here knew about you and—'

'Shhh! We don't talk of such things. We who hate the

Germans all have our part to play. We need you. But we need fit and able Tommies. Not dead ones, which you will be if you are discovered. And you must remember that there are Dutch people who take money and presents from the Germans, then speak ill of their own countrymen. Speed is of the essence to get you away from here.'

'But Arnhem—'

'There are enough British men and Allies to sort out what you cannot do alone.'

'I'm surprised you know what's going on,' he said. 'The secrecy in England is paramount.'

'Which is all the more important that we get you away from here and home to safety. Plans can be wrung out of men in all kinds of ways. You must win this war!'

She had taken his hand and he could feel its roughness where it was used to hard work.

'Arrangements are already in motion. I repeat, you will stay down here. Please don't risk my father's life. He is a good man and has helped many Englishmen.'

A moan from the next bed meant that the sergeant was coming to. Joe looked over as his eyes opened.

'Back in the land of the living, Sarge?'

Renata got up and stood over the sergeant.

Joe watched as she smoothed back the hair from his

sweaty forehead. He knew then that whatever his own feel-ings were about fighting the enemy, he couldn't leave this man on his own to face whatever unspeakable horrors might happen.

Cecil looked at him.

'Sorry, you got no breakfast, Sarge, I've eaten the bloody lot, including yours!' Joe said jokingly.

Sylvie pulled down her skirt and started laughing. The smell of Brylcreem and cologne seemed to fill the small alleyway, where there was hardly room to move. Let alone do what they'd just done.

'What's so funny?' asked Lennie, buttoning his flies.

'Well, I had the son and now I've had the father!' She put her hand beneath his chin and stared into his eyes. 'For an old 'un you're pretty good.'

'And you're a little tease.'

'And you'll come back for more, won't you?'

'Maybe I will, maybe I won't.'

'You will,' she said and stepped away. 'Where are you going?'

He was looking at his watch. 'It's still early. We could go out and get something to eat? I know a few clubs over Pompey that'll still serve a good meal.'

'I've been on my feet with the twelve till two shift at the

Point of No Return and then I've sung my heart out at Lee Tower Ballroom. All I want to do now is go to bed.'

'I could get us a room at the Black Bear?'

'I want nourishment, not punishment,' Sylvie laughed. 'Besides, I'd like to be in my own room trying on those three gowns you got me!'

'Get you a fur coat next time, my little songbird.' Lennie squashed himself against her slight body. 'If you knew how much I've been wanting to do that to you.'

He kissed her, his tongue finding its way into her mouth. Sylvie pushed him away. 'Stop that, you'll get me all hot and bothered.'

Once his body was clear from hers she began walking down the alley and out on to the High Street. She stopped, turned back and waved. The brown carrier bag crackled as she tightened her fingers on its strings. This had been a very profitable evening. Three brand new dresses that her little seamstress could alter to fit, and the promise of a fur coat next time.

At the dustbin outside Burton's Men's Tailoring she paused, opened her handbag and took out a letter. After tearing it in half she put the pieces in the bin, then banged down the metal lid and walked over the road to the Point. That was another one dealt with, Sylvie thought.

*

'Coming, ready, or not!'

Ruby could hear muffled giggling. She stepped away from the tree where she had been standing, hiding her eyes while Marge and the kids hid from her.

She walked further into the wooded area. The brambles were black with glistening fruit and there was a crooked apple tree with rosy apples hanging from its laden boughs. Momentarily she thought of the big blackberry and apple tart Nan had cooked for pudding. Ruby was still full up from the roast dinner they'd eaten. Not a joint of meat, but the sausages had been plentiful and the roast potatoes browned to perfection. Tinned peas and carrots and Nan certainly knew how to make gravy as well. None of that Oxo cube and water stuff. It was marvellous how she'd conquered that little Calor gas oven, thought Ruby.

Another giggle, louder this time, and Ruby parted a bush and looked behind it, finding nothing but a discarded toy soldier of Tony's.

It was a sunny afternoon and neither of them needed to be at the Point until seven o'clock, as opening time was later on a Sunday. Both she and Marge had arrived at Lee-on-the-Solent by bus and walked back along the funny little path to the caravan, where Nan was busy cooking a meal for them all. They'd smelled the dinner from quite far off and it had made both their mouths water.

After eating their fill the kids wanted to play outside and for everyone to join in.

How could Ruby refuse? It was hide-and-seek. Now it was her turn to find everyone. A piece of black cloth showing behind a tree and Ruby had found Nan.

'It's not fair, I can't run as far as the others,' Nan wailed, but using her stick walked alongside Ruby to find the children and Marge.

'I can see you!'

Ruby spotted Chrissie curled into a ball behind the caravan. She had her hands over her eyes.

'She thinks if she can't see you, you can't see her,' said Nan. Ruby rolled the little girl on the grass and tickled her until she begged Ruby to stop. Just as well, really, as Chrissie's nappy was about to fall off and was hanging around her ankles.

Ruby heard a noise from inside the caravan. She motioned to Nan to be quiet and crept in silently through the open door. She saw the big wardrobe door move and yanked it open to discover Marge convulsed with laughter, the empty jerry can perched on her head like a strange hat.

'Gotcha!' Ruby said. She could hardly speak for laughing. 'That leaves one small boy to find.'

She said the words loudly, theatrically, from the doorway of the caravan, knowing Tony would hear her.

He wasn't in the van. Outside they all trooped along, saying, 'Not here!'

'He's not here either!'

'Wonder where Tony is?'

Ruby saw a grey-socked leg slip from the laden apple tree.

Standing beneath the tree she shouted, 'Well, I just don't know where that boy is!' The giggling above her became louder. She made to walk away, then suddenly turned back and looked upwards to find Tony sitting astride a firm branch.

'Found you,' Ruby shouted. The boy slithered down the tree like an eel.

'My turn now,' he shouted.

Ruby said, 'Count me out this time, I need a sit down.' She collapsed on the wooden bench. Nan settled herself next to her and put her wrinkled face towards the late sun. Ruby could hear the sea tumbling on the shore.

'I never thought I'd like it here, but I do. The kids can run wild. They can go out and I'm not scared any harm will come to them,' Nan confided.

Chrissie was holding on to the wooden seat and bouncing up and down. Her mouth was open and dribble showed where new teeth had come through. Now, she was minus her nappy.

'Aren't you scared at night?'

'Bless you, no, Ruby. What's to hurt us? Tony saw an owl for the first time yesterday. When we're all cosy in the van it's lovely.'

'I'm making a pot of tea, then you and I will have to get back to the Point,' shouted Marge. She poked her head out of the door and Ruby nodded her assent.

'It's been a lovely afternoon,' she said to Nan and grabbed her papery hand. 'And that dinner was a real treat.' Ruby laid her head on Nan's shoulder.

'It took me a while to understand the Calor gas, but I got it sussed out now,' the old lady said. 'Same as the oil lamps.' She stroked Ruby's hair. 'That heater's a bugger though. You have to make sure the top's on straight, else it flames up. Made me jump the first time it did it but I got that sorted out now.'

'And how about room?'

'Oh, there's enough for us all as long as we don't leave any stuff out. Got to put everything away. I makes up the double bunk for the two kids and the two single bunks together does me and Marge fine.'

'Sounds all right,' said Ruby.

'Best thing we ever did, leaving that flat. And we don't have to see that bleedin' rent collector. He was a nasty bit of work, never did like him.'

'Well, I hope you like this cuppa,' said Marge, putting down a tray with three mugs on the wooden table.

Ruby grabbed hers immediately. Playing hide-and-seek had tired her out. Marge had put in extra milk to cool it so that she could drink it straight back.

'Is Tony all right that we don't want to play any more?' Ruby didn't want the little boy upset.

'Oh, yes. He's drawing a picture of what we had for dinner,' Marge said.

'I hope he's got a big enough piece of paper. I haven't eaten that much for ages.'

Marge smiled at Ruby. 'Did you write that letter you said was going to be your last one to Joe?'

'Oh, didn't I say?'

Marge shook her head.

'I poured out my heart and told him I was leaving the Point to live as Richard William's housekeeper. I said if I didn't hear from him ever again I'd always love him.'

'Did you say his parents had been right shits to you?' Marge enquired. She took a mouthful of her tea.

'No, I didn't. What's the point?'

Ruby heard Marge sigh. 'You're too soft for your own good,' she said quietly.

'I'll second that,' said Nan. She took off her spectacles and polished the lenses with the end of her apron.

'Sylvie was just leaving for singing. She said she'd pop the letter in the post. I was quite pleased about that as it had just started to rain again, saved me going out and getting wet. Of course, if I'd left it on the hall table, Percy would have collected it in the morning.'

Half an hour later Ruby sat on the Hants and Dorset bus next to Marge.

'I really enjoyed this afternoon, thanks, Marge,' she said. She looked down at the floor that was strewn with dog-ends and used tickets. Then for a while she watched the scenery. 'How about Tim? Have you seen him?'

Ruby looked into Marge's face. She had coloured up.

'I have, as it happens.'

'Well?'

'Well, he's not half as bad as I thought he'd be.'

'I want a bit more than that,' said Ruby. 'C'mon, tell me.'

'As I was leaving the other night, to cycle home, he came out of the shadows and said he'd been waiting for me to finish—'

'Where was I?' Ruby interrupted.

'You'd gone upstairs. Anyway, he said he could fit the bike in the back of his car if I wanted a ride home and I thought, Here it comes, girl, payback time.'

'And was it?'

'That's the funny thing. He parked up near the barbed wire on the beach and began talking. And talking and bloody talking! You know, I think deep down he's lonely, Ruby,' she said. 'Oh, I forgot, he gave me these.' Digging down in her handbag she took out two of what looked to Ruby like lipstick cases. Marge unscrewed one and showed her the blue pop-up eye shadow. 'They're both the same colour, you can have one, I don't need two.'

'Where did Tim get them?'

'I never asked and he never said. But I reckon they're American, I ain't never seen none like this before.'

Ruby drew the colour on her wrist. Then she put her nose to it. 'Smells nice,' she said, adding, 'Thanks.'

Marge carried on talking about Tim. Ruby sat and listened, the bus trundling along. It was dark outside now and she was happy that Nan and the kids and Marge had settled into the caravan and were content. Marge said, 'He kissed me on the forehead, well, I ask you, such a little kiss, then he said, "I'd like to take you out somewhere where we can be together without hiding away." You could have knocked me down with a feather. There was I expecting to be groped and he's all sweetness and light!'

'Then what?'

'Then nothing, until this morning when he puts a note into my hand as I served him.' Marge foraged again in her handbag and came out with a scrap of paper that said, *Lee Tower Ballroom? Saturday Night at 8? Meet you there? Tell me tomorrow.* Ruby handed her back the bit of paper. 'You going?'

'I mentioned it to Nan when you took Chrissie to see that bird's nest Tony told you about. I haven't kept no secrets from her. Nan said I should go.'

'Really?'

'I haven't been out for ages and like I told Nan, he was such a gent, almost like he was courtin' me.'

'But he's older than you and he's married.'

'Don't be such a prude. If it wasn't for Tim I'd be on me arse out in the streets, wouldn't I? So what if he's married? If what he was tellin' me is true, she's a right bitch!'

For a moment there was silence, except for someone coughing at the back of the bus. Then a child cried and a woman was telling the kiddie to be quiet.

'Right, can I do anything? Mind the kids?' Ruby knew Marge didn't make a habit of going out with married men.

The trouble was, this Tim Bracknell had been good to Marge and she no doubt felt she needed to pay him back.

Marge's eyes were like soft pools. 'Thanks, but Nan said it's fine. Anyway, you need all the rest you can get, you'll be dropping that little one soon.' She patted Ruby's stomach. 'And you're moving to Alverstoke as well, so you've got enough on your plate.'

Ruby put her hand over Marge's and stared at her. 'Just be careful, an' . . .'

'An' what?'

'And have a bloody good time.'

Chapter Twenty

'If you could marry anyone in the world, who would it be?'

Marge, Mervyn and Ruby were sitting in the kitchen at the Point eating toast and having a well-earned cuppa after the Sunday night shift. The stench of cigarette smoke had come in from the bar and Ruby was feeling sick. She was playing a 'What if' game with them both and some of their answers were giving her the giggles.

'That's easy,' said Mervyn. 'I'd marry Marge here, like a shot.'

The silence was deafening.

'Why?' asked Ruby. Marge's face was beetroot-coloured.

Mervyn had been packing back the pints tonight. He certainly wasn't drunk, Ruby had never seen her employer the worse for wear, but he was garrulous.

'Marge has got a quick tongue, she's a bloody good

barmaid an' if I was younger I'd have asked her years ago.'

Marge slid off the chair she was sitting on. 'Whoops,' she said. 'This is where I cycle home to me kids.'

'What's the matter? We're playing a game, ain't we?' Mervyn was flustered. Ruby realized he was telling the truth. She'd said, many times, 'He fancies you', to Marge; now the truth was out.

'Game's over,' said Marge. 'I'll see you two tomorrow.'

'I'm sick of this.' Joe threw down the book he was trying to read and began pacing the cellar. 'I need fresh air.' The atmosphere was dank and clammy.

'You can't venture outside, you'll put everyone's lives at risk.'

The sergeant was reading too, but he'd stopped long enough to answer Joe. There was a good supply of books in English left behind by other men who had been helped home to safety. On the floor was the remains of a meal freshly cooked by Renata. There was no denying both of them were being looked after admirably. The sergeant went back to his book.

Joe stood in front of his bed. 'It wouldn't be so bad if you and me had anything in common, but all along you've treated me like scum. I want to know why.'

The sergeant put down his book. 'Now we're getting to the crux of the matter. That's what's bothering you. Not the fact that I'm trussed up like a bleedin' chicken and you've got to babysit me.'

'I want to fight . . .'

'Always what you wants, isn't it?'

Joe looked at him, at the man's bristling moustache that had echoes of grey in it. He reckoned there was no need for him to stand on ceremony with his superior officer now. There was no one around to witness that he wasn't deferring to him. Joe was angry and because there were only the two of them cooped up in that dank cellar he'd spoken to the man as he would an equal. There was silence. Joe thought you could cut the air with a knife. He needed answers to questions going round and round in his brain. But the people who could answer those questions weren't here. The only person who was, was the man who had stopped him going home to find out the truth!

'You ever stopped to think how easy you've had it?'

Joe sighed. 'You don't know what you're on about. Me dad's a fly-by-night who I wouldn't trust further than I could throw him. Oh, don't get me wrong, I love him, but he's out for number one, always. Me mum, who I love dearly, should have stood up to him and his larks years ago. I was tainted before I was born. More so because I got me dad's looks, everyone expects me to be a chip off the old block.'

'And you're not?'

'Are you joking? All I want is a woman to love me for me and a kiddie or two I can love. I've done all that "sowing wild oats", and I thought I'd got the girl of my dreams. Now I'm not so sure. Same as I joined up to fight and now I can't do that neither!'

'You're full of anger.'

Joe picked up the novel he'd been reading. 'Look, bloody words, this book's full of words an' I can't get a fuckin' word out of my girl, I feel like I'm going daft!'

He threw the book against the wall where it slid down and landed face up. The pages fluttered, then were still.

'My mother says Ruby's pregnant with some other bloke's kid. I don't care whose fuckin' kid she's carrying, as long as she's there for me when I get home . . .'

'You'd take her back after she's been with another bloke?'

Joe sat down heavily on the end of his bed. 'I don't know. I love her.'

He put his head in his hands. Then he continued. 'There's something goin' on I'm being kept out of. If I could have got home on leave I could have sorted—'

'Maybe not,' the sergeant said. 'If you'd found the bloke

responsible you'd have clocked him one and been in trouble. You're a para now. You can't just do what you want.'

'Is that why you made me look a bloody chump doin' all that menial stuff?' He closed his eyes and when he opened them Cecil was staring at him. 'Cleaning the fuckin' bogs with a fuckin' toothbrush. You was tryin' to break me.'

'Well it didn't work, did it? I wasn't trying to break you, only to show you that you don't know all the answers, an' you have to take orders from them as does. And if you hadn't grabbed hold of me I'd be dead now, so you can't hate me for it.'

Joe breathed in deeply and blew out his cheeks, letting the air out slowly. He was now beginning to think that the sergeant's falling out of the plane had been an accident, rather than a deliberate choice to die.

'And look where that's got me. Now I got to babysit you!'

'*Que sera, sera!*'

'What's that when it's at home?'

'A Spanish phrase, it means "What will be, will be".' Suddenly, the sergeant grinned.

Joe faced him. 'I smelled the drink on you. I got to know, did you mean to die or was it an accident?'

'We'll never know.' The sergeant smiled at him again.

'You're a bastard!'

'So my boy told me. He's dead now.' The man's eyes filled with bright tears. He blinked them away. 'There's many times I wish I was with him.' For a moment he was silent, then he said, 'You're so like him. You think you know it all, but you know fuck all.'

'You're right! I didn't know enough to let you go on sliding past me, did I?'

'You couldn't do that.'

Joe rubbed his hand across his forehead, wiping the sweat away. 'No, you're right. I couldn't do that.'

'If this bus doesn't get a move on we'll be late.'

'Don't worry, we'll still have time to go to your room and change,' said Marge. 'Won't be your room for much longer, though, will it?'

'Tuesday.'

'Are you worried about moving into that writer's house?'

'I was at first, but it's only a job and I need money for the baby, and a home.'

'I don't like him.'

'So you said already.' Ruby gripped hold of the metal rail and pulled herself upright. The bus had stopped at the ferry. Marge jumped off the platform with ease and then waited, her hand outstretched for Ruby to grip as she stepped heavily down to the pavement.

'I don't think Richard Williams is all that he seems.'

'Who of us is?'

Ruby thought suddenly of the way Joe's mother had embraced her then turned against her. But she was protecting her son, Ruby's reasoning told her. If only Joe had answered her letters.

Hand in hand, Marge and Ruby hurried to the Point of No Return.

The noise came first. The drone of engines, low and growing louder. It was like Marge's hand on the door had set it all off.

'Oh no, we haven't had a raid for a while and just when we think it's all over, here it comes again,' said Ruby.

'Shut that bloody door!' Mervyn yelled as they practically fell inside the pub. 'Don't you two know there's a war on!'

'Don't answer him back, or he'll start on about gas masks. Get up them stairs, Ruby,' Marge urged.

Marge made a beeline for the bathroom and Ruby opened her bedroom door and sat down in front of the dressing table. But no sooner had she sat down than she was up again and rushing to the window to pull the curtains, to keep the light from shining out. At the little sink, she cleaned her teeth and washed her face, then took another blouse from the wardrobe. It took a while to force the buttons closed. If she didn't soon have this baby she'd have to go around naked, because nothing fitted her any more.

The thwump of the bomb made her stagger, leaning against the bed for support as she grabbed at its frame. The light went out. Marge bustled into the bedroom and automatically flicked the switch to off.

'There's no light in the bathroom either,' she said. Another thwump made the room shudder and Ruby felt bits of gritty stuff fall onto her head and hands.

'The ceiling'll come down in a minute.' The siren started up its mournful wail.

'Cheerful,' said Marge. Ruby managed to see she was pulling on a jumper over her head. 'I'm not changing me trousers,' she said. 'The customers only see half of me behind the bar.'

Ruby was at the window now. She'd pulled back the curtain and was watching the criss-cross of beams searching the skies for the planes. She could see sparks rising from the ground, far off, near the barracks. She knew it was the returning ground fire. Already, in the distance, she could see flames reaching into the heavens, orange against the black.

'That's down near the picture house,' she said. 'They've got something. I hope it's not the Criterion.'

'When you gotta go, you gotta go,' said Marge. Ruby knew her words were only forced cheerfulness. As with every raid, Marge worried herself sick that her family were kept safe. 'An' we better get downstairs.' There was another crash and Marge grabbed hold of Ruby. 'I hope my kids ain't frightened,' she said. 'They used to hide in the cupboard under the stairs what led to the top flat. There's no cupboard under the stairs in the van.'

'They're probably safer out there than in the town,' said Ruby. 'The planes only drop the bombs where they think they'll do the most damage. I can't see a bomber dropping one in the woods.'

Ruby stopped at the dressing-table mirror and peered into the darkness. She outlined her lips and pressed them together.

'Come on,' urged Marge.

Marge stayed close to Ruby going down the wide stairs. The noise outside the pub was loud. The sound of breaking glass began, shattering somewhere close by. The stench of cordite was drifting in.

Mervyn had lit small candles in jars and the bar looked like a fairyland, thought Ruby.

'About time you two turned up,' said Mervyn.

'You don't need us,' cheeked Marge, 'there's only a handful of punters in.'

One of the four men in the bar picked up a candle and put it beneath his chin, making a face, hoping to frighten Marge.

'You're better-looking like that, Clive,' she said.

Another crash, so close that even Mervyn dropped to his knees behind the bar.

And then, silence. Followed by a whistling sound, getting ever nearer.

'Oh, no,' shouted Clive. 'It's a bloody doodlebug!'

Marge and Ruby had their arms around each other. Close by was the bulk that was Mervyn. Ruby's heart was beating fast in the silence while they waited for the bomb to find its target.

The almighty crash caused glasses to fall from shelves. One of the men swore.

More silence and the smell of dust in the air.

Nothing, not even the sound of breathing, punctured the air inside the bar. Then someone coughed.

'That's that, then,' barked Mervyn. 'Anyone for a shot of whisky?'

He pulled himself upright. Outside, the sound of running

feet passed the window. 'Get the glasses, Marge.' Marge rose.

Suddenly the lights came on of their own accord. The all-clear sounded. Marge pulled Ruby to her feet and burst out laughing.

'What's so funny?'

'You are,' said Marge. 'Your lips are bright blue!'

Renata set the draughts back on the board. She had won again. The sergeant didn't take enough time to think the game through.

'You will play Piet when he has finished with the wireless?'

Her father knelt in the corner of the cellar. He was connecting wires to the set, eager for the latest news. Ever fearful the wireless would be discovered, it was dismantled and hidden behind a brick in the fireplace after being used. She knew Piet wanted to get both the Tommies to safety as soon as possible. There had been rumours that the Germans were pushing the Allies back.

She too wanted the men gone, but for a different reason. Her feelings were growing for the young curly-haired paratrooper. In another life this might be a good thing. But war was different and she loved the Polish man she had promised herself to with all her heart. For a year she had known nothing of his whereabouts, but a few weeks ago she had heard he was alive at a camp in Bergen-Belsen. Every night she prayed he was still living. News of these camps had trickled through, thousands of men in them were still alive, but many more had been sent to the gas chambers; and not just men, women and children too.

From the corner came a crackling sound, followed by words that her father fought to make clearer by listening intently, using the earphones and twiddling the knobs.

'Shhh!' Her father was writing down words on a notepad. She could hear the scratch of the pencil on the paper.

Music suddenly blared out and Piet began dismantling the radio set to its usual jigsaw of pieces. His face was grim as he turned towards them.

'The airborne operation that might have cut the war short has ended in tragic failure. British paratroopers managed to capture the north of Arnhem Bridge, but the Germans held the town. Atrocious weather halted the landing of reinforcements, so after eight days of bloody warfare and facing overwhelming odds, the British have had to pull back. Of the ten thousand men, only two thousand remain.'

The silence in the cellar was palpable.

'What will be, will be,' said the sergeant.

Chapter Twenty-One

'Are you sure you've got everything?'

Ruby looked at the three carrier bags alongside her on the seat in the back of Richard Williams's car and smiled at Merv and Marge, who were outside the Point, standing on the pavement. She nodded, but she was scared to speak because she thought she might show herself up by crying.

'I'll come and see you, you ain't all that far from me.' Marge ran her fingers through her hair and peered in at Ruby.

'Better let us know when you intend to come . . .'

Ruby saw Marge frown at Richard's words.

'I've never 'ad to make an appointment to see a mate before.'

Her words were sharp. Richard coughed and said quickly, 'I'd hate you to come round and be disappointed . . .'

Merv pushed a big hand in through the wound-down window. 'Put that in your purse for emergencies, love. I know you've got your wages, but buy the baby something.'

Marge was staring at Richard, who sat tight-lipped.

Ruby was choked. Nevertheless, she knew to refuse him would be churlish, so she took the five-pound note gratefully.

'We'd better go,' Richard said. He'd already started up the car and it was idling, but now he gave a final wave to the small crowd on the pavement and Ruby felt the wheels turn towards her next adventure.

She was too choked up to speak. Instead she watched the waving figures grow smaller in the side mirror and then the car was on its way to Alverstoke. A ten-minute ride to a different world. A place filled with retired forces men who had splurged out on huge homes facing the sea or backing on to parkland. There were no Saturday night fights here. The pretty little pub in the heart of the village, the Village Home, was a haven for G and T drinkers where, even in wartime, gourmet food was served with selected wines. Ruby knew she'd be like a fish out of water.

In her heart she would rather have squeezed herself into Marge's caravan. Her head had told her she had to take Mr Williams's kind offer. A job, wages and a home for her and her coming baby was preferable to being a dead weight, dependant on her friend's generosity.

Richard Williams turned to her. 'After I've settled you in, I have to go to work.' Ruby stared at him. He continued, 'News doesn't stop just because it's four in the afternoon. You get yourself acquainted with the house.' He paused. 'Though I'd prefer it if you didn't leave the house to walk too far.' He looked at her startled face. 'If the baby starts, there'll be no one with you. At home there's a telephone, you see, to summon help.'

Her heart began to beat more normally as she realized that he was only thinking about her. She felt a warm glow run through her body and began to look out of the window.

Ruby's eyes opened wide at the sight of so many pretty houses. None of them terraced, like she was used to. No back privies here. No strings of grey nappies on saggy lines.

Richard turned the car into Vectis Road and headed towards the driveway of a huge house. Its five-bar-gated entrance was open and the car rolled to a halt outside a gabled porch.

'Here it is, home sweet home.' Richard Williams climbed out of the car and walked to the passenger side, where he helped Ruby out. He took her arm. In two seconds they were in a wide hallway with parquet flooring that smelled of lavender polish. He pressed a set of keys into her hand.

'This is your home now,' he said and smiled. 'I'll just bring in your things, then I'll leave you to wander about. I have no idea what time I'll be back, so don't bother to cook or wait up for me.'

She stood and watched as he went back out to the car and came in with the rest of her bags, which he set on the floor.

'You'll find everything you could possibly need in the kitchen. Don't forget there's a list of numbers by the phone.' He swept his hand towards the bottom of the wide staircase where a black Bakelite telephone sat on a wrought-iron table.

And then the front door closed on him.

Ruby heard the crank of the car and the rumble as it rolled along the driveway. She wondered if she ought to go out and close the big gate, but as it was open when they arrived, she decided not to bother.

A huge wave of loneliness engulfed her.

She could hear clocks ticking. Carrying her handbag, she walked down the hall and into a bright kitchen with frilled curtains at the wide windows. She gasped: beyond was the garden, it looked enormous!

The back door already had a key in it, so she used it and stepped out. Bad weather had been prophesied. Already, the grass had a sheen of dampness. She walked across to a sort of summer house. It was locked, but she gazed through the windows at the seats and table inside. No doubt the key was on the keyring she had left with her handbag on the kitchen table, but she could look in there properly another day. She walked around admiring the trees and gardens, still with its late-blooming flowers brightly showing pretty faces towards the very last of the day. She marvelled at the high wooden fence encompassing the gardens, giving absolute privacy, and just for a moment was relieved that a child could play safely here without being able to escape on to the road.

As she walked back to the open door she almost tripped over an object hidden in the grass. It was an iron ring firmly embedded in the soil. There were three of them; not rusted, she tried to imagine what they had been used for and couldn't fathom it out.

Back in the kitchen, she filled the kettle from the stone sink tap and set it on the gas stove. Matches were to hand. She found a tin marked 'Tea' with a scoop inside and began making a pot.

The kitchen was spotless. The curtains were evenly spaced and not meant to be touched when a raid came. A blackout curtain was rolled up at the top of the window and a cord released it. There was a wooden bread bin with a loaf inside. In the tall cupboard above the stove was a collection of tinned foodstuffs. She smiled. The larger tins were at the back and the smaller ones in front. Each tin faced outwards, so it was easy to read the contents.

Hanging over the pull-down door of the Aga were three clean tea towels. Each one was blue-edged; all were evenly spaced on the rail, so she made sure she tidied them after she had looked into the sparkling clean oven.

Ruby wondered why on earth he needed a housekeeper when he seemed perfectly able to look after his own house. The kettle was boiling, so she made the tea and put a patchwork cosy over the pot. While the tea brewed she would explore the house and look at her bedroom, which Richard had said was at the front of the house.

The smell of lavender was overpowering, but Ruby decided it was because her sense of smell was heightened by her pregnancy. The first bedroom she entered obviously belonged to Mr Williams. A wealth of leather and polished wood, everything neat and tidy, too tidy for a man, she decided, remembering Mervyn's room at the Point that was a jumble of sweaty clothing and discarded books. On the bedside table were three books, neatly piled, the largest at the bottom, the smallest on the top.

The next room was locked. Ruby stepped back and one by one went through her set of keys, but not one fitted the lock. She decided she would ask him about that room later.

In her own room, she sat on the bed and sighed. It was the largest bedroom she'd ever had. A bedroom like she had seen in American pictures. She got off the bed and went to the wardrobe. Of course it was empty. And she had nothing that would fill it, except her new dress that she couldn't now fit into. Her meagre clothes could be slung in a drawer. But one of the carrier bags contained baby clothes and these she placed in her bottom dressing-table drawer.

Her make-up and hairbrush went on the top of the dressing table. She reverently laid the grass ring in the top drawer. Ruby didn't unwrap it from the white cotton because she knew that if she did she would cry. She left everything where she could get at it easily.

She went downstairs and drank a cup of tea and left her cup and saucer in the sink.

Tonight Marge was going to Lee Tower Ballroom with Tim, and Ruby envied her. Not because she would be dancing to the resident band, but because Ruby wouldn't be at the Point tomorrow to hear all about it.

Ruby didn't begrudge Marge going out and having a good time, of course not. But she'd miss all her excited chatter about the glitter ball that lit up the ballroom and the clothes the other girls had worn. Perhaps Marge might find time to pop in and see her? Mr Williams hadn't seemed too keen on her having guests, but Marge was different, wasn't she?

Ruby yawned. There didn't seem to be anything that needed doing. She had been told not to bother cooking a meal. It surely wouldn't hurt if she went back upstairs and had a little lie-down, would it?

One day perhaps she could have a house like this instead of being an unmarried mother, the lowest of the low, a woman that married women would look down on and talk about behind her back.

Ruby wandered back up to her room and took the grass ring that Joe had made for her from the drawer. She slipped it on her finger. It was falling to bits now, dry and brittle. But she could remember that night and the way her beloved Joe had looked at her. Joe loved her, Ruby was sure of it. She stopped herself from crying; after all, tears wouldn't do the baby any good, would they?

She wanted to see the room where her employer worked at writing those Westerns. She'd never seen where a real writer actually sat and thought about stories. She yawned again.

There was plenty of time to finish exploring.

'The Hospital of Saint Elizabeth has been taken by the Germans. I'm so happy you aren't there.' Renata put down the bowls of vegetable soup. 'I'm sorry too that there isn't more to eat.' Joe could hear gunfire.

Joe hated himself. He should be outside fighting, not here hiding in the cellar.

The sergeant slept a great deal of the day; there had been problems with one of the breaks to his leg and sedation was better than nothing, so the doctor helped Cecil Howard to sleep away the pain. But now Piet had almost run out of medical supplies.

He said, 'We have been under Nazi domination for four years, will it never end?' The noise of mortar fire and shells were close by.

'We all thought we would be able to hold the bridge at Arnhem, but no one could foresee the Germans fighting back. The bridge is sixty miles behind enemy lines; it's a pity Montgomery's daring plan to seize it couldn't come to fruition. It wouldn't be so bad if the Second Army Division could get through with supplies,' said Joe. The old man had previously relayed all this information to him from his wireless set.

Piet started to climb the stairs to the upper house. He went carefully, using his stick.

Renata said, 'He gets cross if I try to help him too much. He's a very independent man.'

Sergeant Howard gave a sleepy snuffle. Renata said, 'He'll wake soon. I have been thinking of what you have told me of your girl at home.'

'Oh, yes?' During a period when the sergeant was asleep, Joe had sat and talked to Renata about Ruby.

'My man may be alive or may be dead. But I love him so much that whatever has happened to him while we have been apart is of no consequence. If your girl has a child by someone else, you do not know her circumstances. These stories you hear from other people are simply that: stories. Only your girl knows the truth.'

He stared at her. 'Forgive, yes, forgetting is much harder—' She stopped his words.

'If I climbed into bed with you, now, you would not turn me down?'

She was waiting for his reply. He thought carefully what he would like to do with her if she was offered to him on a plate and he said, 'No, I wouldn't turn you down. You are a kind and beautiful woman and you would give me comfort and happiness.'

'But you wouldn't love me?'

'How can I? In another time, another place, we might love each other.' He thought for a moment, then said, 'But you love your man.'

Renata sat down beside him and said, 'That doesn't stop me wanting comfort and happiness because the one I love isn't here. Many times I've watched you sleeping and I've wondered . . .'

He picked up her hand and held it to his lips. 'Did anyone ever tell you, you are a very wise and beautiful woman?'

He kissed her hand and she smiled at him and removed it, pretending to fiddle with her hair; running a finger through a long orange curl.

The sound of the furniture moving above caused Joe to look over to where Piet was making his way slowly down the stairs. He breathed a sigh of relief. Always, he thought it might be a German soldier.

Renata went to move away but Joe stopped her. 'Would you willingly sleep with me?' His voice was soft enough for her to hear, but he hoped it didn't carry towards Piet. She pushed his hand away and rose, smiling down at him.

'I have thought of nothing else,' she said. His heart skipped a beat.

'There is fighting about the church,' Piet said to them grimly, his face white, like marble. 'Renata, I forbid you to go outside.'

Joe slid from the bed, went to the other corner of the cellar and picked up his rifle.

'Where you going, mate?' Cecil's voice was hoarse, muffled.

'So you're awake, are you?' Joe threw a handgun onto the sergeant's bed. He said to Piet, 'Would you be willing to give me as many painkillers and sleeping tablets for him as you can spare?'

Piet looked troubled. 'Why? He can't fight,' he said. 'He should not be on his feet.'

Joe was fastening a belt about his waist. 'No, but I can, and you said the hospital has fallen to the Germans, which means that any time now what's left of our airborne men will be told to get out of this town. I can't let this bugger –' he pointed to the sergeant – 'be left in the hands of the enemy, and if they're fighting in the church, they're entering houses too. This house could well be next. You've both been too generous to us. Your repayment must not be being shot by the Germans.'

Piet was searching in his medical bag. He took out a brown bottle of pills, shook it, then handed it to Joe, who tucked it into his top pocket.

The sergeant was sitting up, his hands searching the bed-covers. He found the weapon. Joe looked at his leg, which was covered with splints and bandages.

'You can stay here,' he said, 'if you'd rather, but somehow I don't think you'll put these kind people in any more danger.'

'Did I ever tell you, you remind me of my boy?' the sergeant said.

It was over a week since Joe had parachuted down into the fields around Arnhem.

The mixed bag of men left fighting were hungry. According to the last newscast Joe had heard, they needed water and ammunition and they'd not dared to sleep. Oosterbeek was surrounded by the enemy and as Joe had prophesied, orders were to get out of enemy-occupied territory.

Joe looked like the hunchback of Notre Dame. His nemesis couldn't walk, so Cecil was slung across Joe's shoulder, the best method of transportation he had found since leaving the safety of Piet's house and falling in with a small band of soldiers hiding in the woods.

'Don't the fuckin' Jerries ever have a day off?' asked Joe's new friend Pat. There were four of them in the foxhole near the water. They'd been told to wait for the Canadian boats to take them to the far side of the river. Once on the other side, they'd be ferried home. That's if they lived long enough to get there.

German tanks had nosed about Oosterbeek and loudspeakers were telling them, 'Surrender or we will kill you.'

The seriously injured had to be left behind. Bitter

hand-to-hand fighting resulted in kill or be killed. Joe had lost count of how many German men he had seen fall.

Joe said to his sergeant, 'Can you swim?'

He poked the last of the painkillers into the man's cracked mouth and listened as the weak answer came: 'No.'

'There's a first time for everything,' Joe said and added drops of river water to ease Cecil's thirst.

Under cover of darkness, he crept out from the foxhole, dragging the sergeant with him. He felt like crying.

He remembered the oh, so sweet kisses from Ruby and how she'd felt against his warm body that night late in January when she'd told him she loved him. He remembered how he'd danced in the street with her. If he died, he'd take those precious memories with him.

The River Rhine was icy cold. He put his hand over the sergeant's mouth so that he wouldn't cry out, and he began swimming; one arm now around the man. He felt a sharp pain in his shoulder. Then that too became numbed by the freezing water as he struck out for the other side of the river.

Just when he thought he must stop because there was no feeling in his arms or legs and the weight of the sergeant was dragging him beneath the water, a dull torchlight picked him out. It shone in his eyes.

'Get aboard this boat, bud,' said the Canadian, putting out his hand.

'Tony, if you don't get back into bed this minute I'll clip you one!' Nan gazed at Chrissie, asleep like an angel, her little podgy arms spread above her head. She bent and tucked the covers over her as best she could without disturbing the little girl. It was cold in the van. 'Tony, I'm not telling you again. You wake up Chrissie and I'll skin you alive!' She'd already had a go at him for paddling in the freezing cold sea. He'd got through a break in the barbed wire lying along the beach to stop the Germans invading. Nan thanked God the mines hidden beneath the stones were further up at Browndown.

The little boy leaned across and picked up a book. 'Read to me, Nan.'

Nan took a mouthful of tea, put down her cup and took the battered book that was his favourite: *Gobbolino, the Witch's Cat*.

'Don't you get fed up with this one?' He grinned at her and shook his head. How could she refuse him?

Nan looked at his chubby face. 'Cuddle down in bed, then.' She watched as he wriggled beneath the quilt. He'd be asleep in a few moments. She hobbled to the stove after putting the book on her own pillow. 'I'll just light this and leave it on low. We don't want a cold place for your mum to come back to, do we?' Tony shook his head and yawned.

Nan fiddled with the heater; she didn't like the smell of the paraffin, but it was better than being unable to sleep because of the wind that poked freezing fingers into the van.

'Hurry up and light,' she told the stove. It had been a long day and she was tired.

Tony murmured drowsily, 'Silly Nan, stove can't talk!'

She smiled at him and arranged herself in her own narrow bed before pulling up the covers. She adjusted her spectacles, picked up his book and began to read aloud, wondering if she'd be asleep before Tony . . .

Chapter Twenty-Two

The Dashing White Sergeant was the second-to-last dance before the waltz finished the evening's entertainment at the Lee Tower Ballroom. Marge had laughed so much she thought her stomach would burst when everyone got in a muddle with the steps and it all went wrong. Tim swung her around.

'Enjoying yourself?'

She clung to him. 'Not half,' she said. The glitter ball above was making patterns across the ceiling and walls and the cigarette smoke mixed with perfume was heady. Tonight had been wonderful. Since arriving they had danced practically every dance, only sitting out to drink the beers that Tim had bought at the bar. She found him easy to chat to. He regaled her with stories of tenants he'd met at work and she'd told him about some of the funny happenings she'd encountered while serving behind the bar.

Nan had remodelled a dress for her, using bias binding and a lace collar. Marge knew she looked just as good as any of the other girls. Nan had been all for her having a night out. The old woman had met Tim and reckoned, as did Marge, that the bloke was lonely. Married he might be, but Nan thought he wasn't all that happy with his wife. But then some men weren't, she'd said. Going to a dance with him was small payment for him putting a roof over their heads.

Now clinging to Tim as the last waltz signified the end of her evening out, she heard a sailor call to one of his mates sitting at a table, 'There's a bloody great bonfire up near the woods!'

Earlier Marge had watched him and his girl, a fine-featured redhead, leave the ballroom. Sooner or later the lads found a way to get their girls slightly squiffy and to walk along the dark promenade with them, often snuggling up together on the wooden seats or the pebbly beach.

'There's a war on, you daft lummox,' came the reply.

'No bleedin' bombers tonight though . . .' another voice shouted.

Marge went cold. The sailor in the doorway was pointing in the direction of the caravan. 'I got to look,' she said, slipping out of Tim's arms.

Running for the door wasn't easy. She had to weave past

couples dancing and ignore Tim's voice calling her back which seemed to rise above the sound of the band's music.

When she pushed open the swing doors, there was a crowd of onlookers staring into the distance towards the woods. Orange flames rose into the dark night and even from where she stood, she smelled the stink of burning. The crowd was too far away from the scene to do anything except watch the spectacle.

Marge let out a cry and fell to her knees. Tim had caught up with her. He pulled her to her feet and clutched her to his body. Marge struggled free and was pushing her way through the gawping crowd, her elbows parting the people in front of her.

'Jesus Christ!' Tim cried and started running after her, along the clifftop path.

Stumbling along the uneven ground, Marge knew it was the caravan burning.

Bushes scratched at her legs and tree branches whipped her body. Once, she stumbled, and her hands slid along the stony path, but she was up and running again, the stink of burning growing stronger the faster she ran.

Marge could feel the heat from the scorching van long before she reached it. Tim, who was still beside her, grabbed at her arm to stop her running straight into the inferno.

Then he realized he had let her go and was now leaning against a tree, crying into the bark, as though playing some peculiar game of hide-and-seek, his voice crying, 'I shall say you're squatters! I shall say you're squatters!'

A man was walking towards them through the smoke. Marge breathlessly yelled, 'Where are they?'

The man stopped at the sound of her voice. He peered through the dust floating in the air. 'Keep back. Can't you see it's dangerous?'

Now Marge could make out a fire engine that had ploughed its way from the road and into the clearing. More men, some in uniform, were having trouble with a hose that was barely spurting out water.

'My kids are in there!' Marge was now screaming. 'My kids are in there!'

The noise from the burning caravan sounded like flames rushing up the chimney when she'd held a newspaper in front of a fire to make it draw. The intense heat made her step backwards into the arms of the man who'd told her to keep back.

'No one's in there,' he said. He was holding her tightly so she couldn't move. She saw a man kneel and take photographs. She wrenched herself free and kicked out at the man, and his camera fell from his grasp. He glared at her and swore.

'What the fuck you doin'?' she screeched. 'My kids're in there!'

The man caught her again. This time she felt his arms like bands of steel around her.

'You want to get yourself killed?' he snarled at her. 'There's nobody in there now!'

Marge heard him this time. She felt herself go limp, falling against him like a sagging rag doll.

'It's almost under control, so they're letting it burn itself out.' His voice was soothing.

'Where are my kids?'

It was almost as if he hadn't taken any notice of her question as he asked, 'You the parent?'

'Course I am! Where—'

'I'll take you,' he said. Not letting go of her, he twisted her body around and she saw Tim sitting beneath that same tree, his head on his knees, his shoulders heaving.

Her brain was whirling; her legs matching the man's strides as he walked towards the fire engine, then passed it, going to where another man was straightening a tarpaulin on the ground.

'Mac, this is the mother.'

The man stood up. 'For fuck's sake, take her away!' His voice was like the hiss of a snake.

'She got to identify . . .'

His next words were lost to her as that one word, *identify*, stuck in her brain. Marge heard a scream that rent the air about her like the howl of a thousand demons. And realized it came from herself.

Mervyn had to practically beg the nurses to let him in to see Marge. For the patient's own eventual peace of mind, they finally allowed him into the small room at the War Memorial Hospital.

He'd begged Grace, his cleaner, to take over in the bar and she'd already roped in her granddaughter, Dottie, to help out because they'd lost Ruby.

The caravan fire and the deaths of the two children and their grandmother had shocked the whole of Gosport.

And, as if to compound the horror, the *Evening News* had published a photograph of the burned-out caravan in their early edition. Their reporters had given their take on the story.

Mervyn was frantic. If Grace hadn't helped him out, he'd have willingly closed the pub down so he could go to Marge.

He had been told she was sedated. He couldn't believe that the vibrant girl who'd served behind the bar at the Point of No Return had disintegrated into this white-faced wreck of a woman now lying in bed. He sat down at her side and enfolded her hand in his great paw.

She opened her eyes.

'I killed them all,' she said.

'That isn't what the fire officers said. The fire was caused by a faulty paraffin heater and you weren't even there—'

'Exactly. I should have been there!' Tears spilled down her face. She turned her face into the pillow and away from him. 'I killed my family.'

Mervyn gripped her hand. 'Stop that! Look, they don't want you cluttering up their hospital beds here when there are men who have been sent home from the war with terrible injuries and missing limbs . . .' He paused. 'I'm taking you back to the Point.'

She was staring at him vacantly.

After a long while she asked, 'Why are you being so good to me when I don't deserve it?'

'Because it's about time someone looked after you, for a change.'

She was looking at him, her eyes dark ringed. He longed to tell her how much he cared for her, had always cared for her. But to him she was a fragile little thing and he was an ugly old man. Beauty and the Beast came to mind.

Mervyn was sure she'd understood about him taking her

home. But now she was asleep again, out of it. And he was glad. He also knew he was doing no good sitting there while she slept her drugged sleep, so he got up to leave.

Her feeble grip on his hand tightened, so he looked down at her. 'What is it? What d'you want, Margie?' If she asked him to fly to the moon he would.

'Ruby? Where's Ruby?'

'Don't you worry, I'll get her.'

He saw the relief flood over her face. For a moment he stood, holding her hand until her breathing became more even, then he gently laid it on the sheet and left the room.

When he got into his car he decided he would go straight round to Vectis Road to see Ruby.

He was surprised not to have found her already at the hospital, as Gosport's jungle drums for news beat loud and long and the local newspaper had made a meal of it.

He knew how Ruby cared for her mate. It was possible, he surmised, that the girl wasn't well. After all, she was near her time now and she'd have had to walk or catch the bus to the hospital if that Williams bloke wasn't at home. There was no way that man hadn't heard about the fire, no way at all.

When he reached the tree-lined Vectis Road, he slowed the car, looking for the right house number. By God, these were nice houses, he thought. You had to be moneyed to live along here. Then he spotted the house with its neat garden; he pulled up outside and got out of the car, walking towards the five-barred gate.

The cold air made him shiver. Wind and snow had been forecast. That was stupid, he thought, it was far, far too early for snow.

He looked up into the gun-metal sky, then made two sharp bangs on the door knocker and the sound seemed to reverberate through the house. He waited. No one answered. He knocked again. Mervyn had never expected Richard to be home, he'd be at work, but he thought he heard sounds from within the house, was it someone calling? He let the door knocker resound again, satisfied that if there was anyone in they must have heard, or be stone deaf.

He waited, moving from one foot to the other, eager to get back to the Point. He'd promised Grace he wouldn't be longer than was necessary. She was worried, as she only had very basic barmaid skills. He tutted to himself: he should have closed the pub. He was cross with himself that the one thing Marge had asked him to do, to get hold of Ruby, he hadn't been able to carry out. The strange thing was, he was almost sure there was someone at home.

Mervyn decided he would drive through the heart of Alverstoke village. If Ruby had gone to the shops, it was possible he would meet her coming back. He got back in his car.

There was a greengrocer in the village who sold flowers, when he could get them, and Mervyn thought he would buy some for Marge. A visit to the chemist for toothpaste and soap and other women's toiletries, whatever he could get hold of, might be a good idea. He tapped his fingers on the steering wheel. Marge would also need clothing and nightwear. The poor little cow had lost everything, hadn't she? Those things might be difficult to come by without clothing coupons, but he was sure he could find a way, maybe not today, but certainly tomorrow. He could buy coupons from Lennie, couldn't he?

As his car crawled through the village, his eyes searching for a pregnant long-haired girl, his thoughts went back to the peculiar conversation he'd had with Lennie before the fire had become common knowledge.

Lennie had been in the kitchen making himself a brew when Mervyn went through to pay him for the spirits he'd purloined from the Americans.

Lennie had been in a jovial mood.

'There's talk my Joe could be up for the Military Medal!'

Mervyn, flabbergasted, listened as Lennie told him about Joe's bravery. Apparently, he'd saved a senior officer's life. Mervyn had ways and means of finding out all sorts of stuff.

'Of course, the silly bugger still thinks young Ruby is as pure as the driven snow,' Lennie added. 'One of the hospital nurses wrote, as Joe's shoulder and arm is damaged, but he's alive . . .'

Lennie's eyes were sparkling with happiness. Mervyn was happy, not just for him, but for Ruby, too.

'How is Ruby?' Lennie had asked eventually.

'To the best of my knowledge, apart from sleepin' with your boy and getting pregnant by him, she's all right.'

Mervyn counted out the money he owed and shoved it across the table at Lennie.

'How can you say that when she's left you in the lurch and swanned off with one of your customers?'

Mervyn stared at him. For a moment he was speechless. 'She's keeping house for that funny bugger, the writer. I told her I couldn't keep her here, not with the baby so close. Lennie, you know how it is, I can't have a baby on the premises, it's not healthy . . .'

'Ha! So that's what they call it nowadays, is it? Keeping house? More like "shacking up with", if my memory serves me.'

'No! You got it wrong!' Mervyn banged his fist on the

table. 'I was all for this bloke taking her off my hands. Well, you and your missus wouldn't give her house room, would you?'

'My lad deserves better than a trollop!'

Mervyn had leapt up in defence of the girl. 'She's no trollop! All she's done is moon about these premises after your Joe who, if you don't mind me saying, hasn't treated her well, no, not at all well. At least he could have answered her letters.'

Lennie had jumped up and looked as though he was ready to land one on Mervyn, but then must have thought better of it, remembering that Mervyn had been a professional boxer. Luckily, Mervyn had diffused the situation. 'Let's not fall out over this, mate, we go back far too far . . .'

Lennie confessed he'd been seeing Sylvie and she'd been giving him information about Ruby.

Mervyn said, 'You great fool! The little bitch wants your lad, not you, always has. Can't you see she's out for what she can get? But it don't make no sense why your boy ain't written to Ruby when she's poured out her heart to him on paper . . .' Mervyn thought of all the times he'd consoled her.

Lennie drank back the remains of his tea and shuddered at its coldness.

Mervyn twisted off the top of the brandy and sloshed some in a couple of clean cups. He pushed a flowered cup across the table at Lennie. 'I think me and you ought to have a chinwag about this.'

Chapter Twenty-Three

'I've brought you tea.'

Ruby opened her eyes, startled to find Richard bending over her bed. It took her a few moments to realize where she was. She struggled to a sitting position and saw he'd left a cup of tea in a china cup and saucer on her bedside table.

'I'm sorry,' she said. 'I came upstairs intending to lie down and must have fallen asleep.' She began to move heavily off the bed. The only man ever to have seen her sleeping was Mervyn and she was unnerved at Richard's presence.

'Stay where you are,' he said. 'I don't need you to do anything for me.' He looked around at the clothes that she hadn't put away. She thought a look of annoyance crossed his face. 'Though you could tidy this room,' he said. 'I'm not used to mess. Sometimes my mother made a lot of mess . . .'

'I'm really sorry,' she said, pulling herself back to the

centre of the bed, because she realized if she stood up she might end up showing her underwear, which was stretched to its limits across the baby. 'As soon as I've drunk my tea I'll put everything away.'

'Yes, I found the remains of stewed tea left in the kitchen.' He gave a small laugh. 'I usually clear up after myself.'

'I'll come down and wash up,' she said.

'Don't worry, I've already seen to it,' he said. 'I've also cooked a meal while you've been sleeping, so if you'd like to sample my cooking . . .'

'That's really nice of you,' she said. 'Though if I'm supposed to be the housekeeper I should be the one doing that.'

He picked up the cup and saucer and held it before her. She had no option but to take it from him. He turned on his heels and left the room, saying, 'Don't forget to bring down those tea things. We can discuss your duties while we eat.'

Ruby heard his footsteps descend the stairs. Quickly she drank the barely warm tea and then she clumsily removed herself from the bed, straightening the crumpled candlewick cover before she bent to the task of putting her clothes away. She hurried, not wanting to keep him waiting. She had a feeling of resentment. She wasn't used to being told she had been found wanting in her actions. Perhaps he hadn't meant to be judgemental? Perhaps he hadn't realized he had wounded her? Maybe she was being silly, after all, she had only just woken from a deep sleep. Ruby went downstairs.

In the kitchen she put her cup and saucer on the draining board. Richard had passed her in the hallway, taking a dish of cauliflower into the dining room.

'Dinner's ready,' he'd said. The kitchen was filled with the smell of food; already he'd opened a small window to allow the cooking aromas to escape.

Ruby was about to leave the kitchen to follow him, but she looked at her used cup and saucer on the clean wooden draining board and suddenly decided she would rinse them and put them away. Perhaps he might not like it if she simply left them there to be washed up along with the dinner things. It took her two minutes to perform the task and immediately she felt better.

In the dining room, which was tastefully furnished and highly polished, he'd set places at either end of the table. Covered dishes sat on table mats. She knew she must remember from now on that the meal they ate in the evening was to be called dinner, not tea, which was what she and Marge called it.

She marvelled at the amount of crockery – just for the two of them. There was even a side plate!

Ruby suddenly felt very inferior. Even at Mervyn's he

rarely laid the table when they ate together. She looked at the plates, knives, forks, spoons and condiments and tried to memorize the layout so she could replicate it for Richard. It was obvious he was used to better things!

'Sit down,' he commanded.

From a large dish he took a small cooked chicken and placed it on a stainless steel carving tray.

'White or dark?'

Ruby stared at him, not at all sure what he meant.

'White meat or dark meat?' She breathed a sigh of relief. Of course, white was the breast . . .

'White, please.' She watched as he carved neat slices and laid them on the plate she'd offered him. She was surprised to discover her plate was warm. 'Thank you,' she said as her plate was returned. Chicken? Ruby couldn't remember when she had seen such a sumptuous meal as was set before her.

'Did you turn off the light in your room?'

Ruby had to think. 'I'm not sure.'

'I don't like wasting electricity, it's expensive.'

'Excuse me.' Ruby scrambled from her chair as best as her ungainly body would allow and went up the stairs to where she could see her room was in darkness. 'Yes,' she said, squeezing herself into her chair once more. 'I'll try to remember.'

'Help yourself to vegetables,' he said. She saw every lidded dish had the appropriate serving utensils. Roasted potatoes, cauliflower, peas, and gravy in a gravy boat. The whole dinner set was of the finest china. Ruby groaned inwardly, hoping she never let a piece slip through her fingers; after all, she was used to enamel mugs and chipped cups. Then there were the serviettes, made of linen? How did she use one? Tuck it into her neckline or lay it across her lap? She decided she would wait, watch and learn.

'I'm not used to proper dining,' she said. She tried a smile. 'I hope I get things right for you.'

'Don't worry, I'm sure we'll work together very well once you see how I like things done.'

'I hope so.' She tried to make light of the heavy atmosphere. After all, this was a job, like any other job, and once she'd fallen into the right routine she'd feel a lot better, wouldn't she?

Ruby thought it prudent to wait for him to start eating and when he began she fell on her food with relish. It was all expertly cooked and she imagined him toiling away as she had slept.

'It's very good,' she said. He didn't eat as quickly as her and she saw to her dismay he had plenty of food left on his plate. Ruby began to eat more slowly. He was methodically working his way through his meal.

She wondered how Marge was doing in her caravan.

Ruby swept away the thought that it might have been better to have been squashed into the caravan with Marge and Nan and the children and their easy come, easy go attitude to food and life. Then she was angry with herself. This man had given her a home. All the same, she missed Marge and her chatter. Perhaps tomorrow she could walk up and see her? Already today seemed over before it had started. Afternoon would be best, Marge would be at the Point in the morning and evening.

Ruby began to feel tired. She stifled a yawn. Whatever was the matter with her?

Perhaps if she got a conversation going? She remembered how she had loved the silence and seclusion of the garden.

'The outside grounds are especially nice,' she began.

'Yes, my mother loved being out there.' He dabbed the corner of his mouth with his serviette. 'Of course, she was quite safe.'

Ruby remembered the iron rings hidden in the grass.

'I found rings in the earth, what are they for?'

'My mother took to wandering and I had to make sure she was safe so I secured her wheelchair to them.'

Ruby yawned again. Secured her wheelchair? Whatever did he mean? It was an effort for her to keep her eyes open as she ate. Too late, she realized that despite her best intentions, she'd wolfed down her meal, not realizing how hungry she'd been.

'Why don't you go back upstairs to bed?' He left his place at the table and walked towards her. He put out a hand and helped her rise. 'Do you need help getting undressed?'

Ruby's thoughts were flying around her brain like Hallowe'en witches on broomsticks.

'No,' she said and stumbled sleepily into his arms.

When Ruby woke, her head was heavy. She had no idea what time it was, but by the light shining into her bedroom through the flounces in the curtains despite the blackout blinds being drawn, she had a feeling it was late. Sleep came so easily nowadays, really deep sleep, but when she woke up she often felt still tired. She swung her legs over the side of the bed and stood up. Again there was a cup of tea on the bedside table, and she drank it back greedily, even though it was cold.

The previous evening and the dinner came back to her. So too did Richard's words about securing his mother's wheelchair. Of course, she reasoned, his mother had been going senile, hadn't she? It was more than likely he had kept the wheelchair upright by using the rings and possibly some rope or something so she wouldn't tip the chair over and hurt herself. Of course, that had to be it.

With dismay, she saw she was wearing a nightdress. She felt the colour rise, hot on her neck. Had he undressed her last night? Or had she managed it herself before falling into bed? She hoped it was the latter. Ruby didn't like to think of him touching her; he was quite a strange man. But then he wrote books, didn't he, and she'd heard it said that authors were a breed apart, often quite peculiar people.

She listened carefully. No sounds came from below. She had a feeling that the house was empty and that Richard had gone to work. They hadn't talked about her duties last night. Of course, it was good of him to go to so much trouble, providing a delicious meal for the two of them. Maybe he had left instructions on the kitchen table for her? Again she wondered if he had undressed her . . . Her heart began to beat alarmingly. Put it out of your mind, she told herself. Her head was thumping.

Ruby decided to go in search of some aspirin. She felt heavy and lethargic, convinced her baby had moved downwards, deeper into her groin. How long could she go on like this?

She tied her dressing gown around her bump and went down the stairs carefully. In the kitchen she could find no aspirin. There was, however, a note left on the side.

I've prepared a meal for tonight, having decided to allow you to sleep in this morning. You're going to need all the rest you can get now you're near your confinement. Take it easy today, I'll be home early. We'll have that conversation tonight.

On the top of the oven a shining set of saucepans contained ready-peeled potatoes and fresh vegetables. She opened the oven door and found a pastry-covered pie.

'Well, fancy that,' she said to herself. Ruby had never known a man who could cook, or who could provide such delicious meals when the war decreed that practically everything was on ration. Yet the previous evening she'd eaten chicken! She couldn't remember the last time she'd eaten fowl. A wave of dizziness overtook her. Aspirin? Of course, those tablets would be in the bathroom cabinet, wouldn't they? Richard liked things in their right places, didn't he?

Upstairs in the shining white bathroom that smelled of bleach, she discovered a bottle of aspirin in the cabinet.

The bathroom was well appointed. Ruby would have liked a bath, but decided she might not be able to get out of the high tub and didn't like to think she might slip, so she used the shower and afterwards fastidiously cleaned up after herself, putting the towels back on the towel rail exactly as she had found them. There were four white towels, all evenly spaced, neatly folded.

It was too cold to go outside, so Ruby thought she might go back to bed. She'd already looked around the house and found nothing out of place and nothing that needed cleaning. She thought about going on the bus into the town to see Marge at the Point of No Return, but she honestly didn't feel like going outside. The aspirin hadn't kicked in yet and, looking through the windows to the back garden, she could see a film of frost on the grass.

Ruby decided she would look in the room Richard had designated as his workplace. It might be nice to read one of his Westerns, as sometimes authors allowed a peek inside their heads through the books they wrote. It might be nice to understand Richard a little better.

Inside the highly polished, oak-walled room, shelves surrounded her on three sides and contained books on guns, maps of America, biographies of well-known American personalities and novels by well-known writers. She picked up a copy of *The Ox-Bow Incident* by Walter Van Tilburg Clark and began leafing through it.

A long shelf was devoted to Richard's own books, but she

didn't touch them. What if he didn't like her going into his writing room? On his desk was a bottle of whisky and there was a glass next to his typewriter. She'd heard a little nip sometimes helped the creative juices to flow. Perhaps he'd be angry that she'd touched copies of his published books. She decided it might be more prudent to ask if she could read them first. In the corner was a very large piano. She didn't know anyone who could play, except a friend of Sylvie's who she sometimes used as an accompanist when the band wasn't available.

That he earned good money was evident by the house and the excellent food he'd provided. He also owned a car and had a good job with the newspaper. She wondered why he'd never married. It was difficult for her to guess how old he was, maybe thirties? Early forties? But he'd nursed his mother before she'd died, so Ruby supposed he hadn't had a great deal of time for women. She'd also heard that writers were natural 'loners'.

Ruby heard a noise. It sounded like someone at the door. She looked down at herself, a shapeless lump with her dressing gown tied high above her swollen stomach. The knocking increased. Ruby suddenly felt withdrawn and shy. It couldn't be anyone for her, for Marge would be at work now. Again came the hammering on the front door. Ruby stood in Richard's workroom with the book in her hand, willing the caller to leave. She didn't want to talk to anyone or see anyone, all she wanted to do was go to bed. She stayed quite still and didn't move until she was sure the person at the door had gone. By now she'd convinced herself that the caller had been one of those people trying to entice customers to join a club by bringing around articles for sale that they could pay for weekly. She decided it couldn't possibly be anyone who wanted to see Richard, because he would have told her if someone was expected.

She made herself some toast spread with butter and then washed up after herself, making sure she left everything pristine. She would go back to bed and read, yes, that's what she'd do. But first she'd telephone the Point and ask Mervyn if she could talk to Marge.

Feeling quite excited at the prospect of chatting with her friend, Ruby went into the hall, picked up the telephone receiver and dialled.

It rang for a while before a woman answered. The woman sounded young and breathless.

'Marge isn't here—'

Her voice was interrupted by another voice telling her to be quick, they were busy. Ruby could hear Bing Crosby singing. All the background noise told Ruby she'd definitely phoned during a busy period.

'Can I speak to Mervyn?'

'No, he's with Marge, look I've got to go, who shall I say call—'

Ruby was about to tell the strange voice who she was, but the telephone was put back on its cradle and a buzzing noise after a click told her she'd been cut off.

Ruby put the phone down. Was that a new barmaid brought in to replace her? Thinking about that made her feel suddenly very sad. She'd recognized the other woman's voice as belonging to Grace. A new girl in the bar would have to learn about all Mervyn's funny ways. She wondered if Marge had told her about the gas-mask drill? Ruby suddenly realized her own gas mask was where she'd left it, beneath the bar counter. Not much point in worrying about that, she could pick it up later. Maybe the Germans wouldn't use gas anyway. A lot of people had stopped carrying their gas masks. Well, there was little point in worrying or phoning back now, it sounded as if Mervyn and Marge were up to their eyes in work elsewhere in the pub.

Ruby climbed the stairs and went into the room she now thought of as hers, got into bed and began reading, but it wasn't long before her eyes closed.

Chapter Twenty-Four

Richard stepped inside the King's Head. Smoke and perfumed hair oil enveloped him. His eyes searched the long room for Leon, finally spotting him standing with a group of drinkers at the bar. The wireless was playing music from films.

He took a moment to watch the young man he loved with all his heart before he stepped up behind him and tapped him on the shoulder.

Leon turned immediately and when he saw Richard his face broke into a big smile.

'Hello, you,' he said.

Richard's heart was light. 'Want a drink?'

Leon shook his head and nodded at the half of shandy on the bar top. 'I'm on a break, as you can see, but I'll be finished soon.'

Richard's eyes left the handsome lad and spotted a deserted table.

'I'll get myself a whisky and take yours over there.' He nodded towards the table. 'I've installed her, so you can come home whenever you want.'

The young man's eyes held his. 'I think you're making a big mistake,' he said. 'How do you know you can trust her?'

'The poor kid's so glad to have a home she'll not worry about what's going on between me and you. You know how big my house is. Besides, she's ready to give birth any day, she'll be in hospital then, which will give us more time on our own.'

Just then the music from the wireless ceased and the young man said, 'I've got to get back to work. Will you wait for me?'

'For ever,' said Richard so quietly that only he and the younger man could hear, his voice close to Leon's good ear.

Leon walked over to the piano and sat down on the velvet stool. People waited expectantly, the crowd mostly made up of elderly men and younger boys, although there were a few well-dressed women sitting smoking, their long scarlet nails every so often flicking cigarette ash into shell-shaped trays.

Richard looked at Leon's barely touched drink, and when the bartender set him a large whisky on the bar, he took both drinks to the table. Richard sat down, but he only put his own drink on the table. He took a sip from Leon's glass, hoping his lips were caressing where the young man's lips had touched the rim of the glass.

Leon, at the piano, looked over to Richard and smiled again. Then his long fingers began to caress the ivories. 'Be Careful, It's My Heart', the Bing Crosby song, floated clearly throughout the bar. For a few moments the audience of drinkers listened, then after a while they began once more to chat and drink. Richard hated this disrespectful attitude to Leon's music, but as Leon had told him time and time again, he was background noise in the small popular bar where men went to meet men, hoping to find the love of their dreams.

Richard stared at the curve of Leon's cheek. A lock of hair had fallen across his forehead and it bounced as Leon moved his fingers across the notes of the piano. He put not only his heart into his music, but his soul as well.

Sudden movement caught Richard's eye. A well-dressed man began walking from the bar through the seated tables with a brandy glass in his hand. When he reached the piano, he slid a beer mat beneath the glass and set it down on top.

Leon looked up briefly and nodded and the man smiled at him before turning and walking back into the crowd at the bar.

Anger surged through Richard. He stared after the retreating male figure. Leon rarely drank alcohol. At work he preferred a clear head, hence the hardly touched beer and lemonade, but he enjoyed a brandy every so often. How did that man know that? More importantly, Richard had never seen the man in the King's Head before, so who was he? Now the man was leaning across the bar and talking to Edward, the bartender, who seemed utterly at ease with him. So, it rather looked as though the man was a regular, but he wasn't someone Richard was familiar with.

Richard watched as, with ease, the man, who was dressed in a checked suit, said something to Edward that made him laugh. Yes, thought Richard, the stranger definitely wasn't a stranger here.

The King's Head was a well-known meeting spot, but since it was also frequented by men of power and means, men who were often in the public eye, a blind eye was mostly turned to the happenings there.

A stab of fear pierced Richard's heart.

I must not let my jealousy spoil this evening, he told himself. He looked at his watch. Another twenty minutes and Leon would be allowed another break. Another pianist would take over playing the popular music the clientele loved.

Richard's eyes kept returning to the man at the bar. Who was he?

At last Leon finished his selection of music with some tunes from *Oklahoma!* receiving praise from the patrons sitting at tables. He stood up, closed the piano lid to applause, and walked straight over to Richard.

'You were fabulous, as usual.' Richard smiled at him. He held back from making a comment either about the man in the checked suit or the drink that Leon had left on top of the piano.

'So, I can come home?' This time there was no smile from Leon. Panic rose in Richard's heart.

'We both agreed it was for the best that you leave when my mother died. Two gentlemen living alone and with gossip escalating . . .'

'Don't get het up. You think I wanted the neighbours talking about us?' Leon grinned. His teeth were white and even. Immediately Richard felt better.

'I couldn't ask any more of you than to keep a roof over my head and what's not to like, living in a Southsea hotel?' Leon said. 'But I'd sooner have stayed with you.'

Richard was sure he heard a note of sarcasm. He tried to ignore it as he replied, 'You wouldn't last five minutes, a pretty boy like you in prison with all those sex-hungry men, you know you wouldn't. Better to be safe than sorry, Leon, and if it got out that Hank Wilson is a pansy, a queer, my sales would fall and I'd lose my job at the newspaper. I didn't want you to leave.'

Out of sight beneath the table Leon squeezed Richard's thigh. 'God, that's what I love about you, you're so easy to wind up!' Richard felt his tension leave him. He put down his hand, covered Leon's fingers and looked into his lover's soft eyes that were brimming with happiness as Leon asked, 'Come on, tell me what's happened.'

Richard made himself stop thinking about the man who'd provided Leon's drink. Suddenly he wanted to get out of the place. He wanted air.

'I'll talk while we walk,' he said, finishing his drink. 'You must be hungry, let me buy you supper?'

'I'll grab my coat.' Richard watched as Leon got up and threaded himself through the crowd and out through a door at the back. Momentarily, Richard gazed about, looking for the man in the checked suit, who seemed to have disappeared. His heartbeat returned to normal as Leon came back to him, holding a trilby, with a light-coloured mackintosh slung over one arm.

'Let's get out of this place,' he said.

They walked across the dark common. Richard could hear the sea lapping against Southsea's pebbled beach. The barbed wire stopped people enjoying the waves, but the air was fresh. A small wind came across from the direction of the Isle of Wight.

Richard longed to put his arm through Leon's, but to do so would be foolhardy. Police patrolling the seafront and the public toilets near Clarence Pier were always on the lookout for homosexuals. It was against the law for men to openly show affection to one another and could be punishable by a prison sentence. Yet the Southsea Common and the Rose Gardens were well-established meeting places.

'Does the girl understand . . .?'

'God, no!' Richard didn't let him finish his sentence. 'She's had to leave the pub where she works. The kiddie's due at any time so I've suggested she become my housekeeper.'

He felt suddenly affronted at the gust of laughter that came from the younger man.

'Housekeeper? But you can't bear anyone touching your stuff! You cringe when you have to invite people inside your showcase of a house in case—'

'You touch my stuff.' Richard was indignant.

Leon stopped walking and stood quite still. 'But you love me . . .'

'There you go,' said Richard, still affronted. Leon suddenly smiled at him.

'So you're doing this so we can live together again, like we did when Edith was ill? And you promise to curb your jealousy if I come back to you?'

Richard nodded.

'Your mother was in her dotage. Surely a young woman will understand why I'm living with you. You won't be able to silence her . . .'

'As long as we're discreet, that house is big enough to cover a multitude of sins.'

'So now you consider what we feel for each other to be a sin?'

'Don't put words into my mouth, Leon. Let me take care of things.' He paused. 'If I married the girl, she'd be my wife and unable to testify . . .'

'Jesus Christ! You really mean it, don't you?'

Leon had turned away from him, his hands deep in his mackintosh pockets. He turned back and sought Richard's eyes. 'You'd actually do such a thing?'

'You know how I feel about you,' Richard said. 'I'd do anything for you.'

Chapter Twenty-Five

Sylvie lay back on the pillow and smiled at him.

'Well, you've got a lot of energy for an old 'un!'

'Not so much of the old, if you don't mind.' Lennie lit two Player's cigarettes and passed her one. Sylvie knew he'd seen that done in the pictures in that movie with Bette Davis and Paul Henreid. 'A fag after a bit of the other is always very welcome,' he said. He took a long drag on the cigarette and used his other hand to fondle her naked rump. 'Have you thought over what I suggested about singing for the Yanks in Southampton?'

'I don't know . . .' In truth, she'd done nothing else but think about it. To sing in front of a huge audience was what she wanted more than anything. Sure, she liked being paid for singing in the pubs and clubs around Gosport and Portsmouth, but she wanted more. But what did

Lennie expect in return for doing her such a huge favour? He seemed moody tonight, like he had something on his mind.

A couple of times a week Lennie reserved a room in the Black Bear in Gosport's High Street, where she stripped off and got into bed with him. In return he gave her black-market gear; clothes, nylons and shoes, food, make-up and cigarettes. Sylvie was living on Easy Street. The one downfall was that she was sleeping with the wrong man. It was Joe she wanted, not his father! And she'd spent a great deal of her time denigrating Ruby every moment she could, not only to Joe whenever he phoned, but to his father and anyone else who'd listen in the hope that the romance between Ruby and Joe would be well and truly killed off.

Very early this morning she'd heard the telephone ringing downstairs and had come from her bedroom at the Point of No Return to answer it before the noise woke the whole pub.

Joe had been as excited as hell about being brought home from Holland and was phoning from a London hospital where he'd been taken with a septic bullet wound in his shoulder, bad enough to put an end to his career in the paras, so he'd said. She expected him to be pleased about that, but he wasn't.

'Go and wake Ruby,' Joe begged. 'She can't be working, or out, not at this unearthly hour.'

This time Sylvie was able to tell him the truth. 'She's not living or working here any more, Joe.' She'd heard the intake of his breath. 'She went to live with some bloke, a customer . . .' She waited, but he didn't speak, so she said, 'It's possible the bloke is her baby's father. Look, I'm really pleased you're home again in England. How long before they let you out of hospital?'

'Not sure,' he said quietly. 'This bullet wound I took from a German while I was swimming and hauling this sergeant to safety is pretty bad.'

She'd let Joe talk, after all, he deserved it. Finally she asked, 'I take it you've been in touch with your dad?'

Sylvie didn't care what he spoke to his father about as long as Lennie hadn't spilled the beans about himself and her. She didn't think Lennie was the type to tell tales, but you never knew. She wasn't ready to lose Lennie from her hold yet – he was far too useful to her.

'Yeah, I told him about the possibility of a medal. But I'm phoning him again later.'

'Medal?'

'Do you see my dad?'

'Sometimes,' she answered.

'He'll tell you, I don't want to talk about it, it's a bloody farce. Look, d'you know where Ruby is?'

Of course she knew where Ruby was, and why she'd had no option but to be taken in by that writer bloke. She saw no reason to tell Joe the true story, though.

'No, Joe, she upped and left, like I said, she's gone off with some bloke.'

Joe didn't even say goodbye. He simply put the phone down. Not that Sylvie minded, not at all.

Now, she said to Joe's father, 'I took a phone call from Joe this morning – what's this about a medal?'

'My Joe's in line for the Military Medal. I didn't think he had it in him, but apparently he never left his sergeant's side even though the poor bugger had a busted leg. He carried the man to the river and swam across, taking him to safety. He saved his life.'

'But why didn't he want to talk about it?'

'Because that's my Joe all over. He'll be in hospital for some time. They thought he might lose his arm. It got infected by the filthy river water. Me and his mother, we're so proud of him.'

'He's a hero,' said Sylvie, then she realized the conversation was moving away from her, so she said, 'About this singing . . .'

'Ahh, Marlene Dietrich is over here entertaining in London. I can get you on the bill with her . . .'

'What! Really?' Sylvie was practically jumping up and down on the bed with happiness.

'There's something you have to do first, though.'

'What? I'll do anything!' Sylvie could see it now, her name on a poster below that of the great Marlene Dietrich's. Her career would go through the roof.

'My mate at Southampton who handles all the bookings says he can get you a spot finishing the first half of the show, but . . .'

'But what?' She knew there'd be a hitch somewhere.

'He's like an agent, he can't simply sign you up when he's never heard you sing . . .'

'That's no problem, I'll go to Southampton and audition.'

Sylvie was sure once he'd heard her sing, especially dressed up to the nines in her new silver clingy dress that Lennie had got for her, which had been altered by her lady in Mayfield Road and now fitted like a second skin . . .

He had begun laughing at her. He was lighting two more cigarettes while sitting in the bed with his knees drawn up.

'That's not the way contracts are given out in wartime. Haven't you ever heard of the casting couch?'

Sylvie took the cigarette and dragged on it. She knew exactly what he meant. She looked into his dark eyes.

Lennie was offering her the chance of stardom, but she had to pay for it. 'You want me to sleep with this American friend of yours?'

He put his hand on her bare knee and rubbed her soft skin. 'It's the way of the world, Sylvie, everything comes at a price.'

'And what d'you get out of it?' She wasn't stupid. There had to be something in this for him. She was already giving Lennie her body in exchange for treats and presents, what else could he want? But surely if she was a top-line artist Joe would look at her with respect. Especially if she could move out of the Point and into a nice flat of her own. No one knew how fed up she was with pulling pints to supplement her income. She'd seen the hungry looks in the men's eyes as she'd sung to them from the stage. Surely this boost to her career would make her more desirable to the one man she wanted above all others – Joe?

'I become your manager, Sylvie. Together we'll hit the big time,' Lennie said.

'C'mon, wake up, sleepyhead.' Richard stood over her while Ruby struggled to come to her senses. He had gone to the window and closed the blackout curtains.

Sitting up in bed she said, 'I only lay down for a moment to read a book I borrowed from your collection. I hope you didn't mind me taking it. I must have fallen asleep.' She pulled *The Ox-Bow Incident* into view and continued, 'I only read a few pages.'

He turned to her. When he smiled, it lifted his thin face into a sort of handsomeness.

'Of course I don't mind. I'm sure you'll put it back where you found it, just don't turn the pages down. However, I would prefer you didn't go into the room where the piano is, at all.' He smiled again. 'You must be very near your time so you're bound to feel tired. I've been home for quite a while but I let you sleep. Dinner's ready, if you'd like to come downstairs.'

'I'm beginning to feel like a fraud,' she said. 'I'm supposed to be looking after you, but we seem to have switched places.'

'Don't worry about it,' he said. 'While I was at the *News* today I got to thinking about the arrangements you've made for the birth . . .'

'Actually,' she said. 'I've not made any.'

'But you must!' He looked concerned. 'You should be seeing a doctor or midwife every so often, and . . .' He stopped speaking and stared at her.

Ruby said, 'I've felt fine until the last couple of days. I

thought once I knew the baby was coming I'd telephone for an ambulance and . . .'

He gave a big sigh. 'Suppose the ambulances were attending people who've been bombed out? Suppose a doodlebug brought the phone wires down?'

'I didn't think,' said Ruby. 'I've just been feeling so well . . .' Actually, that wasn't quite the truth. She had headaches, swollen feet and felt ugly. But, not being one to dwell on illnesses, Ruby took it all in her stride.

'Tomorrow I'm making sure someone, somewhere will have a bed ready for you.' He paused and sat down on the edge of the bed. 'You don't mind me sitting here, do you?'

'Well, it is your bed—'

He broke in, 'I wanted to talk to you last night, but it wasn't possible. Look, I've got a proposition to put to you. When I write I get carried away and sometimes take no notice of the time. Then I realize I'm hungry and I can't be bothered to cook. That's one of the reasons I need a house-keeper. But you must know why I particularly picked you?'

Ruby frowned.

He put his hand inside his suit pocket and brought out his wallet. From that he took a folded piece of paper. 'This is a special licence to allow us to marry . . .'

'Marry! But I don't love you. I don't even know you.' The

words were out in a rush before she'd thought about them. Ruby was shaking.

Richard didn't look fazed by her outburst.

'But I know you are an honest girl who's been led astray and had the dirty done on her. I've heard all the gossip that the father of your child is Joe Stark and that you haven't heard from him for ages, that he wants nothing more to do with you.'

Ruby listened, hooked to his every word as he continued, 'I know his family don't believe the child belongs to him. Mervyn's kept you in work as long as possible, and, well, you know the rest yourself, don't you?'

Ruby blinked back the tears; a self-indulgence she could do without. Again he spoke. 'When the kiddie's born, there'll be nowhere for you to go. You'll have no hope of getting a place to live. Landladies won't allow unmarried mothers anywhere near their houses, that's if you have enough money for a deposit and rent, which you probably don't. And how will you keep your baby? You won't be able to work and pay someone to look after the child. The worst thing will be the shame. You'll be talked about and have fingers pointed at you everywhere you go. Alternatively, you can give the baby away, put it up for adoption . . .' She heard herself gasp.

He picked up her hand and stroked it. 'I know you already

love that child and would do anything to keep it safe. I can give you and your baby a home. I can provide the child with a name. I'm well aware you don't know me, let alone have feelings for me, but if you look after me I'll look after you and the child. Perhaps in time . . . Well, who knows?' He sat without moving, staring into her eyes.

Ruby pulled her hand away. She had come to this house because she needed a refuge.

Now this man was offering her more.

No, she didn't love him. And already she had discovered he had some funny ways. He'd had a different upbringing to her. He had a lovely home, a good job, but he was careful with his money. Was that such a bad thing, though? she reasoned. He liked things just so. Ruby had never had anything precious, except her dead mother and the baby inside her.

She would always love Joe, but for all she knew he could be dead. He had to be dead, else he would have written to her. Ruby sighed. She began thinking the one thing she'd pushed from her mind all this time: Joe was like his dad!

She was confused and tired. Was it really possible that Joe had lied to her?

For the sake of her baby she could marry this man. Then she would no longer be looked down on. Her child would have a decent home and a father. She took a deep breath.

'I don't love you,' she repeated. 'And if I agree, you have to understand that it will be a long while before I can be a proper wife to you.' She knew she was blushing. 'I'd like us to have separate bedrooms.' She didn't think he'd disagree with that, after all he wouldn't want to be woken up in the night by a screaming child. 'There must be another reason you want to marry me though?'

'Yes, I'm often asked by other journalists for details of my writing and personal life. My books sell well, you see . . .' He paused. 'I'd like my image to be that of a happily married father. Unfortunately, what with working at the newspaper and writing, which is a solitary occupation, I have little time to meet women. Well, the right kind of women. The times you've seen me in the pub at Gosport are hours that I've stolen from work.'

Ruby felt his fingers on her arm. 'I certainly agree to your having your own room,' he said, 'and for as long as you want.'

He suddenly laughed and Ruby felt relief rush through her.

'On another matter, I have another book contract to fulfil, so I'll need the services of a researcher, who'll stay in one of the other rooms. I can promise you he won't bother you in any way.'

He stood up. 'Come downstairs and eat something, then you can tell me later what you think of my proposal.'

'I don't need to think things over.' It seemed to her that all her prayers had been answered. 'Yes, I'll marry you,' she said.

Chapter Twenty-Six

Ruby sat in the kitchen while Richard telephoned the *News* and told them he was taking some time off, which he was owed. She'd made herself as presentable as she could, after all, today was to be her wedding day. Her wraparound skirt barely fitted, but with a smock over the top and a safety pin holding it all together she was happy that her new swing coat, brought home for her by Richard, covered her. It was a lovely shade of green. Richard had promised she was to have money to spend on new clothes as soon as the baby was born. She was looking forward to a day's shopping for the baby and for herself.

Richard had thought of everything. He had a small bouquet of white flowers delivered to the house. From the cellar he'd produced a bottle of champagne for a toast upon their return. He'd telephoned Fareham register office and they could be married in a few hours, due to a cancellation. He had also telephoned Blake Maternity Home, who suggested Ruby get herself along to a doctor there as soon as possible. She really felt as though Richard had taken a load from her shoulders and would look after her, just as he'd promised.

Ruby would be a married woman. No one would sneer at her for being an unmarried mother.

Now she was gazing around the kitchen, thinking soon this house would be hers. The wonderful garden outside would be a place of safety for her child to play in.

Her one great sadness was that she had wanted her best friend to be with her to wish her luck.

'I didn't want to tell you this, Ruby, but Marge isn't working at the Point any longer.'

Ruby had stared at him, aghast. 'Do you know where she is working?'

'Not yet, but I'll find out for you. Don't worry about her not being around today. It's going to be a small informal service. But after the baby's born we'll have a special party and invite all your mates from the pub.'

'Really?'

He put his hand on her shoulder. 'Of course,' he replied, gazing deeply into her eyes.

In the mirror she touched up her lips with the red lipstick. Richard's words made sense. After all, hadn't a strange woman answered the telephone at the Point when she'd phoned? Was she a new barmaid, a replacement?

She'd informed Ruby that Mervyn had gone to see Marge; perhaps to persuade her to return? Ruby knew how fond of Marge he was. Perhaps she'd found another job nearer to where the van was parked? Ruby had tried to telephone the Point several more times but had received a funny sort of engaged signal.

'Could we drive to where Marge lives?' Ruby asked. 'I'd like at least to tell Nan my good news, she could pass the message on.'

'You silly goose,' he said. 'We've no time now to drive anywhere except straight to Fareham, but when we get back you write a letter and I'll deliver it to her. You'll probably be too exhausted for me to drive you anywhere.'

Ruby realized he was trying to make life easier for her. She hadn't slept well last night and today she felt jumpy with another headache that she'd already taken aspirin for. She looked down at her swollen ankles. They were so misshapen. The wedding would tax her strength, and it was kind of Richard to offer to find Marge.

*

Driving along the road to Fareham Richard Williams thought how great it was that all his plans had come to fruition. He stole a glance at Ruby – she really was a pretty little thing – the sooner he'd trained her to be the wife he wanted, the happier he'd be.

He'd never liked that mouthy Marge and although he'd not been near the burning caravan, with Jamie Foster's photographs Richard had managed to knock up a passable piece for the newspaper. If the editor ever knew he'd not actually witnessed the fire himself, there'd be hell to pay. The *News* was a well-respected broadsheet. Thank God he'd remembered not to bring home the copy.

The last thing he needed was for Ruby to find out the truth. She'd go straight to the hospital to see her mate, no matter how tired she felt. Never mind about the wedding. Then Miss Mouth Almighty would do everything in her power to persuade Ruby not to wed him. He wasn't at all sorry he'd sometimes left his bedroom phone extension's receiver off the hook so that Ruby wasn't able to use the phone.

He'd seen the way Marge had looked at him. Ruby was sweet, in her way, naive too, but there were no flies on Marge. She'd been around the block more times than Gino the ice-cream man.

But from what he'd heard the silly cow had lost everything, and nearly lost her marbles too, with the shock of it all. No, it wouldn't do Ruby any good at all to find out about the fire and the deaths; why, she might even go into early labour. That could stop this visit to the register office. Where would he be then? He wouldn't be able to have Leon living with him and he so wanted to be closer to the young man he loved.

He thought it was clever the way he'd offered her a job when Mervyn wanted her off the premises. When she'd accepted employment, the next step had been to play on the way her child would be bullied when people discovered the kiddie was a bastard. Ruby was such a nice girl that, due to the predicament she was in, Richard was almost certain that had he told her the real reason he needed to marry her, she would understand and agree. But he couldn't take that chance. Marriage would solve her problem and his.

And his problem was that he could no longer bear to live without Leon.

They'd met two years ago on the common at Southsea. It wasn't enough now for him to see him occasionally. It cut deep into Richard's soul, wondering what Leon was doing when they weren't together. The memory of the man in the checked suit buying Leon a drink suddenly flashed into his mind.

When his mother was alive, she had lost her mind and had to be restrained for her own good after his father had been killed in an air raid. He had been able to bring his conquests back to the house.

Unable to move around a great deal, she'd accepted Leon as a researcher. In fact, they'd got on well together. Sometimes too well. He'd had to remind Leon who paid the bills. Leon wasn't stupid, he simply wanted an easy life. He liked nice clothes, good food, going to the theatre and, of course, the piano. Hence the grand piano that had cost Richard an arm and a leg. The doctor had agreed his mother's state of mind had caused the cellar fall. Age, grief and feeble-mindedness had taken its toll.

He stole another look at Ruby. She was looking at the ring he'd given her. Of course it had been his mother's. No need for him to waste money, especially as she thought it was all the more special for belonging to his mum. Ruby would be putty in his hands. He'd show her how to save money on the housekeeping and the utilities. He'd finish sorting out the birthing arrangements for her, have a word with the midwife, play the doting husband. He knew where he could get hold of a second-hand pram, that would please Ruby and it shouldn't cost too much. He'd be able to keep her sweet with only a few kisses and cuddles, she wouldn't expect him to want to sleep with her tonight, or any time soon because of the baby. He was glad that she'd insisted on separate rooms. He wouldn't need to show any prowess in bed with her for ages, thank goodness. He looked at his watch. In an hour she would be his wife. His secret would be safe. Soon he wouldn't have to worry about men buying Leon drinks, because Leon would be living safely beneath his roof.

Joe pulled the chair up close to the sergeant's bed and sat down. 'I'm never getting shot of you, am I? I spent my part of the war in Holland tied to your apron strings because of the damage to your leg, now I got the bloody bed next to you in this hospital.'

'I told you you was like a son to me, didn't I?' Cecil Howard smiled.

'An' I didn't want no fuss made about me carryin' you to safety. But you had to go shouting off your mouth about me saving your life! You're worse than my own dad, but at least he respects my wishes!'

'Yeah, when you cool down, you going to tell me what your girl's up to?' The sergeant lit up a cigarette.

Joe took a swig of the tea provided by the pretty nurse, then set the tin mug down. 'Apparently she's gone off with some bloke.' He looked at the sergeant who had propped his cigarette on the side of his bedside table and was now combing his thick moustache with his fingers. Joe carried on, 'I can't see it, myself. I told her I'd be back for her and she's not the sort to mess a bloke about. The trouble is, I can't do anything until I get out of this place.' He shrugged, then winced.

'That bullet wound playing up?'

'If you mean the bullet that went into my shoulder and turned septic, instead of in your bloody arse where it belonged, the answer's Yes, it bloody hurts!'

The sergeant laughed again, then he grew serious as he picked up his cigarette and continued to smoke. 'You want to remember what Renata said about things happening in wartime that have no place in a normal life. There'll be a good reason for what's happening to Ruby. When you get out of here, don't go back to Gosport with all guns blazing. You keep your own counsel until you've found out the truth.'

Joe stared at him. 'I'm out of here as soon as possible,' he said. 'My dad said my Ruby has a mate who's been stirring things and one or two facts don't add up. My old man deals in black-market gear, you see, and he gets about a bit. He said a few tales have been told that aren't quite true. Ruby's left the pub where she worked, but only because she had to.

My dad delivers stuff to the Point of No Return and is a mate of Ruby's old boss.'

They chatted a while longer, then Joe put the mug back on the side table, and got up and wandered down the ward to the office. He greeted some of the more able and awake patients and thanked his lucky stars he was, at least, still in one piece. He wouldn't be going back to fight; it was all over for him now. Apparently he was always going to have a problem with his shoulder muscles. He thought of his mates who'd died in the Netherlands. He knew he was one lucky bastard and if he could discover what had happened to Ruby, maybe he could put things right for himself and her. His dad, for all his bad points, always put family first. All Joe needed to do was to get out of this place and make a few discoveries of his own.

After a few words with a blonde nurse, he walked back to the sergeant's bed.

'Set these up,' he said, putting down the draughts and the board on the bed's flat surface. 'See if you can beat me this time.'

Chapter Twenty-Seven

Marge wouldn't come out of the bedroom. 'I can't do it, Merv. I'll feel their eyes on me and their thoughts will be like spears in my body. They'll wish it was me what's dead, not my family . . .'

'Marge, not everyone feels like that. You should know that most of my customers love you, they don't want you stuck up here.' He had lost only one regular customer since the caravan fire and he'd heard Tim from the estate agents had moved his family out of Gosport, so that didn't count, did it?

'I don't want no pity, neither,' she called.

He closed the door on her red-eyed and puffy-faced misery. The doctors at the hospital had warned him she would take time to come to terms with the tragedy. The grief and blame that she couldn't shake off, he'd have to contend with. To force her to see and meet with people before she was ready could well tip her over the edge.

Mervyn knew he should be thankful she'd agreed to come back and live at the Point, but this new, depressed woman who was growing thinner by the day because she wasn't eating was worrying him sick.

'In time she'll snap out of it,' Grace said.

'But I can't trust her,' he said. 'She thinks she has nothing left to live for.' He didn't like to tell her he'd removed everything from Marge's bedroom that he thought she might be able to use to harm herself. He'd even taken her medication down to the kitchen and hidden it, doling out the tablets daily and watching while she swallowed them.

The one person he thought might cheer her up, he couldn't get hold of. Several times he'd driven out to Alverstoke and banged on the door in Vectis Road, but no one had answered. Mervyn thought it was possible that Ruby had gone into labour and if that was so, she wouldn't be at the house until she was sent home from whichever hospital or maternity home had taken her in. Richard hadn't been in the Point for a while either and Mervyn was loath to phone the *Evening News* office for him in case the man thought it was an imposition on Mervyn's part. He'd never been over-friendly with Richard, believing him to be a rather secretive person. Well, after all, he was a writer, Mervyn thought.

But people didn't just disappear off the face of the earth, not in Gosport, they didn't. Mervyn hadn't had any joy with the telephone either; it always seemed to be engaged, which didn't make a lot of sense when no one ever answered the front door! Still, until he could get hold of Ruby, he'd just have to take care of Marge as best he could.

Lennie had been in with his usual bottles of alcohol and fags and he'd had to put him straight on a few more facts concerning Ruby. Lennie was convinced Ruby had gone off with Richard Williams because she was in love with him!

'No,' he'd said, 'I told her, Lennie, an' I told you. I couldn't have her here with the baby. Babies and boozers don't go together.' He'd had quite a chat with Lennie. His mate had told him all sorts of rubbish about Ruby. 'That girl only ever went out with her mate Marge, I don't know where you're getting all these untruths from.' Lennie had given him a very funny look, then, after a while, 'I know where it's coming from,' he'd said mysteriously. 'And I'm putting a stop to it. No one hurts my son. No one!'

Grace butted into his thoughts. 'You got anyone else for the bar yet?'

She was polishing the bar with her yellow duster.

'No,' Mervyn said. 'That dark-haired young woman the labour exchange sent round was a waste of time. Couldn't add up! No good having a barmaid what can't add up. I'd go bankrupt in a week!' He tried to make light of it to Grace, but one look at her bunions protruding through the holes she'd cut in the sides of her old slippers told him her swollen feet were getting her down. She needed help with all the chores she'd taken on to help him.

'Your girl wouldn't like a permanent job, would she?'

The punters had taken to Grace's granddaughter.

'She can't, Merv. She's working split shifts at the armament factory down Weevil Lane and they pay more'n you do.' Grace was rubbing at a brass beer pump now. He shouldn't ask her to do more than she could manage, it wasn't fair.

Grace looked over at him. 'I'm going to make a pot of tea. I could do with a sit down before we open. Anyway, we should be all right for tonight, we got Lady Muck coming in to swan about, haven't we?'

Mervyn gave a hollow laugh. 'Just about sums our Sylvie up, that does. Still, her pulling a few pints is better than nothing, I suppose.'

He watched as Grace moved heavily from the bar. To tell the truth, he didn't know a lot about her. She'd turned up one morning just after he'd taken over the licence to the pub and said, 'Me name's Grace, I'm the cleaner, an' I'll live in.'

She did her job and he didn't complain about her methods of changing the upstairs sheets and pillowcases regularly, and there were always fresh towels on the rails. With her salt-and-pepper hair that was forever escaping from her bun, and corns and bunions that stretched her shoes to a funny shape, she didn't say much, but when she did a lot of common sense came out from her lipstick-creased mouth.

Best of all, she knew he loved Marge, even though her spark had suddenly gone out, and Grace loved her too. How Marge was going to cope with the funerals next week was beyond him.

The day of the burials was cold and clear.

Mervyn wasn't surprised to see so many people turn up to see Marge arrive, dressed in black. He helped her into the little chapel. She broke down when she saw the coffins. He had to practically keep her upright at the graveside after the service in Ann's Hill Cemetery, as she was a crying mess. She asked after Ruby; what could he tell her?

Her husband, Alf, the father of her dead children, stood stiffly in his sparkling army uniform. He didn't acknowledge her presence. He spoke to no one.

When the service was over, he came towards Marge. Mervyn expected at least a few words of condolence from him.

'You bitch,' he said. 'May you rot in hell for what you've done. I want nothing more to do with you.'

Mervyn watched him walk away, leaving an even more distraught and damaged woman hanging limply on to his arm.

It wasn't Mervyn's place to interfere between husband and wife, but he would have if the lout had touched her. He made sure Marge got home safely to the Point, in the car, supported by himself and Grace. When Marge disappeared back into the bedroom and he heard the key turn on the inside, it nearly broke his heart.

Later, Mervyn left a tray outside her room. He was glad he'd left nothing in her bedroom with which she could harm herself. He had even removed her stockings from the dressing-table drawers in case she decided to try to hang herself.

At closing time he left Grace and Sylvie to finish cleaning up and drove out to the house in Alverstoke where he banged on the Vectis Road door until the darkened dwelling finally assured Mervyn of its emptiness. He knew if anyone could help Marge, it was Ruby. But where was she?

*

Ruby woke in the double bed alone. Something had woken her. She looked at the hotel's bedside clock that said half past three in the morning and stretched out luxuriously. Then she realized what it was that had caused her to wake. Someone was laughing. Not noisily but softly, more like a giggle. She needed the lavatory. The bathroom was along the hall, so she heaved her bulky body from the bed and slipped her new dressing gown about herself.

Keppel's Head Hotel on Portsmouth Hard was part of her surprise honeymoon. Richard, her husband – how funny to think she was now a married woman – had been the soul of discretion and booked two adjoining rooms, one for each of them. They'd driven in his car from the register office at Fareham, after stopping off at the house so they could toast each other with champagne and pick up a few necessary things from the shops.

Previously, he'd contacted not only the doctor, but Blake Maternity Home, just as he'd promised, and made an appointment for her to see the midwife there. Already it felt good to know Richard was taking care of her.

Ruby marvelled at his kindness. She wasn't ready to sleep with him and he didn't mind at all. After signing in at the hotel's reception they'd taken a slow walk along Southsea front, looking at the warships in the Solent. Just like at Gosport, the beach was strewn with barbed wire.

She hadn't minded at all that upon their return, when she decided to go to her room after an early dinner, he'd suggested that he would prefer a drink in the hotel's bar.

Ruby had gone straight to sleep. The noise of nearby laughter had woken her.

The hall carpet was warm to her bare feet and she pushed open the bathroom door. Afterwards, she made her way back to her room. Passing Richard's room, she heard the laughter again.

Once more in bed, she wondered if Richard was with someone. Instantly, she dismissed the idea. He'd probably been listening to the wireless, some late-night foreign station. Soon Ruby's eyelids grew heavy.

She thought about her wedding ceremony. Richard had called in two people from the street as witnesses and afterwards treated them to drinks in a nearby pub. He'd later produced coupons, enough to buy new nightwear and the dressing gown she'd worn earlier. He'd wanted to purchase an outfit for her, but Ruby declined, saying she preferred to wait until the baby was born.

She'd never stayed at a hotel before. Ruby was content

that Richard didn't intend to claim his rights as a husband. She began drifting back to sleep and thinking.

Earlier in the day Ruby had felt unwell, but the aspirins she had taken seemed to have worked. She wondered how Marge was getting on in her snug little home in the woods. It would be so lovely if she could see her. It didn't seem right for Ruby to have married without Marge there to wish her luck. When she got home to Vectis Road she'd ask Richard to take her out to the caravan. Happily, she slept.

Ruby woke to a wet bed.

She was angry at herself for spoiling the nice starched cotton sheets, especially as she had been to the lavatory in the middle of the night. But as she moved, the pain gripped her; a long, low, digging finger that squeezed her kidneys and probed around to the front of her swollen belly. The pull on her insides made her feel as if her guts were falling through her body. Ruby held her breath; the pain was easing, only a little, but enough for her to think rationally.

The baby was coming!

With her hands supporting her abdomen she rolled from the bed and crawled towards the adjoining door between her room and Richard's.

Another wave of pain engulfed her, causing her to double

up, but not before she'd managed to bang on the door. Ruby hadn't realized the birth pains would be so severe. She thought they would start gently and become more intense as time went on.

Again her muscles clenched. She thumped once more, and this time she definitely heard voices.

'Richard!' Out came her strangled scream of his name. She could hear movements coming from behind the door.

She heard the key turn. Then Richard was kneeling before her in his pyjama top and trousers.

'We must get you to the maternity home,' he said. He began questioning her. 'Have your waters broken? How long is it between pains?'

Ruby couldn't answer exactly, but she was happy to let him take charge of her. Another wave of crippling pain hit her.

'I'm scared,' she said.

'Stop that, it's a natural function,' he said sharply. He rose, grabbed his coat from the back of the door and slung it over her shoulders. Then he picked her up in his arms and strode out into the corridor.

At the reception desk a peak-capped night manager jumped to attention. Richard barked orders to the man and swept through the double doors with Ruby in his arms. The cold air bit into her skin and she was glad of his coat.

When he got to his car, which was parked outside the hotel, he said, 'Can you stand?'

He didn't wait for an answer, but tried to lean her against the car while he opened the passenger door.

Ruby cried out as another unpleasant finger pushed her stomach downwards. He settled her inside his car. Then he stood on the pavement and looked about him. Clenching her teeth as pain ripped through her, Ruby followed his gaze and she saw him raise a hand to a figure standing in the hotel's entrance. Then the pains swallowed her up.

'I'll get you there in time, Ruby,' Richard said. 'First babies usually take longer to arrive.'

In her befuddled state she had no idea what he meant and didn't care. Everything seemed as though it was a dream, a hugely painful dream.

Traffic seemed almost non-existent, but every so often Richard put his hand on her knee, her arm, whichever part of herself wasn't waving around with the excruciating feeling that she was being split open into segments like an orange.

Vaguely she was aware that he was driving up a dark lane and then mercifully she saw a thin light showing the open edge of a door in a large building. That door was immediately swept open, a trolley pushed down a slope and Ruby was lifted from the car on to the stretcher and wheeled inside the building. All the time Richard was close by her and soothing her with words.

A large woman in a white hat and blue uniform searched Ruby's lower region. 'Straight to delivery,' she said in a voice that meant business.

Miraculously, something cold was jammed into the skin on her back above her bottom and Ruby faded out.

When Ruby opened her eyes she knew it was dawn. She could hear birds singing and through the window opposite she could see trees, practically bare of their leaves, but those few remaining were coloured red and gold.

She could hear a muted noise, rather like the sound of a motorbike's exhaust on a machine that had seen better days. The sound grew in intensity, coming nearer and nearer, then she saw a long black pointed plane with fire gushing from its rear end.

The terrible object soared across her vision as she looked out of the window, then the ear-splitting noise suddenly halted. The long thin plane stopped in mid-air, then dropped like a stone, nose-diving past her view.

The mighty explosion that followed showed a plume of black smoke spiralling high into the air. Then came the sound of falling masonry and tall flames that followed the path of the smoke and filled the window and disguised her view once more.

There had been no siren, no warning. Perhaps she had slept through Moaning Minnie.

Presently fire engines could be heard, along with the bells of emergency vehicles. Fear crept up around Ruby's heart. She knew only too well what was happening.

The door opened and the large woman who was familiar to Ruby from the previous evening filled the doorway. 'Just when we think the war's over Hitler sends these V-2s.' The nurse smiled at her. 'How are we this morning?'

The fear dissipated. Ruby looked down at her baggy hospital shift.

'My baby? Where is it?' Joy began to well up inside her. She'd been brought to this place last night in labour. She stared at the nurse, then her eyes scanned the room. It contained her bed, two chairs, a cupboard and a table on wheels. An orange glow, with smoke, dark and whirling, filled the window, which was framed by bright curtains.

'Nothing for you to worry about, dearie. We're safe here. All the babies are in the nursery. Your boy has a slight touch of jaundice that'll soon clear. How are you feeling?'

Boy? She had a little boy! Her heart swelled with emotion.

Ruby realized her lower half was swaddled with pads and towelling. She felt tired and very thirsty.

'Can I see him? And I'd love a cup of tea,' she whispered. Images began crowding into her brain. Of sitting in Richard's car, the intense pain, the trolley being pushed towards the car and then, nothing. 'I can't remember . . .'

'You were in a bad way so the doctor gave you a little something.'

'You sure he's all right, my baby?'

'He needs a name, can't have him called Baby Williams for ever, can we, dear?'

She was then unable to speak, for a thermometer was placed in her mouth. Her wrist was lifted, held. 'Of course he's all right.' The nurse removed the thermometer and studied it. 'Hungry, I should imagine. You have your breakfast first, then I'll bring him to you. His colour is a little golden but it will soon pass.'

Ruby could hear a trolley being wheeled noisily along a corridor. She felt euphoric. A little boy. Baby Williams. She, Ruby, was married. She had a husband. He had brought her to this place. She felt like shouting with joy. It was all over. All that pain, all that dizziness, all that fear, all that heartache. She'd given birth to a boy, her son.

The nurse took a clipboard from the bottom of the bed,

and wrote on it using the pencil that hung from a string. Then she moved towards the door and opened it to reveal an elderly woman in a wraparound pinny. Behind her was a trolley stacked with cups. A wonderful smell of cooking suddenly swept into the room.

'Give this girl a big breakfast, Joan. She deserves it; eight pounds and thirteen ounces, a little boy. And a cuppa, she's gasping.'

'Joel,' said Ruby. The woman drew the wheeled bed table closer with one hand and placed a white plate covered with a metal dish on it. Cups and saucers rattled together on the trolley as she touched them. Brown tea gushed into a cup. Ruby felt unbearably happy. 'Not Baby Williams,' she said. 'Joel. After his dad.'

Chapter Twenty-Eight

Sylvie smoothed her hands down over her hips. She could see by her reflection in the mirror that she looked good. Her hair shone with health and bounced about her face in her usual Cleopatra style and her figure was well defined in the red velvet strapless dress.

She'd already been down to the bar in the Point and made sure the small band that was going to accompany her tonight knew exactly when and where to come in, to make the most of the four songs that she'd chosen to sing. She'd start with 'Falling in Love Again', go straight into 'Body and Soul', then finish with 'I'm Pulling Through'. Always she was asked to sing another and she would shake her head, then let the audience beg, finally finishing with 'Strange Fruit'. The Billie Holiday songs suited her voice and tonight she needed to impress Bertrand Kowalsky.

'Falling in Love Again' was Marlene Dietrich's song, but she would show Kowalsky how she interpreted it. Just imagine, she thought, if she could perform on the same bill as the great Dietrich? But first she had to prove to the American that she had a voice – that wouldn't be a problem. Then she had to perform her casting couch bit by sleeping with him. The actual act of going to bed with him meant nothing to her. After all, he wouldn't be the first, second or even tenth bloke she'd allowed to make love to her so that she could get what she wanted. She smiled to herself and turned the letter that she'd picked up from the downstairs hall table over in her hands.

Was Joe never going to get the message that running after Ruby Garett was useless? She debated whether to open it and read the contents. She drummed her long red finger-nails on the top of her dressing table. She'd already told Joe during one of his phone calls that Ruby was living with one of the pub's regulars. Perhaps, when Joe next phoned, she'd say Ruby hadn't been seen for a while.

Mervyn knew where she was supposed to be living, but had had no luck in contacting her. He hadn't only gone to the house once, either, but several times, because he had some crackpot idea that Marge might snap out of the sadness that enveloped her like a shroud if she saw Ruby.

She wondered what Bertrand Kowalsky would be like. Loud-mouthed, like all the Americans she'd met, she supposed. He was probably married with a crowd of kids back in his own country. Not that she worried about any feelings his wife might have if she found out her husband was sleeping around. That was nothing to do with her. Sylvie saw herself as giving a service in payment for a job, sort of like a special interview. She picked up her red lipstick and dabbed more colour on to her mouth.

'How can he fail to like you?' she asked her reflection, after she'd blotted her lips and examined her perfectly made-up face.

Mervyn had asked her to do a turn behind the bar this evening. He still hadn't got a replacement for Ruby, and with Marge hiding away, was finding things difficult. Sylvie had told him to take a running jump. She was the floor show, not a barmaid tonight. He'd taken the hint and got Grace to do an extra shift.

Mervyn would have to understand that she, Sylvie, wasn't at his beck and call. Why, after tonight she could be moving on to bigger things. Bigger than singing in the clubs and pubs of Gosport! She looked at the clock. Time to go and mingle with the customers; she ought to talk to Lennie and find out where Kowalsky was taking her after she'd performed in the bar. The bloke was based in Southampton, so it could be the Polygon hotel, an expensive place. Maybe he'd drive her out to a small New Forest inn. They'd probably have champagne . . . a nice meal perhaps?

Sylvie looked at the time again. Wouldn't do for her to be late starting, would it? The important man would think she always kept her audience waiting.

Down the wide stairway she walked, slow enough so she wouldn't get herself in a sweat, yet fast enough not to keep the band waiting. A waft of stale perfume and beer greeted her. Outside the open door she could hear Merv telling the punters her story and the success her singing had brought her. The audience began clapping as Sylvie pushed open the door and, with her stage smile fixed on her lips, walked to the piano, where a high stool was kept for her to perch on provocatively. There were wolf-whistles and cheers. She motioned her audience to silence as Mervyn dimmed the lights.

Leaning against the bar was Lennie, a big man at his side. Why were Americans so well-padded? Probably because most of them always had plenty to eat, she surmised. His loud checked jacket barely covered his gut. He was watching her every move, but then, that was his job, wasn't it, to look her over so he could decide whether she had charisma and stage presence?

Sylvie explained to the customers about her choice of songs and ended with, 'Billie Holiday has the voice of an angel, but also of a woman who knows what life is about. I make no apologies for saying I believe her to be the greatest singer I've ever heard. This is my tribute to her.'

The audience whooped and cheered and Sylvie knew she had them in the palm of her hand. The man standing with Lennie gave her a small nod. The pianist and horn player began and Sylvie opened her mouth to sing in the sweaty, smoke-filled room.

She liked to wander amongst the audience, picking out men, and sometimes women who she guessed were especially receptive, to make them believe the words she sang were exclusively for them. She walked through the crowd now, and when she came to Lennie, she paused and smiled.

Then she looked at the man next to him. Despite the smile on his lips, it hadn't reached those dark eyes. They were the colour of slate, cold, and reflected somehow the sharp spicy lemon fragrance of his cologne. Sylvie put her hand on his arm. His suit had fashionable padded shoulders. His shirt was expensive. His cufflinks showed on the white silk of his cuffs, pure gold initials that she couldn't quite decipher. He smelled of money. He continued smiling, then said softly, 'Pleased to meetcha, Miss Meadows.' Sylvie thrilled at his accent.

Sylvie sang, her eyes not letting him go, but allowing the sultry notes to wash over him, then she moved away so he got a good look at her rear view as she walked towards the musicians.

Just as she had anticipated, the applause didn't die down until she'd promised another song. The sad and haunting 'Strange Fruit' left the audience wanting more of her, which was exactly as she had planned.

Sylvie left the bar to tumultuous applause and stood in the hall at the bottom of the stairs. She was breathing hard. She had no need to wait for her money – Mervyn would pay her in the morning. She climbed upstairs to her room and took her fur coat from the wardrobe. When she returned to the downstairs hall the two men were waiting for her.

'I've booked our usual room at the Black Bear,' said Lennie. 'Thought you'd feel more comfortable there.'

'Allow me.' The American lifted her coat from her arm and waited until she turned so he could slip it over her shoulders. Looking back she gave him another smile, disguising the anger she felt that Lennie hadn't thought the man might prefer to take her further afield than Gosport High Street, for what could be the turning point in her career.

'I'm leaving you in good hands, Sylvie,' Lennie said. Sylvie noticed a fine sheen of sweat on his top lip. 'I'm not wishing you good luck, because I know that you are going to get all you deserve.'

Lennie walked to the big glass door of the Point of No Return and pulled it open so the couple could slide out into the darkness. When he walked back into the bar, he caught Mervyn's eye and winked at him.

'Right, little lady, I guess you'd better point us in the right direction.' The American slipped his hand beneath her elbow and, as one, they turned towards the Ferry, for the short walk to the Black Bear. 'I've the key to the side door,' he said. 'Better to spare your blushes by going in that way than fighting through the bar crowd.'

The pavement was white with frost and Sylvie's toes in her strappy evening shoes were frozen. A thought struck her. Whilst it was only a short walk to the Black Bear, nevertheless it was a walk. It might have been better had the American had a car waiting. Of course she wasn't familiar with American niceties and her fur coat was warm, but then . . .

His arm around her waist was firm now and he only let go of her when they reached the small pub's back door in North Street to turn the key in the lock.

'Get up them stairs, little lady,' he said when the side door opened onto the flight of steps that led to the rooms above the main bar. He slapped her on the rump and she forced herself to giggle playfully, despite thinking this wasn't going to be as much fun as she thought it might have been.

Once inside the small room dominated by a sagging brass bed, Sylvie looked towards the bedside table. Usually, Lennie made sure that there was alcohol, clean glasses and a packet of cigarettes set out on a tray, ready for their post-coital chat. This time there was nothing. She consoled herself that this was an American, a bigger fish than Lennie.

Maybe the American would offer to take her out somewhere afterwards.

There were always clubs and bars open after hours for those who had money to spend.

He was standing by the bed now and had delved in his jacket pocket and produced a packet of cigarettes. She saw the familiar Lucky Strikes and put out a hand.

'I didn't think you'd smoke, not with your voice,' he said.

'Everyone smokes these days, Bertrand,' she said. He lit up for her. She saw his hand shake; he was nervous, she thought. As the light caught his cufflinks she saw the initials were at odds with the name Bertrand Kowalsky. A question lingered in her mind, but she pushed it away and laughed, a shrill sound. She hated to admit it, but she too was nervous. The American took a couple of long drags then stubbed out the cigarette on the glass ashtray. He took off his coat, threw it on a chair and put out a hand for her to remove her coat. She extinguished her cigarette, then passed him her fur. Sylvie could see he liked what he saw.

Coming round to her side of the bed, he turned her away from him and unzipped her dress. It fell to the floor and she stepped out of it, leaving it where it had fallen. She had seen Joan Crawford do that in a picture.

His hands were now tearing at his own clothes that dropped where they were thrown.

She saw his legs were thin and white, too thin for his big knees; his lower body was overshadowed by his huge gut, which hid his genitals. He pushed her backwards; she fell onto the bed.

His mouth was wet, his tongue everywhere and she felt his hands grabbing at her underwear. She heard the rip of her silk camisole.

Her lips were being bitten and his tongue was a slithering wet snake. He was bruising her mouth, so she tried to push him off her, but now she was crushed by his bloated body and somehow he had pinioned her wrists together above her head with one hand.

'What are you doing to me?'

She was wriggling beneath him, trying to get out of his grip.

'I'm giving you what you want.' His voice was muffled against her hair. But the American accent had gone, replaced by the harsh-sounding local twang.

Suddenly his other hand gave her a blow to the side of her head that made her sight blur and her one word, 'Why?' sound funny, slurred, even to her own ears. She tried to move her legs, to close them, but his knees were keeping them apart.

His breath was wet on her face. She couldn't breathe with that awful tongue down her throat and him slavering away inside her mouth. She felt his fingers at her crotch, his nails scraping at her soft flesh, a thin hardness pushing at her.

Stunned, she was too slow to do anything except take the next blow he dealt her. Now her face was stinging. He had let go of her wrists.

With her hands at his shoulders she shoved him away. He gasped. She felt him collapse at her side as though his fat body was spilling everywhere.

The stink of his cologne, his sweat, his hair oil sickened her. As he moved she rolled away from him. Her nose was bleeding. A blood-red drop dripped onto the white sheet.

'Bitch!' He was now leaning on his side, watching as she scrambled from the bed. His voice was sarcastic.

Sylvie tried to gather her torn underwear about her.

'Bit late for that, darlin', I already seen it all,' he said.

'You're not an American!' She spat out the words, finding the metallic taste of blood in her mouth. The side of her lip was bleeding. Sylvie wiped her hand across her nose again and winced at the pain.

'And you're not a nice girl, are you? Trying to break up my mate's son's relationship with his sweetheart by lying through your teeth every minute you got!'

Sylvie's eyes narrowed.

It took only seconds to realize that she had been taken in by Lennie. He had discovered what she was up to and was getting his own back for the lies she'd told him, and other people who had turned everyone against Ruby.

She hissed, 'Who are you?' Her face hurt. Sylvie touched her skin. Already she could feel it swelling. She wanted to cry with the humiliation of it all, but she wouldn't, not in front of this despicable fat man. Instead, she forced herself to breathe deeply in and out while she waited for his answer. The bed was between them so she no longer felt frightened.

'I'm a packer at the Southampton USA base. I help Lennie

load up his gear. I'm getting paid for tonight. It's been most enjoyable . . .'

He slipped his legs off the bed and began looking around for his clothes. They were strewn over the floor. She looked at him with loathing.

So there was no American agent, no furthering her career. She'd been conned into giving herself to this nobody. She'd been tricked!

The man had nearly finished dressing now. 'Don't think too badly of Lennie. He loves his boy and only wants what's best for him.' The fat man stood, a rumpled figure with a checked jacket over his arm and one hand on the doorknob. 'Sorry I hit you, but I like a bit of violence.' He stared at her. 'You 'ave got a lovely voice, though.' Then the door opened and he was gone.

As the door closed behind him, then and only then did Sylvie turn her face into the wall, and cry. And cry.

After a while she had no more tears left and was instead taken over by a rage so fierce she wanted to destroy something, anything. But she already had, hadn't she? Lennie had seen through her ruse to get Joe and paid her back. Her own greed had put paid to all her dreams.

She dismissed the fact that she was at fault for causing Ruby pain.

After all, she'd submitted to the groping hands of Lennie Stark, albeit in exchange for paltry gifts, hadn't she? And she had no doubt that Mervyn had been in on the ruse, because those two men were as thick as thieves, but she'd always thought Mervyn incapable of such a despicable trick as this.

She didn't care if she never saw Lennie Stark again. She certainly wouldn't give him the chance to gloat over the trick he'd played on her. Sylvie made her way to the long mirror.

Her face was a mess. One eye was practically closed where that animal had hit her in the face, and her nose, though the bleeding had stopped, was swollen. There was a cut on her cheek where that awful man must have been wearing a ring as he lashed out at her. It had also caught at the side of her mouth. Feeling the tears rise again, she sat down on the bed and put her face in her hands. She must think!

She had no more engagements until next weekend. With a bit of luck and a lot of panstick make-up she could disguise the mess of her face. Her venue was at South Parade Pier over in Southsea and she usually stayed at Ma Barker's guesthouse along the front, as the last ferry back to Gosport had sailed by the time the show ended.

'No.' The word slipped from her lips. She wouldn't give either of the men, Lennie or Mervyn, the satisfaction of seeing her like this. And she would get her own back, Yes, she would.

Putting her coat around her, Sylvie went down the corridor and into the bathroom. While she tried to soak her pain away in the bath she thought about the next part of her plan. The Black Bear was officially closed for the night and so was, for once, silent. Sylvie dressed as best she could, her coat wrapped tightly about her, for her walk back to the Point of No Return.

Her skin tingled, not from the cold but from the nail brush she had used on her bare skin.

She seethed with anger at Mervyn. Hadn't she worked her fingers to the bone for him behind his bar? Hadn't she sung her heart out to make him more money? She ignored the fee she charged him for that.

It was obvious to her now that the two men had discussed Joe and Ruby, and had somehow discovered she had caused trouble.

Lennie, outraged at her deception, had seen no further than the lies. That he could have her as a daughter-in-law hadn't entered his stupid brain. All he saw was his son's unhappiness at losing Ruby. The two of them had concocted the story about an American agent looking for talent to appear with Marlene Dietrich who, incidentally, was here in

England at present entertaining the troops. She had fallen for the lie, hook, line and sinker.

Every step she took was filled with pain. But inside, her anger was a light burning brightly.

Sylvie pushed open the side door at the Point, pulling the blackout curtain aside. The night was silent, until somewhere a long way away, a fox screamed.

The warmth and fug of cigarette smoke filled her nostrils as she closed the door behind her and went first to the kitchen.

There was a box of bottles on the kitchen table. She ignored the alcohol and made for the old Welsh dresser, opening the bottom cupboard door. Right at the back was a tin of National Dried Milk that had once contained baby milk powder. Its heaviness pleased her as she dragged it out and set it on the table top carefully, in case any loose change rattled.

Opening it, Sylvie found what she was looking for. Rolls of notes, a bag of silver and one of copper. Food and clothing coupons.

A smile grew on her lips as she fingered the notes.

Outside, a dustbin lid rattled and she gasped and then held her breath. The cat sang out and Sylvie began breathing again. She stuffed six rolls of notes inside her handbag. The bag of coins was ridiculously heavy. She needed to carry as light a burden as possible. It hurt to leave money behind, but it couldn't be helped. The clothing and food coupons Mervyn had come by dishonestly also went into her handbag, as did a bundle of petrol coupons.

Back into the cupboard went the National Dried Milk tin. Mervyn had no idea she knew where he kept his money, taken from the till each evening. Once a week he deposited it in Lloyds Bank.

The thin moonlight shining through the window was a blessing as she carefully went upstairs, watching out for the creaking step.

Her room felt like a haven of safety. After making sure the blackout curtains were tightly closed, she put on the bedside lamp. Once more she examined her face in a mirror. She would need to wrap a scarf around her head so that she wouldn't draw attention to her injuries.

With her battered leather holdall open on her bed, Sylvie began to pack. A few special gowns; she could mix and match and buy more now she had the wherewithal. Then she undressed, put on clean underwear and warm daywear, finishing off her outfit with her fur coat and matching hat.

Mervyn wouldn't find her. She smiled to herself. The ferry had long since stopped running, but there was a small motor-boat that took latecomers across to Portsmouth for a price. From the harbour she could walk, albeit with difficulty, to Southsea and the boarding house. Thank God she'd packed only her necessities.

She would rest for a couple of days, perform at the pier, and then on Monday take the train to Reading where she was due to sing at a working men's club.

London would be her next stop. Sylvie had read about the Bouillabaisse Club on Compton Street, in Soho. She would go along for an audition. By that time her face would have healed. She thought about Joe. A wave of sadness engulfed her. She would always love him. Alas, by the time his father had poisoned Joe's mind against her she wouldn't stand a chance with him, now or ever.

Sylvie turned off her bedroom light and, carrying her leather holdall in one hand, her shoulder bag slung across her fur coat and her shoes in her other hand, crept quietly, painfully, down the stairs and away to her new life. She might have lost Joe, but she still had her voice.

Chapter Twenty-Nine

'It says on the wireless that the Germans have had their bread ration cut again.' Lilly Allerton put down her knitting on the blue hospital bedspread and looked at the lunch provided by the maternity home. 'It didn't say nuffink about the bloody English havin' cuts as well!'

Ruby, in the next bed, stifled a laugh. 'Come on, Lilly, we get plenty to eat, even if the bread tastes of cardboard.'

'Maybe for a shrimp like you, but I got to go 'ome to seven kids an' I need to keep me strength up!'

'Eight. You forgot the one you just had.' This from Eleanor in the bed by the door.

Now Ruby laughed out loud. In the week she'd been at Blake Maternity Home in Elson she'd been well fed, cared for, and had learned how to feed and look after Joel.

Tomorrow she'd be going home to her house in Vectis

Road and her new husband, Richard. Being in the hospital had given her time not only to recuperate from the birth, but to think about events that had been troubling her.

Richard had come practically every evening at visiting time, bringing flowers and books. For some reason Ruby thought he saw it as his duty. But she was happy to see him and there were times when she felt his concern for her was real. He had even asked to visit the baby in the nursery.

Somehow, it had got out that he was the writer of the popular Western series written under the nom de plume of Hank Wilson. Some of the husbands had even left copies of his books, telling their wives, 'Get him to sign that.'

Richard revelled in the attention.

He also liked being known as Joel's father.

Ruby was more than satisfied to be 'the wife of that writer bloke' and not 'that unmarried mother'.

She liked being in the maternity home with the other women; the free and easy way they treated each other made her smile. The jokes about private parts and heavy milk-laden breasts made her feel like part of a privileged group. She couldn't actually voice any of the worries she had, but she admired the women who talked about all things sexual with an easy manner. It made her think of Marge and their 'girly' chats. She missed her friend.

'Does Mervyn know I've had the baby?' she asked Richard, thinking that if he had gone into the Point for a drink and told Mervyn, Marge would know as well.

'Of course,' he'd answered. 'They all send their regards.'

That was something and nothing, she thought. But once she was home she'd be able to take the baby out and she'd go into Gosport on the bus to see everyone.

Richard didn't talk about the pub unless she brought it up. What he did talk about was the book he was writing, *Riders of the Sage*. He said he'd asked his researcher to stay at the house to help him with some facts about a ghost town called Calico, near Barstow in California. He said he hoped she wouldn't mind if his friend's stay overlapped with her return home.

Mind? Why would she mind? It would be nice to have someone else to talk to.

In the maternity home, she felt cocooned. She knew practically nothing of what was going on in Gosport. Matron frowned on newspapers and often swept away those she found lying around, saying new mothers didn't need more stress than was necessary.

Each day was a baby-learning discovery for Ruby. She was immensely pleased that Joel had taken well to her breast-feeding him. Poor Lilly Allerton's little girl had had to be bottle-fed. Ruby was amazed at the amount of baby stuff she'd need when she at last went home, but Richard told her not to worry, he'd been given a list and was attending to things. Ruby began to feel cosseted.

Some of the women laughed and joked lewdly about their men. Ruby kept her own counsel in this. She had no experience of living with a man, nor his sexual preferences. She could hardly count the one evening of passion she'd spent with Joe! Nevertheless, she had begun to worry about her and Richard's sleeping arrangements. Before Joel's birth he hadn't laid a finger on her. But now he was her husband and would surely expect his rights.

If Richard had been Joe, she'd know exactly what to do and say and how to feel, but Richard wasn't Joe. Yet again she wished that she could confide in Marge. She missed Marge and thought constantly of Joe.

Eventually, she slept.

Ruby sat holding her precious bundle in the waiting room, her bags at her feet.

The baby boy stirred. His eyes opened and Ruby looked down into their dark depths, that seemed to know the answers to great mysteries. She smiled. He looked like his father with his swirls of dark curls, she thought. Not that she was worried who he looked like, this tiny boy who belonged to her. She thought he was perfect; his rosebud mouth, his upturned nose, his small, determined chin. She sought his hand and marvelled at his finely shaped nails and the way he grabbed at her finger with a strength she thought impossible in one so tiny. Ruby felt she could spend days just sitting watching him. She had never felt it possible to have such strong feelings for another human being. Even her love for Joe paled into comparison with her feelings towards this defenceless little person.

'Your husband's here.'

Ruby smiled at the nurse who'd just spoken to her.

'Ready, Ruby?'

Richard was smiling as he bent and picked up her packages and bags with ease. He turned, expecting her to follow him, which she did, across the black-and-white tiled floor to the main entrance.

As the car drove through the Gosport streets, Ruby asked from her seat in the back of the car, 'Have you discovered anything about Marge?'

'To be honest, Ruby, I've not had time to think about your friend. I have a deadline coming up for my latest novel, so I've not been anywhere except to work at the *News* office and to visit you, of course.'

'So is your friend still staying . . .'

'Does it worry you?' His tone was crisp.

'Not at all,' she said. 'It'll be good having someone else in the house.'

Again, there was silence.

'Ruby, Leon is staying to help me with my work, I don't want you to distract him. There are times when I've been unable to write in exactly the way I wanted and Leon has been able to type up my feelings exactly. One day Leon could be a writer himself. The fact that there's a child in my house who will disturb my thoughts will be hard enough for me to come to terms with . . .'

The rest of his words were tuned out by Ruby's thoughts. Was he saying he wanted her to make sure the child cried as little as possible so that he and Leon could finish his book?

'I don't intend to let Joel cry unnecessarily,' she said quickly. 'And I'm sure he'll soon get into a routine. Why, the hospital advised—'

She got no further for he interrupted.

'I thought you'd prefer it if Joel shared your room for a while and I keep to my own quarters. I don't want to disturb either of you if I work late, which often happens. Is that to your satisfaction?'

Inwardly, she breathed a sigh of relief. She'd been

worrying about 'that' side of their marriage. For them to remain in separate rooms would be ideal. She looked down at her son and a warm feeling swept over her. Richard was an intelligent man who understood that she needed time in order to be willing in mind and body to sleep with him.

'If that's what you think is best,' she said, her head and heart already feeling lighter as she settled back to look at the changing face of Gosport.

While she'd been in the maternity home, unusually, the weather had taken a turn for the worse.

Early snow lay piled on the pavements, swept into dirty heaps and discoloured by the salt and sand used to grit the roads. The sky was a lumpen grey, full of rain, or perhaps more snow.

'The house is warm. I suggest you stay in for a while. I wouldn't like anything to happen to you. It's very slippery out.'

Ruby nodded. Her eyes caught his in the reflection of the rear-view mirror and he smiled. Again she felt her heart lift.

She could imagine Marge and her family, snug as bugs in rugs in their small home, possibly with Nan yelling every time the caravan door was opened, 'Shut that bloody door!' A smile crept across her face. When the weather let up she'd walk down and see her friend. All the same, it seemed strange that she'd heard nothing from Marge all these weeks.

Of course, Marge could be tired after working extra shifts in the Point. Or was it possible she had a different job? Mervyn might be finding things difficult in the run-up to Christmas, especially if he couldn't find extra staff. Richard had explained how busy the pub had been. Ruby knew Marge hated letter writing and what with the post being as erratic as ever . . .

When the car drew up outside the open five-barred gates at the house in Vectis Road, the door was immediately opened by a tall young man with long blond hair. Ruby thought he'd have done better to put a clip in it or cut it, instead of the constant flicking back of his head to clear his errant locks from his eyes. He was nervously running his fingers through its silky texture. Ruby liked him on sight.

She'd somehow expected to find an older man helping her husband with his work. The word 'researcher' didn't exactly fit Leon's image. He held out a hand towards Ruby.

'Hello, Ruby, you're much prettier than I thought you'd be. I'm Leon.' The words dripped easily from his shapely mouth.

It had been a long time since anyone had paid her a compliment. 'Thank you, Leon,' she said quietly.

'Let me look at the little one.' Leon moved nearer and Ruby could smell his sweet cologne. The young man put his finger into the bundle and exclaimed loudly as Joel curled his hand tightly around Leon's finger. 'Oh, he's holding on to me . . . He's beautiful!'

'Put the kettle on, Leon.' Richard's words were sharp. 'Then collect the stuff from the car.'

Ruby's eyes met the young man's and he grinned at her. And suddenly she didn't feel so alone.

Mervyn sat on the edge of Marge's bed. She was curled up tightly and staring at the wall.

'Go away,' she said.

'Don't you realize how worried about you I am?' He had a busy pub to run without adequate staff. It was difficult to spend with her as much time as he'd have liked. 'Come on down to the bar for a while. The punters are always asking after you.'

'Only because I'm to blame.'

'Stop it! You're full of self-pity. If only you'd come out of this blessed room you'd see people care about you . . .'

'Even my best mate doesn't want anything to do with me.'

Mervyn stood up. There was no use trying to say anything. If he knew where Ruby was he'd ask her to talk some sense into Marge. But he didn't have the time to run around looking for Ruby, not while he needed to be behind the bar serving. What was the point in going to Alverstoke and knocking on a door that no one answered?

He needed to make up the money stolen by that little tramp Sylvie. Still, he couldn't be angry with her for stealing from him and leaving him in the lurch. He and Lennie had played a dirty trick on her by allowing her to think she was meeting an American who would further her career. But Sylvie had been a bitch. She'd destroyed Ruby's reputation. He was glad Sylvie was gone, but missed the extra pair of hands behind the bar and the extra revenue her singing in his pub had generated. He also missed the money and coupons the girl had stolen from him. If he could only get Marge back to her normally sunny self, he was sure everything would take a turn for the better.

He went downstairs and opened up the bar with a heavy heart.

Chapter Thirty

'They say twelve-thousand-pound bombs, three of the buggers, put paid to the *Tirpitz* . . .'

Lennie was sitting by the side of his son's hospital bed, chatting to the sergeant hovering over Joe.

'Yes, the warship's lying on her side at the bottom of Tromsø Fjord in Norway. God bless the RAF,' answered Cecil. He took a crafty swig of the American bourbon that Lennie had tipped into his teacup.

'Bloody Germans thought she was unsinkable, but our Lancasters soon sorted her out.' Lennie looked pleased with himself, almost as though he'd had a hand in bombing the ship himself.

'You two come to chat about the war or to see me?'

Joe tried to make himself comfortable, but the bandages sticking to his bullet wound grazed his tender skin. He tried not to let the pain show on his face. Somehow the infection in his shoulder had flared up again, rendering him helpless after a bad fever.

'You want me to go back to my own ward so you can chat to your dad?' The sergeant looked worried. Joe knew Cecil had bombarded the staff with questions after they'd wheeled him to a private room.

'No, mate, but I need him to tell me if he's seen my Ruby.'

'Have another drop to drink.' His dad upended the black and white bottle into the three mugs, sploshing indiscriminately. 'You too, Joe.'

Joe groaned as he tried and failed to move his arm to still the flow of alcohol.

'You'll be better soon, lad, and can come back to Gosport and find her. A pregnant woman can't be that difficult to find.'

Joe stared at his father. He didn't believe they couldn't get hold of her.

He'd been appalled when he'd heard about the trick they'd played on Sylvie. For all the hurt she'd caused, she deserved punishment. But what his father and Mervyn had done was terrible. He didn't blame his dad for taking what Sylvie had offered on a plate, for Lennie had confessed he'd had a fling with the girl, but if anyone needed to sort things out, it was him, not his father. Sylvie's biggest crime was in loving him. He wished he'd never become entangled with her when she was younger. The saying was, 'There are none so blind as those who cannot see.' He'd certainly been blind to what she'd been up to! If he could only get out of this hospital and back to Gosport . . .

'I'll get off now,' his father said, rising. He put out a hand to the sergeant, who was managing well on his crutches. Joe was glad the army had decided to keep Cecil on, albeit in a desk job. He seemed content with his lot and Joe was relieved about that.

When Joe finally left hospital, he would be out of the army. Free to look for Ruby.

There wasn't a day went by that he didn't remember Renata's words about war changing people. She was a wise woman. In another time or another place, how different might things have been between him and Renata?

Joe regretted not being around to look after Ruby and the child as he'd promised. Why hadn't the letters he'd written got through to her? Why had she stopped writing to him? Why, she might even have had the baby by now and he could be a father! Whatever was done in the past shouldn't be allowed to haunt the present.

*

Raised voices had woken Ruby, and she looked towards the cot where Joel was fast asleep, thankful for once that it wasn't his strident cry intruding into the quiet of the night.

Ruby had gasped when she'd first set eyes on what Richard had done to her room while she'd been away. A flounced cot, hanging mobiles, drawers full of baby clothes – she was enchanted. She never questioned how he had come by the coupons and was all the more grateful because she knew he hated spending money unnecessarily.

A door slammed along the corridor and then footsteps sounded on the stairs. The front door crashed shut, followed by the roar of the car as it burst into life.

Ruby got out of bed and tied her dressing gown around her. She'd only been asleep for a couple of hours. Earlier, she'd left the two men in Richard's workroom after calling out goodnight to them both, to take advantage of Joel being already asleep.

Joel wasn't sleeping well. She suspected it was because neither she nor the baby had got into a proper routine. Richard wasn't happy about being disturbed at night, as, even though their rooms were far apart, Joel's voice was loud. Being woken up made Richard tetchy in the mornings.

Ruby decided she'd make up a bottle for Joel. It was hardly likely he'd sleep right through until morning. Up until recently she'd been managing to breastfeed him, but he seemed to have taken against her milk lately. She was finding the extra nourishment from the tinned variety suited him better. Ruby wondered if her worry about Richard not sleeping well and becoming increasingly moody had somehow affected her milk production. When she'd first left Blake Maternity Home she'd had plenty of milk, but now her breasts' supply never satisfied Joel.

As she passed Richard's room she saw the door was open, and she wasn't surprised to see Leon in his pyjamas, sitting on Richard's bed. Ruby liked the way the two men were free and easy in each other's company, laughing happily at little jokes. It was obvious they had been friends for a long while and cared a great deal about each other. Richard worried about leaving her alone in the house while he and Leon went out to dinner. They frequently returned in the early hours, giggling and laughing, slightly drunk and very apologetic. She was glad they were happy. After all, if Richard needed to work with Leon, wasn't it better that they got on? Leon told her there was a little pub they both liked at Southsea and they had friends there. It was where he had played the piano. Ruby liked listening to him playing during the day, it gave the house a homely feel, especially when he said, 'Tell me some of your favourites, Ruby, and I'll play for you.' Ruby now knew he was deaf in one ear; it, and his heart defect had prevented him from being called up to fight. She was amazed it didn't affect his glorious playing.

He didn't look very happy now, though, his head in his hands, his shoulders shaking.

'Are you all right?' She knew she was asking a silly question. He looked up at her and she gasped. Leon had the beginnings of a black eye. Then she saw his pyjama top was torn at the collar. 'Whatever's the matter?' She moved quickly towards him.

He turned his head, ashamed of his marked face.

Since she'd been home from hospital the time had whirled by, for two reasons. The first, because her baby took up almost every hour of the day, and the second, because she and Leon got on like a house on fire.

Ruby was never going to match up to the perfect partner Richard required. She never remembered to put things away properly in their right places, so he moaned constantly. She'd certainly not been able to cook to the high standard he required, so he also chastised her for that. He remade the beds, rewashed the crockery and woe betide her if she ever set foot in Richard's workroom.

Living with Richard was like walking on eggshells. The atmosphere inside the house was made worse by the weather that was so icy and cold that Ruby dared not set foot outside while carrying her child, for fear of slipping over. Leon had offered to escort her, perhaps for a stroll into the village, but neither liked Richard becoming upset if he found out.

Richard said he'd ordered a pram for Joel, but maintained orders were slow in coming due to the lack of materials because of the war. If she could have pushed the child out in the fresh air she was sure Joel would sleep better at nights.

Daily, when Richard left the house, she breathed a sigh of relief. It was as though a huge black cloud filled whatever room Richard occupied. But when the door closed on him as he left for work at the newspaper office, the whole atmosphere in the house changed for the better.

Leon seemed to know exactly how to handle Richard. Ruby could see that there was an empathy between the two men that she could never be part of. She dreaded the sound of Richard's key in the door.

It was a sharp contrast to being with Leon. She did nothing but laugh and chatter when he was around.

'What's the matter?' Ruby asked again and sat down beside Leon. 'You and Richard had words?'

Leon pushed his hair back from his eyes.

'Again,' he said. The one word was full of meaning.

'I can't help if you don't tell me.' Ruby put her hand over his fingers to still them as he tapped aimlessly on the counterpane.

'You can't help me anyway,' he whispered. 'Not when you're the cause of the problem.'

She must have looked confused, for he said, 'He's jealous of our friendship.'

Ruby stared at him.

'He doesn't like it that I'm fond of you and the baby,' he continued.

'But there's nothing unusual in that, is there?'

She thought of Leon cuddling Joel. Ruby felt she could talk to Leon. A smile lifted the corner of her mouth, thinking about the visit from the midwife who'd come to check up on her and the baby. Apparently the first time she'd visited no one had answered the door. She'd left a card, and when Ruby had admitted her on her second visit she'd taken one look at the kitchen and said, 'Oh, you are lucky to have such a beautiful home.' After she'd looked at Joel and asked questions, she added, as Leon let her out, 'You must be very proud, I'm glad to see you both coping so well.'

'She thinks you're the father,' Ruby had said, after the midwife had left. She'd been convulsed with giggles.

'I suppose I am closer to your age than Richard,' Leon had replied. But when Ruby had told Richard during dinner that evening, he hadn't seen the funny side of it.

Now Leon gingerly touched his eye and said, 'Has he broken the skin?'

She peered at his swollen eye and shook her head. 'I'll get a cold compress.'

He stopped her.

'His jealousy gets the better of him,' Leon said.

'I didn't think he cared that much about me.' The words were out of Ruby's mouth before she thought about them.

Leon was staring at her. 'You really don't know, do you?'

Ruby frowned. 'Know what?'

Leon said softly, 'It's not you he's jealous about, it's me.'

Ruby couldn't speak. It took a while to assimilate his words. Then all she could think of to say was, 'You and him?'

Leon nodded. 'Don't say you never realized Richard preferred men to women!'

Ruby knew her mouth had fallen open. She gasped, before saying, 'I had no idea!'

Leon said, 'I thought when you agreed to marry him it was because you wanted a name for your baby and you knew he wouldn't lay a finger on you. Surely you don't care for him?'

'Of course not. I told him I didn't love him and he said it didn't matter . . .'

'Of course it didn't matter. His getting married was a cover so I could legitimately stay here without anyone asking questions. And I've never known him spend so much money on anyone as he does on you and the baby. Except me, of course. He really wanted this set-up to work.'

Everything was falling into place inside Ruby's head. Richard had never kissed her, at least, not a proper kiss, not even on their honeymoon . . .

Ruby stared at Leon. 'It was you in the next room in the hotel, wasn't it?' She remembered the giggling. 'Everything has been a sham . . .'

She remembered Marge sometimes pointing to different men in the pub and telling her they were 'pansies'. But Ruby hadn't taken much notice. It hadn't concerned her.

Leon picked up her hand. 'I was living at that hotel. We never meant to hurt you. You needed a home. He thought if he gave the child his name, it would solve all our problems.'

'I thought he cared about me,' Ruby said.

'Come on, Ruby, don't make out you weren't using him. Gosport can be a cruel place for an unmarried girl with a baby, no job and no home . . .'

She looked into his kind eyes. 'I haven't met any men who, who, who . . .'

'Like other men?' Leon finished her sentence for her. 'Unfortunately, the same is true of a lot of people and that's why we're misunderstood and outlawed. It's a crime for men to prefer their own sex, punishable by prison or worse. Please don't be angry with Richard. Not all homosexual men are devious brutes. You both got something out of the marriage.'

Ruby thought about his words. Leon was right. She had a lot to thank Richard for.

'But surely if we're to live together comfortably he can't knock you about for being nice to me?'

Leon shook his head and replied, 'Unfortunately he's not good at controlling his jealousy. You've really not met many jealous men, have you?'

Ruby shook her head, then got up. 'I'll get a wet compress,' she said.

Downstairs in her immaculate kitchen she held a clean tea towel beneath the cold tap until the cloth felt icy to her touch. She took it upstairs and laid it across Leon's eye. He gave her a grateful smile.

She asked, 'Where's Richard gone?'

Leon shrugged. 'Usually he drives out to the beach, finds

a place where the barbed wire is broken and sits down to think.'

'So he could be gone some time?' she said. 'I need to think about all this. How long have you known him?'

'We met a few years ago, not far from the hotel he took you to for your honeymoon.'

Ruby turned towards the door. Leon got up to follow.

'I was walking along the common near the seafront after finishing my stint at the piano in a hotel when he caught up with me and began chatting. That part of Portsmouth is a known meeting place for men like us.'

Ruby suddenly remembered the night she and Joe had made love. It flashed through her mind that she knew nothing of how men went about such things with each other. Her own feelings, that she'd never explored before, had shocked her.

She didn't want to think about it.

'Just let me check on Joel,' she said, 'then come downstairs. I need a cup of tea.'

Standing over her baby's cot, she was suddenly filled with unfathomable and overwhelming love for her son. She took a deep breath of Joel's soothing baby smell.

'He's a lovely boy,' Leon said. He had walked up behind her.

Ruby looked at Leon. 'Yes,' she said softly.

Sitting down, with the teapot between them, Leon explained that he and Richard had been together as a couple for about two years.

'His mother was alive then,' he said. 'She was very frail and I came to this house at Richard's insistence. Like with you, he explained to her my role was to help him with his research for his Western novels. Unlike you –' he grinned at her – 'she knew the ways of the world and despite being proud of her son for his literary achievements, found it hard to accept him as he was . . .'

'But she was his mother!'

'You'd be surprised how many parents reject their offspring. They seem to think it reflects on them, somehow. The Nazis do terrible things to homosexuals. They pretend it's an illness and torture or castrate men . . .'

Ruby felt her tears rise – she had no idea such a terrible world existed.

Leon stirred his tea. 'His mother got spiteful. I think she realized she was never going to become a grandmother to his children.'

'How did you feel about that?' Ruby saw Leon's eyes were filled with tears.

'I had to keep out of her way. That was easy, she used

the wheelchair and couldn't get about without her stick indoors. I knew it hurt him, her taunts. I offered to leave, but it wasn't what he wanted. One night after they'd rowed she said she was going to tell his boss at the newspaper office about his sexual preferences. He locked her in her room that night. Imagine how his life would have been if it was discovered the famous Gosport cowboy writer was a pansy!'

'Surely his mother didn't mean it?' Ruby tried to imagine how she would feel if it was her own son who . . . She knew she would love her boy and stand by him whatever he did, whoever he was. How could she ever hate or be ashamed of anything that came from her own body? But Richard's mother was of a different generation, wasn't she?

Leon wiped his eyes. 'She said she'd never get over the shame. It would kill her, she said. She thought I should leave.'

'So what happened?' Ruby poured out more tea and pushed the refill towards Leon.

'I agreed to go. I thought it better to keep the peace.'

She nodded. 'Very wise.'

Leon shook his head. 'But before I had time to pack up and leave his mother fell down the cellar steps!'

Ruby stared at him. Silence reigned, then she said softly, 'Very convenient.'

Looking into Leon's eyes, she wondered if it had really been an accident.

'I think he must care for you a great deal,' she went on. But now fear was clutching at her heart. Would a similar fate, an accident, await her if she didn't do as she was told?

'But why marry me and bring me to this house when he could live here alone with you?'

'Don't you see, he couldn't do that? People would talk. His career and writing mean everything to him, along with me, of course.' He frowned. 'I left after his mother's funeral and got a job in a bar. His work and my job didn't leave a great deal of time for us to be together. As time went on he came up with the idea of giving you a roof over your head. You would be a foil for him and me to carry on living together . . .'

'That part works! I know you're like a couple of kids together, but if you hadn't spilled the beans I don't think I would have worked out that there was something more than a professional relationship between you two.'

'That's something else that's getting him down. He has to hold back on showing affection . . .'

'But that's an awful way to live!'

'He can't see things changing unless people begin to accept love for what it is and men and women for who they are.'

Ruby sighed, agreeing with him. 'I see it all now,' she said. 'But I'm scared of his moods. He should try to control his jealousy.' Then she remembered the round chain links embedded in the lawn. Were they put there to stop his mother falling from her wheelchair, or something more sinister?

'He does try to curb his jealousy, but he remembers an incident and dwells on it until it grows inside him. I've been trying to convince him lately that there is nothing between a bar customer and myself. This man bought me a brandy after asking the bartender what I really liked to drink, other than the weak stuff I usually have to keep me hydrated while I play the piano. In Richard's head he made something out of nothing.'

'Why, if you care about Richard, are you telling me all this?'

'I wouldn't have done, but tonight you asked me what the matter was . . .'

He pushed his tea away. Ruby realized it was probably cold by now.

'Do you love him?'

'Yes, I do. No one can help who they fall in love with, Ruby.'

She looked into his face. The bruise around his eye was changing colour now, taking on a purple hue.

'Does he often hit you?' Then without waiting for his reply she asked, 'Didn't the doctor or police wonder how his mother came to fall down the stairs?'

Leon looked away. 'He concocted a story about some photographs being in a suitcase in the cellar. The authorities made a few enquiries, but her health wasn't good, so they decided it was accidental death.'

'Why did you say the word "concocted"?'

'Only because I never heard either of them talk about a suitcase and photos, but that's not to say they didn't. You asked if Richard has hurt me before. A few months ago he broke my arm. He was mortified. He cried and begged me not to stop seeing him. He said he'd turn over a new leaf. Of course it put a stop to my piano playing until I healed and I hated him for that. He gave me money because I couldn't keep myself by playing. The music is a release for me for all my thoughts and hopes . . .'

Leon gave a big sigh. 'I think he's forgotten about that now.' Then he added, 'He's definitely been drinking more lately and that fuels him.'

Ruby got up and walked towards the kitchen door; she'd heard her child cry.

'I'm going to leave you to wash up and put the stuff away,' she said. 'You'll make a better job of it than me. I need to go upstairs, think over all you've told me. And it wouldn't do for Richard to come home now and find us together, would it? Perhaps I ought to think about moving on . . .'

'No! If you leave, the gossip will start up again. You mustn't go. I've told you all this so you can be aware of his moods and understand the reasons behind them.'

With his words ringing in her ears Ruby went upstairs to her room. Joel's cry had come to nothing. She took off her dressing gown and crept into bed. She hated arguments of any kind. Perhaps it wasn't safe here in this house any more. Her mind was still turning over all she'd learned about Richard and Leon's relationship when, in the early hours, she heard the car's engine halt outside, and the front door open and footsteps come up the stairs. She wondered how it was possible she had lived on this earth for as long as she had with truly no idea of how other people managed their love lives. It was a long time before she slept.

Chapter Thirty-One

Ruby had taken to staying in bed until she'd heard the front door slam behind her husband as he left for work. One of the gifts Richard had bought was an electric bottle warmer, so she had begun preparing a bottle for Joel at night to feed him in her bedroom in the mornings.

Richard's increasingly black moods made her feel uncomfortable. She felt scared to voice an opinion and even something as simple as going to the kitchen for a drink of tap water became an action that might be examined in detail.

Ruby prayed that the pram would be delivered soon so she could at least get out of the house and its heavy atmosphere. She became worried about incurring Richard's wrath, so she stayed out of his way as much as possible.

If only there was a break in the weather so she might

be able to go outside with the baby. She would feel so much better. But day after day the ice showed little sign of thawing.

While Joel slept, Ruby read and listened to the wireless. Winston Churchill celebrated his seventieth birthday and the lights went on again in Piccadilly and the Strand in London, and all over the rest of the country after five years of blackouts.

She left most of the housework for Leon, as Richard preferred it that way.

Ruby realized many women would be happy to exchange places with her. She lived in a lovely home, had plenty to eat and she had only to ask her husband for whatever she needed for herself or the baby and he brought it home with him. She didn't need money, so never asked for it. She was, however, unhappy that whenever she asked Richard if he would take her out anywhere in the car, he made excuses not to go.

Was he really so worried that people might ask questions and discover his secret, or was it simply because he had no time to take her?

Her plan was that when the weather broke she would carry Joel – for she had now almost given up hope that Richard's promise of a pram for the baby would ever materialize – along to the woodland near Browndown and visit Marge in her caravan.

She didn't blame Marge for not contacting her. Surely her friend would have heard by now that Ruby had married Richard Williams? She might be thinking that Ruby didn't want anything more to do with her; after all it had been a long time since the two friends had spoken together. She'd been stupid to marry the man. She was aware of that now. She had tied herself to someone who didn't love her, for the sake of giving her child a name. This was a mess she had to get out of, but how?

Ruby had given up hope of seeing Joe again, although, like her dead mother, he was constantly in her thoughts. She realized that because of the war anything could have happened to him. She often looked at the plaited grass ring he had given her and knew she would keep it for ever. She hoped with all her heart that he was safe.

That she seemed to have slipped so easily from her friend Marge's thoughts she put down to Richard's intervention. Knowing his nature now, there was no way he would have wanted Marge visiting the house in Vectis Road. Marge was nobody's fool. Richard's secret would soon be out in the open if Marge had come calling.

Ruby stared out of the window. Oh, how she wished she could put her plan into operation.

Joel quivered in his sleep, but didn't wake. With her dressing gown tied about her, Ruby descended the stairs. She could hear from the rattle of pots that Leon was already up. He was probably making tea.

Much as she valued Leon's friendship, she decided to keep her secret to herself. One slip of his tongue and she'd never be able to go to Marge's caravan.

Richard might even decide to keep her locked inside the house!

Leon was swirling hot water in the teapot.

'Good morning, Princess,' he said. Ruby grinned at him. As he threw the hot water away she saw his wrist was bruised. He caught her gazing at his hand and tried to conceal it.

'Has he hurt you again?' She came straight out with the question. But as she spoke she realized that she already knew the answer.

When Richard had arrived home last night, Leon wasn't in. He'd insisted on going up to the postbox in the village for Ruby as she'd written a letter to Marge, care of 'The Caravan at Browndown'. Not that she expected an answer, but hope was in her heart.

Leon had thought it best to take the letter out of the

house and put it into the postbox before Richard saw it and began asking questions. Unfortunately, Richard had arrived home before Leon returned.

'I thought his moody silence, once I'd told him where I'd been, was all the grief I'd get, but I got the old, "Where did you really go?" followed by, "Who did you talk to?" and it just went on and on after you'd gone to bed until things got ugly.'

'I'm sorry,' Ruby said. 'It's all my fault . . .'

'Don't blame yourself for his jealous actions.' Leon began spooning tea into the warm pot. 'I used to believe his jealousy showed how much he cared. But it becomes wearing after a while.'

'I'm sorry.'

'If you say you're sorry once more I'll, I'll . . .' He smiled at her. 'Just don't say you're sorry again.' Leon paused. 'Before the argument he was actually in a good mood, we'd got quite a lot of work done on his novel.'

Ruby was glad about that; if Richard was writing well he would be less likely to find things to moan about concerning her or Joel.

'I've been thinking,' she said. 'What if I told him I know he's a homosexual?'

The long whistle Leon let escape through his teeth surprised Ruby.

'Not a good idea,' he said. 'He's gone to all this trouble to conceal the truth and would be terrified you'd tell someone. You'd have a hold over him, see?'

He looked enquiringly at her.

'I could promise not to say anything that might incriminate either of you. I just thought he might be happier if things were out in the open. It might be better for all three of us. At least then he wouldn't have to hold back on his true feelings for you when I'm there.'

'Let me think about it.' He bit his lip. 'Richard definitely wouldn't like it if he thought we'd been discussing him behind his back.'

Leon began taking down the china cups for the tea. Ruby wandered out of the kitchen and opened the door to Richard's workroom. French doors opened out on to the gardens and the bookshelves covering the walls held many books she would have liked to read.

Richard had stated emphatically that he didn't want her to go in his study again. While he was at home, she did as she was told. He and Leon spent their evenings together alone, working in that room, but it gave her great pleasure to look at the books that he'd had published that lay on the shelves.

There were times when she wanted to tell him how proud she was of his success, but courage failed her.

Books, magazines and leaflets also stood in piles on the floor, on chairs, on the tops of cupboards.

Ruby had thought at first that the piles represented an untidy streak in his nature, but upon closer inspection she noted they were little mountains of information on the various states of America where battles had been fought, where Indian reservations were sited, and on cemeteries where gunfighters had been buried. All the names were magical to her, places and people she'd read about or seen in films. Calamity Jane, Buffalo Bill, Tombstone, Deadwood. Ruby so wanted to talk to Richard about his writing, his work, but he kept this part of his life separate from her, too.

She moved towards the French doors and in so doing knocked against a pile of papers on Death Valley. Magazines scattered, and Ruby hastily piled them up again, her heart beating fast. Her eyes alighted on the whisky bottle on the floor next to the desk.

She often smelled alcohol on Richard. If it helped him relax, then she was happy with that. Ruby gazed out into the garden. It looked like a freezing lunar landscape with the icicles and snow. She shivered. If only the weather would change!

'Good piece of work you did for yesterday's front page.'

Richard looked up from the notes he was trying to put

in some sort of order for a piece on the work of rebuilding Coventry after the terrible bombings.

'Thanks,' he said to his associate on the paper. He didn't like the man very much but he liked the praise. He was expecting and hoping for a new contract from his book publisher. He'd have liked to tell his colleague about it, but felt uncomfortable talking about himself. Besides, what right had he to feel pleased with himself?

He thought of the look on Leon's face when he had hurt him last night.

Why couldn't he get it into his head that Leon stayed with him because he loved him? Where did these awful feelings come from that made him angry with Leon for doing things without him? Why couldn't he reconcile himself that Leon being with Ruby and the child day after day didn't mean they were doing things that excluded him? And what if they were? They were friends, for Christ's sake, nothing more! He ought to be happy they got on well together.

He wanted this strange family to work. It was almost a '*ménage à trois*' but without the sexual gratification.

To keep Ruby sweet, he had spent money on her and told her she only had to ask for anything she needed and he would provide it. Leon knew how he hated wasting money, but it was necessary for Ruby to be well cared for, the child, too.

He felt she wasn't happy but he wasn't sure how to correct that. He was glad that the house was large enough that they didn't have to live on top of each other.

Of course, he didn't doubt Leon's feelings towards him. Why then did he feel it necessary to pick away at their relationship as if it were a scab?

Perhaps his insecurity stemmed from his mother's unwillingness to accept him as he was. People shouldn't have to be afraid of who they are. Perhaps one day something wonderful might happen and other men like him would be able to shout out loud that they were proud of who they were!

Mervyn crashed the telephone down with a bang.

The brewery was unable to fulfil his order. 'This bloody war!' he swore.

He remembered when back in 1943 the brewers had been asked to cut back on barley by ten per cent. Other materials had been suggested for use by the government in the brewing of beer. Oats were used and the result tasted so awful that it was laughingly proposed that the brewers serve it to Hitler to help them win the war! Potatoes were also tried, but the resulting beer tasted of potatoes and made the customers pass wind!

And now Brickwood's had telephoned and told him his usual beer order couldn't be met. He'd asked when he could expect a delivery and was told to leave his cellar door unlocked and they'd get to him as soon as they were able.

Mervyn knew it was no good remonstrating about delivery dates. Every pub was experiencing difficulties. Coming up to Christmas, he'd been told things were likely to worsen.

The trouble was, so one excuse went, fewer people than ever went on their annual hop-picking break to Kent and its surrounds, fearing an invasion by the enemy while their homes were left empty! Mervyn drummed his fingers on the table.

He'd begun to rely more and more on whatever alcohol his mate Lennie could filch from the American stores. Two boxes and two casks sat on Mervyn's kitchen table. Lennie sat there drinking tea.

'I wish you could get hold of a good barmaid for me,' Mervyn said. 'No one wants to be run off their feet all day and night when the armament yards are paying good wages.' He thought back to happier times when Marge and Ruby were like two people-magnets behind his bar.

It still pained him that he couldn't get Marge to snap out

of the doldrums. She only left the bedroom occasionally, and wandered around looking like a wraith. Only this morning Mervyn had had to wipe a tear from his eye while searching beneath the bar counter, where Grace never investigated, for his spectacle case. The three gas masks in their containers lay together: Marge's, Sylvie's and Ruby's. Like three strangely boxed, unwanted Christmas gifts.

Thank God that blasted Hitler hadn't bothered sending along bombers to shower Gosport with death missiles recently. The horrible little man was more interested in flying over his unmanned buzz bombs to kill people.

But at least Mervyn knew where the gas masks were if they were needed suddenly.

'You're not the only one with troubles,' said Lennie. 'My lad walked out of the hospital, said he's had enough of lying in a bed recuperating and wants to find Ruby. Well, he won't have to look far, will he? Her shutting herself up living in that big house in Alverstoke all lovey-dovey with that writer chap?'

'That's as maybe, but pinning her down is another matter,' Mervyn argued.

'I went there and no one's answering the door. I've given up now.'

Mervyn added, 'Well, when he does get hold of her, I

hope he tells her Marge needs her.' He thought fondly of the days gone by when Marge and Ruby had chattered together constantly. He thought too of how he missed Marge's little boy.

A lump filled his throat. It couldn't be easy for Marge, who wouldn't stop blaming herself for her family's deaths. 'I don't understand how Ruby could abandon her friend when she needed her the most. I never thought she was like that.'

'Bad business all round,' said Lennie. 'Who'd have thought that little tramp Sylvie could cause so much bother with the lies she told?'

'Yes,' said Mervyn. 'Who'd have thought it?'

Chapter Thirty-Two

'You don't look well. You shouldn't have left the hospital—'

'Mum, please stop going on at me.' Joe looked at the worry lines on her face and his heart softened. That was the trouble with parents, they never let go, never wanted to admit their children were grown up. He got up from the kitchen chair and went over to her, enfolding her in a bear hug.

'Look, Mum, if I don't find out the truth I'll go daft wondering about Ruby.'

His mother sighed. For all the lies that had been bandied around about Ruby, she had to admit she hadn't done her duty by the girl. If only she'd believed her when she said she'd had no other feller except Joe, instead of swallowing all those lies spread about by that Sylvie, Joe wouldn't be worried sick now. And maybe Ruby wouldn't have married that writer bloke . . .

'You'd best start with Mervyn and your dad. Marge is stopping at the pub as well. She may shed some light on things, but take it easy, she's fragile.'

Joe knew about the fire and guessed his mother was referring to that. He nodded. His mother was putting the finishing touches to the Christmas cake, such as it was this year with all the shortages. She smelled of vanilla and icing.

In the hall he put on his coat and threw a scarf around his neck. Every arm movement pained his recovering shoulder wound. He went back into the kitchen and dropped a kiss on his mother's forehead. Then he said, 'I don't want you blaming yourself, Sylvie always was pretty persuasive when it came to lying for her own ends.' He didn't want to elaborate. His father had told him about sleeping with Sylvie and Joe didn't know how much his mother knew about their affair. He didn't want his mother upset, though he knew she was well aware of what his father was capable of.

Neither did he need to tell anyone that he'd spotted a news item in a London paper he'd found on the train saying Sylvie was appearing at a well-known Soho club. He'd read the cutting, complete with a large photo of her looking, as usual, quite gorgeous, and then said aloud, 'Good luck, Sylvie, just don't come back to Gosport!'

Cecil was coming for Christmas. Emily Stark had readied

the spare room downstairs at the front of the house. To do that she'd had to get his father to move his contraband to the upstairs box room. He hadn't been pleased about that, but he got on well with the sergeant and didn't really mind as much as he made out.

Cecil couldn't manage stairs too well, but he'd graduated to a single cane to walk with instead of the crutches. Joe was looking forward to having a few drinks with him. Maybe if he got him in the right mood he'd discover whether Cecil was so drunk he didn't know what he was doing that day when they baled out of the plane or if there was something in his life that had made him want to end it. The sergeant was a funny bugger, there was no doubt about it. But after the jump, Cecil was definitely easier on Joe, almost fatherly, that's when he wasn't complaining about his injuries!

Ruby was up early. She'd had very little sleep. She was gazing out of the window into the garden, pleased that at long last the icicles hanging from the summer house had begun to drip and thaw.

Joel had refused to settle and had grizzled continuously through the night. She'd encountered Richard on the stairs very early in the morning and could sense by his frosty greeting that he'd been kept awake too. Worrying about Richard's demeanour made her feel on edge.

She'd laid a place at the table for his breakfast and she was making tea when Richard said, 'I thought I told you to stay out of my workroom.' Ruby realized he must have noticed that the books hadn't been placed back in their right order.

She faced him. 'I'm not going to apologize,' she said. 'Not when I'm proud of what you do, I simply wanted to see what you're working on.' She swept past him and carried on upstairs to fetch Joel down, who was crying loudly.

Joel had messed himself and sooner than take him downstairs and change his nappy she decided to do it in the bedroom. She didn't think Richard, eating breakfast, would appreciate Joel's offering.

Later, carrying her son, she descended the stairs to hear a fast bubbling sound.

'Oh!' she cried out. Stupidly, she'd forgotten about the saucepan on the stove and now the water was boiling and along with it, Joel's milk.

She rushed to the stove and automatically grabbed the handle of the pan, which was hot and seared the palm of her hand. She screamed, almost dropping Joel.

Richard quickly lifted the child from her arms. The

saucepan had fallen to the floor, the boiling water hitting Ruby's foot.

She sank to the lino. Leon, close behind Richard, fell to the floor and pulled her away from the spilled liquid, the pan and the bottle of milk that had rolled and spilled out over the kitchen floor.

'Joel!' Ruby cried out her son's name.

'He's all right! What about you?' Leon was looking at her anxiously. The smell of spoiled milk filled the kitchen. He knelt beside her and turned the palm of her hand towards him. The skin was red, but not broken. Stricken, Ruby looked at Richard standing with the little one safely in his arms, her relief evident on her face.

Richard's face was inscrutable. Leon scrambled to his feet, saying, 'Give me the baby. You go to work. I can sort this out. Go on, go!'

The last word was practically a shout. Nevertheless, Richard handed over Joel, who was now screaming, to Leon, and immediately Joel left Richard's arms the screams fell to a whimper. Richard, wordlessly, turned and left the kitchen. Leon found a space on the lino where it was dry. 'You stay there, poppet. I'll sort you out in a moment, after I've seen to your mum,' he said, laying the child down.

Ruby had already scrambled up and was examining her

foot at the same time as casting an anxious eye on her baby.

The front door banged shut.

Ruby kicked off her slipper – underneath the fabric, the hot water was soaking her foot. The redness was fast creeping up her ankle.

'You could have really hurt yourself and the baby. You need cold water on that foot.'

Ruby knew Leon was being aggressive with her because she was in the wrong. It was she who had forgotten about the milk heating on the stove. Joel was screaming again by now, and Leon began to do what he could to calm the child.

Ruby breathed a sigh of relief. 'I shouldn't have gone inside his room . . .'

'Don't be foolish! Don't make excuses for him. He's at fault, not you. You were probably worrying about that and so forgot about the milk. I'll make a bottle for Joel. He sounds ravenous. How's your foot?'

Her foot, dry now but red and painful, was the least of Ruby's worries.

'I'm all right.' But she was lying.

The highly charged atmosphere in the house was getting to her and to Joel.

'Shall I telephone for a doctor?'

Ruby shook her head. 'They have far more serious things to attend to than this.' She examined her hand. 'Richard's going to be in a right mood this evening,' she said softly.

She was scared. That one moment's thoughtlessness had hurt her. She'd get over the scald, it wasn't serious, but what if it had been Joel who had been hurt? In that moment Ruby knew she had to get away from this house before something really bad happened.

Leon looked at the redness on her hand and foot. She wriggled her toes, knowing she was fine, and Leon returned her baby to her while he made tea, milk for Joel and then cleaned the floor. Ruby hummed to Joel, soothing his restlessness. Leon passed her the freshly made baby's milk in the bottle, then began making toast.

'I'm going out for a while. I need to get away to clear my head.' Ruby stared at Leon. She looked down at Joel, who was pulling on the rubber teat, his eyes wide and anxious. Ruby realized she was shaking with emotion.

'A good idea,' Leon said. 'I think at last the weather's broken. I'll come with you.'

She shook her head. 'I need to think,' she said. She'd go to the woodland near Stoke's Bay. While she realized Marge wouldn't be at the caravan because she'd be at work, Nan would be at home and it would cheer her up to chat with the old lady.

Well wrapped up against the cold and with a spare bottle of milk for Joel and a change of clothes and nappies in a bag slung over her shoulder, Ruby left the house.

Leon waved to her from the window, after admonishing her to be careful and warning her to return before five o'clock when Richard came home. Ruby couldn't face an inquisition from Richard, so she promised Leon she wouldn't be late.

She refrained from telling him where she was going.

Stepping carefully on the icy pavements, her plan was to stay with Nan for a while and chat, then catch the bus down to Gosport. Tied in a handkerchief in her pocket, Ruby had brought all her money with her. She still had the five-pound note given to her by Mervyn and cash left from her wages that she'd saved as well as the money sent to her from Joe for their bottom drawer.

There was plenty for bus fares and cups of tea, and later if she needed it she could pay for a bed and breakfast. Maybe Marge might offer to put her up? Or if she stayed in the caravan she could pay Marge rent, until she decided what to do next.

Her foot and hand pained her, but they'd soon heal. She

could feel the heat from Joel's body through the shawl and it was comforting. She walked slowly, watching the icy pavement carefully in case she should stumble. A sharp wind had risen and it made the day seem even colder. There was little point in waiting at a bus stop because during the day the bus she needed came hourly. In that time she could easily walk to the caravan hidden in the woods.

'Good morning.' An elderly gentleman with a dog tipped his hat to her.

For a moment she wondered if he knew her, if he would tell Richard she'd left the house. She told herself not to be silly. It was simply a man out walking his dog, being polite. Being indoors for such a long time had narrowed her outlook on life.

The cold on her cheeks was invigorating. Her child slept snug and warm and she took a deep breath of the chilly air. Now a drizzle had begun to hasten the thaw. She looked up into the sky and saw it was a gun-metal grey, full of ominously bad weather. She hoped she'd reach the warmth of Marge's caravan before the heavens opened.

Ruby looked down and smiled. Joel had opened his eyes. Big blue circles stared up at her, trusting her to do the right thing. Yet what was the right thing to do?

Ruby knew Leon understood. If he had any sense he would leave Richard.

What made a person stay with someone who was cruel to them? She knew the answer to that. Leon loved Richard. He would stay because he believed all the rows and punches meant that Richard cared enough to chastise him when things weren't to his satisfaction. Ruby didn't believe love was cruel. Surely it was forgiving? If you loved someone didn't you want what was best for them?

Joel was making tiny sucking noises with his perfectly shaped lips. She wondered what Joe's mother would make of her grandson. Emily Stark couldn't say Joel didn't belong to Joe. The baby was a tiny replica of her son, with his large eyes and curly dark hair.

Joel's eyes closed again. The gentle jogging in her arms had lulled him to sleep once more. There was little early morning traffic, the pavement had disappeared and she was now walking close to the side of the road.

Now that she was away from the houses, Ruby could hear the sea. Across the road, the field looked magical covered in a thin layer of white. The snow didn't seem so heavy here. On the leafless trees, tiny buds were promising new growth. Holly bushes were glossy and green. Ruby saw ahead the small road that led eventually to the clearing and began to cross over.

'Watch it, missus!' The deep voice rumbled in the still air, followed by a bicycle bell, shrill and insistent.

Ruby stepped back. An automatic response to the policeman wearing a cape, riding his bicycle, who had swerved to avoid her.

'Watch where you're going!' He was wobbling on the seat of his bike and staring back at her as he carried on down the road towards Lee-on-the-Solent.

'Sorry! Sorry!' she called out. He put out a hand and waved as he rode onwards.

'How stupid am I?' she enquired of Joel, oblivious, asleep. 'I'm thinking so much I'm not watching where I'm walking!'

Trees were high on either side of the lane, which was little more than a wide path. Ruby could see the pebbly beach and the barbed wire. Underfoot, the grass was crisp where it hadn't been trodden down. She knew soon she would come upon the clearing and she began to feel excited.

But when she came upon the space where she thought the mobile caravan should be, the earth was frozen and blackened, partly covered with snow. Trees were devoid of branches where it looked like they had been burned, and there was a smell of singed wood in the air. Then she noticed pieces of charred wood scattered about. They were snow-encrusted, but it was obvious that a sizeable fire had taken place here. Ruby looked about her, walking further into the undergrowth. She was unsure if this was where the caravan had stood. Yet common sense told her that the home which had once stood here was now gone, burned out. She leaned against the trunk of a tree.

What had happened here? More importantly, where were Marge's family?

'You all right, miss?'

Ruby looked about for the voice. It was the policeman. He was pushing his bicycle and walking towards her with a worried look on his face.

'When I saw you turn in this way I thought I'd take a look-see. No one's been here since the fire . . .'

Ruby saw he was a fatherly figure, so she felt easy in his company. As he stood beside her she could smell peppermints.

'I don't know anything about a fire . . .'

'Bad business that. A while ago now.' He peered at her.

'The family who lived in the caravan, where are they?'

The man frowned. 'You really don't know what happened?' Ruby shook her head. Her heart was thudding against her chest. How could this terrible thing have happened? Why had news of the fire been kept from her?

'Three people died . . .'

Ruby gasped. The policeman leant his cycle against a tree,

stepped forward and pulled her and Joel to the safety of his warm cape as her knees began to buckle.

'Who?' began Ruby.

'The young woman's all right, but her children and the old woman died . . .'

'Where is she?' She had to see Marge. She pulled away. Ruby had to find out why she'd been kept in the dark about this awful thing.

'I believe the young woman is living in the town. Haven't seen hide nor hair of her though, she went to a pub, the Point of—'

'No Return?' finished Ruby for him. He studied her as she asked, 'What time's the next bus into town?' Ruby knew she had to get to Gosport, had to find Marge.

He looked at his pocket watch. 'Should be one along in the next ten minutes.

'I'll walk back and wait with you to see you safely on the bus. You look like you've had a shock. I don't want to leave you on your own with the baby in this godforsaken place.'

Ruby stared at him gratefully. 'Thanks,' she said. 'I'd appreciate you walking me to the stop.'

There were questions going round and round in her head. How could Nan and those beautiful children be dead? But Ruby knew the only person who would tell her the truth was

Marge. She stood close to the man, glad of his nearness, but she couldn't ask him a thing. If she did speak, she knew she would cry.

When the green Hants and Dorset bus trundled along the road, her escort helped her on board. She realized the reason she hadn't seen or heard from Marge was because she was nursing her own terrible grief. Ruby willed the bus to go faster so she could get to her friend.

Chapter Thirty-Three

'Where's she gone?'

Richard's voice was harsh. His eyes had narrowed and his face looked dark and cruel. Leon could smell the alcohol on his breath. Richard was late. He'd obviously stopped off somewhere before coming home. It was dark outside.

Leon took a deep breath. He'd spent the day tidying the house and preparing a meal, hoping that Richard would come home with a smile on his face. Every time he'd heard a noise outside he'd prayed it was Ruby returning. Now he watched as Richard lurched down the hallway to his workroom. Once inside, Richard poured whisky into a tumbler from the bottle on his desk.

He offered a drink to Leon, who shook his head.

'She went out earlier, I wouldn't be surprised to see her come back any time now.'

Richard glared at him. 'Don't try to soft-soap me. Are you hiding something from me?'

'Why would I do that?'

'I think you've a soft spot for her . . .'

'Don't be silly.' Leon pulled on his arm. 'Come back into the kitchen and have a meal with me. I've kept it all ready—'

Richard pushed his hand away and drank from the glass.

'Don't have any more . . .' Leon pleaded.

'If I want to drink, I will.'

Richard threw out an arm. Unfortunately, the whisky splashed from the glass down Leon's shirt. Leon turned away in disgust, but Richard had already seen the look on his face and it angered him.

'Who the fuck d'you think you are to tell me what to do in my own house?'

He threw his glass against the wall, where it shattered and the remains of the alcohol dripped down the wall.

Leon moved out of Richard's reach.

Richard's eyes looked Leon up and down. 'I won't have you telling me what to do.'

Leon's face crumpled. Now Richard had started taunting him he was unlikely to stop. Richard didn't seem to be able to help himself, he knew how easily hurt Leon could be.

'I picked you up – a bloody beach bum boy from Southsea – and gave you a home . . .'

He got no further, for again, waving his arms about, he stumbled against the table. Leon put out a hand to steady him. 'Get the fuck away from me!' Richard swore.

Leon tried to snatch the bottle from the desk, but he wasn't quick enough and Richard grabbed at it, swigging from its neck as though it was water. Then he threw the bottle across the room, laughing as Leon cowered.

'I'm going out to bring that cow back,' he mumbled. 'She'll be down the bar in the town. If she shouts off her mouth about what's been going on here between me and you I could lose my job. Where would my pretty boy be then?' Richard's voice was slurred. He lurched past Leon, knocking him aside. He didn't bother to reclaim his overcoat but walked unevenly to the front door. Cold air charged in as Richard swept out to the car. After a couple of false starts the engine purred into action. He left Leon nursing his pride.

As Richard drove past the Criterion picture house his wheels clipped the pavement.

He shouted an expletive but didn't slow, carrying on down Forton Road towards the ferry. The steady rain didn't help.

He had a thumping headache. Parking with difficulty, he

left the car by the kerb, its rear end pointing out into the street, and staggered from the vehicle towards the Point of No Return. The road was empty, not only of traffic, but also of people. The shops and the many public houses that lined Gosport's High Street were closed.

Richard banged at the door of the Point, but to no avail. The front of the pub was in darkness. Richard hoped to persuade Ruby to come home with him to Vectis Road. That was if she was there.

His memory of the look on Leon's face as he'd pushed past him was haunting him. Why on earth had all that hatred and rubbish spilled from Richard's lips into the ears of the only person he had ever really cared about, beyond himself?

Even more, he despised himself for hurting Leon. It had been a terrible thing to have done to the talented boy.

Again Richard hit the door. Above, a light showed faintly in one of the bedrooms. Had it been on before? He was too befuddled to think properly.

Of course, Ruby could be anywhere. But Richard thought that sooner or later she'd end up here. This pub was the one place that he'd tried to keep her from. Living with him as his wife showed the people of Gosport he was a decent man, a husband, someone who'd married her to do right by her. He'd tried to keep the truth from her of his double life, but she wasn't stupid. If she started talking about their domestic arrangements, he could lose everything. And probably gain a prison sentence! Again, his fist hit the sturdy door. No one answered.

'Only another half-hour, mate, can't your thirst wait that long?' the elderly man with the scruffy dog shouted at him from across the road. He had his collar turned up against the rain.

Richard swore at him. In his pocket was a half-bottle of whisky he could finish any time he wanted. He wondered if he could get inside the pub around the back. His head was thumping badly. His own fault for his greediness in swallowing whisky like it was going out of fashion.

At the side of the pub, near the alley, he saw that the chute doors were unlocked. He smiled to himself. Surprisingly, he also yawned. The lack of sleep due to the baby crying and, of course, the alcohol, had made him weary. If he could get inside the pub and Ruby was in there, surely Mervyn would understand a man's need to drag his wife back home where she belonged?

He hauled up the heavy trapdoor and saw the metal slide that the barrels rolled down. No doubt there was an inner door leading to the bar somewhere in the cellar. He could smell the cool interior and the stench of beer and hops.

Richard, feet first, gave himself enough room to slide into the hatchway, then he let the heavy wooden door set in the pavement close behind him. He didn't expect the chute to be so slippery and he slid, tumbling drunkenly to the bottom, knocking his head against the wooden side of the chute. By the time he'd rolled in a shapeless heap onto the floor, the pain, the whisky and his exhaustion caused him to black out into unconsciousness.

Joe was walking down the Avenue at Alverstoke. He didn't want to think about the pain he was experiencing in his shoulder. The decision he'd made this morning was that he wasn't going to close his eyes tonight to sleep without first finding answers to where Ruby was and what the hell was going on. He'd been out all day. Darkness had fallen. The light wind brushed against his cheeks, cold and sharp, accentuating the rain. In his pocket was the address in Vectis Road of that writer chap, Richard Williams.

'Wait until tomorrow, lad,' his father had pleaded. 'You can have my van then. It'll make it easier for you.' His father had gone to Southampton to replenish his stocks of contraband from the American stores. Joe, however, was determined to find out the truth. Ruby had married Richard Williams. Married!

Why would she marry him? To marry someone you must have feelings for them. He'd believed her when she said she loved him, but if she hadn't lied to him that night beneath the stars, and he didn't believe she had, why hadn't he had answers to his letters and why had she married another man?

Joe's heart was heavy. Having come from the Point of No Return, he'd had to physically brush unbidden tears away after talking to Marge. That's if you could call the few words they'd exchanged talking. Where was that vibrant cocky little girl that had been his Ruby's closest friend?

When he'd entered the pub, Mervyn had clasped him to his body like a long-lost son. 'After talking to your dad, I've been waiting for you to appear, lad, but you got to know how lies get mixed in with the truth. Marge hasn't seen hide nor hair of Ruby.'

Mervyn had tried to put him off talking to Marge. Joe could understand why now.

She was withdrawn and sullen and couldn't get over why Ruby hadn't been to see her after the fire had taken Nan and her two children. Joe held her hand, which was practically skin and bone, and agreed there had to be something more going on.

Why hadn't Ruby come when her friend needed her?

He was appalled by what had happened out there in the

woods. Like Mervyn, he hoped Marge would forgive herself for what was, after all, a terrible accident.

Marge had to move on with her life.

'I believed Ruby and I had something special. Why did she stop writing to me? Why did she feel she couldn't share what was going on in her life with me?

'I prayed for letters from her and I wrote as often as I could.'

Marge had stared at him. 'But she was always writing to you! She was devastated not to hear from you.'

Joe had sat down on the edge of the bed in Marge's room and cupped his head in his hands. It doesn't make sense, he thought. It just doesn't add up.

Mervyn had put his hand on Joe's shoulder to comfort him. Joe winced.

'You shouldn't have left the hospital until they'd given you the all-clear . . .'

'Mervyn, I can't go on not knowing. Especially with her being so near to having the baby. I couldn't just sit around waiting for my shoulder to heal properly.'

Marge interrupted. 'Joe, Ruby never put a foot wrong.'

'But she's married another bloke! Being in another country and not knowing whether I was going to be alive the next day didn't stop me feeling angry when letters from my mum told me she was out having a good time. I didn't mind that, why should I? But I was told there were other men. And listening to snippets of conversation from Sylvie who always seemed to want to say something derogatory about Ruby's actions . . .'

'Sylvie was like a viper in the nest. You've heard what happened to her and how she left with my money?' Mervyn voice had risen.

'Sylvie's one of those people who'd fall in a cesspit and come up with a rose in her mouth,' said Marge.

Mervyn said, 'You and Ruby have both been through a great deal together.

'But I've not been as charitable as I should have been towards the girl.' He looked at Marge. 'I wish to God I'd allowed her to stay here when she told me she had nowhere else to go.' He frowned at Joe. 'That's the only reason she went to live with that bloody writer chap, weren't no funny business, she was going to be his housekeeper, you know?'

'Housekeeper, I can understand. Why marry him? And it still doesn't alter the fact that she's out there somewhere and doesn't want to be found. Maybe she's already had my son or daughter. I've got to find her.'

Marge reached across and kissed him on the cheek. 'Go and find her, Joe, and bring her back here to me.' She looked at Mervyn. 'To us,' she added.

And now he was walking through Alverstoke's suburbs,

determined to find another piece to the puzzle of what had happened to the girl he loved.

Or was he simply angry because he'd been deceived?

If she'd married this writer bloke, who was he to interfere? Ruby wasn't the first girl Joe had made love to, but she was the only one he'd loved.

He was the first man who'd touched her. His mind was in a turmoil and the aggravating pain he was experiencing certainly didn't help.

Could he love her as wholeheartedly as before, knowing she'd slept in another man's arms, been touched by him? He couldn't get it out of his head that she'd actually married Richard Williams. Why would she do that if she loved him?

When he found her, if she told him she'd married Richard Williams because she loved him, after falling out of love with Joe, he'd bow out gracefully. He'd like contact with his child but he'd leave Ruby in peace to enjoy her life.

He still couldn't shake off the feeling that something was wrong, though.

The lack of letters was at the bottom of everything. Marge said Ruby had written. Surely she wouldn't lie about a thing like that? And it still didn't answer the question of why his letters hadn't got through to Ruby.

So what had he found out so far?

Ruby had been pregnant, homeless and jobless.

She'd asked his mother for a home and been refused. His mother hadn't believed the child was his because there'd been gossip. Ruby, destitute, had become a housekeeper. All that made sense. Then she had married. Given up house-keeping for the writer bloke and married him. She must have loved him, she must!

If only he had been here in England. Maybe he could have prevented things going the way they had.

Joe stood outside the house in Vectis Road and watched for signs of life. He knocked hard. From inside came the strains of a popular song being played on the piano. He knocked again. The music eventually stopped and Joe was pleased when he heard footsteps coming towards him.

The door opened and a good-looking young man stood there.

Joe took a deep breath, 'I'm looking for Ruby—'

He got no further before the man interrupted, 'Has something happened to her?'

Surely this couldn't be the writer chap? Joe had been told the man was older.

'I hope not,' Joe said. 'Where is she?'

The young man had the remnants of bruising on his face. He was staring at Joe.

'She went out earlier. She's not back yet. Look, I have to go.' He went to close the door.

Joe blocked the door with his foot. 'I'm asking you one more time, where is she?'

'She went out to see her friend who lives in a caravan. That's what I think, anyway.'

'Don't be bloody daft, mate! Did she really say that was where she was going?'

'Not exactly, but I can't think where else she would have gone as she was walking with the baby . . .'

'The baby?'

'Little boy. This awful weather kept her inside.'

Joe felt tears near the surface of his eyes. So he was father to a little boy! His heart began to swell with pride. All kinds of questions moved around his brain. Why hadn't she been to see Marge? And more importantly why was she going to a caravan that wasn't there?

'Look, I've got to go inside.'

Joe didn't see the point in stopping him shutting the door. The young man seemed ill at ease, nervous. Joe turned away. At least he was a little nearer to finding Ruby. She definitely was living in this house. He could come back later.

He glanced back at the size of the place. He could see why Richard Williams needed a housekeeper.

The young man's face had told Joe he knew nothing of the tragic fire. It was surprising how much information had been exchanged in so little time.

Joe walked down to where he'd been told Marge's caravan had stood.

He had no expectation of Ruby being there, but he was determined to leave no stone unturned.

It was wet underfoot, and dark, but the moon had decided to show her face so that Joe was able to find the scene of the tragedy. He could smell the bitterness of the burnt trees and bushes.

Joe said a little prayer inside his head, for of course he remembered the kiddies and the old lady. His heart ached for Marge, remembering her thin face as he'd left the pub.

'Two visitors in one day, I don't bally well believe it.'

The voice startled Joe. Then he made out the caped figure of a copper pushing a bike with a very weak front light in the gloom.

'I heard you can get picked up by the police for not having a suitable front lamp,' he said. The policeman laughed.

'I suppose you're going to tell me you're looking for the young woman with the baby?'

'I am,' Joe said. 'Obviously you've seen my Ruby? But how did you guess that?'

'Oh, her and I talked, not much, mind. Besides, you don't get many visitors to this place, and two in one day? I put her on the bus to the ferry. You haven't seen a little mongrel dog around on your travels? One of my Lee-on-the-Solent old ladies left her front door open and her pet's wandered.'

Joe shook his head. Then he walked over to him, took his arm and pumped his hand. 'That's the best news I've had all day, that you've seen my girl. When was this?'

'A while ago. She was upset. She knew nothing about the fire or the deaths . . .'

'No, both me and her seem to be like mushrooms, stuck in the dark about things. Was she all right?'

'Tired and cold and looking for her mate, the girly who'd lived in the van here. Can I do anything to help? I was just riding on my rounds and looking for Mrs John's Laddie when I heard you charging about like a bull in a china shop.'

'No, I'm fine, and all the better now I've heard where she was headed.'

'If you're off to catch the bus, I'll step along with you,' the policeman said.

'You home on leave?'

'Sort of,' Joe answered. 'Thanks for helping her.' They walked together companionably towards the main road, the rain beginning to ease.

Chapter Thirty-Four

Ruby had walked along the High Street, glad to be on familiar territory. Her arms ached from carrying her precious bundle. She was amazed that Joel had barely whimpered all the time they'd been out. Was it the cold fresh air? Or was he sleeping because there was no bad atmosphere keeping him awake? He could probably do with a nappy change, but in another few moments she'd be at the Point of No Return. She couldn't change him in the cold street.

She was excited, yet worried about seeing Marge. How was she coping without her children and her nan? Why hadn't Richard told her about the fire?

Inside her head the question answered itself. If Ruby had heard about the fire she'd have gone immediately to be with Marge. Richard hadn't wanted that. Had Leon known? Somehow, she didn't think so. There was a rapport between her and Leon and she was sure he would have confided in her. Ruby was beginning to believe that Richard had gone to great lengths to keep secrets from her, all in case she inadvertently spilled the beans about his homosexuality. A lifestyle that he'd tried so hard to keep from her.

How simple-minded she must appear to him. Would she have cared if he'd told her the truth, that he'd married her to protect himself? No, she wouldn't have minded at all. It would have been a relief that he never expected her to share a bed, like a proper husband and wife.

Happiness had to be grabbed with both hands and held on to as tightly as possible. There wasn't that much love in the world that it should be discarded simply because that love was between a couple of the same sex.

The law was an ass, thought Ruby. In the future surely it might be possible to openly show love to whoever you wanted? Richard had given her a home and her son a name. She would always be grateful for that. She would keep his secret. And that secret included Leon. Leon had been especially kind to her.

Ruby stopped in the doorway of Burton's Tailoring to adjust the shawl about Joel's head. It was raining and she was pleased, as the rain would help the ice to melt further. Who would have thought the weather could make her a prisoner? It wasn't only Richard who had been her jailer.

Ruby didn't want to go back to Vectis Road to live. Perhaps if Marge was staying with Mervyn, it might just be possible that he would allow her to spend the night with Marge.

She had enough clothing and milk to last Joel overnight. If Mervyn said she couldn't stay, she could buy herself one night's bed and breakfast, either at the Black Bear or the scruffy little café on the corner of North Street, the Central Café.

She had enough money to tide her over for a while. After that she would think again.

Sylvie came to mind. Ruby wondered if she was writing to Joe. Had Joe ever received any of the letters Ruby had written?

She knew she'd lost him for good now. If he came back from the war he wouldn't want anything to do with her. She was a married woman.

Wherever he was, she hoped he was safe. Jesus, would this war never end?

She crossed the road. She could hear wireless music coming from the Point.

Sadness caught at her heart. If only the clock could be turned backwards!

She mentally chastised herself. She couldn't imagine life

without her beautiful boy; he was all she had left of the love of her life, her Joe.

Her heart felt as though it was a caged bird fluttering to be released from her chest as she managed to push open the door and step inside to be enveloped in the familiar fug of cigarette smoke and beer fumes. The heat hit her like an old warm overcoat. Should she enter the bar or should she go through to the kitchen where Mervyn might be?

Her decision was made for her as a door opened and Mervyn stepped in front of her.

The look of pure joy on his face told her she'd done the right thing in coming back. Then she saw Mervyn was crying!

'Oh, my love. It's like looking at an angel,' he said, crushing her and the child in his brawny arms. He stepped back and took Joel. Ruby relinquished her prize, amazed and delighted that he was pleased to see her.

'Where's Marge?'

Mervyn was already on the stairs. 'Come with me.'

Every familiar step brought further hope to her, but outside a room Mervyn stopped, handed back her baby and whispered, 'She's not like she used to be.'

Ruby thought Mervyn looked a shadow of his former self, but his happiness at seeing her was genuine.

At first Ruby wasn't sure who the thin girl sitting in the chair by the window was. As the young woman turned, she said, 'Ruby?' The girl came towards her and she saw the unmistakable signs of joy spread over Marge's gaunt face. 'I've missed you.' Then her eyes settled on the bundle in Ruby's arms. 'Is this . . .?'

'Joel,' finished Ruby for her. 'I've missed you an' all.'

Marge put out her arms, gathering Ruby in a huge cuddle and Ruby promptly burst into tears. 'I didn't know,' was all she said.

She was aware of the door closing and a male voice mumbling 'Tea' and then she was alone with her baby and Marge.

The muffled voice from Marge could barely be heard as the bundle was taken from her arms. 'Oh, God, Ruby, he's so beautiful!'

Marge was now engrossed in sitting with the baby in her lap, unwrapping his many layers. 'Ruby! When did you last change him?'

Ruby let her bag slip to the carpet and kicked it towards Marge. Now she was warming up, the pain from her foot and hand was reminding her it existed.

'I been too busy trying to find you to worry about that,' she said. 'Anyway, it would have freezed his little whatsit off to change his nappy outside in the cold.'

The throaty laugh from Marge reminded Ruby of good times gone by.

Already Marge was undressing the little boy, exposing his rounded limbs and all the while talking to him and exclaiming over him to Ruby. Unused to all this sudden attention, Joel began to cry and this made Marge laugh harder, but it was laughter tinged with sadness that she wouldn't hear the same cry from Chrissie ever again.

'Hungry, he's hungry,' she said. 'I'd know that cry anywhere. Have you a bottle? Or are you feeding him?'

Ruby foraged in the bag. The wrapped bottle of milk was stone cold. Before Marge had time to call for Mervyn, he opened the door, arriving with steaming cups of tea on a tray. Without a word, still with the same daft smile on his face, he took the cold milk and closed the door again.

'I didn't know—' began Ruby, but Marge hushed her. 'We can talk properly later,' she said. 'I'm so glad you're here. Can I give him his bottle?' Ruby managed to answer her barrage of questions and even get some in of her own. It wasn't long before Mervyn returned and Marge leaned forward, took the bottle and tested the milk on her wrist, then happily began to feed the child.

Mervyn picked up the wet discarded nappy and motioned for Ruby to follow him outside the bedroom.

'I haven't seen Marge with so much energy since before the accident,' he said. 'You don't know what it means to have the two of you here. I can see we're going to be discussing things well into the night. Do you have to return home soon?'

Ruby took a deep breath. 'I'd appreciate it if I could stay here tonight.'

'I wouldn't have it any other way,' Mervyn said quickly.

'Richard might come looking for me. I really don't want to see him.'

'I won't tell him you're here,' he said. She saw him frown with the knowledge that there was more she hadn't told him. Then, 'Are you hungry?'

Ruby said, 'I'm starving.' He looked pleased at her reply. 'If you eat, perhaps Marge will eat along with you.'

'I'd like nothing more than that,' Ruby said. Mervyn looked as if he was about to say something, but then he clammed up.

'What's the matter?'

She saw him frown again. Then he shook his head and said, 'It's nothing, love. Why don't you go back in that room and stay with Marge.

'You're doing her a power of good and that's what she needs.' He looked sheepish.

'You know how much I care about her, don't you?'

Ruby grabbed at his hand. 'Of course—'

Mervyn interrupted her. 'At this moment in time, I'd do anything for you and your little one.' Ruby breathed a sigh of relief. Tonight, she didn't have to go back to Vectis Road, and tomorrow could look after itself.

'There is something,' she said. 'Can you get hold of some National Dried Milk? I didn't bring enough.'

Mervyn threw his arms about her. 'For what you've done, I could get you the bloody moon!'

He slipped back downstairs. He had customers to serve. Grace was already in the bar; the punters liked her easy banter, but she couldn't work alone during the busiest part of the evening.

Frank Sinatra was singing on the wireless. Later, Mervyn thought, when they'd all eaten a meal, he would tell Ruby that Joe was safe and looking for her.

Maybe he should have already told her? But he didn't want anything to spoil either girl's happiness at finding each other once more. Yes, he decided, let Marge have her fill of Ruby before he gave Ruby the good news. He wondered what her story was. Why had she come here now?

He must get hold of some baby milk. Organize a meal for the girls.

'Pour us a pint, Mervyn,' said Ol' Tom. 'I'm dyin' of thirst here!'

'Coming straight up,' said Mervyn, feeling happier than he'd felt in ages. 'In fact, have it on me!'

Mervyn was in the bar alone, wiping out the last of the ashtrays, when he heard a knocking on the window and looked over to see Joe's face peering in. He threw down the cloth and hurried to the main door. 'Come in, lad,' he said. 'I suppose you know your Ruby's here? And your son?' He stood aside so Joe could enter.

Mervyn saw how tired he was. His hunched shoulder told of the pain he was in, but at his words Joe's face lit up like a Christmas tree.

'Thank God they're here,' he said. 'I got no proper answer at Vectis Road; I've been hunting everywhere.'

Mervyn could feel the excitement coming from the young man. But his heart sank. If Marge and Ruby were still in the throes of gossiping upstairs, the happiness of Marge could soon dissipate when Joe saw Ruby and his son. Why, he could even take Ruby away from the Point!

Mervyn decided that first he could at least ask Joe for the biggest favour he would ever ask of him. He poured

Joe a half pint and some beer for himself and bade Joe be comfortable on a bar stool.

'She was in a bit of a state when she got here, mate. But she's eaten and with Marge's help, the little one's been looked after. She talks constantly of you now she knows you've left the hospital and are safe, and if I live to be a hundred I'll never be able to thank Ruby enough for the change she's brought to Marge.'

Joe leaned over and put his rough hand on Mervyn's arm. 'Spit it out, mate, what are you trying to say?'

Mervyn took a deep breath. 'I'm asking if you'd postpone seeing your girl just a while longer? I need you to go home and ask your dad for some baby milk for your kiddie. If there's any to be had, Lennie can get hold of it, though it's more than likely he's already got a stack somewhere. Ruby doesn't want to go back to Vectis Road. She hasn't said why, an' I'm not pushing her for answers.'

He saw the stricken look on Joe's face.

'Now wait a minute, old man. Do you realize what you're asking of me?' Joe slid from the stool and stepped uncomfortably from one foot to the other. 'I haven't seen the girl I love for ages, she's had my child and you are asking me to come back another time?'

Mervyn saw the anger in Joe's face and the incredulity

in his eyes. He might once have boxed for a living, but he knew he was certainly no match for this young soldier who so desperately wanted to see Ruby.

'It's for your son, Joe.' He thought for a moment. 'Take my van if you want.' Joe was about to speak when a voice cut into their conversation.

'Hello, Joe.'

Mervyn saw the couple looking at each other as though there was no one else in the room. Then Ruby seemed to snap out of it and said to Mervyn, 'Marge is asleep with Joel. If a bomb dropped on that bedroom, heaven forbid, she wouldn't wake.'

Mervyn saw the happiness leap into Joe's eyes as Ruby came towards them. She wore his dressing gown, which swamped her small figure. She'd bathed and washed her hair. She looked like a fragile child. He knew it was time to leave.

'Don't forget that dried milk, National Dried,' he grumbled good-naturedly.

Then he heard himself saying, 'Ruby's staying the night and I daresay I can find a bed for you as well, Joe.' Then he left them.

'I don't know whether to sit with you or run errands,' Joe said.

He wanted to enfold her in his arms, but something held him back. This was the girl he loved, the woman who'd borne his child. He been looking for her, found her, and now was at a loss what to say to her. Without being able to stop himself he blurted out the first words that made sense in his head.

'Why did you marry him?'

'Come and sit down,' Ruby said. She sat down on a bar stool and Joe sat down beside her. He could smell the soapy freshness of her.

He listened while she told him she'd been devastated to discover she was homeless, pregnant and very frightened.

'Somehow I seemed to have obtained a bad reputation. I was a pariah. The only friend I had was Marge and she had problems of her own that I didn't want to add to . . .'

'I've heard that, but why marry him?'

He wasn't brushing away the awfulness of her life, but he wanted her to get to what he considered the crux of the matter. To think of her in bed with another man was killing him. To think of her saying, 'I love you' to someone else was cutting him in two.

She sighed and fastened the large dressing gown over her knees, where it had slipped back, exposing her legs. There was a red mark which was almost a blush, covering her foot.

So too he noticed a similar mark on her hand. She was also wearing Mervyn's slippers. They looked ridiculously big on her small feet.

'I hadn't heard from you. This is no excuse, but even though in the bottom of my heart I knew you loved me, people were telling me you were like your dad. "The apple doesn't fall far from the tree," was something said to me more than once.'

He opened his mouth to protest, thought better of it and listened.

'Maybe I was still in shock from losing my mum, maybe I just wanted someone to help me, I don't know.' She paused, moved strands of damp hair from her face and he thought how delicate her wrists were. 'I wrote and kept on writing. I poured out my heart to you in those letters. You were writing to your mum, but when you stopped enclosing little letters for me I guessed it was all over between us.

'It was like you went off the face of the earth, until I heard via Gosport's jungle drums you'd been phoning Sylvie . . .'

Now Joe couldn't help himself. 'I was looking for you. When I got back from Holland, I couldn't get hold of you. She answered the phone . . . I always—'

'You want me to go on or not?'

'Sorry,' he said. 'I just wanted to explain.'

She nodded understandingly. 'Richard came up with the offer of a job, a housekeeper. He was kind to me, Joe.'

Joe turned his head away. He didn't want to look in her eyes or at her face when she told him how living with the bloke had turned into love.

'I got to thinking how it would be after the baby was born. I was trapped. I'd never get a job, a place to live, people were going to point their fingers at me and call my little one a bastard. I was really down about it all. When Richard mentioned marriage, I jumped at it.' She paused. 'I told him I didn't care for him, not in that way. He said it would solve problems to have me as his wife, he'd lost his mum, you see . . .' Again she paused. 'It was a marriage of convenience so that I could hold my head high once more.' Ruby put her hand to her forehead. He saw her shoulders rise and fall with emotion. He wanted more than anything to hold her, tell her everything would be all right. He held back. Thoughts of intimacies between them. Of her touching another man. It was as if he had an open wound and someone was pushing in a knife and turning it.

'But, marriage?' He slid from the stool and began pacing up and down the bar.

He looked at her, she was staring at him, her cheeks wet with tears.

This wasn't how it should be between them. He dismissed the notion that she was lying to him, because he'd known her all his life and never known her to tell an untruth.

'How do you feel about him now?'

She looked surprised at his question. He sat back again on the stool and picked up a beer mat, turning it in his fingers.

'I'm not happy. I never expected to be. But it's not something I want any more, staying with him. I've discovered lies, things he's kept from me . . .' She paused. 'I never found out until today about the fire.'

Joe was irritated, he didn't want to talk about Marge; his own problems with Ruby were uppermost in his head.

'Has something happened in Paradise?' His voice was sarcastic. He saw he'd hurt her.

'Yes, something's happened. That's why I'm here and not at home in Alverstoke.'

'Ah, yes, home, Alverstoke, the big house in Vectis Road—'

'You don't know what you're talking about.' Her eyes had filled once more with tears and he longed to simply pull her towards him and tell her she needn't ever go back to Vectis Road, that he would look after her and everything would be all right. But he sat perfectly still, unable, unwilling to move, except to twist the beer mat backwards and forwards. Until bits of cardboard fell on the shiny surface of the bar.

Ruby took a deep breath. 'Why don't you go and see if you can get some food for your son?'

He couldn't believe it: she was dismissing him. He wanted to shout at her. Say how much she'd hurt him. He turned and walked from the bar, throwing the broken beer mat across the counter.

Chapter Thirty-Five

Ruby heard the front door of the pub slam shut. She sighed. This wasn't how things between them should have gone. There was a barrier and she didn't know how to break it down.

'Is everything all right?'

Marge came and sat down beside her. 'I heard raised voices. Joe's . . .'

Ruby tried to laugh things off. 'Oh, you know how men are.'

'He loves you, anyone can see that.'

'He's got a funny way of showing it.'

Marge put her hand over Ruby's. 'It's a lot for him to take in; me too. I never thought you'd tie the knot with Richard Williams.'

'I did it because it seemed like the best way to get out of a bad situation.'

Ruby didn't want to talk about a marriage that wasn't a marriage. She knew then that she would say nothing about the love affair between Richard and Leon. It would be on her conscience for ever if she hurt Leon, who'd been almost like a brother to her. As for Richard? He'd delivered what he'd promised.

'I don't want to go back to him,' she added.

'Now we're getting somewhere,' said Marge. 'Has he been cruel to you?'

'Why d'you think that?'

'Because you're different . . .'

'I've had a child, I'm a mother, of course I'm different. I'm not going to talk about my life with him, but I will tell you he's a very possessive man who now makes life intolerable for me and for Joel.' She thought of her child sound asleep upstairs and how contented he'd seemed with Marge looking after him.

Ruby knew it was because the atmosphere here in the pub was totally different to the strained silences in the Alverstoke house. Joel deserved a happy home and somehow she'd find a way to give that to him.

'I'll suggest to Mervyn that you stay here. He'll be all for it, I know he will.'

Ruby looked at her friend. 'For a few days that would

be good, but nothing's changed from before. Mervyn's not running a nursery, he's running a pub.'

Marge's face fell. 'I want you to stay,' she said.

'For a little while, until I sort my head out, that would be great.'

Then she'd set the wheels in motion to leave Richard permanently. She hated that flavour of fear that had been her daily companion at Richard's house, but nevertheless the men's love affair was their business. She didn't want to be a scapegoat any longer.

'What about Joe?' Marge released Ruby's hand and tucked a stray lock of hair behind one of Ruby's ears.

'I think Joe's finding it hard to come to terms with what's happened to us both. We need to sit back a bit and find out if there's anything left between us.'

Marge looked horrified. 'But he loves you,' she said again.

'I think he's having a hard time remembering that,' said Ruby.

Joe shook the brown carrier bag containing the tinned milk. The box room upstairs, just like the shed in his mother's house, was packed to the rafters with contraband.

But then he'd never known his father to be anything else

but a wheeler and dealer and the war had provided ample opportunities for Lennie to make money.

Lennie and Emily had been out when Joe had arrived back at the house, so he hadn't had to explain why he was looking for dried milk.

He remembered the marks on Ruby's skin. A well of anger rose from deep inside him. If Richard Williams had laid one finger on Ruby . . . He shook away the thought. Until he knew for certain what the problems between them were, it wasn't his place to interfere between man and wife.

But husband or not, he'd kill the bloke if he had harmed her!

'You made a right mess of it.' His intense thoughts caused him to speak aloud.

He tried to remember Renata's words about war changing people. Had he wanted the Dutch girl, she would have slept with him, hadn't she said so? But it wasn't the woman he had desired, only the act of intercourse to make him feel wanted. It would have meant absolutely nothing to him at all. A comfort fuck, the lads would call it.

He didn't think for one minute that Ruby had loved Richard Williams.

But she'd married him. Again jealousy gnawed at him. Oh, he knew what was wrong with him. He hated it that his Ruby had been touched by another man. Now she was beyond his reach, a married woman. Whatever could he do about it?

He pulled his coat collar higher up his neck. The cold rain was seeping down his back.

His problem was whether he could bear to touch Ruby after she'd been handled by someone else. That was it, in a nutshell. He comforted himself by thinking most men would feel the same.

There was little point in begging her to come away with him if it wasn't going to work. And what about Joel?

He hated to think of his son being brought up by another man. He'd have to do something about that. Joel was his blood. That's if he ever got to meet him! He knew in his heart that he'd do anything for the boy. Like walking in the rain to provide his breakfast. He smiled. The walk had given him time to think. He was longing to see Joel, to hold him.

Just as he was longing to hold Ruby. To tell her he'd sort out whatever was worrying her. To tell her he loved her. He couldn't stop loving her. Love wasn't something you turned on and off like a tap. He couldn't bear to lose her again.

She'd married that Williams chap because there was no other way out of her predicament. And let's face it, he thought, Ruby would never have been in that predicament if it hadn't been for him! So what was going to happen now?

He'd better hope that when he saw her again he put himself in a better light, otherwise he would lose her for ever. Together – that was the word, together – they'd look at things rationally. And if she didn't want to tell him everything, he'd accept that. He smiled again – bit like the army, he thought, accepting things when you didn't know why you had to. Well, he'd simply wait until she felt able to unburden herself to him. Love was about trust. He thought again of Renata. He hoped when the war was finally over she'd be reunited with the man she loved. She deserved it.

Joe used the side door to get in, using the keys Mervyn had given him. He was wet through, but glad he'd walked instead of using Mervyn's van. He put his coat on the hook, went through to the kitchen and left the tins on the table. The carrier bag was soggy and had stuck to the blue and white tins. The place was quiet, and a dull landing light allowed him sight of the upstairs. He wondered whether he should bed down in the bar or use one of the guest rooms, as Mervyn had suggested.

He crept up the stairs and quietly opened the first door he came to. He focused on the two girls, asleep, between them a sleeping baby.

His heart swelled with emotion. That was his son, there, safe with his mother.

He stifled the desire to wake them, now wasn't the time.

He blinked back the wetness that had come unbidden to his eyes.

The room beyond the bathroom had its door open. He smiled, hearing a drawn-out snore from along the landing. Mervyn was a good bloke, he thought.

He pulled the door closed behind him and switched on the bedside lamp. He'd slept in foxholes, in tents, beneath trees and many nights he hadn't slept at all, because any moment he could have been blown up, killed. He thought of the letters he'd written to Ruby. She hadn't received them. Strange that his mother had received letters, though.

He knew he would sleep lightly. Just in case Richard Williams decided on a late-night visit, looking for his wife. He thought of the money he was due from the army. If he could persuade Ruby to help him look for a house . . . Joe finished rubbing his hair dry with the towel that had been left on the bed and climbed into the clean sheets.

He wasn't setting out to break up a marriage, but if Ruby would forgive him, allow him to make her happy . . .

The shouting woke Joe the following morning. Hauling on clothes as he descended the stairs, he found Mervyn trying to pull his braces on while opening up the side door. A blast of cold air enveloped him. One of the draymen burst into the hall. 'Oh, God, it's awful.'

The middle-aged man, eyes wild, stared about him. 'Get an ambulance, the coppers, anything. We just tipped the three barrels down. We just did what we're asked to do when the hatches are left unlocked . . .' He paused, clutching at Mervyn. 'We didn't know anyone was down there . . .'

Joe left him with Mervyn and stepped outside the door.

'Joe?' It was Ruby's voice.

The man yelled, 'No, don't you go in there!'

Joe reached the corner of the pub where the gaping mouth of the cellar was wide open, its doors laid back like two wooden floppy tongues. The horse was snorting heavily and Joe saw the wooden ramp leading from the cart to the cellar's open doors.

Several men were peering into the darkness. Joe pushed a man wearing a knapsack aside, and stared down. Mervyn, at his side, gasped.

'Take Ruby back inside,' he growled at Joe. She was almost upon them.

'It's her bloody husband. Must have fallen down the chute, and these daft buggers of draymen didn't bother to look.'

Joe leapt towards Ruby and pushed her back. It suddenly

occurred to him that she had no shoes on and her feet must be cold.

'Oh, Joe, is it really Richard? Is he hurt?'

Mervyn must have heard Ruby for he shouted back, 'Course I'm sure. Those wooden barrels weigh a bleedin' ton. He's not writing no more cowboy books . . .'

Marge, her face grey, was making tea. The drayman sat slumped at the kitchen table. Joe pushed Ruby towards a chair. 'Let the police deal with it,' he said.

One glance had told him the man was dead. 'I reckon the men need a drop of something more in that tea.'

'I'll get brandy from the bar,' Marge said. 'Then I'm going upstairs to take care of the baby. Joe, you look after Ruby.'

Joe stared at Ruby. She sat slumped like a rag doll, her eyes wide, her lips pressed in a straight line. He'd seen it before, that shocked look, on men in Holland.

Her body was trembling.

He knew she wasn't listening to him but he said quietly, 'I'm here, Ruby.'

Later, when the police had left and the body had been removed, Mervyn, Joe and Ruby were left in the kitchen. Ruby spoke.

'I must tell Leon. He'll have to be told.' Joe realized she

was still deeply shocked. He put out a hand as she struggled up from the table.

'Where are you going?'

'Upstairs,' she said. 'To my baby, it's not fair to leave Marge seeing to Joel.'

'Who's Leon?' Joe followed her.

Mervyn shouted, 'Marge can cope, it's doing her the power of good.'

Marge was in the bathroom, bathing the little boy in the sink.

'I hope you didn't mind, Rube. I heard him cry. I've made him a bottle.'

Joe watched Marge carefully soaping the little boy's hair. It was plastered to his head in dark curls. Joe felt his lips curve into a smile. 'He's not so little,' he said. He felt as though someone had reached into his body, taken out his heart and was squeezing it tightly. 'He's lovely,' he said. And immediately put his hand to his mouth in case he said anything else they thought was silly, but he couldn't take his eyes from the child, wriggling and kicking in Marge's capable hands.

'D'you want to take over?'

Joe wasn't sure if Marge was talking to him or Ruby, but as he realized Ruby was no longer at his side he said softly, 'No fear! I'd best go to her.'

Ruby was sitting on the dishevelled bed. He sat down beside her. Her fingers were working on the fringe of the bedspread, curling and uncurling the cotton.

'Look,' he said. 'I didn't wish that Richard any harm.'

He wanted to put his arm around her, touch her, will some of the energy from his body to flow into hers, because she'd become a shell of a person. But then who wouldn't?, he thought, she'd just found her husband dead.

'I have to tell Leon,' she repeated.

'I don't think you're in a fit state to go anywhere or see anyone . . .' he began.

'You don't understand . . .'

'Then tell me.'

Ruby got up and went into the bathroom where Marge was sitting on the stool, with Joel, partly dressed, lying in her arms and taking a bottle. The tins of food that had been left on the table downstairs had been discovered. The bathroom smelled of talcum powder.

'I need to go out, will you look after Joel?'

Marge looked at Ruby. 'Of course. But are you sure you need to leave?'

'There's something I have to do.'

Joe intervened. 'You're not leaving here on your own.

Where d'you want to go?' Joe didn't like the idea of her traipsing the streets on her own.

'Trust me, I'll be all right. I need to go to the house.'

'Get yourself dressed, then come downstairs.' He left the two women and found Mervyn putting a notice in the window telling customers he was closing for the day.

'It's the least I can do,' Mervyn said. 'He wasn't anything to me except a customer, but he was Ruby's husband.'

Joe said, 'You'll get twice as many customers tomorrow, you old rogue. They'll be wanting to know the ins and outs.'

Mervyn asked, 'She all right?' He rolled his eyes towards the rooms upstairs.

Joe shook his head. 'Can I take your van?'

Mervyn took keys from his trouser pocket and handed them to Joe. Joe was glad he'd asked no questions.

Chapter Thirty-Six

'I don't know . . .' began Joe.

Ruby put her hand on his knee. 'I know you don't,' she said. The van stank of fags and it was littered with rubbish. 'You will understand,' she said. 'Thank you for driving me to Alverstoke.'

It was bitterly cold. She was glad Joel was warm and safe with Marge.

Everything that had happened since she'd set foot in the Point yesterday was like a film. Nothing felt real. She couldn't quite believe she was sitting in this smelly vehicle, hurtling along the road back towards the house she'd escaped from.

It was better she told Leon than he discover the truth about Richard from someone else. Of course, he'd be worried sick that Richard hadn't gone home last night. Leon deserved to hear about Richard's death from her. But for now she was glad of Joe's silence. Her eyes stole over his face, taking in his beloved profile as he drove.

From the moment she'd set eyes on him yesterday she'd wanted to fly into his arms. But time apart had changed them both. He'd gone away to war a boy and come home a man, and she'd pushed him away from her by creating fences between them.

She could almost see inside his mind – he was holding himself back. And why? Because he believed she'd married Richard Williams for love.

Of course he understood how bad things had been for her while he was away.

She'd tried to explain, but only time would show Joe that she'd never stopped loving him. All right, she'd wait. She had all the time in the world for him to come to his senses, to realize she had only ever loved him.

But now her thoughts were with Leon.

He was going to be distraught.

She saw the pain cross Joe's face as he came round to open the door for her.

'Your shoulder isn't right. You shouldn't have left the hospital.'

'I thought you were more important.' He slammed the van's door shut.

There was no answer to their knocking at the front door. 'I can hear the piano,' Ruby said. 'Let's go round the back. Leon has difficulty hearing.'

The musical notes came sweet and clear. Ruby knocked on the French doors and called out Leon's name.

She saw at once that he hadn't slept. His hair was unkempt. It took a moment for him to register who it was, but as soon as he saw Ruby he smiled. He opened the door wide for them to enter, yet tied the belt of his silk dressing gown tighter about his slight body.

'What's happened?' It was as if looking at their grave faces had given him the answer. Leon's face went white.

Ruby pushed him towards the sofa and sat down next to him. 'Go and make tea, Joe.'

Joe stared at her. 'Tea can wait,' he said.

Ruby picked up one of Leon's hands. She didn't know how to approach this, but decided to be open and frank.

'I'm sorry, Leon, but Richard's dead.'

His eyes were still upon her as he digested her words. Then he fell against her.

His arms went around her and she felt his tears wet on her neck. Leon cried out, 'No! He wouldn't leave me.'

Ruby looked at Joe, who stared questioningly. Then he frowned and suddenly, as though a light had been switched on in his brain, his face was full of understanding, and he said, 'I'll leave you two alone and find the kitchen.'

Leon pushed away from Ruby. 'How? What happened?'

She held both his hands once more and told him all she knew.

'The police said he'd been drinking. It was a terrible accident, Leon, but that's what it was, an accident.'

'Does anyone know—' As the words fell from Leon's lips, Joe entered, a tray in his hands. Ruby knew Leon had learned early to guard the secret of his and Richard's sexuality. He was thinking of Richard's good name. He stared at Joe.

'You've got nothing to worry about from me.' Joe set down the tray on the table and held up his hands in a mock surrender.

The relief on Leon's face was evident. 'Thank you,' he said. 'I knew if Ruby loved you, you'd be a good man. I can see you're Joel's father. He's so like you.' Then he looked at Ruby.

Joe now knew she had never been in love with Richard Williams. How could she have been? Already he looked happier.

Ruby also realized that Leon could do without small talk with visitors. He was the real victim in this sad affair. Richard hadn't been a perfect man, but Leon had loved him.

'I'll stay as long as you want,' Ruby said, 'but I do need to collect a few items.'

Leon shook his head, interrupting her. 'I'd rather be alone.'

'You can come back to the pub with us, if you'd rather?' Joe's voice was gruff. Again, Leon shook his head.

'If you'll allow me to stay here, Ruby, until I sort myself out . . .' She must have looked confused, for Joe broke in.

'Richard was married to you, so this house is probably yours now.'

Ruby cried out, 'For God's sake!'

She didn't want the place. But she was concerned that Leon should be able to stay wherever he wanted and as long as he wanted. His grief wouldn't dissipate overnight. Perhaps the Point of No Return wasn't the best place for him to be, even though she was sure Mervyn would find room for him to stay in one of the guest rooms for the time being.

'Stay here,' she said. 'I'll come back later and make sure you're all right.'

'I'd prefer to be here with his things about me,' Leon said.

'If that place doesn't get a hit from one of Hitler's doodle-bugs during the next Gosport raid, I'll tell Leon he's welcome to stay there as long as he wants,' said Ruby. 'I don't want to live there again.'

Joe said, 'Don't let your heart rule your head, Ruby. One day you might be glad of that piece of land with a house on it.'

'Leon's lost the man he loved, so if he feels closer to Richard there, fine. I'm the lucky one. Do you see now why Richard married me?'

Joe changed gear and stopped at the crossroads. 'Yes. But I don't see why you couldn't tell me the truth yesterday.'

'It wasn't up to me to destroy two lives. To have everyone talking about Richard. You can't help who befriends you or who you fall in love with, can you?'

Joe thought suddenly of the strange relationship that had developed between him and his sergeant and how he couldn't imagine not having his friend in his life, now. The last time he'd asked him if, that day of the parachute drop, he'd meant to take his own life, Cecil had said, 'My head was in a mess, and the drink didn't help. *Que sera, sera.*' Joe knew they'd never refer to it again.

Joe thought too of the red-haired girl in Holland who had cared for him, Renata. She'd saved his life. She had spoken little, but when she had, every word made a great deal of sense.

'I'll not speak of this to Mervyn,' Joe said. 'No one needs to know the ins and outs of your marriage.'

The traffic had cleared and they were on their way again.

'It's gossip that gets about, shredding reputations,' whispered Ruby.

'And we both have first-hand knowledge of the damage that can do, don't we?' He pressed his hand on her knee. She looked up at him and his heart did somersaults.

'Are we all right? Together, now?' she asked.

A tear made a track down his cheek. 'I think so,' said Joe.

He quickly removed his hand from her knee and brushed the tear away. 'I'm sorry.'

'Cry if you want to.' Ruby handed Joe a grubby handkerchief. 'I've cried a lot.'

'I love you,' he said.

'And I love you,' Ruby said.

It was almost dusk when Joe pulled up outside the Point. The pub was closed. He parked the van and went into the kitchen, dragging Ruby by the hand.

The big old table was surrounded by Mervyn, Marge and both Joe's parents.

They were talking about Christmas, which was fast approaching, his sergeant, who was to be invited to Gosport, and of course Richard's death. Empty cups and saucers littered the table as well as glasses, some containing alcohol.

The air was fuggy with cigarette smoke, warm and

welcoming. On the table sat cardboard boxes containing bottles of spirits.

'All you lot need to know was that Richard Williams married Ruby to help her out of a nasty situation when I wasn't around to look after her. Don't any of you make any more out of it, because there's nothing to make.' Joe glared at his father, who put up his hands in mock horror. Ruby smiled at Marge. Marge winked back at her.

'I saw by the stuff in the shed and box room you're still duckin' and divin',' Joe said to his father.

'You can't teach an old dog new tricks,' said his mother. She was knitting something using soft white wool. 'About time you two got back. I'm glad to see you've sorted everything out.'

'What's that?' Joe asked, looking at her knitting.

'It's a matinee jacket for your son. I hope Ruby'll accept it in the spirit it's being knitted with.' She looked at Ruby sheepishly. 'I'm sorry, Ruby. Can you find it in your heart to forgive me?'

The pride that Joe felt was instant, though he said, 'You blow hot and cold like the weather, Mum,' but he meant it kindly.

Ruby walked over to her mother-in-law and said, 'It's all done with now.'

She bent and kissed the top of the woman's head. Mervyn's

voice cut through the big band music on the wireless. 'You've done wonders for Marge, Ruby. You gonna tell us why you came back? Your old man falling down my cellar was an accident. The silly drunken bugger was no doubt looking for you.'

Marge's voice cut in, 'Mervyn, everyone's got secrets and everyone should be allowed to keep those secrets. You can't know every blessed thing about a person.

'Leave her alone, she'll tell us when she's good and ready.'

For a moment, silence reigned in the kitchen. Joe gave Marge a grateful smile. His Ruby had a good friend in her.

Ruby said, 'See? Marge knows me better than anyone, almost.' She looked at Joe and he could feel the truth binding them together, but she broke that gaze and asked Marge, 'Joel all right?'

'Fast asleep upstairs,' Marge said. Ruby nodded.

'Where are you off to now?' Mervyn asked. Joe had thrown his coat over the back of a kitchen chair.

'It might have escaped your notice, while you've all been sending me on errands, that I met my Ruby last night only for a short while, and believe it or not I've yet to properly introduce myself to my son. So if you lot want me for anything else you're going to have to wait in line!'

Joe grabbed Ruby's hand and pulled her after him, through the hall and up the stairs to meet his son.

Chapter Thirty-Seven

It was New Year's Day in the Point of No Return. Mervyn had opened up because he had more light beer than he knew what to do with, courtesy of the American Supply Depot and Lennie.

Dejected-looking decorations hung askew after the merriment of the previous night seeing in 1945. The wireless was playing loudly, yet was still almost drowned out by the laughter and chatter from the people ignoring Bing Crosby.

Mervyn stood with his arms folded and a smile that reached from ear to ear.

He was surveying his kingdom, his empire. Grace was methodically wiping out ashtrays after emptying the dogends into an old biscuit tin. Her slippers, as always with cut-outs for her bunions, were new, a Christmas present from her granddaughter.

Joe's parents sat at a round table with a huge blue and white pram blocking the way of anyone who needed to pass. The pram was new, very shiny and had fallen off the back of a lorry and into Lennie's hands before any damage was done to it.

Inside was a sleeping child. Dark curls were damp on the little boy's forehead and his chubby arms were spread above his head.

One hand on the pram's handle belonged to Joe's sergeant, Cecil. Every so often he rocked the big pram to make sure the child inside slept on undisturbed. On the table in front of him was a large sheet of paper. He was costing materials, rent and rates on a nearby garage and workshop. Ruby smiled at him. He was excited about him and Joe going into partnership together. His desk job with the army didn't suit him, but life in Gosport and cutting down on drinking did.

Mervyn sighed. He gathered glasses to be refilled and hummed along to Bing. When there was a lull in the music he announced, 'I got a special treat for you lot today. I hope you're going to invite him back again to play for you.'

Then, still holding the glasses, he made a dramatic bow

and swept one hand towards a slight, good-looking young man at the upright piano that Lennie had saved from being dumped by the manager from the Gypsy Queen. It had taken three of them, Lennie, Joe and Mervyn, to push it along Forton Road. Mervyn had it tuned especially for Leon, but Ruby knew the cost of the piano tuner still rankled. Beer dregs splashed over the floor from the glasses waving about in Mervyn's other hand.

The piano player struck a chord and 'The White Cliffs of Dover' spilled into the room. 'Turn the bleedin' wireless off,' shouted Mervyn.

Wireless silenced, the customers listened quietly, politely at first, then the piano became, like the wireless, background music. But the punters voiced their approval by slipping coins in a pint mug that was doing the rounds.

'Leon's bloody good,' Mervyn said.

'Don't get too used to him, he's going back to live in Southsea,' Ruby said.

Behind the bar, she was waiting for the Guinness to feed into the glass. It was a long, slow business. Marge stood beside her at the Brickwood's pump. The two young women grinned at each other.

'When's the wedding?'

Marge stared at Ruby. 'Easter. How did you know?'

Ruby said, 'Mervyn can't keep secrets.'

'Well I thought it was about time I let Mervyn make an honest woman of me. My divorce will be finalized by then, hopefully. Just imagine, from a barmaid to a bar manager's wife!'

'And who'd have thought Leon would have agreed to play the piano in this pub,' said Ruby.

'I reckon he'll draw the customers in before he ups and leaves,' Marge said. 'The money he was left in your ex's will will tide him over nicely,' she added.

'Swinging On A Star' was being played and a few people were singing along. Leon must have felt Ruby and Marge discussing him, for he suddenly looked up from the keyboard and winked at Ruby. Earlier, he'd told them he'd been in touch with Richard's publishers and offered to finish a novel that Richard had started.

They'd told him to send it to them after completion, but not to raise his hopes. They'd been interested in the suggestion, though.

'You all right about Leon living in your house at Vectis Road until you find a buyer?'

'Course I am, we both are. That two-up and two-down along from Joe's mum and dad has come up for sale and Joe's already put down a deposit. It'll be nice to be able to invest in the garage in Mumby Road as well. But Joe's funny. He's heard from the authorities about the medal presentation and he's not sure he wants to collect it.'

Marge gasped. 'Not sure he wants the Military Medal?'

'He's shy about it, that's what it is. He hates fuss and bother. It'll all work out, you'll see. But fancy us going to Buckingham Palace for the Spring Investiture!'

Ruby grinned. 'King George himself is going to present it. In the ballroom, the letter says. Cecil is coming with us. We'll go up to London on the train. Cecil says we'll go out and celebrate afterwards and stay overnight at a hotel. Dinner in a posh club. He's found out Sylvie's singing at the Bouillabaisse Club in New Street, Soho. Let her see me and Joe are happy, despite all her tricks.'

'I wouldn't go and see her if you paid me. Watch out!' Ruby's Guinness had overflowed into the drip tray. She pulled a face at Marge, who'd started pulling another pint of Brickwood's.

'Whoops! Regret is a waste of time, it's like the past crippling the present and future. His family know how I feel about the way Sylvie was treated . . .'

Just then the air-raid siren began screaming.

The electric lights went off, Mervyn swore and stomped off to find candles.

Patrons sitting at tables tried to cower beneath them for safety. Joe had entered the bar with a wooden crate full of American Budweiser beers that he placed on the top of the counter. He lifted the flap in the bar top and joined Ruby and Marge.

'What a bloody time to start messing us about with bombs again,' he said.

One of the pub's regulars, Harry, came over to the bar. 'I swear that man Hitler has a screw missing. I expect it's in retaliation to Patton's men and their tanks entering the Saar Basin. Apparently, Adolf's men are running all over the place and our boys are advancing on Cologne.'

'Well, Moaning Minnie or not, I'm staying here. There's no way I'm going out in the cold to a shelter,' said Ruby. Marge took the money for the customer's drinks and put it in the till.

'Take one for yourself,' called Harry. Marge blew Harry a kiss. His neck went bright red as he left the bar area clutching three pints. Marge nodded in agreement at Ruby's words. 'We're as safe here as anywhere,' she said.

Mervyn shouted above the noise, 'This could be a gas attack! Girls behind the bar, check your gas masks. The rest of you in here should have carried in your own!'

Joe began to laugh. 'Do you think he means me as well, calling me a girl behind the bar?'

Marge was scrabbling beneath the counter, sorting through cracked glasses and polishing cloths. She drew out the three box-like contraptions with long straps.

'I thought I'd seen the last of these,' she said. 'Which one's mine?'

Ruby held up her gas-mask box. This was something she entirely forgotten about, Mervyn and his gas-mask exercises. Still, she thought, he meant well. Overhead she could hear planes. The candles flickered, sending spirals of smoke curling upwards. Ruby looked over at the pram. Joe squeezed her shoulder.

'Get your head down, lad,' shouted Mervyn at Leon.

'Try not to worry. If we go, I hope we all go together. I couldn't bear it without you,' said Joe. Ruby raised herself to her full height and kissed him on the nose.

Marge thrust another box at Ruby, who passed it to Joe. 'Humour him,' she said, nodding towards Mervyn. Joe began fiddling with the catch on the side.

Suddenly, a shower of papers flew up into the air and began falling like autumn leaves on to the floor behind the bar.

'Bloody hell!' Joe said.

Marge bent and picked up a letter. After reading the name and address she passed it to Ruby.

'I don't know what more proof you need that Sylvie tried to wreck your lives,' she said. She scanned another letter, then handed that one to Joe, who was also picking up unopened letters.

'These look like some of the letters we never received from each other,' he said.

'They're in Sylvie's gas-mask case, so you don't have to look far for the culprit.' Marge had to shout above the roar of the planes overhead.

Bits of ceiling were falling. Joe's face was as white as the plaster tumbling about them. Ruby fled to Joe's parents and was bending over the pram in an effort to stop any stray pieces of masonry falling on Joel. Not that it was necessary, for Cecil had already pulled up the hood and buttoned the apron. Ruby thrust a letter into Joe's mother's hands so she could look at it.

Then the terrible noise spluttered across the night sky outside like an old car exhaust coughing up its last choking sounds.

Ruby scrambled to a window and peeked outside in time to see the sinister cigar-shaped rocket, flames issuing from its rear, hurtling through the sky. Then the ear-splitting sound cut out. Silence reigned. Ruby could almost taste the fear from the people in the bar as they waited the inevitable long wait for the nose-diving bomb to reach its target, hoping against hope it wouldn't land on their homes.

Seconds seemed like hours until finally the crash came.

It wasn't the Point.

Ruby saw a mass of dangling telephone wires and a crater so huge it seemed to have swallowed the boatyard it had landed on.

'It's hit Camper and Nicholson's,' she cried. 'Thank God the place is shut down today!'

While the smoke cleared it seemed funny to Ruby that the landscape outside had been dramatically altered so quickly.

Local people were emerging from their hiding places and still Ruby went on watching as vehicles arrived and went trundling down the High Street. ARP vans, ambulances and fire engines rolled up simultaneously as the siren sang out the all-clear.

'After the calm that bugger Hitler is starting again,' said Mervyn. He was sloshing whisky into tot glasses to take everyone's mind off the carnage outside.

'Ruby!'

Joe was at her side and then his arms were around her and he held her tightly.

'By the look of all those letters we never had, Sylvie really meant to keep us apart,' he said.

'It didn't work, though,' said Ruby. 'I don't wish her any more harm. I hope one day she can be as happy as we are.' She looked into his eyes before she foraged in her pocket and drew out the grasses which she'd wrapped in a handkerchief.

Joe had plaited them in a ring that night almost a year ago.

She pushed it on to her wedding ring finger. Except for her mother's ring on her right hand, her fingers were bare.

'When I told you that night that I loved you, I meant it. I was fragile then and I needed you to look out for me. But this war has changed us, for the better, I hope,' she said. Ruby saw Joe was looking at her with his eyes full of love.

'Some changes are wonderful,' he whispered, before his lips met hers.

Acknowledgements

Thank you as always, to Juliet Burton, my patient agent, and to Jane Wood, editor par excellence. To Alainna Hadjigeorgiou, Therese Keating, Katie Gordon and the many lovely people of Quercus who are so kind to me. Also to the special people who buy my books, a great big thank you.